PEVNEE RIVER

MLOK
ISLAND

KZHADEE
MARSHES

MOUNT
KERRUB

CITY OF
NEDOBYT

THE NAMELESS MOUNTAINS

A CLOCK OF STARS

THE GREATEST KINGDOM

A CLOCK OF STARS

THE GREATEST KINGDOM

FRANCESCA GIBBONS

Illustrated by
CHRIS RIDDELL

HarperCollins *Children's Books*

First published in the United Kingdom by
HarperCollins *Children's Books* in 2022
HarperCollins *Children's Books* is a division of HarperCollins*Publishers* Ltd
1 London Bridge Street
London SE1 9GF

www.harpercollins.co.uk

HarperCollins*Publishers*
1st Floor, Watermarque Building, Ringsend Road
Dublin 4, Ireland

1

HB ISBN: 978–0–00–835513–5
TPB ISBN: 978–0–00–835514–2

Francesca Gibbons and Chris Riddell assert the moral right to be
identified as the author and illustrator of the work respectively.

A CIP catalogue record for this title is available from the British Library.

Typeset in Adobe Caslon Pro by
Palimpsest Book Production Ltd, Falkirk, Stirlingshire
Printed and bound in the UK using 100% renewable electricity
at CPI Group (UK) Ltd

For Zemira, who is the bravest child I know
and who has many adventures ahead of her

A Cast of Characters

IMOGEN AND MARIE

MUM

ANDEL

ANNESHKA

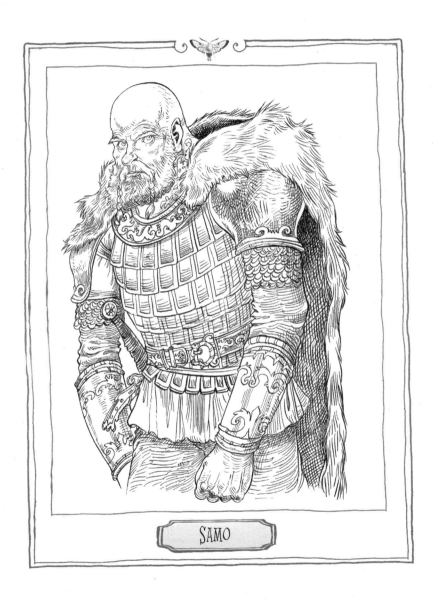

SAMO

MIRO

KAZIMIRA and KONYA

LOFKINYE

OCHI

GRAND LIBRARIAN OTAKAR

GRAND MAGE BOHOOSH

QUEEN NELA AND QUEEN OLGA

PROLOGUE

High up in a tree house, Andel squeezed a spring between his fingers. He was making a wind-up toy, and he wanted it to be perfect.

The room where he worked was something between a carpenter's yard and a magician's workshop – full of wood and weights and all manner of tools, bubbling liquids and gems.

The forest canopy swished around him, squirrels gossiped in the trees, and Andel leaned closer to his work. He had to get the settings just right if the toy frog was to hop like the real thing.

There was a creak on the steps and Andel glanced up. He wasn't expecting any visitors . . . If the woman from the tree house by the lake had come to ask for more singing boxes, he would have to find somewhere to hide.

But the footsteps were swift. Perhaps it was his daughter, Daneetsa, come to summon him home. She was always teasing him, saying that he only went to his workshop to nap.

Well, Andel would tease her right back. He hurried to his

sheepskin armchair and sat, struggling to keep the grin off his face.

The creaking on the steps grew louder. Daneetsa was near the top.

Andel closed his eye and pretended to snore. He couldn't wait to see his daughter's reaction.

The thrush that had been singing went quiet. There were footsteps on the balcony, approaching the entrance. They were heavier than Andel had been expecting.

He opened his eye just a sliver. A figure stood at his doorway – not Daneetsa, but a man. Andel's eye snapped open.

'Erm . . . hello?' he said.

The man stepped into the workshop. He wasn't especially tall, but he was strong. Andel could sense it from the way that he moved. His head was shaven and his beard was cut to a point. He turned his cool gaze upon Andel . . . and Andel felt himself shrink.

But there was no reason to be frightened. Just because the man had come at the end of the day, it didn't mean he intended any harm. Just because he carried a sword and two daggers . . .

Andel tried to remember where he'd put his small knife.

'I'm Andel,' he said, getting to his feet. 'They call me The Clockmaker, although I make other trinkets. Is there something in particular that you're after?'

The man cleared wood shavings off Andel's worktop with

a single sweep of his hand. Then he placed a package on the space that he'd made.

There was something in his face that Andel did not like – a mocking expression that reminded Andel of the men who had taken his eye.

Anger and fear rose inside him.

He thought he'd made his peace with that, he thought—

'What do you want?' he blurted.

Finally, the man spoke, as if he'd been waiting for Andel to look afraid. 'Commission,' he grunted.

Ah . . . so he was just a customer, after all. Andel let out his breath. 'Well, there's a bit of a waiting list,' he said. 'But if you don't mind leaving your details, I'll send word when I've got a slot.'

The man unfolded the package on the worktop, revealing a shiny black book. The cover was scorched, as if it had been pulled from a fire, but the title was still visible: *The Book of Winged Things.*

The man opened the book and Andel saw that it was full of moths. They were drawn in exquisite detail. He leaned in, in spite of himself. The man kept turning the pages.

But wait. Those moths were not drawings – they were the real things, killed and flattened, like flowers in a press. Andel suppressed a shiver.

The man stopped on a page with a silver-grey moth. He cracked the book's spine and pushed it closer. *Mezi Mūra,* the scrawled words said. The name was familiar, though Andel had never seen an insect like it. It had huge antennae and a velvety body.

'Very nice,' he said, straightening, and he looked the stranger in the face. 'What exactly is your commission?'

'A moth,' said the man. 'Like that.' He jabbed the page with one finger.

Andel considered the request. He liked working on a small scale and the silver-grey moth *was* beautiful. To make something that could fly would be an excellent challenge . . .

But why would such a man want a moth? Surely, it wasn't a toy?

'Must be exactly the same,' said the stranger and he reached into his pocket and pulled out a purse. He slapped it on to the worktop.

Andel heard footsteps in the forest below. Light feet, fast feet. *Daneetsa*. And, for a reason that he couldn't quite name, he didn't want this man to meet his daughter.

'I'll do it,' he cried, ignoring his misgivings. What the man wanted with such a contraption was not his concern. Surely, it could do no harm.

'One month,' said the stranger as he stalked out of the tree house. 'You have one month to make the moth.'

CHAPTER 1

Imogen walked barefoot across the kitchen. Feet slapping cold tiles, she reached for the biscuit tin and took a fistful of Bourbons. One in her mouth. Two in her pyjama pockets.

Munch, munch, munch. They were good.

She loved Sunday mornings. Mum slept in and, until Marie was awake, Imogen got the computer to herself. It was just her, *Cosmic Defenders*, and the biscuits.

A man's jumper lay by the sink. It had been thrown there casually, as if it belonged here . . . and it did. Mark had moved in last month and his things were scattered throughout the house.

Imogen had decided she didn't mind the extra coat, extra keys or the big squeaky shoes. It was good to be reminded that Mark was a permanent fixture – like a sofa, or a rug, or a dad.

She picked up his jumper and slipped it over her head. The sleeves finished down by her knees and the wool smelled of coffee. There was another scent too, a smoky aroma, as if Mark had been sitting by a bonfire.

Imogen wondered if her real dad smelled similar, before pushing the thought aside.

She glanced at Marie's drawings, which were stuck on the fridge next to Mum's lists. The mundane was mixed with the magical: river sprites, bread and bleach. Imogen picked up a pencil and added 'biscuits' to the shopping list.

Then she took a Bourbon from her pocket and ate it, slower this time, savouring the chocolatey middle. It was several months since she'd returned from the world beyond the door in the tree, but the novelty of being home hadn't worn off.

She enjoyed the comforting sounds of the house – the faint hiss of water in pipes, the gentle hum of the fridge. Soon Mog the cat would appear, miaowing until he got food. Better make the most of the peace.

Pulling up a seat at the kitchen table, Imogen reached for Mum's laptop. She was allowed to play *Cosmic Defenders* as long as she kept the volume off. She ran her finger over the mousepad and the screen flashed awake. Imogen felt a little thrill at the thought of playing her favourite game.

But Mum must have been reading the news before bed because a browser had been left open. Imogen was about to close it when a picture at the top caught her eye.

It was a photo of the prime minister, stepping out of his house. He looked defeated, sagging inwards like a hoover bag. Imogen cocked her head. Perhaps this wasn't how he thought being prime minister would be.

The photo was a swirl of movement; jostling microphones,

blurry police uniforms. Only the woman at the top of the steps was still. She looked straight at the camera, as if she'd known this moment was coming, as if she'd been *born ready*.

Imogen recognised her in an instant.

The blonde hair.

The violet-blue eyes.

Imogen blinked in the laptop's light. Then she slammed the screen shut and backed away. The kitchen cabinet pressed into her spine. She could hear the throb of her heart. *It's her, it's her . . .*

Anneshka.

But Anneshka couldn't be in this world! It wasn't possible!

Surely, this was a look-a-like . . . or some kind of Photoshop prank.

Imogen tried to gather herself. She reached for the laptop, prised it open, waited for the screen to flicker back to life.

The news article was still there. Imogen scanned the headline:

New Scheme Given the Go-Ahead

She studied the photo more closely. The woman's body was hidden behind the prime minister, who was hurrying away from the cameras as quickly as his suit-bound legs would allow.

The woman was in no such rush. Her long hair was swept back from her face. Even her make-up was of this world – flicky little lines at the sides of her eyes.

A smile ghosted her lips. It felt like her gaze was cutting through the screen, piercing her way into the kitchen.

That was Anneshka Mazanar, as sure as chocolate's sweet. What was she doing with the prime minister? What was all this talk of a 'scheme'?

Imogen pulled the biscuit tin on to the kitchen table and stuck another Bourbon in her mouth. Crumbs fell on the laptop, but Imogen didn't even notice. She was transfixed by the article.

Annabelle Clifford-Marbles spent several years rescuing orphans abroad, before launching her new business in England. She already enjoys the backing of—

'Imogen?' Mum was standing at the kitchen doorway. 'Is everything okay?'

Imogen looked from the laptop to her mother, who was tying her dressing gown round her waist. Mum raised her eyebrows, waiting for Imogen to speak.

'I know that woman from the news,' whispered Imogen. Her voice was as dry as crumbs. 'She's the woman who kidnapped Marie.'

CHAPTER 2

Mum sprang into action before Imogen had even finished her sentence. First, she ran to the phone and called Grandma. 'Yes, come over,' she said. 'You can have your cup of tea here.'

Then Mum dashed upstairs, dressing gown flapping. 'Mark!' she called as she ran.

Imogen sat alone in the kitchen, stomach churning. Anneshka Mazanar was here . . . in England . . .

The world had felt so soft and sunlit. But now a shadow had appeared.

Mark came thundering down the stairs, face serious, dried toothpaste on his top. He put a heavy hand on Imogen's shoulder. 'Can we – are you sure that it's her?'

Imogen nodded.

Marie came downstairs more slowly. Her hair was tousled and her eyes were large. Imogen wanted to say something to make her little sister feel better, but all words of comfort had fled.

Imogen's mind drifted back to the prophecy . . . For that's

what had started all this. Anneshka was destined to rule the greatest kingdom, that's what the clock of stars said.

The clock had also shown a little figure in a raincoat – a figure that looked like Marie. After that, Anneshka had been convinced that Marie would help her become queen.

'It's all right, darling,' Mum whispered. She gave Marie a protective squeeze. 'I'm here. You're safe with me.'

But Imogen wasn't so sure. She couldn't forget what Ochi, the forest witch, had told her: *The child is part of Anneshka's prophecy. Their destinies are tied.*

A screech of brakes signalled Grandma's arrival. She burst into the house, rollers stuck in her hair, blouse inside out. 'I came as soon as I could!' she declared.

Even the cat joined in. He launched in through his cat-flap and sprang on to the table, miaowing, as if to say, *Did you come to see me?*

And so, the family was assembled. They each took a seat round the kitchen table, with Imogen sat at one end. 'Go on, Imogen,' said Mum. 'Show us what you found.'

Imogen opened the laptop as if unlocking the cage of a wild beast. Mum, Grandma and Mark leaned closer. Marie stayed where she was.

Imogen wished she hadn't eaten so many biscuits. She felt a little bit sick. But at least her family were taking this seriously. Not one person had said she was making it up. They were all here – all listening.

She turned on the laptop and *there* was the photo. *There*

were Anneshka's violet eyes. Imogen swivelled the computer so the others could see.

Marie let out a funny noise. Grandma sucked the air between her teeth. The cat rubbed his face on the laptop and purred.

'That's her,' said Mark through clenched jaws. 'That's Anneshka Mazanar.'

Mum shook her head. 'She looks so – so—'

'Where does she get her hair done?' cried Grandma, with a mix of horror and awe.

Marie buried her face in Mum's side and, even though it was a bit babyish, Imogen didn't mind. She knew what Marie had been through – kidnapped by Anneshka and used to do her bidding.

'I thought you said she lives overseas?' said Grandma, securing the roller in her fringe.

'Not overseas,' said Imogen. 'She's from another world. But she can't have come through the door in the tree. The shadow moth's the only thing that makes it open.'

'And the moth would never let her through!' cried Marie.

'Hmm,' said Mum. 'There must be another way.'

Imogen tried to picture it – a second magical door . . . Where might such a thing be? Close to their home or in another country? Perhaps there were many such portals, hidden at the back of old graveyards, tucked behind ivy in the corners of parks, buried deep in ancient woodlands . . .

Mark spoke in a whisper. 'You don't think Anneshka has

come for—' He caught himself, but they all knew where that sentence had been heading. *You don't think she's come for Marie?*

Tears filled Marie's eyes. 'I'm not going with her! She can't make me!'

'Of course not,' said Mum. 'That woman's not coming anywhere near you.'

'I'd like to see her get past me,' said Grandma, stamping her walking stick on the floor.

Imogen glanced out of the window, as if Anneshka might appear at any moment. She knew that was silly, but she couldn't help it . . .

The sisters' eyes met across the kitchen table. 'Anneshka will do anything to make her prophecy come true,' said Marie. 'It's the only thing she cares about.'

'I thought she'd already found the greatest kingdom,' said Mark. 'I thought that's why she let you go.'

'But what if she didn't?' gasped Marie. 'What if she's still searching? Then she'd want – she'd want me!'

Imogen tried to squash her rising panic.

The thought of Anneshka being in this world made her feel like she was on the edge of a very steep cliff. The moment she took her eyes off the drop, she was sure she would slip.

Mark propped his elbows on the table. 'You don't think this is it? The greatest kingdom, I mean?'

Grandma snorted so hard she had to grab a tissue. 'No, Mark. I don't. If there *is* such a thing, it's Italy. The opera, the architecture, the—'

'What are we going to do?' cried Marie, looking from Mark to Grandma to Mum.

'I'll write a letter to the prime minister,' said Mark. 'Tell him the truth about Anneshka. She ought to be locked up for what she's done.'

'A letter?' Grandma looked at Mark with disbelief. 'What good will that do? She needs some sense knocking into her. Why, she can't be much older than twenty. Barely out of short trousers. I'll go over there and give her a good talking-to.'

'No,' said Mum, rather loudly. Every head turned her way. 'No letters. No lectures. You must all stay away from Anneshka or Annabelle or whatever she's calling herself. And I mean it. I don't even want you in the same county as her.'

Imogen had to admit, she didn't fancy meeting Anneshka again. Just the thought of it made the skin on the back of her neck prickle.

'I don't want you girls worrying, either,' continued Mum. 'Mark and I will work out what to do. In the meantime, there's no reason to think Anneshka being here has anything to do with us. She doesn't even know where we live. It's best if you forget all about this.'

Hearing Mum speak with such confidence made Imogen feel a bit better. Although she wasn't sure she could just *forget*.

'I need tea,' muttered Grandma, and she put the kettle on. 'Tea with an orange juice chaser. Anyone else want one?'

Mum nodded and got to her feet. Mark stayed put, reaching

for the cat. But Mog, who was normally so keen to be stroked, hissed and hopped to the floor.

That's strange, thought Imogen. She looked at Mark – properly this time.

He stretched across the table and ruffled her hair. 'What's going on in that head of yours, Imogen? Didn't you hear your mum? We'll take care of this Anneshka situation. There's nothing to worry about.'

CHAPTER 3

Imogen started spending her lunchbreaks in the school computer room. Her friends said this was boring and refused to join her. They couldn't understand why she'd become obsessed with 'some random businesswoman'.

But Imogen couldn't stop thinking about Anneshka. Even though Mum had told her to forget it. Even though Mark said it would be fine.

It was as if Anneshka was a planet and Imogen was a rock, trapped in an endless orbit. Her mind kept circling back.

Imogen didn't want to worry her mother, and she still didn't have her own phone, so school breaks were her only chance to investigate.

She started by searching Anneshka's fake name. Several news articles popped up.

Annabelle Clifford-Marbles is a good friend of the Duke of Sconfordshire. They were riding together through his Little Piddlington Estate, when they came up with the idea.

What idea? wondered Imogen.

She kept reading . . .

Ms Clifford-Marbles explained: 'And I just thought, look at all this green. Isn't green marvellous? Wouldn't it be lovely if more things were green?'

Well, that didn't sound much like Anneshka.
Imogen scrolled down the page.

'We're calling it Green & Pleasant. A stylish way to save the world.'

That *really* didn't sound like Anneshka. There was even a photo of her, pretending to plant a tree.

None of this made any sense . . .

Had Anneshka Mazanar really changed? Did she feel sorry for trying to kill Miro? Did she regret kidnapping Marie?

Imogen tapped at the desk as she thought . . .

No.

It was more likely that Anneshka had made a mistake than she'd become an environmentalist. *She must no longer think that Valkahá is the greatest kingdom, must be searching for a new throne . . . just like Marie said.* This 'new Anneshka' was just another disguise.

Imogen typed in 'what is greatness?'

The computer had thousands of answers:

A natural ability to do better than others.

Imogen had to admit, she would like to have *a natural ability to do better.* She'd like to be better at singing and maths. Once, she'd wanted it so badly that she'd copied the answers for an algebra test.

Imogen shook off the thought and kept searching.

Ah, here was a new definition:

The quality of being great (in size, ability or power).

Her gaze lingered on the last word.

Power.

Now that sounded more like Anneshka.

Pow-er, power, *power*—

The boy at the next computer gave Imogen a funny look and she realised she must have been chanting the word out loud.

'Sorry,' she said, and she began an image search. There was a photo of Anneshka kissing a baby, Anneshka painting a fighter jet green, Anneshka pulling a sad face next to a piece of litter.

A symbol was sewn on to the pocket of her dress. Imogen zoomed in. It was a small green crown . . . Was that Anneshka's logo?

In the corner of the litter photo was a man who looked a bit like a Viking. He had a pointy beard and a close-shaven head. He was in the next photo too, standing beside Anneshka. A badge was pinned to his jacket, shaped like a crown.

Imogen peered at the screen more intently. There was the same man, making way for Anneshka. There he was growling at a child. The Viking man was in every shot.

Imogen gripped the sides of the computer screen. 'Who *are* you?' she whispered.

The boy at the next computer gawked, but Imogen didn't care. She had to work this out. It felt like the only way to guard against Anneshka was to know more about her than she knew about them.

Perhaps the Viking was friends with Anneshka . . . or perhaps he was a new bodyguard? There was something a bit frightening about him. He didn't look like he knew how to smile.

Brrring! went the school bell.

Lunch was over.

Imogen banged the desk with frustration. She would have to leave her research for the weekend – just when she felt like she was making progress too.

It's okay, Imogen reassured herself. *It's not as if Anneshka's going to turn up tomorrow. I've still got time to work this out.*

CHAPTER 4

I mogen tried not to think about Anneshka when she got home from school.

She tried not to think about her that evening, while eating Mum's famous chicken casserole; tried not to think of her as she climbed into bed, where Marie was already snoozing.

Marie had been sharing Imogen's bed ever since she'd been kidnapped. She was having trouble falling asleep in her own room and she seemed to feel safer here.

Imogen was still trying not to think of Anneshka the next morning, when Mum announced that they were going to the Haberdash Gardens. 'Mark says, if you're good, he'll make a campfire,' said Mum.

Imogen knew this was code for *don't you go wandering off*.

She didn't mind though. She was surprised that Mum let them go at all. After all, the door was in the gardens . . . the door that led to the magical world.

It was embedded in the trunk of an enormous tree, and it

had a tendency to slam shut. That was how Imogen and Marie had got stuck in Yaroslav. That was how Mark had got stuck too.

It would be easy for it to happen again . . .

But Mum had got into the habit of visiting the gardens when the girls were missing. It was where she'd felt closest to them. Now they were home, she took the girls to see Mrs Haberdash and her overgrown estate most weekends.

Mum said it was all about 'trust'. She said she knew the girls wouldn't go looking for trouble (which meant the door in the tree). And the more Mum acted like she trusted Imogen, the more sensible Imogen wanted to be.

As Mark pulled into the car park, Imogen experienced a familiar tingling, remembering her other-world adventures and how it had all begun . . .

Mum was in the front passenger seat. Marie and Imogen were in the back. And *there* were the Haberdash Gardens, with plants pressing themselves against the fence, vines creeping under the gate.

The land had been in Mrs Haberdash's family for centuries. But the money had run out, and she'd stopped being able to afford gardeners many years ago.

Luckily, Mrs H had the tea rooms: a mobile home on the other side of the car park, where she sold hot drinks and cake. This, her pet dogs, and her many friends seemed to keep her happy.

Friendly letters hung above the garden gate, saying *Welcome to the Haberdash Gardens.* Less friendly letters were painted across it: *NO TRESPASSING!*

But Mrs Haberdash said the sisters could trespass as much as they liked.

Mark parked and the girls sprang out of the car, racing each other to the gate. Soon, the whole family was walking along the garden path, surrounded by birdsong and leaves.

A worry creature was standing on top of a tall flower, pulling a scary face. Marie, Mum and Mark kept walking. They couldn't see the little beast.

Imogen paused. She could see it. She could see it very well indeed.

It was about the size of an onion, with short wrinkly legs and pale eyes. The worry creatures often appeared when she was anxious. They never made things better – only worse – although Imogen had got much better at managing them.

Anneshka could be behind that bush, hissed the worry creature.

'Keep up, Imogen,' called Mum. She was further up the path, almost out of sight behind the wall of shrubs.

Imogen swatted the creature off the flower and it fell, screaming, into the weeds. Then she trotted to catch up.

The family kept walking until they reached Mum's tent. It had become a permanent fixture of the gardens, pitched beneath the branches of a horse chestnut tree. The grass around it had grown long and wild, apart from a bit that had been flattened by repeated picnics.

As usual, Mum had brought snacks and a book. Mark arranged stones in a circle and collected sticks to stack inside. 'You can't beat a good campfire,' he said. 'I learned how to do it in—'

'Scouts,' cut in Imogen, because Mark had said this before. But she couldn't help cracking a smile.

A short while later the girls were sitting by the crackling fire, nibbling crisps. 'Hey, Marie,' Imogen whispered. 'I looked up Anneshka.'

'Mum said not to think about that,' her sister replied.

Imogen groaned. It might be easy for Marie to stop thinking, but Imogen couldn't just switch off her brain.

As if to prove her point, the onion-sized worry creature came back into view. It was hopping from plant to plant, using the cow parsley heads as wobbly stepping stones.

Imogen shuffled closer to her sister. 'But did you know Anneshka's friends with a duke?'

Marie was very quiet. She'd been quiet over tea the night before too. Imogen had thought she was just tired, but now she wondered if something else was going on.

Mum and Mark talked on the other side of the campfire. They looked very serious and their voices were low. Imogen suspected they were talking about Anneshka too . . .

The worry creature slid down a stem, like a firefighter whizzing down a pole. *You can't be safe from Anneshka if you don't know what she's doing,* it hissed.

'She says she's making things greener,' Imogen continued. 'But I don't think that's true.'

'In case you haven't noticed, I don't care,' snapped Marie.

Imogen blinked, startled. She often spoke to Marie about her fears and anxieties. It was the best way to make the worry creatures go.

And Marie never responded like that.

Then Imogen felt very silly, because how could she forget? She might be stressed about Anneshka, but this was much harder for Marie.

In the quiet moments before sleep, as the girls lay in bed, Marie would talk . . .

She'd talked about the time Anneshka had threatened to feed her to a dragon. Marie had thought she was about to die.

Sometimes, Marie talked about the old queen – the one she'd seen murdered. Imogen had told Marie that it wasn't her fault, there was nothing she could have done. But Marie still had nightmares about that evening.

Imogen ate the last crisp and sighed. Her worry creature was getting closer, hissing, but Imogen fixed her attention on her sister.

'Sorry, Marie,' she whispered. 'You're right . . . I shouldn't talk about Anneshka if you don't want to. I won't bring it up again.'

Marie stared at the tangled undergrowth, not giving any sign that she'd heard.

Anneshka could be out there, said the worry creature.

Imogen booted it away.

'Besides,' she added, focusing on Marie. 'There's nothing for us to talk about. Mum and Mark are here. It's totally different – much safer – in this world.'

On the other side of the campfire, Mum and Mark sat closer, fingers touching when they thought the girls couldn't see.

CHAPTER 5

Anneshka Mazanar had achieved a lot in our world, just as Imogen's investigation had shown.

She'd interrogated religious leaders. She'd successfully blackmailed the Queen. She'd even considered strangling the prime minister. It would have been easy enough. She'd seen stewed fruit more capable of defending itself than that man.

But, for now, the prime minister was more useful alive. He didn't seem to object to the 'disappearance' of Anneshka's enemies. He was even happy to help with her money-making schemes, so long as he profited too. In this United Kingdom, Anneshka could grow very rich.

And yet, wealth alone wasn't greatness. Anneshka had learned that. The five queens of Valkahá had been slick with silver and look what had happened to them. They'd drowned like metal-plated rats.

Even the five queens' legacy was in tatters. Miroslav Krishnov had seen to this during the duel, when he'd whipped off the krootymoosh's mask.

Still . . . when Anneshka had left Valkahá, she'd filled

several trunks with the five queens' silver – as much as one carriage could hold.

Money may not be *all* there was to greatness, but it helped to have plenty to hand.

After the duel, Anneshka had pretended to be Princess Pavla again, and King Ctibor had fallen for it. He'd been distracted, searching for his youngest daughter, and he said 'Pavla' could do as she wished.

So Anneshka had taken his money too, helping herself to it in the castle vaults. With this stolen fortune, she bought a legion of Yezdetz; fierce warriors who fought for pay.

The Yezdetz had travelled with Anneshka to England, through the door in the tree. They disguised themselves as the local nobility, in green wellington boots, tweed clothes and flat caps.

With soldiers, the remaining silver, and her own cunning, Anneshka had no problem wriggling into the English elite. Here, she had multiplied her wealth many times over, and made influential friends.

But not everything had been simple. Anneshka had discovered a powerful magic that ran all of the UK, from how people made money to who they married. It was in their pockets, in their handbags, in their homes. It had the power to take lives or save them.

The locals called it *technology*.

And, although none of the peasants seemed sure how it worked, Anneshka knew it was the meaning of greatness.

It controlled everything. And what could be greater than that?

Anneshka just needed to find the source of the magic. To make it hers. Only then would she rule this kingdom. Never mind politicians or royalty . . . They weren't in charge around here.

Anneshka would sit on the *Throne of Technology*.

If only she could find it.

After a frustrating few months, where she'd uncovered more questions than answers, Anneshka returned to her own world. The people of England may not know about magic, but she knew someone who did.

Anneshka stood in the Kolsaney Forests. Samo, the leader of the Yezdetz, was at her side. He was bald with a rather impressive beard.

In the half-light of dusk, the forests were made of abstract shapes. No matter which way Anneshka turned, there was a never-ending pattern of vertical lines. The trees were repeating themselves.

'How I hate this place,' she muttered, and, in that moment, she had the horrible feeling that nothing had changed. Despite everything she'd been through, despite all the people she'd fooled – the forest was just the same as it had always been . . .

She was just the same . . . no closer to ruling the greatest kingdom than when she first began.

Anneshka took a deep breath. 'Ochi,' she called. 'Where are you?'

Only an angry squirrel replied.

Perhaps the witch is afraid, thought Anneshka. 'Lay down your weapons,' she told Samo.

The leader of the Yezdetz removed his sword and daggers. He placed them at the foot of a tree.

'Ochi,' Anneshka shouted once more. 'Will you show us the way to your house? This man wishes to purchase a prophecy. He's ready to sell his soul.'

Samo's cool eyes flicked to Anneshka's face, but he didn't object. He was almost always silent, and Anneshka liked him for that.

A velecour squawked and Anneshka pivoted, startled by the sound. When she turned back, she noticed a gap in the trees – a path that hadn't been there before. It seemed to lead to an old cottage.

'Follow me,' Anneshka commanded, and she walked towards the house.

Samo's footsteps were silent behind her.

There were eyes in the trunks of the trees.

'Ochi owes me answers,' Anneshka muttered. She remembered a phrase from the other world; one that suited her current mood well. 'No more Mr Nice Guy.'

CHAPTER 6

Ochi was in the cottage garden. Young and willowy, she greeted Anneshka with a smile. Although, Anneshka noted, the smile didn't reach the witch's eyes.

'Come in, child,' said Ochi. 'My, haven't you been busy? The trees have told me so much.' She bowed to Samo. 'You too, brave warrior. You are most welcome.'

Anneshka stepped into the cottage. It looked the same as the last time she'd visited. There was a writing desk and a fireplace, clay pots on every surface, a chicken asleep in a drawer.

As soon as the witch passed the threshold, her figure crumpled and her dark hair turned white, thinning until there was almost none left.

Anneshka had seen this transformation many times, but it never failed to disgust her. The real Ochi was no more a young woman than an ancient oak was an acorn.

The change was over in a matter of seconds and the old witch hobbled to her chair. 'So,' she croaked, eyeing Samo. 'What can I do for you?'

'Never mind *him*,' snapped Anneshka. 'It's me who needs your help.'

'But your soul is already—'

'The stars said I'd rule the greatest kingdom,' said Anneshka. 'And I have found the right place. There is a world with flying machines and underwater ships, where houses are lit by un-burning fires called elec-trici-tee.'

Anneshka had to pause for breath. 'If I could just understand the enchantment behind it . . . there must be a system of spells. Then I'd be a powerful ruler – not just a queen, but a mage – with mastery over all living things. *That* is greatness. *That* is my destiny.'

The witch brought her bony fingertips together, so they formed a steeple in front of her face. She took her time before she answered. 'Magic? I know very little of the stuff.'

'Nonsense,' shrieked Anneshka. 'You're a witch!'

The chicken woke up and started fussing. Ochi looked uncomfortable. 'My powers are humble and of this world. Besides, you are already a princess, heir to King Ctibor's throne . . . Is that not enough?'

'You call that a throne? The Lowlands are half-flooded and rotten with damp!' Anneshka stepped closer to the old woman. 'How do I control England's magic? Where is it kept?'

'I don't know,' insisted Ochi.

'Very well,' said Anneshka and she signalled to Samo. He stalked across the room, quick as a shadow, and reached for one of Ochi's pots.

'What are you—' the witch started.

Samo threw the pot at the floor. It smashed, clay shards flying.

Ochi screamed.

The chicken in the drawer looked alarmed.

And among the smashed pot was some kind of vapour – a soft and glittering mist.

So that is a soul, thought Anneshka. It was so small, so flimsy, so easy to miss. It hardly seemed worth all the fuss . . .

Still, releasing it had the desired effect on the witch.

Ochi threw herself on to her knees and tried to grab the little cloud, but it would not be contained. It seeped between her fingers, circling her wrists. 'Noooo!' she croaked.

The soul swirled for a moment as if gathering itself, then it flew, shrieking, up the chimney.

Anneshka winced. It felt like the scream would pierce her eardrums.

'How could you?' cried Ochi. 'I earned that soul, fair and square! I need it – I need it to live!'

'How can I control England's magic?' asked Anneshka. 'You know, don't you? Tell me the truth!'

Ochi only shook her head. She was quivering, frantic.

Samo seized another pot and let it fall. This one landed with a dull thump. The soul slithered out from a crack, shimmering and shimmying. Then it too flew, screaming, up the chimney.

The other pots started trembling, as if they wanted to be

freed next. There were hundreds of them – lined up on the windowsill, tucked under the stairs, stacked in the corners of the room.

Samo kept going. He took two pots and smashed them against each other – *thud, thud, crack!* The clay broke and souls oozed out.

'Stop it!' cried Ochi. 'Stop!' She grasped Samo's arm, but he shook her off.

Anneshka watched, amused.

She picked up a pot and felt its weight in her hand. It was solid enough. She threw it against the wall.

The chicken ducked as the pot hurtled over its head. Clay smashed and the soul fled, shrieking. Anneshka felt a tremor of joy.

Samo was slow, methodical, working his way round the room. The chicken took cover beneath the desk. The freed souls pooled on the ground, misting Anneshka's ankles, waiting their turn to soar free.

The more pots Samo broke, the weaker Ochi became. She was sprawled on the ground, hardly able to lift her head. Each released soul seemed to layer on the years, bringing the witch closer to death.

Anneshka raised her hand and Samo stopped. 'Something to tell us?' she asked.

'I don't know – about their – magic,' gasped Ochi.

Anneshka peered down her pretty nose. 'You really are pathetic, aren't you? You're not a messenger for the stars! You're just a broken old instrument, no good for—'

Her eyes passed over a clock. It was sitting on the mantelpiece with scratches all over its face. Tiny jewels, that looked like stars, were suspended in the air before it. All five hands were still.

'Talking of broken old instruments . . .' Anneshka remembered what Ochi had told her, that the clock was tuned to the time of the stars. 'Samo, take that timepiece.'

The leader of the Yezdetz obeyed.

'Let us return to England,' said Anneshka and she stepped over the collapsed witch. 'Ochi is just a translator, and a poor one at that. With the right apparatus, I can find the source of magic for myself.'

CHAPTER 7

The next weekend, Mum and the girls returned to the Haberdash Gardens. It was a warm May Sunday, and Imogen was determined to keep her promise. She would *not* talk about Anneshka. Not even if Marie brought it up. Not even if one thousand worry creatures were waiting in Mum's tent.

'I don't know why,' said Mum, as she drove down the road to the Haberdash Estate, 'but I feel strangely calm in this place. I'd come every day if I could.'

Imogen knew what Mum meant. She liked being with the birds and the frogs and the insects. In the evening, it was a good place to watch stars.

Mark was helping Imogen learn the stars' names. He didn't know them all himself, but he'd got a special astronomy app on his phone.

There was no Mark in the car today though. He'd taken up mountain biking and he'd gone to do that instead.

'I'm going to draw a skret,' said Marie, from the back seat. She'd perked up in the last week. Imogen suspected that the shock of Anneshka's appearance was beginning to fade.

She glanced at Mum, wondering if she'd say that skret don't exist. But Mum only smiled. 'Sounds like a good plan,' she replied.

As Mum turned off the engine, Imogen heard barking. It wasn't coming from the gardens. It was coming from the tea rooms, on the other side of the car park.

That was strange . . . Mrs Haberdash's dogs didn't usually bark, unless they were *very* excited.

The girls leaped out of the car. There was a sign on the tea rooms' entrance: Unexpected Visitors. Closed early.

Something smashed on the other side of the door.

Mum came hurrying over. 'What is it? What's—'

Bang, clatter, SMASH!

Whoever was in there, they were getting through Mrs Haberdash's plates.

Mum knocked on the door and was answered by a very loud squawk. She knocked harder. 'Mrs Haberdash?'

'I'm not in,' replied Mrs H's voice.

Imogen and Marie exchanged glances.

'Are you . . . is everything okay?' Mum tried the door handle, but it didn't budge.

'We're not open,' cried Mrs H. 'I've got—' She was interrupted by more crashing, smashing and the yapping of dogs – 'visitors!'

'All right, Mrs Haberdash,' said Mum, backing away.

Imogen was about to say that they couldn't leave her like this, that there was clearly something wrong, when Mum started climbing in through the window. 'You wait here,' she said to the girls, before slipping between the net curtains.

Imogen's imagination went into overdrive. Perhaps Anneshka was in the tea rooms. Perhaps she was holding Mrs Haberdash hostage and the old lady couldn't ask for help.

'Catherine!' cried Mrs H.

Squawk, squawk, CRASH!

'Oh no, not the carrot cake!'

'Mum!' cried Imogen, banging on the door. 'What's going on?'

'Are they safe?' asked Mum's voice.

Imogen wished she could see who 'they' were. Surely, Mum wouldn't stop to ask questions if the visitor really was Anneshka?

Imogen didn't hear Mrs H's reply, but she'd had enough of waiting. 'You stay here,' she told Marie . . . just in case.

Then she scrambled up and through the tea rooms' window. Nothing could prepare her for the scene inside.

The counter, which was always so well ordered with scones and slices of cake, was a mess of trampled sponge. There were smashed saucers by the door, and the dogs, that were normally so lazy, were hurtling around the room – barking, scrabbling under tables, leaping off sofas and chairs.

In the centre of this chaos was Mrs Haberdash, sitting on her mobility scooter. She was brandishing an umbrella with both hands, holding it out like a shield. 'They're out of control!' she cried, with a look of pure desperation.

Imogen peeped around Mrs Haberdash's umbrella.

And *there*, on a cake stand, was a creature that looked nothing like a cake. It didn't look like Anneshka either. It was scrawny, with stunted wings and a long sharp beak. Its feathers were downy – not yet having their adult colours – but there was no mistaking it. *That* was a young velecour.

CHAPTER 8

The bird on the cake stand let out a squawk. It had pale tufty feathers and ping-pong ball eyes. It looked like a bad art project. There was a second chick on the counter, trying hard to swallow a scone.

Imogen had never seen such small velecours. There had been young birds in Castle Yaroslav's gardens, but even they'd had adult plumage. This pair must have been freshly hatched.

'They're enormous,' said Mum, shouting to be heard. The dogs were still running in circles, yapping as they bounced off the walls.

'You should see the fully grown ones,' muttered Imogen.

'They're not dangerous,' said Marie, who had climbed in through the window – despite Imogen and Mum's instructions. 'Or, at least, not on purpose.'

'They've eaten all of my cake!' cried Mrs H. 'And smashed my best china!'

'What are they?' cried Mum.

'Velecours,' said Marie.

Mum glanced at her youngest. 'Vela-what?'

'They're not from here,' said Imogen, remembering Zuby's words. The skret had warned of the perils of letting things slip between worlds. He'd said there was no knowing what kind of destruction it would bring. Well, the velecours were certainly destructive, although this probably wasn't the kind of destruction that Zuby had been worried about.

'Do you mean to say they're from *the other realm*?' asked Mrs Haberdash, in a quavery voice.

The girls nodded. They'd told Mrs H about the door in the tree – and the world that lay beyond. She was the only person outside their family who knew.

'Oh,' said Mrs Haberdash, lowering her umbrella. 'So they're not exotic geese?'

That set everyone laughing. The dogs stopped barking, wondering what was going on. Even the velecours looked confused.

In the quiet that followed, Mum asked, 'Where did you find them, Mrs H?'

'They came through my gardens with the tourists. They must have fallen out of their nest as they can't even fly.'

The velecour on the cake stand stretched its wings and flapped, as if to prove the old lady wrong. It lifted a few centimetres into the air, before falling back down with a plop.

'Sorry, I don't follow,' said Mum. 'What tourists?'

Before Mrs Haberdash could answer, the velecour on the counter did a poo and that set the dogs barking again. Mrs H raised her umbrella.

'Well,' cried Mum. 'We might not be able to solve all the world's problems, but we can at least save your tea rooms from these two.' She grabbed a tablecloth and advanced on the closest bird.

The velecour on the cake stand let out a battle-cry. Imogen and Marie tucked themselves behind Mrs H, bracing themselves for a fight.

But there was no fight. Mum threw the tablecloth and the baby velecour let out a strangled squawk as the fabric fell over its head. Then it went very still.

'There,' said Mum, dusting her hands on her jeans. 'I thought that might do the trick. They think it's night, just like budgies.'

Imogen eyeballed the turkey-sized lump under the tablecloth. It didn't look much like a budgie.

The other velecour made a retching sound and everyone turned its way. There was something wedged in the bird's throat – something shaped like a scone.

'It's choking!' cried Marie. The chick threw back its head, trying to force the scone down.

Mum grabbed the velecour and stuck one hand down its gullet. For a split second, it looked as if the velecour was eating Mum, but she pulled out the scone, brandishing it above her head.

Imogen, Marie and Mrs Haberdash cheered. The velecour struggled and screeched. Mum placed it back on the counter and covered it with a second tablecloth.

The velecours quietened. The dogs retreated to a wicker sofa.

'Right,' said Mum turning to Mrs H. 'Now . . . what's all this talk of tourists?'

CHAPTER 9

'The tourists have come a few times,' confided Mrs H. 'They're not like my regulars at all. They always wear horrible red trousers and wellies. Even when the weather is fine!'

The old lady shook her head, pearl necklace tinkling.

'At first, I thought they were on holiday, but I'm not sure they're *proper* tourists. They said they're part of a business, said they want to buy my estate – the mansion, the tea rooms, the gardens, the lot.'

'What did you say?' asked Imogen. She had an uneasy feeling, deep in the pit of her stomach. She'd never seen anyone else in the Haberdash Gardens, never even heard of people wanting to visit.

'I told them the land's not for sale,' said Mrs H. 'Those are my gardens and you girls warned me about the secret door. I didn't want the tourists to find it . . . Besides, I need these tea rooms.'

Mrs Haberdash rearranged one of her dangly diamond earrings and pulled a thoughtful face. 'The tourists were a lot less friendly after that. They weren't very clear about *why* they wanted the estate. Just said they'd make it greener . . . more exclusive.'

Greener?

The uneasy feeling crept out of Imogen's stomach, spreading along her limbs.

Do not ask about Anneshka, she told herself. *Do not even mention her name. That's the last thing Marie and Mum need.*

'Why have I never seen these people?' asked Mum.

'They come very early,' said Mrs Haberdash.

Don't mention Anneshka – not a word . . .

'I saw them again this morning,' continued the old lady. 'They left just after dawn. Then I found these geese in the car park and they looked so lost.'

Anneshka, Anneshka, Anneshka . . .

'What's the name of the business?' blurted Imogen.

Mrs H paused. 'They're called something like *Purple and Plenty* or *Pleasantly Green* . . . No, no, that's not right . . . *Green and Pleasant*! That was it!'

Mum's hand shot to her mouth.

'But that's Anneshka's business!' cried Marie. Her face was milky white.

Imogen wished she could undo it, wished it wasn't so. But the truth was clear. Anneshka hadn't found a new way to pass between worlds. She was using *their* secret door, in *their* favourite gardens.

She must have let the baby velecours through by mistake.

44

'Hello?' said a voice from outside.

Everyone stared at the tea-room door and one of the dogs growled.

'It's Teddy, from Save Our Birds. I've come to collect the geese.'

'Oh, good,' said Mrs Haberdash and she whizzed towards the door.

'No!' cried Imogen, spreading her arms. Mrs Haberdash looked surprised, so Imogen lowered her voice. 'I mean, we can't let him in. He can't see the velecours.'

The old lady blinked. 'It's all right, Imogen. They'll be well looked after at the bird sanctuary.'

'Velecours don't exist in this world,' said Imogen. 'They're a whole new species. And, if a new species is discovered in your gardens, people will want to investigate.'

She tried to speak calmly, but Zuby's words kept repeating in her head. *Just think what would happen if we had humans slipping between worlds. There'd be wars and diseases and who knows what else.*

'Don't you see?' she pleaded. 'People will find the door in the tree – more people.'

'Imogen's right,' said Mum.

'But I can't keep these birds,' said Mrs H, gesturing at her smashed-up tea rooms and the velecours, who were still under tablecloths.

The bird man knocked again. 'Hello?' he called. 'Is anyone in?'

45

'No!' Mrs H replied.

'We have to take them back,' whispered Marie.

Imogen stared at her sister, her heart beating fast in her chest.

'You don't mean . . . back to the other world?' asked Mum.

Marie gave a solemn nod.

CHAPTER 10

'Absolutely not,' said Mum. 'There's no way you're going anywhere near that door. Not after you got trapped there. Not after Mark almost died.'

'But baby birds need their parents,' said Marie.

Marie was right. Imogen knew it. The velecours wouldn't survive on their own.

Mum seemed to know it too. She took a shuddering breath. 'I'll take them back myself.'

Imogen considered her mother. All spring, Imogen had avoided that part of the garden – the part where she'd found the door in the tree. She didn't want to break the trust that had grown between her and Mum. She also didn't want to get stuck in the wrong world . . . Not *again*.

But every night, Imogen had imagined the journey to Yaroslav. She hoped that, even if she couldn't return in real life, she might visit in her dreams.

She wanted to see Miro more than anything. He'd have something to say about Anneshka's sudden appearance. He'd help to investigate . . .

'Look, I don't have time for this,' shouted the bird man from outside.

'I'll send him away,' said Mrs Haberdash, zipping towards the door. Her dogs trotted after her, tails up.

Now it was just Mum, Marie and Imogen in the tea rooms. And two dozing velecours.

'It might be hard to find the door in the tree,' said Imogen, watching for her mother's reaction. And then, in a quieter voice, she added, 'I still remember the way.'

'I know it too,' squeaked Marie.

But Mum was looking at Imogen. She ran her fingers through her hair. 'You would have to do exactly as I said . . .'

Imogen fizzled with excitement. 'Yes, I would!'

'And you'd need to stay back from the door. Only the birds would go through.'

Imogen knew this was for the best, but she couldn't help wishing she could see Yaroslav one last time. She fiddled with a thread that had been pulled loose from her jumper. 'How will we know if the velecours have found their families?'

Mum's expression sharpened. 'We won't. We'll just have to hope that they're close.'

The velecours were still sleeping under the tablecloths, breathing slow squeaky breaths. Smashing up the tea rooms had clearly tired them out.

Finally, Mum turned to Marie. 'You stay here, with Mrs Haberdash.'

Marie's smile fell and Imogen's heart dropped with it. They

couldn't leave Marie, even if they were only going into the gardens.

'That isn't fair!' cried Marie.

Mum took another deep breath.

Imogen could understand why Mum might be nervous. She and Marie hadn't always done as they were supposed to . . . They hadn't always listened to their mother. And she hadn't listened to them.

But things were different now.

'You can trust us, Mum,' said Imogen. 'Can't she, Marie?'

Marie nodded vigorously.

Mum looked from sister to sister. Finally, she straightened her shoulders. 'Okay,' she said. 'But we're doing this quickly. And neither of you goes within ten feet of that door.'

Marie threw Imogen a grateful look. 'Yes, Mum,' they chorused.

It took all three of them, plus Mrs Haberdash, to cram the velecours into rucksacks. The chicks protested and tried to scrabble free. But, eventually, only their tufty heads stuck out.

Imogen, Marie and Mum set off into the gardens, with Mum and Imogen carrying a velecour each.

Squawk! said the bird at Imogen's back.

'This way,' cried Imogen, pacing down the path.

It felt strange to know that Anneshka and her people were using these gardens to pass between worlds. It made them feel dangerous. Even though Mrs H said the 'tourists' left at dawn, how could she be sure no one had stayed behind?

Imogen led the way across the river, balancing on a fallen tree. The velecour in her rucksack seemed to sense the precariousness of its situation and it kept very still.

When all three of them stood on firm ground, Imogen looked around.

'Where to now?' asked Mum, and for a moment, surprise silenced Imogen. Not so long ago, Mum hadn't believed in the door in the tree. Yet here she was, asking to be shown the way.

Imogen cleared her throat. 'Follow me.'

But the further she walked, the less certain she was that she was going in the right direction. 'Imogen, I don't remember this bit,' whispered Marie.

So Imogen turned back, passing a row of cherry trees.

The velecour in her rucksack became restless, kicking and clawing at the inside of the bag. 'Hey!' cried Imogen. 'Enough of that!'

The chick squawked back.

Imogen didn't recognise this part of the garden either. It was as if the trees were cards, and someone had shuffled the pack.

The path twisted to the right and she felt a surge of recognition. 'This way,' she cried. 'Follow me.' She broke into a run, velecour-stuffed rucksack bouncing on her back.

Buk-buk-ba-gaaaaaaawk! cried the chick.

But when Imogen turned the corner, it wasn't the door in the tree that she discovered – but the river. They'd come full circle.

Imogen kicked at the earth. This was a disaster! Just when Mum had started to believe in her . . .

'Imogen,' said Mum. 'I'm not saying you don't know the way, but perhaps you've just slightly forgotten?'

You're going crazy, whispered a worry creature. *Yaroslav doesn't exist.*

'No!' said Imogen, a little more petulantly than she'd intended. 'It's not me. It's – it's the trees! They're not in the right places!'

'I know what you mean,' Marie muttered. 'It feels different without the moth.'

The moth.

Yes, that was it.

Only Mezi Můra can make the door visible . . . That's what Zuby had said.

Imogen threw up her hands. 'Of course! The door won't show itself without the moth. I forgot.'

'Right,' said Mum. 'And how do we find the moth?'

'You can't,' said Marie. 'The shadow moth finds you.'

'Oh dear,' sighed Mum as the velecour in her backpack started pecking her neck. 'I suppose that's it then. We're stuck with these ridiculous birds.'

CHAPTER 11

When they got home, Mum put the velecours in the bathtub. The chicks clucked with joy as they burst out of the bags. *Free, at last*, they seemed to say.

Marie brought up a bowl of water and Imogen locked the bathroom window. 'We'll have to work out what they eat,' muttered Mum. 'Surely it can't really be cake.'

'Giant worms,' said Imogen, remembering the courgette-sized grubs that the velecours at Castle Yaroslav were fed.

Mum's forehead crinkled. She was clearly trying to think what to do. It wasn't every day that you found yourself responsible for two soon-to-be giant birds that had come from another world.

'It's okay,' she said, more to herself than the girls. 'I'll work something out. The bathroom is just a temporary solution.'

Just like you'll work out what to do about Anneshka? thought Imogen. The list of problems that needed solving was growing. And the solution to them all seemed to be 'wait and see'.

Imogen wondered how long it would be before the

velecours outgrew the bath. They were already scrabbling out of it, stepping on each other in their rush to explore.

After they'd poked their beaks into every corner of the bathroom, they settled down to sleep. One bird curled up in the sink. The other hopped into the laundry basket. They, at least, seemed content.

Mum, Imogen and Marie backed out of the room.

'Girls,' said Mum. 'I'm afraid we can't go back to the Haberdash Gardens. Not if Anneshka and her employees have been there . . . It just isn't safe.'

Imogen felt her body sag. She knew Mum was right. They could hardly sit and make campfires right under Anneshka's nose. She had thought she was far away, in London . . .

The idea of her being close made knots tighten in Imogen's chest. 'How come Anneshka can find the door?' she muttered. 'Surely, the shadow moth wouldn't help her?'

'Perhaps it didn't have any choice,' Marie whispered. And the imaginary safety shield that Imogen had constructed started to buckle and crack. She had thought that Anneshka was busy, meeting the prime minister and going riding with dukes; far too busy to come to *this* part of England.

Mum was staring at the bathroom door with a faraway expression on her face. 'Temporary,' she said. 'It's only temporary.'

As the velecour chicks settled into their new home, temporary became semi-permanent. The girls called the birds Fred and

Frieda. And, soon, they were as much a part of family life as Mog the cat.

The key difference was *these* pets were secret. And growing at a rapid rate.

Imogen would rush home after school and collect slugs from the back garden. Then she'd carry her slimy stash upstairs, where Fred and Frieda gobbled them up, as if they were jelly sweets.

Soon, the whole family had developed a slug habit. Whenever they saw one – in a park or under a hedge – they grabbed it and took it home for the birds.

Of course, the Haberdash Gardens would have been an ideal place to go slug hunting. But Mum still said it was too risky. And Imogen agreed.

Everything felt more dangerous now Anneshka had been spotted nearby. Even walking to school felt hazardous . . . Even stepping out of the house . . .

Imogen tried to look up Anneshka's movements, tried to work out who the 'tourists' really were, but she couldn't find any information online. There were only photos from glitzy parties, where Anneshka sipped fizzy wine, escorted by the pointy-bearded man.

At home, Imogen spent a lot of time in the bathroom. It felt safe because there was only a small window, too small for an adult to climb through, and there was a lock on the door.

Imogen didn't read books on the loo, like Grandma. Nor

did she enjoy Mum's candlelit baths. She hated the cold showers that Mark took after cycling.

No, Imogen spent her time with the velecours, teaching them to do tricks. Marie would often join her, and while Imogen held a slug behind a hula-hoop, encouraging Fred to jump through, Marie would sketch the scene.

There *were* a few downsides to keeping giant birds in the bathroom. The chicks always wanted to join in with showers. And they stared when you sat on the loo.

Worst of all, the velecours were not toilet-trained so the girls, Mum and Mark had to clean up after them. And, the bigger the birds, the bigger the poo.

Within a few weeks, Fred and Frieda were as large as Labradors. By summer, they were sized like Great Danes. They still didn't look like adult velecours, but their pale fluffy feathers had been replaced by more colourful plumage.

'What are we going to do with them?' asked Mum, worry writ large on her face. 'We can't keep them here much longer. They're too big.'

Imogen didn't have an answer for that. She didn't have the answer for anything much. Frieda stood on the edge of the bathtub, stretching and flapping her wings.

'Temporary,' said Mum. 'It was supposed to be temporary.'

CHAPTER 12

The clock did not work. Anneshka tried everything to fix it – to force the jewelled stars into motion, to make the mechanism tick. But the clock's hands were as still as a dead man's fingers.

She thought she knew how to make it tell the future. It involved promises and blood. She'd seen the forest witch do it. So why didn't it work for her?

Anneshka took the clock to a jeweller. She was back in England, and determined to find the source of all magic with the timepiece's help.

The people in the jeweller's tried to sell her a digital watch. Anneshka had never seen such an ugly lump of metal. 'I'd rather not know the time, than be forced to look at that thing,' she told the assistant. 'It looks like it was made by a skret.'

That night, Anneshka stood on the balcony of her manor. Electric light flooded out through the windows, creating pools of brightness on the terrace floor.

Apart from that, Anneshka was surrounded by darkness.

A breeze rustled through the parkland around the house. A deer grazed at the edge of the lawn.

And Anneshka had the feeling that someone was watching.

She looked up. A group of stars peered down on her. Anneshka stared back, defiant. It was the first time she'd felt that perhaps – just *maybe* – the stars were not on her side.

'I will find the Throne of Technology,' she said to the stars. 'Just you see if I don't . . . I'll come up there and kill you if I have to. I'll rule London and Vodnislav, Valkahá and Hull.'

The stars seemed to dim a little. But they did not reply.

And that was when an idea struck her . . .

The clock read the future, as it was told by the stars. But what if the constellations in this world were different? What if they spoke in strange ways?

Anneshka returned to the Haberdash Gardens before sunrise. Samo and his most skilled warriors were with her: a tall woman, called Gunilla, who wore a furry hat – she was an expert tracker, and the best axe thrower the Yezdetz had.

There were also two men who looked like brothers, but might have just worn matching clothes. Their names were Erik and Ulf. Apparently, in their own lands, they kept giant war elk, which they rode into battle.

The five of them stood in the empty car park. There were no lights in the Haberdash Mansion or the tea rooms. The world was sleeping and so was the clock. Anneshka had it slung over one shoulder, in a specially made velvet bag.

Samo dug his hand into his front pocket and pulled out

a moth. It didn't have any wingdust, nor did it have blood in its veins. This creature was made by humans.

Samo released the mechanical insect and it flew into the gardens, taking a far straighter line than any living moth. Anneshka hitched the clock-bag up her shoulder and gave chase. The Yezdetz followed, weapons clinking beneath their tweed jackets.

The moth led them through the gardens and across the river, right up to the door in the tree. Then it flew at the keyhole, whipping back its silver-leaf wings.

The door in the tree clicked open and the Yezdetz ducked through. They checked the forest, before signalling to Anneshka that it was safe.

Anneshka passed into her old world, crouching low so she didn't bang her head. It was nightfall in the Kolsaney Forests, and, for a moment, she couldn't make out her companions in the gloom. They had a habit of fading into the darkness, as if they were made of shadow-stuff.

Gunilla turned on an electric torch and the trees appeared without warning, huge and unexpectedly close. Anneshka almost jumped.

The Yezdetz were visible now too – standing in defensive positions, eyes scanning the forest. Gunilla drew an axe with her free hand. Erik and Ulf touched the hilt of their swords.

Samo recaptured the moth with one swift movement, attaching it to a chain and placing it in his pocket. Then he reached for his blade.

Watching the four of them, Anneshka felt very glad they were on her side. It would not do well to have such people against you. With the Yezdetz forming a protective ring around her, she lifted the clock out of its bag and placed it on the ground.

'It is time,' said Anneshka. 'Let us do as we practised.'

Samo cut the skin on his palm. 'I pledge to make you the queen of the greatest kingdom,' he declared. 'Stars, help us find the way.'

It was the most Anneshka had ever heard Samo say.

Gunilla stuck the torch under one arm and cut her hand on the edge of her axe. Then she echoed Samo: 'I pledge to make you the queen of the greatest kingdom . . . Stars, help us find the way.'

Erik and Ulf used their swords to pierce each other's hands, repeating the same words.

Now it was Anneshka's turn. 'I pledge to make you the chiefs of a great army,' she whispered, and she cut her palm without looking. 'Stars, help us find the way.'

The Yezdetz warriors and Anneshka reached over the clock, joining their bloods. The forest creaked around them. A breeze spoke through the leaves. And, on the mossy floor, the clock of stars stirred.

It began with a minuscule clicking, like the *tip-tap* of a centipede's legs. The cogs and gears inside were connecting. Then it started to tick.

Anneshka and Samo stepped closer, peering down at the device.

The clock's hands were moving, tracing circles round its scratched face. 'It's working!' cried Anneshka. The hands accelerated to an insect whirr, while the mechanical stars buzzed about.

Anneshka leaned even closer. Samo was still holding his dagger, as if he expected the clock to attack, but, finally, the hands slowed and the little hatch opened. A figure walked out. It was small, no bigger than Anneshka's little finger.

Anneshka's breath caught in her throat. The curly red hair. The pink skin. The raincoat. She knew that face very well – although, here, she was seeing it in miniature, painted and carved into wood.

The figure lifted one arm and pointed, then it trundled back into the clock.

Anneshka closed her eyes. She did not understand. Marie had already played her part . . . hadn't she? She'd told Anneshka about the door in the tree and the moth that made it open. She'd helped her to murder a queen.

What more could the girl possibly offer? Had Anneshka released her too soon?

Samo angled his close-shaven head. Erik and Ulf crossed their arms, clearly unimpressed by the wooden child.

But Anneshka straightened. 'We need to find that girl.'

CHAPTER 13

Imogen and Marie stood outside the old council building, near the centre of town. They'd just been to Drama Club and were waiting to be picked up.

Imogen watched the passing cars, checking each one to see who was inside. It was a habit she'd developed since learning that Anneshka had been to the Haberdash Gardens. Imogen was always worried she was close.

Normally, Imogen would have told her sister what she was up to. But she'd promised not to speak about Anneshka and she meant to keep that pledge.

She tried to remember what Mum had told her. *There's no reason to think Anneshka being here has anything to do with us . . .*

Then she replayed Mark's words. *We'll take care of this, Imogen. There's nothing to worry about.*

But these reassurances had failed to silence Imogen's worry creatures. As the weeks passed, she had become more nervous – not less. She wished Mark would hurry up and collect them.

At least there wasn't long left before the summer holidays.

Imogen couldn't wait to break up. Surely, Anneshka wouldn't dare to do anything when there were grown-ups around. Plus, Imogen had big plans for the velecours – new tricks she wanted them to learn.

One by one, the other children were met by their adults. 'Are you girls okay for a lift?' one of the mothers asked.

'Our stepdad is coming,' said Imogen, feeling a bubble of pride swell in her chest. She hadn't called Mark that before.

Marie's eyes flicked to Imogen's face. Nothing got past her.

Soon, people were arriving for the next class and there was still no sign of Mark. Marie hunted for slugs on the verge. Imogen sat cross-legged and pulled at the grass.

There's nothing to worry about. There's nothing to worry about.

She took a deep breath and glanced up.

Her gaze settled on a man on the other side of the road. He wore green trousers, a green jacket and green welly boots.

Imogen felt that she knew him from somewhere . . . She recognised the sharp beard and the close-shaven head. In one hand, he held a newspaper, but he wasn't reading. He was looking at her.

Imogen's body stiffened.

As soon as the man saw that she returned his gaze, he went back to his paper.

Imogen tried to brush it off. He had probably been looking *in her direction*. That's not the same as looking *at her*.

Where was Mark anyway? He wasn't usually late. Perhaps he'd forgotten about them . . .

Her bubble of pride popped.

A fleet of dads with prams rushed by, temporarily blocking her view. When they'd gone, she saw that the stranger was still there. And he was staring at her.

A chill ran down Imogen's spine.

She knew where she'd seen him before. He was the Viking man from the internet. The one who'd been in the photos with Anneshka.

Imogen fiddled with her laces, buying time. Then she got to her feet and paced up the road. The man's eyes followed her.

She turned on her heel and hurried back to Marie, who was placing a large slug in her pocket.

Imogen *knew* it had been a bad idea to go to Drama Club.

She *knew* they should have stayed at home.

Imogen couldn't help glancing the man's way. To her horror, he got to his feet. He started walking across the road. Imogen grabbed Marie's hand and tugged her towards the council building's entrance.

'Imogen, what's going on? You're scaring me!'

But when Imogen glanced over her shoulder, the man was walking faster. Imogen dragged Marie through the revolving doors. 'Mr Evans,' she called. 'Mr Evaaaaaans!'

The drama instructor appeared at the far end of a corridor. 'Imogen, Marie, you're still here?'

Imogen squinted back through the revolving doors. The man with the shaved head was nowhere to be seen.

'I don't want to leap to any conclusions,' said Mr Evans, 'but I think your stepdad might have forgotten to pick you up.'

CHAPTER 14

Mum arrived like a mini thundercloud. 'Mark promised he'd do Drama Club!' she cried.

Imogen and Marie climbed into her car, with Imogen still checking over her shoulder, making sure that the strange man had gone.

Marie glanced at Imogen, perhaps wondering what she was doing.

'There was a man – a spy for Anneshka,' Imogen whispered.

'Don't say that,' hissed Marie. She clearly thought Imogen was making things up, and it stung.

'I'm so sorry you were left there, girls,' said Mum.

'That's okay,' said Marie and she patted her bulging pocket. 'I found three slugs while we waited.'

Why was she acting like everything was fine? Everything was not fine. Quite the opposite!

The velecours were outgrowing the bathroom. Anneshka was in this world. And now they were being followed by Anneshka's spy or bodyguard – or whatever that man was.

But Imogen didn't want to reveal that she'd been researching

Anneshka, that she'd seen the man online. And it was possible that she'd made a mistake. There must be millions of men with bald heads and beards. It might not be the same one.

'Mark had better not be at Crickley Chase,' muttered Mum. She gripped the steering wheel tight. 'It's all very well deciding he's committed to cycling, but what about his commitments to us?'

'Didn't want to go in his stupid car anyway,' said Imogen, surprising herself with her own bitterness. She'd got into the habit of trusting Mark. Being forgotten didn't feel very nice.

Mum's mood only got worse as the day wore on. Mark still wasn't home by the evening and Mum cooked tea in a rage. She mashed the potatoes with a violent passion.

'I think Mum's imagining the potato's Mark's head,' whispered Marie.

When Mark returned, it was dark outside. Imogen heard his car as she brushed her teeth. She recognised the lazy hum of the engine, the bleep as the doors locked.

The velecours snored in the bathtub beside her. Mark's footsteps crunched on the path outside.

Was it Imogen's imagination or had his walking slowed? He probably knew he'd be in trouble – was probably in no rush to come home.

For a moment, Imogen felt a pang of sympathy. Mum was scary when she was cross.

But she smothered the feeling, spat out her toothpaste,

and locked her toothbrush in the box that they used to keep things safe from Fred and Frieda.

Mark had left Imogen and Marie at Drama Club. They'd almost been caught by that man. Whatever Mum said to him, Mark deserved it.

As the girls climbed into Imogen's bed, voices drifted through the floorboards from below. Then the voices got louder and louder.

'I wasn't gallivanting,' said Mark. 'I was mountain biking. I'm allowed my own hobbies, Cathy.'

Mum's response was hard to distinguish. Imogen just made out two words: 'THE GIRLS'.

The argument seemed to go on forever. Imogen and Marie lay very still beneath the duvet, united by a single wish: *Please don't let Mark and Mum break up.*

Imogen's eyes were closed, but she could not shut her ears. It wasn't like with Mum's other boyfriends. Not like with Gavin or Ross. Imogen had been pleased when those relationships ended. But Mark was part of the family. If he left, a bit of Imogen would leave too.

A few minutes later, there were footsteps on the landing, followed by a knock on the bedroom door.

Marie shifted under the duvet. 'Hello?' Imogen croaked.

The door opened and the light from the landing spilled in. Imogen recognised his silhouette.

'Hello,' whispered Mark.

She rubbed her eyes and tried to scowl. She wasn't angry any more; just relieved that he'd decided to stay.

'Can I come in?' Mark asked.

'I suppose so,' said Imogen.

'I just wanted to apologise . . . for leaving you girls like that. It won't happen again.'

Imogen smiled. 'It better not,' she said, trying to mimic her mum.

'Where were you?' asked Marie. 'Why didn't you come?'

Now, for the first time, Imogen looked at her stepdad properly. Her vision had adjusted to the light from the landing and Mark was close to the bed.

What she saw shook her to the core.

There was a faint glow in his eyes. Not the normal shine that eyes have, when light reflects off them. This was a light that seemed to come from within, as if flames burned inside his head.

Imogen clutched at the duvet.

She remembered a conversation she'd had with her sister, when they'd got home after their last adventure. Marie said Mark had changed – that he walked slowly and his eyes seemed to glow.

At the time, Imogen had dismissed it. She'd thought Marie was confused. She'd wanted to reassure her . . . but perhaps she should have listened instead.

'I lost . . . track of time,' Mark said. He seemed to be struggling to find the right words.

'It's okay,' whispered Imogen, a new urgency in her voice. She wanted him to get out of her bedroom. She dug her fingers into the sheets.

Beside her, Marie had gone very still.

'If you're sure,' said Mark. 'I don't want—' his words stuck again. 'I care about you – about you both.'

'We know,' said Imogen, and now she could smell it: the scent of a freshly struck match. 'We're tired, Mark, okay? Goodnight.'

She lay down and pulled the duvet right up to her neck. It was only when she heard his slow footsteps retreat that she let herself exhale.

'Did you see that?' Marie breathed.

Imogen had a sinking, sinking, falling feeling. She knew what she'd just witnessed. She recognised the tell-tale signs. That was the smell of a yedleek.

Chapter 15

On a different evening, in a different world, another child was struggling to sleep.

Miro lay curled on a giant waxy leaf. He was floating downstream on the Pevnee River. It was the night after the duel, and memories of defeating the krootymoosh were still fresh in his mind.

Champion . . .

That's what they'd called him.

The Champion of Vodnislav.

The river carried Miro through the darkness – away from the water dragon and the place where he'd done battle, away from Patoleezal, his adviser, away from his people and his throne.

His people . . .

The phrase jabbed at Miro. He'd always thought 'his people' were the ones that he ruled.

But Miro did not wish to be King of Yaroslav. He did not wish to live in Patoleezal's mansion and marry when he came of age. He did not wish to spend years in a mirror-filled room.

With time, Miro hoped Patoleezal would understand. He *had* to leave Yaroslav. There was nothing there for him any more. Besides, Miro wasn't only from Yaroslav. His mother had grown up somewhere else . . .

The water strained beneath the enormous lily pad and Miro tried not to think of it – tried not to think of the eels and the weeds and what would happen if the leaf split.

Konya, the giant cat, stirred beside him. The sněehoolark was in the middle of the lily pad, watching the darkness with every inch of her body. Her ears swivelled this way and that.

On the other side of the leaf was Princess Kazimira. She'd stopped screaming for her daddy hours ago. Instead, she lay shivering in a great mass of bows.

Miro curled up even tighter. He was getting cold too. After the duel, he'd shed his armour and now he wore just his shirt, trousers and boots.

His people . . .

His people . . .

What did it mean?

Miro closed his eyes.

Both his parents were dead. They'd been killed years ago, when Miro was small, and he'd been left in the care of his uncle. But now Uncle Drakomor was dead too – the last relative from his father's side of the family – and Miro had never felt so alone.

For a long time, he had pretended this was everyone.

Patoleezal had pretended too. When pushed, he'd said Miro's mother was from 'distant lands'. Miro did not like it when Patoleezal talked like that. It made Miro feel distant from himself.

And, although Miro's mother was gone, although she was with the stars, surely she looked down on him from time to time . . .

He wondered what she thought. Was she ashamed of her child, who knew so little of her realm? Did she recognise who he'd become?

Miro ached to know.

So he was travelling towards the Nameless Mountains, where his mother had been born. Or, at least, he thought he was. It was difficult to know which way the river was going.

Miro hoped to find his mother's family when he got there. He especially wanted to meet his mother's mothers – Grandmother Olga and Granny Nela.

They had married young and, together, they ruled Nedobyt. In this beautiful mountain city, waterfalls threaded the slopes. There were birchwoods and mineral springs and shape-shifting magicians, who called themselves *slipskins*.

Miro had heard all about it from his mother, although he'd never seen Nedobyt for himself. He couldn't remember meeting his grandmothers either, didn't even know how old they would be . . . He couldn't wait to be with them.

But why hadn't they responded to his letters?

He pushed the thought aside.

Overhead, the stars ran like a river. All around, the air vibrated with the croaking of frogs. The rocking of the lily pad lulled Miro, and he must have fallen asleep, for when he opened his eyes it was dawn.

Kazimira was still dozing. Her cheeks were tear-stained, her fingers clenched into fists. Konya lay in the centre of the lily pad, nose tucked under tail.

Miro sat up, unpeeling his face from the rubbery leaf. He tried to make out his surroundings in the soft light.

The first thing he noticed was the water. Yesterday, the river had been beer-brown and wild; full of the dragon's power. This morning, it ran slow and smooth.

The second thing Miro noticed was the riverbank – or rather, the place where he guessed it might be. It was no longer clear where the land ended and where the water began.

The sun inched up and Miro could see a little further. The river had expanded to such a great width that it was not really a river any more. It was a sprawling marsh, dotted with grassy mounds.

Miro shuffled to the edge of the leaf, careful not to disturb his companions. The landscape around him was empty. No trees. No boulders. No rolling hills. Nothing but standing water and tiny islands.

He couldn't make out any people, or signs that they might exist. Not so much as a lonely fisher-hut. It was as if Miro and Kazimira were the only humans left in the world.

'I'm not bathing without my dollies,' mumbled Kazimira, eyes still firmly shut. Miro's gaze lingered on the princess.

She'd ended up on the lily pad by accident, after falling from her castle on Konya's back. Miro hadn't asked why she'd been sitting on the sněehoolark . . . or why Konya had jumped.

Kazimira's father must be searching for her, thought Miro. *He'll be turning the Lowland kingdom upside down.* In many ways, King Ctibor was not a good person, yet he loved his daughter very much, and Miro envied her that.

The princess was not the companion he'd have chosen for this journey. He would have much preferred Imogen or Perla or Marie. He wondered where they were now . . .

But Miro was grateful for what company he could get. He'd spent enough time alone to know that *someone* was better than *no one*.

Another layer of dawn lifted and Miro could see snowy summits, far away in the south. *Those must be the Nameless Mountains*, he thought, with considerable relief. *That's where my grandmothers live.*

He tried to picture his mother's face. These days, he struggled to remember what she had looked like, but he remembered a song she used to sing:

My little Miro, fly swift as a falcon . . .

He let the melody play in his head.

The lily pad jolted and Miro turned to see it butting up against one of the little islands.

'Where are we?' squawked Kazimira, suddenly awake and outraged.

Miro looked around at the vast flooded marsh. 'I was hoping you'd be able to tell me.'

CHAPTER 16

Miro considered sticking his hand in the water and paddling round the tiny island, but he wasn't sure where he'd paddle to.

There were similar mounds on the left and the right – and many more beyond that. Steering the lily pad through this maze would be impossible.

If Miro wanted to go anywhere, he'd have to jump from islet to islet, using them like stepping stones.

With his arms out for balance, he got to his feet. It had been many hours since he'd used his legs and they'd gone as stiff as old reeds.

Miro put his heel on the island, half expecting it to sink. But, beneath a layer of moss, the ground was solid enough. He stepped off the lily pad.

'Where are you going?' cried Kazimira. She was still sitting on the leaf. Konya yawned and stretched at her side.

'To the mountains,' said Miro and he nodded at the horizon. 'You have permission to accompany me . . . if you'd like.'

'I don't like,' yapped Kazimira. 'I want to go back to my daddy.' The princess beat her fists up and down. 'Daddy wouldn't like me to be here! Daddy would say it isn't safe!'

If she says I've kidnapped her one more time . . .

But there was no point in making threats. The truth was, Miro would probably cry. His triumph from the duel had faded, so had his excitement about his new quest, and he was left feeling drained.

'I already told you,' he mumbled. 'You can do whatever you like.'

Miro hated to admit it, but Kazimira had a point. She *was* too small to be out here, wandering the marsh by herself. Mark would say Miro was too young as well.

Miro often found himself thinking about what Mark would say . . .

But he'd spent his whole life trying to please others, trying to be a good prince – a good king. Now it was his turn to do as he wanted. And he wished to find a way across the marsh, to find his mother's family and, perhaps, his place within it.

Kazimira was not his problem.

The princess's eyes flicked towards Konya, who was sitting with her back to the child. 'Make the kitty carry me home,' she commanded.

'She's not my kitty,' cried Miro. Then he grimaced. He hadn't meant to call Konya 'kitty'.

If Imogen had been there, she would have got the princess

to obey. She was good at saying things with confidence. Marie would have talked Kazimira round.

But Miro didn't know how to make people like him.

He didn't even know how he was going to reach the Nameless Mountains. It was all very well deciding to find your family – it was another thing managing to do it without any food or a map.

His mother's song drifted through his head. *My little Miro, fly swift as a falcon . . .*

How he wished he knew the rest of the words. Perhaps Grandmother Olga and Granny Nela would remember . . . They'd certainly know what his mother had been like. They might even have some stories about him.

Miro had to take the first step towards them. He leaped at the nearest island, swinging his arms as he jumped. He was soaring – soaring – *thwack!* His boots landed in the mud.

Sinking to his knees, he smothered a shriek. *Don't want Kazimira to think I'm a coward.*

Miro shook himself. What did it matter what she thought? She was going in the other direction. Back to King Ctibor, her father – back to Vodnislav Castle, her home.

I bet Konya won't stick around either, thought Miro, with more than a little self-pity. *She'll run back to Perla, her mistress, as soon as she gets the chance.*

Miro jumped to a third island and a wading bird squawked. 'I don't need you,' he called. 'I don't need anyone.' But there was no strength in his words. For Miro no longer believed them.

He moved towards another islet, plotting his route across the marsh. There was a row of larger knolls to the left – a temptingly easy passage. Miro suspected they led to a dead end. Perhaps he should try the small mound to the right.

A splash interrupted his thoughts.

Startled, Miro turned.

Kazimira was standing on the edge of the second islet, with fresh water soaking her dress. She gave Miro an evil look, daring him to laugh.

But Miro didn't feel like laughing. He felt . . . something else.

The princess let out a shrill sound of frustration, before scrambling on to the island.

'W-well done,' said Miro.

Kazimira scowled, but her expression was slightly less furious. 'I did it,' she said. There was a twitch in the corner of her mouth.

Miro's lips twitched in response. 'Yes,' he said. 'You did.'

And so the children continued, with Miro picking out the path through the marshes and Kazimira following as best as she could.

Konya brought up the rear, making sure neither child fell behind. She made the leaps between islands look easy. Her eyes darted between Miro, Kazimira and the small fish that swam below.

Miro surveyed the wetlands with a new sense of purpose. As soon as they found a grown-up, he'd hand over responsibility for the princess. Someone else could take her back home. But, until then, they'd travel together. Until then, they were . . . what did Mark call it?

Oh yes, a *team*.

Miro had no idea how far away the Nameless Mountains were but, surely, if he could see them, they couldn't be that far. Perhaps things would be all right. Perhaps they'd make it to his mother's homeland in time for supper. His stomach growled at the thought.

CHAPTER 17

Miro and Kazimira did not make it to the Nameless Mountains in time for supper. In fact, as the watery sun reached its highest point in the sky, Miro wasn't even sure if they'd moved any closer.

It was a strange place, the marshes. Space seemed to lose its meaning. One mossy island was much like the next, surrounded by tall grass and water of varying depths.

With no distinguishing features, and no way of measuring their progress, the landscape felt eternal.

It was deceptive too. A few times, Miro jumped to an islet, thinking that his foot was about to land on solid rock, only to feel the earth give way beneath him and cold marsh water fill his boots.

After a few hours of walking, his shoes seemed to contain a boggy kingdom of their own.

Kazimira was soaked from head to toe. Konya's long whiskers were limp.

'Daddy says you aren't really a king,' said Kazimira, batting reeds from her face. 'Daddy says you're just a jumped-up noble from a valley no bigger than a millpond.'

Miro was surprised to find he didn't much care what Kazimira's 'daddy' might think. Once, he had wanted King Ctibor's approval. Right now, it didn't seem very important.

'Daddy says people from Yaroslav are cannonballs.'

Miro stopped walking. 'Do you mean cannibals?'

'That's what I said,' replied Kazimira. 'Are you going to eat me?'

It hadn't occurred to Miro that, just as his old nurse told him stories about the people who lived beyond the mountains, a nurse in Vodnislav was busy telling Kazimira stories about people like him.

He'd always been led to believe that foreign lands were terrible. Now he was here, beyond the mountains, and there was some truth to those tales . . . but there was also a lot that was false.

Miro's homeland was no better than its neighbours. In many ways, it was worse. *There are good bits and bad bits in every kingdom*, he thought. *There are horrors and wonders and joys.*

'No,' he said to the princess. 'I'm not going to eat you.'

Although he *was* very hungry. The excitement that had sustained him during his journey down the river had worn off and he was left feeling weak.

By the time the sun started slithering downwards, Miro was bone-weary and Kazimira complained with each step. 'I want my daddy. I want a bath. I want fish and onion soup. I want – I want!'

Even Konya held her tail low. The sněehoolark was soggy up to her belly and, despite being brave about most things, she was not a big fan of water.

Miro saw dark shapes on the horizon. They were buvol; the wild cattle that grazed in these parts. But there were no humans, no one the children could ask for help.

'What do people eat in this swamp?' cried Miro, turning to face the princess. Kazimira shrugged and all the bows on her dress shrugged too.

Miro's gaze returned to the buvol. 'Perhaps we can eat one of those cows?'

In Yaroslav, Miro didn't get involved in the killing of his dinner. It just appeared on his plate, slow-cooked and covered in cream.

Kazimira laughed – a high-pitched laugh that sounded more like a shriek. 'Nobody eats buvol. They're too fierce. You can't even milk them. That's why they're called *wild* cows . . . You really are a ninny.'

Miro scowled. 'I knew that,' he muttered. Desperate, he snapped off a leaf from a plant and stuck it in his mouth.

Urgh! It was the most bitter thing he'd ever tasted. Miro spat it out. His saliva was green and frothing. He spat more, trying to get rid of the taste.

'I'm going to die, aren't I?' said Kazimira, all trace of laughter gone. 'In the middle of nowhere, with no one to even see me do it!'

'Don't I count?' cried Miro, wiping green spit from his mouth.

'I DON'T WANT TO DIE!' screeched Kazimira.

'Me neither,' yelled Miro and panic stirred inside him. He certainly didn't want to die before he'd met his mother's family . . .

'I'M HUNGRRRRRRRYYYYYY!' wailed Kazimira. Her voice seemed to fill that flat land, rolling across the moss-padded marshes. For a moment, Miro was tempted to do the same.

And why not?

There was no one around to judge . . . Miro threw back his head and joined Kazimira's protest, screaming at the top of his lungs.

'I'M HUNNNNGRRRRY!' he bawled. 'I WANT DUMPLINGS AND MEAT!'

He directed his rage at the afternoon sun and its uncaring stare. Then all trace of words disappeared and Miro was just screaming sounds.

Kazimira matched him, scream for scream. She jumped up and down on the springy earth, punctuating her rage with foot stamps.

It felt strangely good, this shedding of shame, this refusal to be well behaved. Miro set his panic free – let it run. Perhaps *this* was how they'd die: shrieking like wild animals.

The screaming was interrupted by a wet *thud*. Miro turned and there was a brown fish on the moss, tail flapping, mouth gasping for air.

Was it . . . a gift from the stars?

No. It was not.

Konya sat beside the fish, looking very pleased with herself. *For you,* her amber eyes seemed to say.

'Thank you, Konya,' said Miro and he thought about stroking the soft fur behind her ears, like he'd seen Perla do, but he was still a bit wary of the snĕehoolark.

'Good kitty!' cried Kazimira and, much to Miro's surprise, the princess grabbed a weed-strewn rock and clubbed the fish over the head. The fish's tail stopped thumping.

Kazimira picked up the carcass and held it level with her eyes. 'Marshfish,' she whispered. Then she peeled off the skin with expert skill and sank her teeth into the flesh.

Miro recoiled. 'D-d-don't you want to cook it?'

But Kazimira already had fish juice running down her face. 'No stoves on the marshes,' she replied. Once she'd eaten half the fish, she passed it to Miro.

'I'm not sure I'm hungry enough to eat raw swampfish,' he muttered, as a load of coiled innards tumbled out.

Kazimira shrugged. 'You die then. It'll just be me and the kitty.'

Now it was Miro's turn to scowl.

He turned away, willing himself to remember why he was here. He thought of his grandmothers. It seemed to be getting harder, but he could still do it, if he scrunched up his eyes.

Miro opened his eyes again. He took a tiny bite of the fish. The meat was slimy, yet the flavour was mild.

He made himself swallow and take another bite – hardly enough to line his stomach. Then he threw what was left to Konya and knelt on the edge of the island. He cupped his hands into the water. It was deep blue-green, with things swimming in it. Miro drank.

Kazimira stuck her chin in and slurped. Miro had never seen a princess drink like that . . . But, to be fair, Miro didn't know many princesses. At least the colour had returned to her cheeks.

When Miro looked back at the fish carcass, all but the tail had disappeared. Konya was licking her paws with a satisfied expression on her broad face.

Miro got to his feet, feeling less weak, and fixed his sights on the mountains. There were many miles between him and his destination. *Still*, he thought, with some effort, *it's closer than I've ever been.*

CHAPTER 18

'What are we going to do about Mark?' asked Marie. The sisters were at home, facing each other on the sofa. Marie had paint all over her school uniform, which was nothing new. She chewed nervously on the ends of her hair.

Mum and Mark were both working, so Grandma had picked the girls up from school, and made sure they were safely inside, before heading off to her bridge club.

'I don't know,' Imogen admitted. She really hadn't seen this coming. She'd been so busy worrying about Anneshka . . .

Marie pressed her lips together. 'I told you Mark's eyes looked different. I told you his walking was slow. And you said I was imagining things. You said—'

'I know,' muttered Imogen. She was annoyed with herself. Marie *had* told her all that, several months ago, and Imogen hadn't listened. 'I'm sorry,' she said. 'You were right.'

Upstairs, the velecours were making a lot of noise. They'd just been given slugs and, even down here, Imogen could hear their excited flaps.

Mum said Fred and Frieda couldn't stay for much longer; she said they were getting too big. But Imogen didn't have the headspace to worry about that at the moment.

'Let's think this through logically,' she said. 'When Mark got stuck in the mines in Valkahá, we thought the yedleek had eaten him. Then he turned up and we thought he'd escaped . . . But what if he didn't?'

'What do you mean?' breathed Marie. She reached for the cat, who was curled up between them.

'What if—' Imogen paused, afraid to say the words out loud – afraid that it would make her worst fears turn true. 'What if the real Mark got eaten and this Mark is a fake?'

There was a moment of silence. Even the velecours were quiet.

'You think yedleek can dress up as humans?' Marie whispered. 'You think our stepdad's a monster in disguise?'

Imogen's heart ached at the thought.

But if the man she'd been calling Mark was a yedleek, then the real Mark must be . . .

No.

It was too horrible to think about, too horrible to look at directly. There was no way that Mark could be dead. She'd seen him just last night, hadn't she?

'Fake Mark wouldn't know how to make campfires,' said Marie, twisting at the sleeve of her school jumper. 'Fake Mark wouldn't crack bad jokes.'

Imogen stared at her sister. Marie was right. Fake Mark wouldn't bang on about business stuff over breakfast. He wouldn't help Imogen learn the names of the stars.

'Perhaps Mark *is* Mark,' said Imogen. 'But the yedleek did something to him and now he's changing . . . into . . . one of them.'

The doorbell rang and both girls jumped. 'I'll get it,' cried Imogen, remembering what Mum had said about her being in charge when they were home on their own.

It's probably Grandma, she thought. *Forgotten her glasses again.*

Imogen skidded across the hallway, using her slippers like skis. Reaching up, she pulled the front door open.

Green trousers. Green jacket. Shaved head.

It was the spy from Drama Club.

Panic flooded Imogen's body. She tried to push the door shut, but the man wedged his welly boot into the gap. 'Parents home?' he asked.

Imogen pushed against the door. The man shoved back and she flew across the hallway, crashing into the wall.

'I'll take that as a no,' said the man, stepping into the house.

Imogen was too shocked to think. All she knew was this wasn't right. She scrambled to her feet. 'Marie!' she shouted, 'Marie, run!'

Imogen hurtled into the lounge. Marie was still sitting with Mog on the sofa.

'Don't move,' said the man, entering the room behind her. Marie's face fell.

Imogen glanced at the window, wondering if they could escape, but it was too risky and this man was fast. 'Stand by the hearth,' he instructed.

The sisters shuffled in front of the gas fire, with Imogen cradling the shoulder she'd hurt. And now she could see the man properly. His beard was thick and pointed. He was dressed in funny clothes.

It was as if someone had taken a waxwork from the museum, one of the Viking men, and stuffed it into Prince Charles's clothing.

'You shouldn't be here,' Imogen said to the intruder. 'Why are you? What do you want?'

The man didn't show any sign that he'd heard. Instead, he glanced back at the hall.

'Imogen,' Marie whimpered. 'What's going on?'

'He's the spy from Drama Club,' Imogen whispered. 'I told you he was up to no good!'

The man signalled over his shoulder, as if there was someone else. Imogen realised, with a lurch, that there was. She heard the tramping of feet.

'You can't – you shouldn't be here!' she cried, as more people entered the lounge. 'My mum will be home soon!'

None of the strangers replied. They all had a stern, efficient look. And, Imogen noticed, they were wearing little crown signs. It was stamped on the front of their wellies. It was stitched on to their coats. Some of them were even sporting crown badges. Was it . . . a uniform?

Two men in red trousers stood by the television. A tall woman, with a rifle slung over one shoulder, guarded the door. She was dressed head-to-toe in tweed and wearing a big fur hat.

Marie eyed the woman's gun. 'What is that for?' she asked.

'Shooting party,' sneered the woman.

By the time the strangers had settled into position, Imogen was trembling . . .

Even Mog the cat looked afraid.

'Imogen,' peeped Marie. 'Who are they?'

Imogen had a horrible feeling that she knew the answer . . .

But this was her home. Her safe place. She could hardly believe that it would be *invaded*, could hardly process what happened next.

There were footsteps in the hallway – a heavy, squeaky tread. The woman with the rifle stood aside and Anneshka walked into the room.

CHAPTER 19

Marie seemed to shrink. She pressed herself closer to Imogen, as if she was trying to climb into her school uniform, as if they could become one girl.

'It's okay,' whispered Imogen. 'I won't let her take you.' Although she had no idea how she would keep such a pledge. Every inch of her wanted to run – wanted to take Marie's hand and bolt for the door, but there was no way they'd make it past that many people.

If only they'd stayed in the bathroom with the velecours. At least there was a lock.

Imogen scowled at Anneshka, channelling her fear into rage. She couldn't believe that, despite all her research on the school computer, all her careful piecing together of the facts, she'd *still* failed to keep Marie safe.

Anneshka looked the same as before. Same blonde hair. Same piercing blue eyes. Same princess-perfect face.

But her clothes were totally different. She wore a long floral dress and wellies. In one hand, she held a pair of pheasants. They were dead – tongues out, feathers gleaming, swinging at her side like a tote bag.

'Hello, Marie,' said Anneshka. 'What have you done to your hair? Would you like me to plait it for you?' She reached out and Marie flinched.

'Get out of our house,' snarled Imogen.

But Anneshka continued as if Imogen hadn't spoken. 'You wouldn't talk to Samo,' she said, nodding at the man with the pointy beard. 'So we were left with no choice but to pay you a visit.'

Anneshka's gaze ran over Mog, the old comfy sofa and the paint-stained rug. She wrinkled her nose. 'You know why I'm here, don't you?' she said, eyes latching on to Marie.

'You're looking for the greatest kingdom.' Marie's voice was sandpaper dry.

'Yes,' said Anneshka. 'Very good.' She sauntered across the room. It was hard to saunter in wellies, but she managed it well enough.

'You weren't quite honest with me, were you?' she continued. 'I asked if your kingdom was rich, and you said it was not. But there are people here with millions upon millions of . . . what do you call them? Ah yes, *pounds*. Not even the five queens of Valkahá had such reserves.'

She lifted both hands like a priestess. The pheasants swung from side to side.

'But it's not only money,' mused Anneshka. 'I've seen all the things that you have: carriages that move without horses, animated paintings that can talk.' She raised one eyebrow at the TV. 'This is a kingdom *rich in magic*. And what could be greater than that?'

'It's not magic,' said Marie. 'It's—'

'Silence,' snapped Anneshka. 'I'll say when you can speak . . . I suppose you've heard about my new business? I'm the CEO of Green & Pleasant, and these are my associates – also known as the Yezdetz, the fiercest warriors of any world.'

Imogen eyed the men in red trousers and the tall woman with the gun. They stood with their heads slightly dipped, eyes flashing. It was like the lounge had been taken over by a pack of wolves.

But, despite all this, the Yezdetz seemed uncomfortable. The tall woman kept scratching at her hat. The men wore their ties far too long. Even Samo looked awkward, as if he was stuck in those big welly boots.

They're not wearing their usual clothes, thought Imogen. *The Yezdetz aren't from this world . . .*

'As far as people know, Green & Pleasant exists to defend the countryside,' said Anneshka. 'We look after all those *green things*, of which you peasants are so fond. But that is not our true purpose.' She lowered her voice to a whisper. 'We've been searching for the source of all magic.'

Imogen thought Anneshka was joking, but her face was serious. Imogen had to stifle a laugh. 'How is that going?' she asked, unable to help herself.

'I have been making enquiries,' said Anneshka. 'Speaking

to the Duke of Sconfordshire. Meeting your prime minister. It's amazing what you can do when you move in the right circles.'

She tossed her head and her hair rippled gold. 'And yet I still haven't found what I seek. All of these mobiles and computers, combine harvesters and microwaves.' She pronounced the words slowly, sounding them out. 'What is the use of such *greatness*, if I cannot harness it for myself?'

Imogen listened with disbelief, but a new feeling was wheedling in. Was it pity? Hope? Anneshka might have made friends in high places, but this was not her world . . . She was clearly very confused.

Even confused people can be dangerous, thought Imogen.

'So here I am,' said Anneshka. 'Hunting for greatness on this wind-blasted isle. And apart from the huge quantity of magic and the excess of rain and sea, it is much the same as anywhere else.'

There was a clucking noise from upstairs and all eyes swivelled to the ceiling. *The velecours*, thought Imogen, fresh panic rising.

'Gunilla, what was that?' Anneshka asked the woman with the rifle.

Imogen didn't know what Anneshka would do if she found two giant birds in the bath, but – and she glanced at the dead pheasants – she didn't want to find out.

'Oh—' said Imogen, thinking fast. 'It's just the central heating. It always clucks when it comes on.'

She prayed that Fred and Frieda wouldn't do anything else. If the velecours started squawking, Anneshka was sure to recognise the sound. Imogen squeezed her hands together.

The tall woman, called Gunilla, looked suspicious. She pointed her rifle at the ceiling, tracking the clucking sound. But after a few seconds of silence, she lowered the weapon, and Imogen let her hands relax.

'Then I remembered you,' said Anneshka. Her eyes seemed to pierce through Marie. 'You are the missing piece of the riddle – the final part of my prophecy.'

'I'm not going with you!' Marie burst out.

Anneshka tipped back her head and laughed. Then her face snapped into serious mode. 'What is the root of this kingdom's power? Where does the magic come from? Tell me, and I'll never bother you again! . . . I'll even throw in a gift.'

She tossed the dead pheasants and they landed, wings splayed, at Marie's feet.

'But if you don't tell me,' said Anneshka, 'Samo will kill you all.' There was an angry miaow as Samo seized Mog. 'Starting with your cat.'

Chapter 20

'No!' cried Imogen. 'Don't hurt Mog!'

Samo held the cat by the scruff of its neck and Imogen felt totally powerless. There was no way she'd beat that man in a fight. No way to reason with him either.

Mog squirmed and lashed out with his paws, but Samo had a tight hold on him.

Imogen glanced at the clock on the wall, willing it to tick faster. There were at least twenty minutes before Mum or Mark would get home.

Then something caught her eye . . . it was poking out of the top of Samo's front pocket, glinting in the light. At first, Imogen thought it was a pocket watch, chained to his button hole.

But that was no watch.

'Do not test us,' warned Anneshka.

Imogen had to do *something*. She couldn't just watch Mog being killed.

'Let go of my cat!' she screamed and she launched herself at Samo. She managed to land a thump on his chest.

Samo was taken by surprise, Mog yowled, and there was a moment of total confusion.

It was all Imogen needed.

She reached for Samo's front pocket – snapped the thin metal chain.

A strong hand caught her arm and twisted. Imogen yelped, falling to the floor. With her face squished against the carpet and her arm bent back, it was hard to see what was going on.

Marie's feet were nearby, next to some posh leather shoes. And, even closer to Imogen's face, were Anneshka's clean wellies.

Grandma says you can tell a lot about people from their footwear . . .

'Miiiiaaaaooooow,' cried poor Mog.

'Stupid children,' hissed Anneshka. 'You cannot fight me. My victory is written in the stars.'

Imogen wanted to say that it wouldn't be a very impressive victory if it took five adults to defeat two children, but Samo was still twisting her arm. It was all she could do to stop herself crying out.

How she *wished* that Mum would hurry up. Imogen could no longer see the wall clock. Surely, there were only fifteen minutes left?

But that was fifteen minutes too long.

Anneshka's wellies stepped closer to Marie's socks and it was all Imogen could see. 'Fulfil your part of the prophecy,' Anneshka shouted. 'Fulfil it or we'll slit your throats! What is the source of this kingdom's magic?'

Marie scrunched her toes and, as Anneshka's voice became more furious, Imogen knew this was it. They were done for. The intruders would kill Mog. Then they'd kill the girls. Then, perhaps, they'd kill Mark and Mum.

Imogen felt a scream rise inside her.

But Marie didn't sound afraid when she spoke. 'I will tell you the source of our greatness.'

The welly boots were very still. 'Go on . . .'

'It's Stonehenge,' said Marie.

'It's *what?*' asked Anneshka.

Imogen wanted to say the same. What was Marie playing at? Stonehenge was just a load of old rocks. Anneshka would never fall for that.

'Marie—' warned Imogen, but Samo twisted her arm tighter and she gasped with pain.

'The place you want is called Stonehenge,' Marie repeated. 'You can look it up, if you like. It's very old . . . *very magical.*'

The Yezdetz were silent. They seemed to be waiting for Anneshka's next move.

'Very well,' said Anneshka. 'I will seek out this stony henge.'

Imogen made a noise between a sob and a laugh. Samo let go of her arm and Mog landed on all fours, just a few inches from Imogen's face. The cat fled the lounge as if his tail was on fire.

Then Imogen scrambled across the carpet to her sister. Stunned, she watched the intruders file out.

Anneshka was the last to leave. She peered down at the

girls. 'I am sure that I don't need to tell you that my people will be watching. If you squeak a word about this, or so much as *think* about running away, I will be the first to know. I have friends in very high places: the Houses of Parliament, Buckingham Palace, the police. Just because you are not being held hostage, do not imagine you are free.'

Anneshka strolled towards the door. 'Oh, and if I find that stony henge is not the source of all magic – if this is some kind of trick – I will hunt you down like two stupid pheasants. And, this time, I won't be so nice.'

CHAPTER 21

It was Kazimira who first spotted the midges. 'Bitey things,' she complained, from the islet behind Miro. 'Make them go away.' She still seemed to think that he was in control of their surroundings.

Miro waited for the princess to catch up, then he wafted his hands at the little cloud of insects that had appeared above her head.

For a few seconds, the flies floated off. But they returned in even greater numbers, as if they'd gathered their family and friends.

Now they swarmed around Miro's head too, looking for an opportunity to land. He fanned his hands in ever more frantic movements, but one fly must have got through because he felt it bite. Miro gasped and slapped his own neck.

The flies weren't the only creatures plaguing the marshes. There were spiders too. Miro hadn't seen them, but he'd noticed their webs. Indeed, they were impossible to miss.

Enormous spiderwebs were strung across islands, glistening

with opalescent silk. They rippled in the breeze like the finest sheets.

Miro tried not to think about the webs' owners . . . about how large they must be to spin structures like that.

Instead, he focused on navigating around the pearly nets. Sometimes, this meant that Miro, Kazimira and Konya had to wade in the water, dragging each other when the marsh got too deep.

'Don't like it,' whined Kazimira.

Miro was inclined to agree. His mind conjured images of his bed in Patoleezal's mansion – of warm fires, grilled sausages, and steaming cups of mint tea.

Perhaps he'd been a fool to leave all that behind. Especially since he might reach Nedobyt only to find no one waiting for him . . .

For a moment, Miro longed to be back in Yaroslav. There would have been no risk of being rejected if he'd stayed put.

But had he ever been fully accepted? Patoleezal's words rang in his head. *I'll shape you into a king . . . Kings don't have silly stuffed toys . . .*

The toy lion that Patoleezal had tried to get rid of had been a gift from Miro's mother. It was the last piece of her that he had.

No, Miro could not return to Yaroslav.

He took a deep breath and waded on.

Konya was also struggling with the midges. They weren't an enemy she knew how to fight. She kept swiping at the insects with her front paws, but it only cleared the air for a moment. The flies regrouped and came back strong.

As the sunlight faded, the midges thickened, until Miro, Konya and Kazimira were wading, not only through water, but through clouds of flies.

'They're going up my nose holes,' screamed Kazimira.

'They're getting in my hair,' Miro cried. If he hadn't known any better, he would have said the swarms of midges were eclipsing the sun. But the sun was setting on its own account, slinking behind the horizon, as if it too was fed up with this place.

Miro squinted through the mist of insects, searching for somewhere to hide. He didn't need a palace or a mansion – just a room with walls and a roof. A shepherd's hut or a pigsty would do. But Miro saw no such thing.

There were midges in his eyes, midges in his ears, midges swarming round the back of his neck. He could even feel midge bites on his bottom. How had they got through his clothes?

He wanted to scream like he'd done before, to tip back his head and shriek. But that would mean opening his mouth, and *that* would mean eating flies.

Desperate, Miro lowered his body into the bog water. He kept going until only the top half of his face was above the surface and he had to breathe through his nose. There were no midges underwater.

Now Miro regretted trying to cross the marshes. *Now* he

felt like a fool. Surely, if his grandmothers had wanted to see him, they would have written months ago.

They hadn't come to his coronation. Hadn't sent word when Uncle Drakomor died. Perhaps they didn't want to know Miro. And now he was being eaten alive by insects for two old ladies who didn't even care!

Kazimira saw Miro and came splashing towards him. The cloud of midges parted as she threw herself into the shallows.

The water closed over her head. The midge-cloud closed too – hovering just a few inches above the water's surface.

Kazimira came up panting. 'Arghhhh!' she screamed. 'I HATE THIS PLACE!'

Miro had never expected to agree with the princess so many times in one day.

As the sun set, the children shivered in cold water. Konya also immersed her body, a look of utter misery on her big whiskered face.

The last of the light glinted off a spiderweb. And that was when Miro noticed . . . The air above the web was thick with midges, just like everywhere else.

But under the spider-spun net, there weren't any flies.

CHAPTER 22

The spider's web covered several small islands. It was strung from the tall grass, like a tent. *Perhaps I can take refuge under that*, thought Miro.

He hauled himself on to the nearest islet, fingers plunging into mossy earth. He had to creep up the mound on his belly, so his head wouldn't break the spider's silk.

It was worth it – it was really worth it – because there were no midges here.

In the middle of the island, Miro rolled on to his back. He breathed in the fly-free air. Above him, the web glistened and, even in the low light, Miro saw that it was splattered with flies. There were hundreds of them, perhaps thousands.

Miro heaved a deep sigh. He'd never been so relieved to see a spider's web in his life. 'Oi, Kazimira,' he called. 'There aren't any midges under here!'

Kazimira didn't hesitate. Miro heard her splashing towards him, then the quiet as she dipped underwater, and, finally, the squelchy mud noises as she wriggled up the little mound.

Konya followed the princess. She was surprisingly good at staying low for such an enormous cat.

The web here was high enough for the children to sit, but Kazimira lay down beside Miro, curling into a dripping ball. Konya began the mammoth task of licking flies from her fur.

For a long while, the children lay still beneath the spider's net. The princess was making little huffs of outrage – half fury, half sobs.

Miro couldn't help it. He started crying too. Why not? Kazimira was at it. He cried for his dead parents. For his dead uncle too. For the grandmothers who he'd never meet.

But most of all he cried for his own foolishness, for believing that he could cross this great wasteland, and for attempting to do it alone.

This had all been a terrible mistake.

A bite on his ear itched so badly that Miro wanted to rip it off.

The marshes were black now, reduced to a soundscape. Reeds tapped against reeds, mice scuffled in the mud, and fish surfaced with wet slips and slops.

When Miro had lived in a castle, he'd lit candles to keep the dark out. But he was too exhausted to be afraid now – exhausted and hungry too.

Through the tiny holes of the spiderweb, Miro saw the cold light of stars. *What?* they seemed to whisper. *You didn't think it would be easy . . . did you?*

'You're right, Kazimira,' Miro muttered. 'This is the worst place in the world. Tomorrow, we'll go back to the Lowlands.'

Kazimira only sniffed.

Exactly *how* they'd get back there was a question for tomorrow. In this swamp, nothing was easy.

Miro wondered how his friends were doing. Had Perla managed to find her brother? Had Imogen gone home with . . . what was she called?

Imogen and . . .

Hmm, that was odd. Miro couldn't remember the other girl's name.

Imogen's sister is . . .

Nope.

His mind was like a hook going into the water and coming up without a fish. Ah well, this wasn't the time for mental gymnastics. He had to focus on surviving.

Miro tried to make himself comfortable on the islet and Kazimira did the same. Konya snuggled between them and neither child complained.

They fell asleep surrounded by tall grass, with a warm cat pressed against them, and with spiderwebs and stars overhead.

CHAPTER 23

The next morning, Miro awoke to something cold and wet, slapping against his face. He opened his eyes and saw a fish.

Behind the fish was Konya. She was lying with her chin on her great floofy paws. Her eyes were fixed on Miro as if she'd brought him the most exquisite gift.

Miro sat up and the events of yesterday washed through him. Island hopping. Midges. Hunger.

The hunger was still there, like a fist gripping his stomach, reminding him that he'd hardly eaten for days.

'Thank you,' said Miro to Konya, unsure of the etiquette. The fish flipped and flapped on the moss.

In Castle Yaroslav, the cook had owned a cat. That cat used to bring the cook presents – mice, rats and, occasionally, frogs. The cook would complain and throw the 'gifts' out the window. She certainly didn't eat them.

But Kazimira had already clubbed the fish with a rock. Now she was peeling off the skin, exposing pink flesh underneath. The sight turned Miro's stomach. How he longed to eat something else.

He wished for honey-roast pig and hot buttered veg, for orange and cinnamon cake. He could almost see little lemon-curd pastries dancing round Kazimira's head.

Miro shook himself.

'Eat it,' said Kazimira. She was holding out the half-chewed fish.

'You don't get to tell me what to do,' muttered Miro, but he nibbled the meat.

'Eat it properly,' snapped the princess. 'I'd like you to live. Don't want to be here on my own.'

Miro looked up, startled. That was the nicest thing the princess had ever said. He forced himself to take a bigger bite, chewing many times before swallowing the raw fish.

At least the midges had gone. If it hadn't been for the bites that still itched across his body, Miro would have said the insects were a mirage – no more real than his fantasy of lemon-curd pastries.

The spider's web still hung above the children. It was so fine, almost transparent against the sky. The midge bodies, that had peppered the web in the evening, were nowhere to be seen. Something must have collected them in the night.

Don't think about the spider, thought Miro. He handed Kazimira the fish.

As she ate, Miro noticed a purple jewel suspended above her head. No, not a jewel . . . a spider. So *this* was the weaver of the web. It was smaller than Miro had expected.

Its gleaming body was the size of a blueberry. Its legs were spindly thin. And it was lowering itself towards Kazimira.

'S-spider,' said Miro, raising a hand.

Kazimira went very still. Then, slowly, she looked up. The princess and the spider made eye contact, and Kazimira let out a piercing scream.

Before Miro's thoughts could catch up with reality, Kazimira slapped the spider to the ground. She held the fish carcass up like a club.

'I think it's all right,' said Miro. 'It might not be dangerous.'

But Kazimira wasn't listening. She started beating the ground with the fish.

Miro didn't know what to do. Neither, it seemed, did Konya. The sněehoolark's tail dropped low and she backed away from the girl.

Finally, Kazimira stopped. 'Got it,' she grunted, pointing to a crumpled purple splodge. Miro didn't dare to crawl closer.

'You killed it,' he whispered. He should have felt relieved. The spider had looked poisonous.

'You killed it,' Miro repeated. Konya kept backing away, down and off the island, like a tiger stalking her prey in reverse.

'Bad spider,' said Kazimira, and she tossed it into the water.

The ground beneath him seemed to tilt and Miro shook his head, willing his dizziness away. He really should have eaten more fish.

But Kazimira seemed to have felt it too. 'What was that?' she demanded.

The island jerked in the other direction and Miro dug his fingers into the moss. *It's an earthquake*, he thought, his mind sluggish.

But the other islets didn't move.

The ground shuddered and tilted further. Kazimira slipped, screaming, through the web and the long grass, into the water below.

Miro held on for a second longer. The horizon slid sideways and wading birds took flight, screeching at the wrong-way-up sky. Then the moss between Miro's fingers ripped and he fell.

He landed with a splash. Water and algae rushed up his nose. Luckily, this bit of bog wasn't deep. Miro's feet pushed against earth and he came up, flailing.

Kazimira's scream was a constant sound, streaking across the marsh.

Konya gave a low hiss.

Miro pushed back his wet hair and there was no making sense of it . . . The island they'd slept on was rising. Water cascaded from the edges, rushing through sedges and reeds. And, as the islet unfurled itself, Miro realised that the mound was not a mound at all – but an enormous back.

CHAPTER 24

Marie sank to the carpet, next to Imogen. The sisters were alone in the lounge once more.

'You saved us,' whispered Imogen.

'That was – it was – horrible!' cried Marie. 'I thought that Samo man was going to kill Mog!'

'But he didn't,' said Imogen, gripping Marie's arm. 'And you were brilliant! Where did you get the idea? Stonehenge, the source of all magic? That's inspired!'

Marie still looked concerned, but a smile inched on to her face. 'You gave me the idea,' she confided. 'You said the velecours were the central heating, and Anneshka fell for it. After that, I knew she could be tricked.'

Imogen wondered at her sister. Marie's was a special kind of cleverness.

'Imogen, I should have believed what you said after Drama Club. You told me that man worked for Anneshka . . . I didn't want it to be true.'

Imogen shrugged, trying to look casual, but Marie's words meant a lot. 'That's okay,' she murmured. 'I should have trusted you when you said Mark had changed.'

'No more doubting each other, okay?' said Marie and there was a new intensity in her eyes. 'From now on, we back each other up.'

'No more doubting,' Imogen agreed.

She shifted on the carpet, so she was facing her sister. One of her arms ached, where Samo had grabbed her. In the other hand, she held something cold. She opened her fingers, revealing a moth.

Marie's hand shot to her mouth.

'It's not real,' said Imogen quickly. 'Look.' She held the moth up to eye-level. Its wings were finely hammered sheets of silver. Tiny jewels sparkled in its eyes. 'I took it from Samo.'

'Why?' gasped Marie.

'I thought it was the shadow moth and it looked trapped.'

Unlike the Mezi Mŭra, this fake moth sat still, like a watch that had run out of battery.

Marie tucked her knees under her school jumper. 'Anneshka is going to want that back, you know.'

'I know,' said Imogen, placing the moth in her pocket. 'And she's going to realise that you lied about Stonehenge.'

Marie's eyes widened. 'Imogen, what will she do?'

She'll come back and kill us. That was Imogen's first thought, but she could hardly say it out loud.

'I don't know,' said Imogen, carefully. 'But at least you've bought us some time. It will take her a few days to work out the truth. Before then we need to make a plan.'

Several plans, thought Imogen. *For the velecours, for Anneshka, for Mark . . .*

The girls barricaded themselves in the bathroom. It was a tight fit now the velecours were so big. Fred pecked at Imogen's school uniform, trying to get her to play. But she wasn't in the mood.

A few minutes later, she heard the front door click. 'Hello, girls!' called Mum's voice.

Marie ran out of the bathroom, thundering down the stairs. 'Mum!' she cried. 'Mum, Mum, MUM!'

Imogen followed, slower. She was trying to filter through events in her head, trying to arrange them into a shape that would make sense.

Anneshka broke into the house. No, not just Anneshka – Anneshka and a load of people in weird clothes. But it's okay, we've dealt with it.

She practised saying it as she walked down the stairs.

But when she saw her mother, all pre-prepared words failed. 'Mum!' she cried and tears sprang to her eyes, making it hard to see.

'Darling? What is it?' Mum was hugging Marie with one hand, still clutching her keys with the other.

'Squ-squ-squwaaaaak!' came the answer.

Imogen had forgotten to close the bathroom door. The velecours came hurtling down after her, flapping. Frieda lifted into the air, but she failed to turn with the staircase and both birds collided with the wall.

Imogen ignored them. She had to deliver her news. 'Anneshka has been here,' she said as she gripped the banister. 'Anneshka broke into the house.'

For a split second, Mum looked confused.

'She came with lots of people,' said Marie. 'She wanted us to help her find greatness.'

'How does she know where we live?' cried Mum.

'Cluck, cluck,' said the velecours as they toddled into the hallway.

Imogen gathered herself. 'We don't know. But she gave us some dead pheasants and we sent her to Stonehenge.'

Now Mum looked really confused and more than a little panicked. 'Are you hurt?' she asked, and she gripped Marie as if she was about to check for damage.

Imogen and Marie shook their heads.

'I'm going to call Mark,' muttered Mum.

Imogen sat on the bottom step, hugging her knees to her chest. She looked at the fast-growing velecours, at the familiar shoes and coats by the door. Nothing felt the same now Anneshka had been here. Just like the Haberdash Gardens, the house felt tainted . . . unsafe.

'Hmm,' said Mum. 'He's not picking up.'

She called his office instead, but the man on reception said that Mark had left early, which was unusual for him.

'Oh,' said Mum to the phone. 'In that case, I'm sure he'll

be home soon.' Imogen watched Mum hang up and noticed her hand was shaking – just a bit.

CHAPTER 25

Bm ut Mark was not back soon. Mum stuck the pheasants outside, by the bins, then she made beans on toast. Imogen squished the beans beneath her fork. She didn't have the stomach for food.

Mum seemed more agitated with every minute that passed. She went from annoyed – 'why won't he pick up?' – to angry – 'after all our talks' – to worried – 'I hope he's okay'. Eventually, she went very quiet.

Imogen looked at Marie across the kitchen table. She wondered if her sister was thinking the same thing . . . Mark must have finished turning into a yedleek, with a clay body and a flaming head.

Perhaps he'd gone to live underground, like the yedleek in Valkahá did. How could they explain that to Mum?

Imogen stared at her plate of mashed beans. 'Sorry, Mum,' she said. 'I'm not hungry.'

'Me neither,' muttered Mum. Her eyes kept darting to the window. 'We can't stay here. Not now Anneshka knows it's our home.'

Fred and Frieda were waiting by the kitchen table. They were tall enough to steal food from the plates, but they knew that wasn't allowed. Instead, they tried their best to look appealing.

'Shall I put the velecours back in the bathroom?' asked Marie.

'Oh . . . no,' said Mum. 'I give up.'

Imogen handed a slice of toast to Frieda and the bird swallowed it whole. Then Frieda folded herself on the floor beside Imogen, letting her head flop on Imogen's lap.

'Mark and I had a bit of an argument,' confessed Mum. 'I was cross that he'd left you at Drama Club. I hope he's not – I hope he hasn't—'

. . . *left us*, thought Imogen, finishing Mum's sentence in her head. She felt a twisting pain at the idea.

He's left her, he's left you, hissed a worry creature. It was sitting on the window ledge.

Imogen stroked the soft feathers between Frieda's eyes and tried not to listen to her fears.

It was only after several deep breaths that she realised the worry creature was making no sense. Mark . . . abandon them? Mark had crossed several kingdoms and faced the yedleek. He'd risked everything to make sure they were safe.

There was no way he'd leave because of an argument.

'Okay,' said Mum, standing up. 'I'm taking you to your grandma's. Get your pyjamas, girls.'

Frieda lifted her head.

'But where are *you* going?' squeaked Marie.

'Crickley Chase. It's where Mark goes mountain biking. I bet that's where he is.'

'Are there any mines in Crickley Chase?' asked Imogen, trying to keep her voice even.

'No, I don't think so,' said Mum. 'Why do you ask?'

Imogen heaved a sigh of relief. Of course Mark wasn't a yedleek. All this stuff with Anneshka had rattled her – sent her brain into overdrive. Mark was probably cycling, just like Mum had said. 'Oh, no reason. I was just wondering.'

'I'll drop you girls off with your grandma,' said Mum. 'You'll be much safer there.' She stacked the plates, not bothering to scrape off Imogen's mashed beans. 'Then I'll find Mark and we'll report Anneshka to the police.' She half-threw the plates into the sink. 'Surely, they can arrest her, now she's broken into my house!'

Imogen wasn't sure about being left with Grandma. The last thing she wanted was to spend time apart from Mum. The world felt less stable, less safe, than ever.

'Can't we stay with you?' asked Imogen. 'At least until you've found Mark?' She stroked Frieda's long feathered neck, trying to draw comfort from the dozing bird.

'Please, Mum,' said Marie. 'Pleeeeaaase.'

Mum's eyes flicked between the sisters. She could never resist when Marie asked in that voice.

'I suppose it won't do any harm . . .' she sighed. Fred

hopped on to Mark's chair and let out a squawk. 'But what on earth am I going to do with this pair?'

Marie cocked her head at the giant birds. 'Perhaps they should come to Crickley Chase too.'

CHAPTER 26

The little island that Miro and Kazimira had spent the night on seemed to be growing and gathering itself. Weeds and old reeds, mud and rotting stuff – it all got swept up into the great shifting mass that was – that was . . .

Miro didn't know what it was.

Konya let out a dynamite hiss.

Kazimira and Miro started screaming.

The island rose higher, trailing stringy grass. Spiderwebs cloaked one side and Miro realised that the land he'd been sleeping on, the land he'd thought was solid rock, was actually a living creature.

Miro had to stop screaming so he could breathe, and, in that instant, he was hit by a smell.

A rotting, rancid stink wafted out from the island. Miro's stomach clenched, threatening to bring up the raw fish he'd forced down.

And still the creature rose.

Its limbs were taking shape now. Mud and moss twitched

into position, forming two arms and two legs. The monster straightened, unfurling its body.

It let out a wet, throaty roar.

Even Kazimira stopped screaming.

The monster's groan rattled through the marsh, sending ripples across the water, making the islets shake. Miro could feel it vibrating through him too. His bones buzzed with the sound.

'Kill it!' shrieked Kazimira. She was pointing at the creature. 'KILL IT NOW!'

Miro didn't even reply. What did Kazimira think he was? Even if he wanted to kill the thing in front of him, he couldn't. This wasn't a fish or a spider. It was some kind of troll and it was over ten feet tall.

The troll shuddered and stretched its shoulders, as if it had been curled up for a very long time. Then it turned its face to the children . . . and what a face it was.

Water poured from the bog creature's eyeholes. Its mouth was ringed with reed stems, which were busy rearranging themselves, trying to remember how mouths worked.

Miro's whole body started shaking. In that moment, it didn't matter that he'd faced the Lord of the Krootymoosh. It didn't matter that he was a king. Miro was absolutely terrified.

Konya lowered herself into the water, until just her face was visible. Then she slunk behind the nearest islet.

'DESTROYYYYYYYYY . . .' groaned the bog troll.

Miro thought it was a threat. The monster was going to destroy them. But no, the word stretched out: '. . . YYYEEEEER-RRRRSS.'

Water cascaded from the troll's shoulders. 'DESSTTTROY-YYYYEEEEEERRRS,' it bellowed again. And Miro realised that the word was an accusation – directed at Kazimira and, no doubt, at him.

Kazimira turned and ran. She splashed and crashed through the marsh, moving as fast as she could over swampy terrain.

Miro tried the opposite strategy. Perhaps if he stayed very still . . .

The bog creature watched the princess. It breathed mist from its mouth.

Then it seemed to decide. It broke into a messy four-legged gallop that was more like a rocking horse than the real thing.

And, was Miro hallucinating, or were the troll's legs lengthening as it ran? Its limbs were becoming stilts, raising its body above the boggy ground.

Miro stared in horror. What *was* this thing?

The troll closed in on the princess. *This is it*, thought Miro, *she's going to die.*

The monster overtook Kazimira and swerved to a halt, blocking her path. Water dripped from its great mossy body, shellfish clattered on its chest.

'DESTTTRRRRRROOYYYYERRRRR,' it roared from its sad fishy mouth.

The troll was reshaping its front legs again – from stilts into colossal arms. Sticks and weeds writhed into position.

Konya poked her head up between the reeds and looked Miro dead in the eyes. Boy and giant cat were united in that moment. Much as they found Kazimira annoying, they *had* to do something to help.

CHAPTER 27

Miro forced his tired limbs into motion, half running, half crawling across the marsh. Konya followed, leaping over islets.

Kazimira seemed to shrink as her enemy grew. The troll drew weeds into its body. The water bubbled as earth was snatched and reeds were snapped into shape.

Miro was moving as fast as he could, but the marsh made running difficult. He could feel the mud clinging to his feet, pulling against his heels like underwater hands.

At last, Miro took fistfuls of grass and heaved himself on to an island. The grass's sharp edges cut his palms, but Miro hardly noticed.

He wasn't far from Kazimira.

The troll reached down and picked up the princess.

'My daddy is the king of the Lowlands,' she shrieked. But her voice sounded like the whine of a fly.

'YOUUUUUUUU,' boomed the monster. Its voice was as rich and layered as the marsh's black soil. 'YOUUUUUUU KILLED THE SPIDERRRRRRRRRRRR.'

Is that why it's so cross? thought Miro. *Because of a small purple spider?*

The troll shook Kazimira like she was a pot of pepper. It had restyled itself as a monstrous squid, with a body the size of a battleship and ten long, flailing limbs.

'Argh-gh-gh-gh,' said Kazimira.

'SPIIIIDEEERRRRRRRRRRRRRRRRRRR,' roared the troll.

Konya ran up the side of the beast, clambering along a tentacle. Even the sněehoolark looked small against the monster's glistening bulk.

She mounted the troll's back. But the bog creature brushed the giant cat off, with one flick of a tentacle.

Konya landed with a splash and Miro's heart skipped a beat. 'Konya!' he cried. The sněehoolark resurfaced and crawled on to an island. She lay there, panting and wet.

The bog monster still had Kazimira. It was holding her upside down, dress flipped over her head. Kazimira wasn't screaming any more.

'Release her!' cried Miro, trying to make his voice loud.

The troll's terrible gaze turned upon him. Water was streaming from its eyes.

'Sh-sh-she didn't mean to hurt the spider,' said Miro, feeling the lie stick in his throat. Kazimira had known *exactly* what she was doing.

The monster angled its great green head. It was terrifying and also, Miro realised with a jolt, it reminded him of his uncle.

Uncle Drakomor . . .

Remembering was hard, but Miro forced himself to do it.

Uncle Drakomor shouting, sending me to my tower . . .

Drakomor had often seemed angry.

But now Miro knew the truth, he wondered if his uncle's fury had been a mask for something else, something more like guilt . . . or sadness.

Miro pulled himself out of the memory, back to the here and now. More water rushed from the troll's eyeholes, making rivers down its face. There were shells on its belly, clams of some kind. They were opening and closing, opening and closing, screaming a tragic chorus.

I wonder, thought Miro . . .

CHAPTER 28

'You're right,' Miro called. What was the point in lying? There was nowhere to hide the truth in this place. 'Kazimira did kill the spider on purpose.'

'NOOOOOOOOOOOOOO,' bellowed the bog troll, waving its tentacles about. Miro had to duck as one whistled through the air at the same height as his neck.

But he kept his eyes on the monster's face, and this time it was clear. Miro saw the pain in the creature's expression. It hit him like a punch in the gut. 'I'm sorry,' he said, weakly.

'WHHYYYYYYYYYYYYYYYYYYYYYYYY?' cried the troll, swinging Kazimira round its head. It was like a gigantic toddler mourning the death of a pet.

How could Miro explain *why* Kazimira had done it? How could he say that sometimes humans killed things because they were afraid . . . or just because they could?

How could he tell the troll that – even though it loved the tiny purple spider – humans only loved beings like themselves?

Miro felt the terrible wave of grief emanating from the troll. It almost knocked him sideways.

'Because she's a ninny,' said Miro. 'She's a spoiled little royal, who's never had to think about anyone other than herself.'

Miro was allowed to say such things because, once, it had applied to him.

The troll let out another groan, but it held Kazimira still. Its chest rose and fell with each breath, making the shells on its front clink.

'But please,' continued Miro, his voice sounding thinner by the second, 'give her another chance. She can do better. I know she can . . . She is very young.'

'SPIDERRRRRR WAS YOOOOOOOOUUUNGG TOOOOOOOOOO,' said the monster, but its voice was quieter; the anger less dominant, the sadness more obvious.

Miro felt grief rise within himself too, although he couldn't pinpoint the source. It was as if he contained a deep well of sadness and someone had removed the lid. The grief flooded through Miro's body, rinsing his heart and his thoughts.

The monster was right. The spider had been a living creature, with every right to exist. And its web had saved Miro and Kazimira from the midges.

Miro felt his lower lip quiver. Suddenly, the killing of the small purple spider felt like the greatest tragedy in the world. Perhaps Kazimira *did* deserve to die.

Miro shook himself. No, that wasn't right. 'Please,' he repeated. 'We'll do anything – take any punishment. But don't kill us . . . because we're sorry and it *was* a beautiful spider.'

The bog troll leaned in, so its face was only a few feet away from Miro's. 'WHHHHOOOOOO ARREEEE YOUUUUUUUUUU?' it asked, breathing mist all over Miro. Its breath smelled of fish guts and rot.

'I was a prince,' began Miro. For a strange moment, he couldn't remember the rest. His uncle's face was clear. His parents' faces were blurry and his own name felt very far away.

The monster sniffed Miro, as if it could identify him through scent alone, as if it wanted to suck him in. Miro felt his damp hair being pulled towards the troll's massive nostrils.

'Then I became a king,' Miro continued. 'And now . . . now I'm just Miro.'

He paused, half-choked by his name. Miro is what his mother used to call him. How he longed to remember her fully. How he longed to see her face, even if it was just in a statue or a painting. The memories were fading too fast . . .

'HMMMMMMMMMMMMMM,' grumbled the monster.

'W-who are you?' asked Miro, trying to imitate the troll's way of talking.

'MEEEEEEEEEEE?' The monster moved backwards. It was still holding the princess in one tentacle. 'I AM THE GUUUUUARDIAN OF MOKZHADEEEEEE.' It gestured at the surrounding marsh.

Miro gulped. 'And what is your name?'

The troll looked confused. A pale crab scuttled out of

its nose and disappeared down its back. 'PAAAAANOO-OOVNÍÍÍÍÍK,' it replied.

'I see,' said Miro. 'Well, Panovník, name your punishment. I'll do whatever you ask. Please, just don't kill Kazimira.'

The shells on Panovník's underarms trembled. 'ANYYY-YYY PUNISHMENT?' it asked.

'Anything,' said Miro.

The troll lowered the princess and, for a terrible moment, Miro thought it was going to drown her, dunking her in the water upside down. But instead it swung her aside, slapping her on to an island like a dead fish.

After that, the monster started shrinking, tentacles retreating into its body, moss shuffling back into the bog. It looked more troll-shaped by the second. Two arms. Two legs.

It was still massive – five times taller than any man Miro had met. But, perhaps, it fitted the title of *bog troll* better than *giant murderous squid*.

'FIIIIIIIIIIIIIIIIIIINNEE,' said Panovník in its slow voice. 'I WIILLLL LET YOUU LIIIIIIIIIIIIIVE.'

Miro was breathless with relief. 'Thank you,' he cried. 'Thank you!'

The bundle of bows that was Kazimira stirred. Konya scrabbled on to Kazimira's island and nudged the princess with her nose.

The bog troll's eyes were still streaming water. Its mouth was still turned down. 'NOOW FOOOOR YOOOUUU-UURRRRR PUNISHMENT,' it groaned.

Miro straightened his back, determined to accept his fate as bravely as he could.

'REMOOOOOOVE MY SUCKERRRRRS,' said Panovník.

Miro thought he'd misheard. But the troll gestured to the shells that were nestled all over its body, hanging like unholy fruit.

Parasites, thought Miro.

The suckers were shaped like pears, with hard polished shells. He had no idea how they were attached to the troll, but he shuddered.

'ORRRRRRRRRRRR WOULD YOUUUUUUU RAAATTHERRRR DIIIIIEEEEEE?'

Miro rolled up his shirt sleeves. 'It's a fair punishment,' he said.

CHAPTER 29

It was much harder fitting the velecours into Mum's car than it had been the first time round, when they'd transported the birds from the tea rooms.

Back then, the velecours had fitted on the girls' laps. Now, they were tall enough to stick their heads through the sunroof. Not that Mum let them do this.

Fred was folded into the boot. Frieda got the back. Imogen and Marie squidged into the front passenger seat, with Marie squatting in the footwell.

'Cycling on a school night,' said Mum. 'Can you believe? . . . I hope everyone is strapped in! Are you ready?'

Frieda stuck her beak forward and squawked.

'I'll take that as a yes,' muttered Mum. And with that, she hit the accelerator.

Mum drove faster than usual, so fast that it made Imogen feel sick. She was grateful when they pulled into the car park at the edge of Crickley Chase.

The sun was low and the car park was empty, apart from one other vehicle.

Imogen's hand went to her mouth when she saw it . . . a sporty red car. It was Mark's and it was parked at a funny angle, with the bike rack mounted on the boot.

There was no bike attached.

'Caught red-handed!' cried Mum. 'To think he didn't even send a text! He should have been at home, should have been protecting . . . He's got a lot of explaining to do.'

Mum, Marie and Imogen climbed out of the car, into the fresh evening air. It had been raining, and everything was gleaming, from the fern fronds to the car park bins.

'What should we do with Fred and Frieda?' asked Marie. 'They look like they want to come too.'

It was true. Frieda was peering through the car window, doing her best puppy-dog eyes. Fred was leaning over the back seats, with his neck at an uncomfortable angle.

'Perhaps they can,' said Mum, who was still staring at Mark's car. 'There won't be anyone around at this hour.' She ran her hands over her face. 'No one except for Mark.'

Mum attached collars and leads to the velecours. She'd bought them for using in the back garden, although they hadn't done this yet. They were supposed to be for dogs, and the velecours were much taller than any dogs Imogen knew, but their necks were very long and thin.

Fred and Frieda clucked as they clambered out, eyes rolling this way and that. Mum took Fred's lead. Imogen took Frieda's. Marie was in charge of the torch. It wasn't dark – not yet – but it might be by the time they returned.

And, with that, they left the car park and headed down the waymarked path.

Had anyone seen them, they would have been quite a sight, parading across Crickley Chase. From a distance, it might have looked like they were walking pet ostriches.

Crickley Chase was a rolling heathland, speckled with heather, bracken and trees. Imogen could see why Mark came here to cycle. It felt very big and free.

'Mark!' called Mum. 'Mark, where are you?' Her voice travelled across the open space. Butterflies danced in the evening sun. Crickets chirruped after the rain.

'I need you to come home now,' Mum shouted. 'I need – *we need* to call the police!'

Imogen wondered how they would find Mark in this place. Surely, he'd be tired of cycling soon. But she couldn't stop thinking about the strange fires she'd seen burn in his eyes . . .

'Hey,' cried Marie. 'What's this?' She picked up an old jumper from the ground.

Imogen's heart started beating too fast.

The jumper had been thrown there casually, as if it was disposable, like a sweet wrapper or an old orange skin. But it was Mark's favourite jumper; the one he wore round the house. It smelled of wool and coffee and smoke . . .

Mum tucked the jumper under one arm. Without saying a word, she walked on.

As the path led them deeper into Crickley Chase, Frieda

lifted her beak and sniffed. Then, without warning, she stood still. 'Come on,' grunted Imogen, tugging at the lead. 'We have to find Mark.'

Frieda spread her wings and flapped. The gust of air almost knocked Imogen off her feet. 'Frieda!' she gasped. 'Don't do that.'

But Frieda could smell her freedom. She thrust out her chest and flapped again. 'Frieda, stop!' shouted Mum.

Frieda squawked in defiance and took off.

Imogen's arms were above her head now. She was holding the lead and being stretched up.

Marie wrapped her arms around Imogen's waist. Both girls pulled against the bird and it felt like they were winning, but Frieda flapped harder still.

Imogen's heels left the ground.

'You have to let go!' cried Mum. She must have released Fred because she also grabbed Imogen, anchoring her to the earth.

Imogen's arms ached and she knew Mum was right.

She unclasped her fingers from the leash.

Imogen, Marie and Mum collapsed on to the footpath in a jumble of arms and legs.

Fred was trying to follow his sister. His belly bounced on the bracken as he struggled to get enough air beneath his wings. Frieda squawked her encouragement and Fred lifted up.

Imogen felt as if she was back in the mines, watching the

yedleek close in on Mark. She'd looked down and Mark's face had got smaller and smaller—

The velecours were also getting further away.

'No!' cried Imogen, reaching up. Something was tearing in her chest.

'It's okay,' said Mum. 'They'll come back when they're ready.'

But Imogen wasn't so sure – about the velecours, about Mark, about any of it. Why had Mark dropped his jumper? Why hadn't he said he was going out? How long did they have before Anneshka returned?

Mum hugged Imogen and Marie. For a moment, they just sat on the path, watching the velecours fly.

'Are you sure you don't want to go straight to your grandma's?'

'No,' said Marie, without missing a beat. 'We want to help find Mark.'

'Come on then,' said Mum, and she stood up, offering the girls a hand each. 'We should hurry before it gets dark.'

CHAPTER 30

They found Mark's shoes at the foot of a hill. Along with his wristwatch.

It was like a treasure hunt, except the clues were items of clothing. And the prize was not treasure . . . it was Mark.

Mum squinted up the slope. 'Girls, I think you'd better wait here.'

The hill rose above a cluster of trees and there was a hole near the top, as if an enormous worm had burrowed through. Imogen felt a twinge of fear. It was the mouth of a cave.

'Please, Mum,' she said. 'Let us come with you.'

Mum had gone very quiet. She was no longer saying things would be okay. She didn't even seem angry with Mark.

The three of them walked up the hill as the sun set. Marie turned on the torch and Imogen's mind filled the blanks. She saw a tall figure in the shadows, a movement behind a tree—

But it was just her imagination.

At the entrance to the cave, they found Mark's bike. It was lying on its side, as if it had been dropped.

For a terrible moment, Imogen thought the bike was a

skeleton. It was because of the darkness and the bike's sharp-angled frame. She gulped and tried to steady her nerves. 'It's just my worry creatures,' she whispered.

'What the hell is going on?' muttered Mum. She dumped Mark's clothing at the top of the hill; the things they'd collected as they walked. Then the three of them peered into the cave.

A route was marked down the edge of the grotto, with a handrail bolted into the wall. There was a sign for tourists, explaining how it had formed.

Imogen couldn't see the back of the cave, even when Marie shone the torch down there, so it must have been very deep, shaped more like a tunnel than a bowl.

'Mark?' Marie called into the darkness, but there was no reply.

'Why would he go in there?' Mum whispered. 'He doesn't like enclosed spaces . . .'

The sisters looked at each other, horror etched on to their faces. They must have been thinking the same thing. *Mark might not like enclosed spaces, but yedleek certainly do . . .*

'Girls, I need you to wait here,' said Mum.

'But—'

'No buts,' snapped Mum. 'I'm serious. There's something very strange going on . . . I should have left you with your grandma. I'm sorry to have brought you this far.'

'But it might not be safe,' cried Imogen.

'Exactly,' Mum replied. 'That's why you're staying put.'

The sky above the Chase was deep blue and starry. Lights

glowed from nearby towns. There was no such illumination in the cave.

Mum took the torch and flashed it round the weed-fringed edges. A few metres in, there were patterns on the walls – fossils shaped like bullets; long-dead creatures trapped in the rock. Beyond that, the torchlight failed.

Imogen's eyes strained, trying to spot hands reaching from within the stone. But there was no sign of yedleek. There was nothing but graffiti and fossils, a handrail and some bird poo.

'Don't worry, I won't go far,' said Mum. 'It's your turn to trust me. Okay?'

Reluctantly, Imogen nodded. She stood with Marie at the mouth of the cave as Mum walked deeper in.

Imogen thought of Mark's abandoned clothes, of the way he'd left his bike. It really wasn't like him . . . She remembered a rhyme she'd heard in the other world, the world where yedleek came from:

> But there are creatures shaped by fire,
> who hunt for human meat.
> They say the young are under-ripe.
> They say the old taste sweet.

'What if Mark has finished turning into a yedleek?' Imogen whispered, half-stiff with dread. It seemed to coil around her like a boa constrictor, making it difficult to think – making it harder to breathe. 'What if he tries to eat Mum?'

'Mum said to trust her,' Marie answered. But Imogen could tell she was scared too.

> *I fear the men of burning light.*
> *I fear their molten forms.*
> *I fear their deep volcano eyes*
> *and yawning, hungry jaws.*

The girls stood for a long while, watching Mum go deeper, watching the circle of torchlight shrink.

'I don't like underground places,' Marie whispered, and Imogen understood why. Marie had spent several weeks in the mines, trapped beneath Valkahá. Imogen remembered the smothering dark, the taste of rock dust between her teeth. Her terror coiled tighter still.

When Imogen couldn't take the suspense any longer, she shouted into the cave. 'Mum, what's in there? Are you okay?' Her voice echoed down the tunnel.

'There's something,' Mum called. She sounded strangely off-key.

Imogen squinted, trying to see further.

'What is it?' cried Marie.

Silence.

'Mum?'

There was no answer.

'Do you think we should—'

Then Mum screamed.

CHAPTER 31

'THEY'RRREEE TOOOOOO SMAAAAALL,' grumbled Panovník, the bog troll. It gestured at the shells attached to its body. 'I CAAANNNOOOOTTT MAAAAKE THEM LEEEEEAAAAAVE.'

The troll sat down, creating a wave with its arse. The surf washed over the island Miro was standing on, flooding his boots.

Kazimira was sitting on the neighbouring islet, looking very sorry for herself. Even when Konya licked her face, the princess didn't respond.

Right, thought Miro. *I suppose I'd better do this alone.*

He waded into the water towards the troll. Up close, Panovník really did smell. Miro tried to hold his breath, but that would only do for so long.

Instead, he snapped off two rushes, that were growing nearby, and poked their sausage-shaped heads up his nostrils. That did the trick. He would just have to breathe through his mouth.

The bog troll was sitting with its legs out in front and its fungus toenails on show. Even sitting, its head seemed far away. Its back was as tall as a tree and, like a tree, Miro noticed that it had a bird's nest on top.

Miro placed one foot on the troll's thigh. It was slimy and glistening green, with water dripping from it. He heaved himself on to the monster's leg and shuffled towards its belly, putting his arms out for balance.

At the troll's gut, Miro encountered his first sucker. It was tucked inside two glossy shells.

He took hold of the shell and tried tugging. But there was something keeping it in place – a pale muscle that extended from the base of the shell, deep into the troll's vegetative flesh.

The muscle stretched when Miro pulled at the sucker. The troll gave a low growl.

Miro tried again, pulling harder. The shell stretched several inches from the monster, its rubbery muscle becoming thinner and thinner until, surely, it must break.

But it didn't. And Miro had to let go.

The shell pinged back into position, snapping against the troll. Miro almost lost his balance.

'OOOOOOOOOWWWWWW,' grumbled Panovník.

'I can't do it!' cried Miro. 'The suckers are too strong!'

'TWWWIIIIIIIIIIIIIIIIIIIIIIIIIIIIIIIIIIIIIIIIIISSSST IT,' boomed the bog troll.

So Miro reached for the shell a third time. He pulled it with both hands, twisting as hard as he could. The thick muscle connecting the shell to the troll released with a wet pop.

The thing in the shell let out a squeal, and Miro almost dropped it with surprise.

He looked down at the sucker. It was pulling itself into its shell, tucking its feelers out of sight. Then it slammed shut.

'I did it?' Miro cried, his words coming out like a question.

The troll closed its eyes and gave a satisfied sigh.

Miro wasn't sure what the troll wanted him to do with the parasite. After what had happened with the spider, Miro guessed killing it wasn't the answer. But if he just dropped it, wouldn't it wriggle back and latch on?

'Throw it here,' came a voice. It took Miro a moment to realise the voice belonged to Kazimira. She was standing up now, holding out the skirt of her dress. Miro had seen peasants doing that when they picked fruit.

He threw the sucker and Kazimira caught it in her skirt. 'Got it!' she cried and Miro grinned.

'KEEEEEEEEEEEEP GOOOOOOIIIIING,' moaned Panovník.

Miro looked up at the troll's chest. There were clusters of suckers all over it – many more to remove. He paused to stuff the rushes further up his nose. Then he started to climb.

It was harder than he'd expected. The troll's flesh was as soft as the marshes, and sometimes Miro's whole hand was absorbed before he found something firm enough to grip.

He wondered what was underneath the troll's weeds. Could the whole monster be like this – just sponge and moss and mud?

No, there must be something at the core of Panovník . . . something of flesh and bone.

Perhaps not. Out here, the normal rules didn't seem to apply.

Miro's mind swam with hunger. He stood on the troll's belly, reaching. The parasites seemed to have tucked themselves into the most tender places, hanging like tassels beneath Panovník's arms.

They waved their feelers as Miro approached, as if trying to shoo him away. But Miro showed no mercy. It was him and Kazimira – or the suckers. Someone had to go.

He grabbed and twisted, becoming more confident with every parasite he removed.

Suck, squelch, thwack!

He threw the suckers and Kazimira ran around her island, catching and collecting them. Konya nudged the shells back into the middle, should any of them try to escape.

By rights, it should have been Kazimira who was climbing the bog troll. She'd got them into this mess. She should shoulder the punishment . . . But at least she was getting involved.

Soon, the troll was shell-free. And there was a pyramid of parasites on Kazimira's island. The pile was so big, there almost wasn't enough room for the girl and the sněehoolark.

Miro sat on Panovník's shoulder, holding on with his legs. The ground seemed a long way down. The rushes that were stuffed up his nostrils made it hard to take deep breaths.

'Is that better?' he asked. There was no need to shout any more. He was right next to Panovník's weed-frilled ear.

The troll rubbed its hands over its torso, feeling for any suckers that Miro might have missed. Then it rubbed its belly, as if pleased by its own velvet-moss skin. 'HHHMM-MMMMMMM,' it groaned. 'MUUUUUUUUUUUCH BETTTEEER.'

Finally, Miro slid down the troll's back, landing in the water with a splash. If he hadn't been so exhausted, it would almost have been fun.

He pulled the rushes from his nose and went to join Kazimira. The shells were all shut – tight-lipped in the face of their defeat.

The bog troll got to its feet. There was still water running from its eyeholes, but, somehow, it seemed less sad.

'What should we do with the suckers?' asked Miro, gesturing at the gleaming pile. Konya was toying with one of them, batting it between her front paws.

'RELLEEEEAAAAAASEE THEM WHEEEEN I'M GOOOOOOOOONNNNNE,' said the bog troll. 'ORRRR EEAAAAT THEMMM . . . IFFF YOU LIIIIIIIIIIIIKE.'

Eat them? Miro hadn't been expecting that.

The suckers looked even more disgusting than the fish Konya had caught. Besides, wasn't that as bad as killing spiders?

But Miro was so hungry . . . and his encounter with the bog troll had left him hungrier than ever – not only for food, but for life. He was determined to get off these hellish marshes.

And if he wanted to survive, he must eat.

Kazimira was already picking up the suckers, holding them to her ear, as if the secret to opening them would be whispered.

'How does one eat a . . . parasite?' asked Miro.

The troll's great belly rumbled and shook. It was, Miro realised, laughing.

'THERRRRRREEE ARREEEEE MOOOOOORREE WAYSSSSSSS TO EAAAAAAAAAAAATTTTTT A SUCCCCKKKERRRRRRRRRRRRRRRRRRRR THAN THERRRRRRRREEEEEE AAAAAARRRRRRREEE STAAAAAAAARRRRRRRRRSSSSSSSSS IN THE SKKKYYYYYYYYYYYYYY.'

CHAPTER 32

Kazimira placed a sucker on a lump of rock and smashed it with a stone. The shell broke into several pieces. Then Kazimira plucked out a creature that was all pale jelly and slime.

She popped it into her mouth.

Miro watched with open disgust. Even Konya looked confused, tilting her head as Kazimira chewed and swallowed.

The troll nodded its great head. 'THHAAAAAATT'S ONE WAAAY TOOOO EEEAAAAAT THEEM.'

Panovník seemed to be in a much better mood now. Much more friendly. Much less kill-y.

Seeing this, Miro felt emboldened to ask, 'Is there a better way? I am very hungry . . . but I don't like raw fish.'

'WEEEELLLL,' grumbled Panovník. 'WE CAAAAN'T HAAAVE THAAAAATTT.'

The troll made a fist and there was a faint smell of gas. Then it opened its hand and green flames danced on its palm.

'MAAAARRRRSSH GAASS BUUURRNS EVERRR-RRYTHINGG,' said the troll and it pulled up a fistful of reeds. 'EVEN DAAAAAMMMP THIIIINGGS.'

It placed the reeds at the centre of an island and lit them. Miro and Konya gathered round.

The green flames took hold and the bog troll fed them with black earth.

The warmth was very comforting – a dry heat Miro hadn't felt for an age. He inched closer to the fire, holding up his hands. His skin had been in water for too long and his fingers looked wrinkled.

Kazimira came splashing towards him, skirt full of suckers. She threw them on to the bonfire and Miro would have felt sorry for the shellfish, if he hadn't been so hungry.

The fire hissed and steam rose with the smoke.

'How will we know when they're done?' asked Miro.

He was answered by a loud pop.

'LIIIIIKKE THHAAAAAAAAATT,' said Panovník. Miro crawled closer, so the heat from the fire was almost too much. And there, among the green licking light, he saw that one sucker shell had burst, revealing roasted meat within.

Kazimira nudged the sucker out the fire using a long stem. Then she blew on it, before removing the meat, which had cooked white, like chicken.

'How is it?' asked Miro, his mouth watering. He had to admit, when they were cooked, the suckers smelled good.

'Mmmmm,' replied Kazimira. She chewed with a thoughtful expression. 'Juicy and sweet.'

Pop, pop, POP! went the suckers.

Konya watched with great interest.

Kazimira flicked the split shells out of the flames and lined them up to cool. Then she worked her way through them, methodically removing the fish.

Miro opened the closest shell with trembling hands. He *really* was very hungry. He would have eaten his own fingers if he'd thought it would help him survive.

'Oh, Stars,' he whispered as steam wafted up from the sucker. Miro stuffed it into his mouth. It was sweet as a prawn, and as juicy as Kazimira had promised.

It was . . .

Miro couldn't believe it.

It was delicious.

There was more popping in the fire. Suckers were exploding this way and that, jumping as they burst.

The children sat together on the edge of the island, stuffing meat into their mouths. They chewed with great abandon, not bothering to close their mouths.

Sucker juice ran down Miro's chin, but he didn't care. He'd never been so hungry. He'd never tasted such tender meat.

He threw some cooked shellfish to Konya and the sněehoolark snapped it up. Kazimira watched with narrowed eyes. Then she started doing the same, throwing the meat a shorter distance each time so the sněehoolark had to come closer to collect the food. Eventually, the giant cat was sitting next to the princess, almost eating out of her hand.

Panovník had shrunk even more now. He was only twice as big as a man.

'Right,' said Miro, dusting himself down. 'I suppose we'd better get going.'

Kazimira scrunched up her face. 'Get going where?' she asked.

Miro opened his mouth, but he was surprised to find he didn't have the answer. 'Off the marshes,' he said, and he lifted his chin to hide his embarrassment. 'We need to get to the other side. To . . . our destination.'

Kazimira thrust her neck forwards. 'Which is . . .?'

Miro couldn't keep up his bluster. 'That's funny,' he said. 'I can't remember.' There was a small voice at the back of his head. *We were going – we were going—*

But he couldn't finish the thought.

He looked at Konya. She was satisfied after a meal of warm suckers, licking her lips and cleaning her paws.

'We were doing *something*,' cried Miro. 'Something important!'

Kazimira let herself flop back on the island, close to the heat of the fire. 'Be quiet,' she moaned. 'Some of us are trying to sleep.'

Then Miro looked at the bog troll. It was hunched over the flames, watching the children.

'What about you?' said Miro. 'Do you remember where we're going?'

The bog troll shrugged its great shoulders, sending water cascading down its chest. It glinted, mud-brown and flecked with wildflowers.

'HOOOOOOWWWW SHOOOOOOOUULD I KNOOOOOOOWWW?' it grumbled.

Miro's legs were very heavy. He'd already travelled many miles.

Perhaps he'd only been awake because he was hungry. Now his stomach was full of shellfish, and a lovely warmth spread outwards, along his limbs, right to the tips of his fingers and toes.

Perhaps if he had a little rest, he'd remember . . . remember where he had to go.

He lay down a few feet from Kazimira, and Konya settled nearby. The clouds were wispy. The sun was weak. Cradling his happy, full belly, Miro closed his eyes.

Perhaps, whatever they were doing could wait . . . just for a little while.

CHAPTER 33

Imogen started running into the cave. Mum's scream echoed all around.

The yedleek, the yedleek. Mark's become one of them.

Imogen sprinted towards her mother. Marie was behind, running too.

Please don't let Mark have hurt Mum, prayed Imogen. *Please let me be wrong.*

Up ahead, she could see a figure, backlit by torchlight.

It was Mum. She was kneeling, and there was a second shape slumped on the ground. 'Mum?' Imogen slowed and Marie almost crashed into her.

Mum's expression was set.

'Mum, what is that?' asked Imogen. She could feel the blood whooshing round her body, hear her pulse hammering in her head. *Tick-tock, tick-tock—*

The thing on the floor was not a monster. It had not come from another world. It was Mark, their stepdad, who lived in their house. Mark, who danced to the radio and made their mother laugh.

He lay on his side, wearing only his boxers. His skin looked very pale. 'Mark!' cried Imogen, but his eyes didn't open.

'What is it?' asked Marie. 'What's happened?'

Mum's breathing went all ragged. Then she crumpled and made a sound, like an animal that's been wounded.

Now Imogen wanted to run.

Mum tried to smother her sobbing, but it kept leaking out. 'Go back to the cave entrance,' she gasped. 'Go back to – go back – go back—'

And Imogen could only think one thing. *Mark crossed several kingdoms to save us, he risked everything to get us out of the mines . . .*

She crouched beside his body and reached out a hand.

'Imogen, don't,' Mum was saying. 'I already . . . He's cold.'

Imogen touched Mark's neck.

Mark had gone all that way to find them. And now they had found him too late.

His skin was clammy, just like Mum said. Imogen moved her hand closer to his jawline.

Thu-thud—

There it was.

Thu-thud, thu-thud—

Beneath her fingers, hope flickered.

'There's a pulse,' said Imogen.

Mum looked up, and Imogen repeated herself. 'Honestly, it's there – feel!' She moved out of the way so Mum could touch Mark's throat.

Mum's face changed after that. She pulled out her phone. 'No reception.' She stumbled to her feet and ran to the cave entrance, leaving the torch behind.

Imogen and Marie stayed by Mark. They talked to him, just in case he could hear.

'Ambulance,' said Mum, her voice echoing down the tunnel. 'Catherine Clarke. Yes – yes, that's right – there's been some kind of accident. We're at the cave on Crickley Chase.'

They stayed with Mark until the paramedics arrived and carried him out. 'He's very cold,' said Mum, hurrying after them. 'His skin feels like it's made out of stone.'

Mum had covered Mark with his clothes, but his jumper slipped off at the mouth of the cave. The medics wrapped him in a silver blanket and made their way down the slope.

Then they loaded Mark into the ambulance, which they'd managed to get to the bottom of the hill. Mum answered their questions. Imogen and Marie watched from a little way back.

Imogen had picked up Mark's jumper and slipped it over her head, comforted to have part of him close. Marie cuddled against her.

The medical people seemed to be asking Mum if she wanted a lift. Mum turned, before responding and gesturing at the girls.

The ambulance sped off, blue lights illuminating the Chase.

Imogen, Marie and Mum watched it retreat. 'Do they know what's wrong with him?' Marie asked.

'I-I don't think so,' said Mum. 'At the hospital – they'll do tests. They said that he's stable. Said that . . .' Her voice trailed off.

Then Mum switched into action mode. No more tears. She hurried back towards the car park, with Imogen and Marie trotting in her wake.

'I'll drop you with Grandma,' Mum called without stopping. 'Then I'm going to hospital. I want to be with Mark when he comes round.'

Imogen recalled Mark's cold white skin. How could Mum be so sure he *would* wake?

Mum didn't slow until they neared Mark's car. 'I should have known that something was wrong,' she said, a little wobble in her voice. 'He hasn't been himself for weeks.'

She unlocked her car and the girls got in.

Imogen was exhausted and a little stunned. She watched the road rise up to meet them as Mum drove along dark country lanes. The hedgerows went galloping on either side. It didn't feel like the car was moving. It felt like the world was rushing at them.

Imogen pulled up the collar of Mark's jumper so it sat over the bridge of her nose. She inhaled the smell of old coffee. She let her tired eyes close.

'Come inside,' said Grandma, when they arrived at her bungalow. 'You must be exhausted, poor little loves.'

Imogen took it all in – the orange-coloured lights, the ceramic ornaments, the embroidered cushions and the little footstool.

Grandma and Mum whispered in the porch. Imogen couldn't make out very much, other than Grandma saying, 'Off you go. I'll take care of the girls.'

Mum left, and Grandma set up the sofa bed. Then she made cups of hot, sugary milk. The sisters sipped their drinks in silence. Imogen felt weirdly numb.

But it was comforting to be somewhere familiar and it was nice to be looked after by Gran.

She peeked out between Grandma's velvet curtains, looking at the street beyond. There was nobody out there – no sign of Anneshka or Samo.

'What a horrible day you've had,' said Grandma. 'But those doctors are very clever . . . Mark probably had a stroke like my friend Mildred. Strokes make people do funny things. Mildred was never the same after her third one. She went from being afraid of her own shadow to skydiving! . . . Do you think you'll be able to sleep?'

Marie looked up at Grandma. 'Not without a story,' she said.

CHAPTER 34

The next evening, Imogen and Marie went to visit Mark in hospital. He wasn't awake yet. He was in a coma – which, according to Mum, was a very long sleep.

A doctor led them into a white room, with machines and a window and a bed. Imogen's first thought when she saw the figure beneath the sheets was: *That isn't Mark – it's not him.*

Mark doesn't need tubes going into his body. Mark doesn't need machines that beep. Mark doesn't sleep with his arms so neatly arranged at his sides.

Mark sleeps like a starfish, with his limbs splayed out. He drives a sporty car very slowly and tells bad jokes and – this – this isn't him.

'Imogen and Marie have come to see you,' said the doctor. She was talking as if Mark was awake. But Mark did not respond.

Imogen remembered a conversation she'd had with Mark several months ago . . . 'Does space go on forever?' she had asked.

'Of course – I mean – no – I'm not sure.'

Imogen liked Mark better for this confession. She liked that he didn't pretend to know.

'Shall we try to find out?' he'd suggested.

After that, Imogen and Mark had started looking things up. Mark had shown her the best websites about space and helped her find library books.

'Scientists disagree,' Imogen had said, reading the book out loud. 'Some of them think the universe is limited to what we can observe. Others think it is infinite.' She spelled out that last word. '*In-fin-ite.*'

'Interesting,' Mark had said. 'Infinite means something goes on forever. And, if that theory's correct, there must be infinite worlds. Think about it,' he'd added, with a smile, 'infinite worlds with infinite Imogens. Must be a right handful.'

Imogen dragged herself out of the memory.

Today, the world seemed *not* infinite. The world seemed very small. It was just this room. Just Imogen, Marie and Mum and the horrible hospital bed and the horrible machine that helped Mark to breathe and the horrible talkative doctor.

'You can go closer, if you like,' said Mum.

Marie drifted towards the bed. The doctor was saying things like, 'keeping him comfortable' and 'monitoring his condition'.

Tears spilled down Marie's face. She slipped her hand into Mark's, but his fingers didn't return her squeeze.

Imogen did not want to go closer. If she only saw Mark

from this distance, she could pretend that it was like a fairy tale – where a princess slept for hundreds of years because she was under a spell.

But when *she* slept, the whole kingdom slept with her. What were Imogen, Marie and Mum supposed to do, while Mark was in his coma?

'When will he wake up?' asked Marie, sniffling.

'We're not exactly sure,' said the doctor. 'We're seeing some unusual activity in his vitals.'

Mum cleared her throat and the doctor stopped.

'In his what?' said Imogen.

The doctor hesitated, and Mum stepped in. 'Mark's not in any pain, girls,' she said, using her gentlest voice. 'But his body is . . . it's not getting better.'

Marie dropped Mark's hand and backed away from the bed. 'He's going to be okay . . . isn't he?'

Mum's mouth opened, but she didn't speak.

No, realised Imogen. *He's not. He's not going to be okay.*

Marie turned and ran from the room.

'Marie!' cried Mum, chasing after her. The doctor followed, white coat flapping, door banging shut as she left.

Now it was just Imogen and her stepdad.

It was hot in the room, and it smelled of school dinners. Imogen tried to open the window, but the handle was locked.

In that moment, she wanted nothing more than to feel fresh air. She wanted Mark to feel it too. Perhaps it would help wake him, perhaps—

She pushed her hands against the glass. She'd break it if she had to – and then – and then – between her splayed fingers was a star.

Imogen peeled her hand off the window. The more she looked, the more stars she could see . . . Faint specks; they were almost invisible, peeking between the clouds.

Imogen blinked at them, refusing to cry.

Was there a different Mark in a different universe, lying in a bed like this one – a Mark who would never wake up? Or was that *this* Mark? Was *this* the world where he died?

'I thought you don't believe in other worlds,' Imogen had said to Mark, when they were reading the book about the universe.

Mark had scratched his nose before responding. 'Well, I've changed my mind . . . It's very important. Scientists do it too. They investigate and, when new evidence emerges, they change the way that they think.'

Imogen turned back to the hospital bed. Mark's chest rose and fell, breathing in time with the machines, as if he was an extension of them.

Imogen shuffled closer. She almost felt afraid . . .

What happened in the fairy tales? How did they make the sleeping princess wake?

Imogen got as close to Mark as she dared, leaning over his pale waxy face. And, as she inhaled, she smelled it.

Underneath the smell of school dinners, of old sweat and

hospital soap, was a scent that didn't belong there. The scent of a freshly struck match.

Imogen breathed it in.

Evidence.

Mark smelled just like the yedleek.

'Mark,' said Imogen, feeling a bit silly. 'Mark, I've changed my mind.'

Of course, he didn't respond.

'You're not a yedleek . . . But the yedleek did *something* to you, didn't they? And I'm going to find out what. Like the scientists, I'll investigate . . . I'll get you out of this mess.'

Imogen leaned a little closer and planted a kiss on his cheek.

CHAPTER 35

There were no maps of the Marshes of Mokzhadee. Those who needed to travel that way took the road to the west, riding many extra miles to avoid the wetlands.

The earth was too damp to explore on foot, and too dry for boats. The few people who had attempted to cross Mokzhadee had never been seen again.

And yet, there was a boy . . .

Miro had lost his boots. What use were shoes when everything was squishy? Sometimes, he lifted a foot from the water and was surprised to find that it wasn't webbed.

He'd lost his rings too. He wore his trousers rolled up and his shirt tied about his head, shielding his face from the sun.

He had been walking for many days
and still the marshes wandered
and still the marshes grew.

Clothes weren't the only thing that Miro was shedding. He'd also lost his way. He could no longer remember where he wanted to go . . . let alone how to get there.

Sometimes, he was seized by a sudden desire to be off the

marshes. He'd glance left and right, the muscles working in his throat. It was the same in every direction: sinking bogs and spiderwebs.

Miro thought he remembered something about his grandparents – about getting to the other side . . .

But then he saw a patch of woolgrass.

He splashed over and snapped off a stem, which was hollow and thick as a flute. Miro placed the stem to his lips and let the sap ooze out. It was so sweet that it made his teeth ache. Draining the last of the syrup, he dropped the stalk.

He had been thinking of something – something else . . .

There was a girl nearby.

'Oi,' said Miro and he snapped off a second stem. 'Would you like a bit of this?'

The girl waded over and split the woolgrass with her fingers, before scooping out the flesh and shovelling it into her mouth. She was wearing a soggy dress made almost entirely out of ribbons and her damp hair was plastered to her head. Miro smiled as syrup rolled down her chin. He wondered who she was.

Perhaps she was his sister . . .

Perhaps they were old friends . . .

Perhaps she was a visiting queen and it was his job to show her round.

And so Miro and the girl dawdled between islands, pausing when they saw something new.

They had been walking for many weeks
and still the marshes wandered
and still the marshes grew.

A giant cat followed the children. Her fur was slick with snotweed, her claws had grown long from walking on the too-soft earth. She was always on the lookout for fish.

Occasionally, she seemed to remember. Her ears would twitch and she'd sniff the wind, as if thinking of going somewhere new . . .

But the impulse never lasted long. She'd spot movement in the shallows and pounce. Miro and the girl would laugh, before going to see what the giant cat had caught.

Last of all came the bog troll.

It followed the children and the cat, moving with great dripping strides. Sometimes it looked like a man, ten foot tall and made out of woolgrass, and sometimes it looked like a great shaggy beast that ambled along on all fours, and sometimes, if Miro looked from the corners of his eyes, it seemed to grow long stilt legs, just like the wading birds that built their nests in the reeds.

The bog troll knew the names of the plants and which ones were safe to eat. It was the troll who had taught Miro how to identify woolgrass. It was the troll who helped him find hairy violets with their edible petals, and spiralled slug-mint with its tangy aftertaste.

And there were always more suckers. Miro and the girl climbed the bog troll, twisting the shellfish free. It didn't matter how many they removed, more appeared the next day.

Miro asked if it was all right to eat the suckers and the fish and the bog troll said it was allowed. It said that death was a good thing, so long as it sustained life. And life was good too . . . so long as, one day, it would die.

'NOOO WAAAAAASTTTTEEE,' rumbled the bog troll. 'NOOO KILLLLINNNG SPIIDEERRRRRRSS FOOOR FUUUUUUUUUUNNN. EVVVERRRRRYY CRRREEEEATTTURRE IS PARRRRRRT OF THE MARRRRRSSSSSHHH.'

'What spider?' asked the girl. 'Who kills them for fun?'

The troll looked at her intently, before shrugging its great leaky shoulders and continuing on its way.

At night, when the midges came, the troll made a fire, lighting marsh gas on its palm. The fire scared off the insects, and the children huddled round.

Miro stuffed suckers with wild frogwort, pushing the shells into the flames and waiting for them to pop. They came out soft and sweet.

Then the children curled tight against the giant cat. *There are so many connections between us*, thought Miro. *Between fur and moss and skin. We're all part of a great swampy soup.*

And one day, when Miro died, the suckers would reclaim him. He felt strangely soothed by the idea. They'd been eating the marshes, so it was only fair if, eventually, the marshes ate them.

THE GREATEST KINGDOM

The cat yawned and stretched her front paws. The bog troll
gave a contented growl. Miro and the girl snuggled closer.
They had been walking for many months
and still the marshes wandered
and still the marshes grew.

CHAPTER 36

Days go by quickly on the marshes
    each one faster than the last
the sun rises and sets
    rises and sets
        until
            eventually
                it seems only to flash
                    on and *off*

                on
                    Miro walks among buvol
                    wild cows with moss on their horns
                    and the buvol hardly glance up because
                    they know he is part of the marsh

off
The air dances with midges
as suckers pop in the fire

The Greatest Kingdom

on

Woolgrass is flowering, dusting pollen
Miro's shoulders turn yellow
and he's dizzy with joy

off

Violet spiders spin their webs
silky nets catching flies
and overhead
the stars
they're spinning too . . .

CHAPTER 37

Imogen and Marie stayed with Grandma for several days. Mum reported Anneshka, and a policewoman started sitting in a car outside Grandma's house. She was supposed to be on watch, but whenever Imogen looked out, she seemed to be taking a nap.

Meanwhile, the girls weren't allowed to go to the park across the road. They weren't even allowed home to fetch their stuff. They had to ask their neighbour to feed Mog.

It was, without a doubt, the worst start to the summer holidays ever.

Mum split her time between Grandma's bungalow and the hospital. Grandma tried to distract the girls with card games and TV.

But Imogen couldn't forget what Mum had said. *Mark is not getting better . . .*

Every time Mum returned from hospital, she seemed a little more defeated than she had been. She tried her best to hide it, but it was clear things were serious.

'Even the specialists are stumped,' Mum said to Grandma

one evening, when she thought Imogen couldn't hear. 'They say he's deteriorating quickly. He can't go on like this . . .'

'Oh, love,' whispered Grandma, putting her arm around Mum.

And yet Imogen had evidence. She'd smelled yedleek through Mark's skin. She *had* to find out what the monsters had done to him. She *had* to make it stop.

But she didn't even know where to start. There were no library books about yedleek, no internet articles, no blogs.

Everything was going so badly, Imogen half expected to hear that Fred and Frieda had been found tangled in electricity wires. But, in the end, it was not the velecours who made the news . . .

Imogen, Marie and Grandma were having breakfast with the radio on, as was Grandma's routine. She was against anyone talking to her before ten o'clock. Said it interfered with her digestion.

Mum had gone to the hospital.

'The incident was reported to the police in the early hours of this morning,' said the woman on the radio. 'They're calling it a national emergency.'

'Imogen, will you pass the jam?' asked Marie.

Grandma drank her tea with her eyes closed.

'Mike Schmidt, senior warden for the charity, denied that it's a publicity stunt. "We have more than enough visitors to the stones. Why would we try to attract more?"'

Marie hummed as she stirred the jam into her porridge,

apparently in her own world. But the man on the radio caught Imogen's attention. What was all this talk of stones?

Here he was, talking again: 'They were there yesterday evening – just as they have been for thousands of years.'

Imogen nudged Marie and nodded at the radio. They listened to the next bit together.

'And then, when we opened this morning,' said the man, 'I couldn't believe it. They were gone. Every single stone that makes up Stonehenge, disappeared without a trace!'

Marie dropped her spoon. 'Grandma!' she cried. 'Grandma, Grandma!'

'Hush,' said Grandma, eyes still shut. 'It's far too early for that.'

The radio woman was speaking again: 'Police have dismissed rumours of alien abduction. With tyre tracks all over the grass, the culprits are very much of this world.'

'But, Grandma, she's stolen Stonehenge!'

'I don't care if she's taken Tutankhamun himself. I'm trying to enjoy my . . .' Grandma opened one eye. 'Who has?'

'Anneshka!' the girls chorused.

Grandma opened the other eye and placed her elbows on the table. 'What would *that woman* want with a load of old rocks? She's supposed to be a super-villain, not a geologist.'

Marie chewed at her bottom lip. 'We might have told her it's the source of all magic.'

'You did what?'

'It was the only way to make her leave,' said Marie. 'She wanted to know what made this kingdom great.'

Grandma cackled and almost choked on her porridge. 'And you told her it was a load of old stones?' She rocked back in her chair, slapping her thigh. Imogen didn't get the joke.

'Police are appealing for witnesses,' blared the radio.

There was a jangling of keys as Mum returned. 'Sorry,' she said. 'I just had a meeting with Mark's doctor and—'

'Catherine,' cut in Grandma. 'Sit down. You've got to hear this.'

CHAPTER 38

Grandma told Mum about Stonehenge going missing, but Mum didn't think it was funny. 'This isn't good news,' she said. 'If Anneshka has got hold of the stones, it's just a matter of time before she realises they aren't magic.'

'And then she'll come looking for me,' said Marie.

Grandma leaned in across the table. 'It's okay, Marie. We'll sort this out.'

'No, it's not!' cried Marie. 'You can't sort it out! Anneshka won't stop until she's got what she wants – until *I've* helped her find greatness! I'll never be safe. None of us will!'

Imogen didn't think she'd ever heard Marie lose her temper . . . They were all quiet for a while. Marie frowned at her porridge. Mum and Grandma exchanged worried looks.

The radio played an upbeat pop song, which was totally at odds with the mood so Grandma turned it off. 'How's Mark?' she asked, taking her seat.

Mum shook her head. 'Not good.' She looked very tired, like the skin beneath her eyes was bruised. 'The doctor keeps asking if he's been abroad,' Mum continued, 'as if he's got a tropical disease. I think they're getting desperate.'

Grandma threw her hands in the air. 'Good Lord, what if that's it?' she cried. Mum, Marie and Imogen all stared. 'What if Mark picked something up from the other place? From the other world, I mean? Mightn't the cure be there too?'

It was a very good point . . .

If the yedleek had done something to Mark, the answer wouldn't be here. It would be back in the world where the monsters lived.

Imogen pushed her porridge bowl aside and gave Marie a significant look.

We have to tell Mum about the yedleek.

But would Mum believe them?

She'd trusted them so far. She'd listened to what they said about the door in the tree . . . She'd even adopted the velecours.

Marie took a deep breath. 'Mum,' she said. 'We've got something to tell you. We think the yedleek did something to Mark in Valkahá, when he was down in the mines.'

'The yedleek?' said Mum. 'What is that?'

So Marie told Mum about the rock monsters – about their endless hunger for human flesh. 'They live in dark places,' she explained. 'The deeper the better.'

Mum looked alarmed. 'You've been near these things?'

'Oh, I saw them lots of times!' said Marie, looking rather proud.

'They don't eat children,' Imogen added.

Mum closed her eyes for a long time. When she opened them, she placed both hands on the tablecloth, as if to steady herself. 'I suppose I *could* ask the doctors in – what's it called? – Yaroslav.'

Imogen could hardly process what she was hearing. Once, Mum hadn't believed that Yaroslav existed. Now she was talking about going there herself?

Mum cleared her throat. 'But there's no way I'm leaving you girls. Not with Anneshka on the loose. We'll just have to make do with the doctors in this world. I'm sure they'll work something out.'

She didn't sound very sure.

He can't go on like this. Wasn't that what Mum had said? Mark was slowly slipping away . . .

'Think about it, Catherine!' cried Grandma, almost spilling her tea. 'It could solve your Anneshka problem. Take the children with you!'

Imogen watched this with something like whiplash. She couldn't keep up with the speed with which things were going. What had got into Grandma?

'It's not safe,' said Mum, sounding angry.

'It's not safe here, either,' replied Grandma, with a great flourish of her hands. 'It's the summer holidays, so the girls won't be missed, and it'd be the last thing Anneshka expects! She won't think to look for Marie in Yaroslav. You'd be killing two birds with one stone!'

Imogen thought of Fred and Frieda and wished Grandma would use a different phrase.

But Grandma bulldozed on. 'And by the time you return, Anneshka will have been arrested in this world for stealing Stonehenge. Come on, Catherine, you have to admit, it's a brilliant plan.'

Imogen didn't dare open her mouth. It was everything she wanted – find a cure for Mark, show Mum the other world, keep Marie safe from Anneshka and perhaps, if she was *really* lucky, she'd get to see Miro again. She longed to hear about his adventures, to thank him for his help rescuing Marie.

Grandma was waiting, eyes gleaming and, for a moment, Imogen forgot that she was the oldest one there. She was like an excitable girl. Child became mother, mother became child, and everything that Imogen knew to be true was turning on its head.

'You know, Mum,' whispered Marie. 'It's not a bad idea.'

'Not bad?' cried Grandma. 'It's *magnificent*!'

Mum glanced out of the window at the police car. 'And what about Mark?' she said. 'We just leave him here . . . on his own?'

'You said it yourself,' replied Grandma. 'He's not conscious. He doesn't know what's going on. And I could visit him while you're away.'

Now Mum turned her eyes to the girls. 'You're forgetting one thing,' she said. 'Only the special moth can open the door

179

in the tree. And we don't have it. So, even if I did approve of this plan, we can't go anywhere.'

Imogen's belly fluttered. She got up from the table and ran to her coat, which was hanging by Grandma's front door. She reached into the zip pocket.

'Imogen?' called Grandma. 'What are you doing?'

Imogen ran back to her family. She parted her hands and there, resting on her palm, was a small mechanical moth.

CHAPTER 39

The mechanical moth sat motionless on Imogen's hand. It was so still. Like an expensive brooch. 'Where did you get that?' gasped Mum.

'I borrowed it from Samo, Anneshka's sidekick. I saw it poking out of his pocket when Anneshka was threatening Marie.'

'Borrowed?' Grandma raised an eyebrow.

'It looks just like the shadow moth,' said Marie.

Tiny silver threads lined the fake moth's body, imitating fur. The wings were made from the thinnest metal. The antennae were fine wires and, instead of eyes, it had gems.

Imogen waited, half expecting to be told off.

'May I hold it?' asked Mum. Imogen tipped her hand and the moth slid on to Mum's outstretched fingers. 'Hah,' she breathed. 'It's so light.'

Grandma and Marie crowded round.

Just like an old-fashioned pocket watch, there was a chain attached to the moth's back. When Imogen snatched it from Samo, the chain had snapped. Now it hung like a glittering tail.

'Do you think this is how Anneshka got here?' said Mum.
'Is this a key to the other world?'

Imogen shook her head. 'I don't know . . . It could be.'

Mum turned the fake insect over and there, on its belly,
was a wind-up key. 'I can't believe I'm saying this, but I think
Grandma is right. I think we should go through the door in
the tree.'

'Thanks very much!' huffed Grandma.

'We can ask the doctors in Yaroslav if they've heard of this
yedleek disease. And there is something reassuring about the
thought of having you girls in a different world to Anneshka . . .
at least until the authorities get hold of her.'

Imogen didn't know whether to cheer or cry. Instead, she
gave Marie a tentative smile. She was so excited to see Miro.
And so afraid that Mark might die . . .

The girls and Mum left the bungalow soon after that.

Grandma hugged them tight on the doorstep. 'Good luck,'
she whispered. 'Take care of each other. Don't worry about
bringing me a gift. Just a postcard will do.'

'We're not going on holiday,' said Mum. 'This is serious.'

Grandma rearranged her face into a sombre expression.
'Yes, of course, dear,' she said.

The policewoman was still snoozing, face smushed against
her vehicle window. She didn't stir as Imogen, Marie and
Mum snuck past.

They bundled into Mum's car, with the girls lying down
on the back seats, in case Anneshka's spies were close.

'It's going to be okay,' Imogen whispered to her sister. 'We won't let Anneshka get you.'

Marie closed her eyes and squeezed Imogen's hand.

Stonehenge was on the news again, blaring over the car radio. 'The public are left shocked as ancient stones are stolen.' Mum turned it off.

When they pulled in to their road, Imogen poked her head up so she could see out of the car. The neighbours' houses looked normal, but their own house had all the curtains drawn.

'Do you think it's safe?' peeped Marie.

'I'll go in first and check,' said Mum, and she climbed out of the car. A few minutes later she came back out to get them. 'There's no one,' she said. 'Let's grab the things we need and be quick.'

Imogen's excitement was punctured when she saw Mark's shoes in the hall. It was a reminder of why they were doing this – of how important their mission was.

She rushed upstairs and looked around her room, trying to work out what to pack, but her thoughts came tumbling fast.

What would Mum make of the world through the door in the tree? Would the doctors in Yaroslav have a cure for Mark? Would they really be safe from Anneshka? How long did they have before she showed up at their house?

Imogen grabbed some clothes, her pocket money and her secret chocolate stash. She didn't have a sword or a dagger. She didn't even have a mobile phone.

She poked her fingers into her coat pocket, checking the moth was still there.

Then she carried her belongings into Mum's bedroom and, together, they rammed them into a backpack, along with Mum and Marie's stuff. After a few frantic minutes, Mum picked up the bag.

Together, they slipped out of the house.

CHAPTER 40

Outside the house there was a strange noise. It sounded a bit like a chicken.

Imogen paused and looked up. 'Come on, Imogen, there's no time to lose,' said Mum, trying to hurry her into the car. She threw the backpack into the boot.

But Imogen could see two familiar shapes, circling over the house. 'Look, Mum,' she cried. 'It's Fred and Frieda! They've come home!'

But as Mum and Marie looked up, another sound filled the air. The rumble of a car engine. No, not one, but several. A long line of 4x4s turned down their road.

'Girls, get in the car,' commanded Mum, her voice low and urgent.

Imogen didn't need asking twice.

Mum started the engine and crawled along the street, in the opposite direction. Imogen turned and peeked through the back window. The 4x4s were parking at the side of the road by their house.

Anneshka stepped out of the first car. She was giving orders

to the tall woman with the fur hat. Samo was there too –
along with the men in red trousers.

There were more people this time. They poured out of the
shiny black cars and on to the street, lining up like soldiers.

And that's what they are, thought Imogen, remembering
what Anneshka had said. *The Yezdetz are the fiercest warriors
of any world.*

Samo turned and looked in Imogen's direction. She ducked,
but it was too late. Samo was pointing at their car.

'Mum, they've seen us,' gasped Imogen.

Mum hit the accelerator. Behind them, car doors slammed.
Marie stared wide-eyed, like a rabbit. Imogen's heart ran fast.

Mum sped on to the main road, taking little notice of
junctions. Imogen had never seen her drive like this. She
jumped three red lights.

Mum's eyes flicked to the car mirror. 'Imogen, is that them?'
she asked.

Imogen turned and saw a fleet of black 4x4s. On the bonnet
of the closest was an ornamental crown. Imogen swallowed.
'Yes, Mum,' she said. 'That's them.'

Fred and Frieda seemed to be following too. Imogen
couldn't see them, but she could hear their squawks from
somewhere overhead.

On the fast road, Mum's car couldn't compete. It was old
and small and the engine revved without going any faster.
The black cars closed the gap.

Imogen and Marie both turned to look at their pursuers.

They could see the people in the cars now, and *there* was Anneshka, in the front passenger seat. She smiled when she saw the girls peeking out of the back window, and waved – moving her fingers one by one.

Imogen pulled Marie down and they lay flat.

'Mum!' cried Marie. 'They've caught up!'

There was a piercing cry from outside and Frieda swooped in front of the closest black car. The driver of Anneshka's vehicle turned sharply, trying to avoid the velecour, and almost veered off the road. Fred dived at the next car, making the driver sound the horn and hit the brakes.

The velecours were big, as big as ponies. Anyone who hit one would know about it. Even in a 4x4.

Imogen wound down the window and shouted out: 'Well done, Frieda! Well done, Fred!'

But Mum didn't even respond. She was a demon driver, focused only on the road ahead.

There were more horn blasts, from behind the black cars, as ordinary people were caught up in the chaos. Motorists gave Mum dirty looks as she wove in and out of the traffic. Some of them had seen the velecours and they were slowing, reaching for their phones.

The next time Imogen looked back, one of the 4x4s had crashed into a lamppost. The others were still chasing, but there was a bigger gap. The tall woman, Gunilla, was shouting at her driver. She'd taken off her fur hat and was gesturing wildly, telling him to go faster.

Mum took the turning for the tea rooms at such speed that the back of the car skidded. Marie and Imogen screamed as they were flung to the side.

'You girls had better be strapped in!' shouted Mum.

Fred and Frieda were flanking the car now, flying just above the trees. They called squawks of encouragement. Mum swerved into the tea rooms' car park. 'Out!' she cried, and she grabbed the bag from the boot.

Imogen hoped that Mrs Haberdash would stay out of sight.

The girls and Mum ran towards the gardens, hurtling through the gate, as the screech of tyres sounded behind them.

Imogen didn't look back. Leaves batted her shoulders and chest. Digging her hand into her pocket, she pulled out the mechanical moth. 'Please help us,' she said. 'Please show us the door in the tree.'

Boots crunched on car park gravel. 'Quick,' cried Mum. 'They're closing in.'

Imogen turned the key in the moth's belly and for a moment she was afraid it wouldn't work. But the machine clicked into motion, wings fluttering so fast they blurred.

The moth lifted from her palm and flew deeper into the gardens.

CHAPTER 41

Imogen, Marie and Mum sprinted through the Haberdash Gardens.

The trees seemed to have inched sideways. The path had flicked to face the other way. The garden had subtly rearranged itself, and Imogen knew why – they had the moth, the magic key.

The mechanical moth flew ahead, silver wings shining. The velecours called from above.

Imogen kept running.

They took a different route to normal, not passing by Mum's tent and the place where Mark made campfires.

Imogen's eyes stung at the memory of her stepdad . . .

But there was no time to get emotional. She could hear voices behind, and Mum and Marie were ahead – disappearing down a tree-fringed path. Imogen tore after them.

There was the river that divided the garden. *There* was the fallen tree. The moth fluttered across the water.

'Quick, girls,' hissed Mum. 'You go first.'

Imogen and Marie moved across the dead tree as swiftly as they could.

'Careful,' called Mum, when they were halfway.

As Imogen stepped on to the wild side of the river, the mechanical moth fluttered off. It didn't dance round her head like the real shadow moth.

But Mum still had to cross the water. She shuffled along the tree, backpack wobbling, forehead creased.

Behind Mum, through the tangled undergrowth, Imogen could see the movement of many arms and the swiping of axes and knives. She could hear sticks breaking too, as the Yezdetz forced their way through the garden.

'Faster, Mum, faster,' cried Marie.

Mum clambered off the tree trunk, panting. 'Which way?' she gasped.

Imogen pointed in the direction of the moth and, with that, they took off.

This time, the trees were more helpful. They seemed to move aside to let Imogen, Marie and Mum pass. Imogen hoped that they would shuffle back into position before the Yezdetz caught up.

She could almost have cried when she saw the huge tree with the little door in its trunk. They'd made it. Now they just needed to get through.

A squawk alerted Imogen to the velecours' arrival. They swooped under the tree's canopy, landing with surprising grace.

'Frieda!' gasped Marie and she ran to hug the giant bird.

Imogen could hear their pursuers, shouting and cursing. 'Where are they?' came a man's voice.

'Over there,' said a woman. 'I saw movement to your left.'

'We need to get through that door *now*,' whispered Mum.

Imogen watched, breathing hard, as the mechanical moth landed on the door. It folded its wings across its body, just like the real moth had done, then it shimmied through the keyhole.

The door opened, revealing a world of autumn light. It seemed to float in the shade of the tree; an opening to a golden world.

'Go,' hissed Mum, and she hurried Marie through. Then Mum gestured to Imogen, 'You next.'

But Frieda had other ideas. The velecour dashed at the opening.

Yet the bird had underestimated how much she'd grown and she got stuck – wedged with her head in one world and her behind in the other.

'No, Frieda!' cried Mum and she tried to pull the velecour back. But Frieda could not be reversed. So Mum started pushing against Frieda's feathered bottom.

Imogen joined her, shoving with all of her might. Frieda's talons scrabbled against the threshold, and then, with a squawk, she was through – launching like a cork from a bottle.

That was lucky. A few more inches of velecour growth and they'd have been in a lot of trouble.

Imogen was about to follow, when Fred gave a warning

squawk. He was running, head-down, for the door. Imogen and Mum jumped aside.

With his beak lowered, legs bent, and a flurry of feathers, Fred disappeared through the door in the tree.

'Over there,' said a gruff voice, and Imogen glanced back to see Samo. He took a few steps towards her, stealthy as starlight.

There were more Yezdetz with him, glowering beneath their flat caps. 'Stop,' called a freckled man. 'We only want to talk.' He was brandishing an axe.

Mum grabbed Imogen and shoved her through the door. Imogen lost her footing and tumbled out of our world.

She fell across the forest floor, soil rubbing against her knees – hands – face. Light dazzled her eyes and Imogen rolled over just in time to see Mum stepping through the door.

Mum had to duck to fit and she was about to lift her head when she jerked backwards. Samo must have got hold of her bag.

Mum clawed at the doorframe, desperately trying to hold on.

'Mum!' shrieked Marie.

The sisters ran to their mother and seized hold of her clothes. Frieda and Fred seemed to understand and they clucked, nervously.

But Samo was winning and Mum was slipping back through the door in the tree.

This was it. They were about to be caught. After everything – after all that they'd planned—

But Mum had other ideas. She moved quickly, letting go of the doorframe and slipping her arms through the bag's straps. It fell from her shoulders and flew backwards.

Mum stumbled forwards, into the forest.

Samo, who was still holding the bag, fell back into the gardens. And Imogen slammed the door shut.

Except she didn't.

Samo's foot was in the gap. He lay spreadeagled, with the backpack on his face, but he'd managed to stick one welly over the threshold.

'Come on, Imogen,' cried Mum. 'Leave him!'

Imogen did as Mum said. She sprinted after Marie and Mum, into the bright autumn forest.

CHAPTER 42

Imogen could hear Anneshka's people behind her. She was running at full pelt, and Mum and Marie were ahead, scrabbling over a fallen branch.

Imogen had no idea which way they were heading. Towards Yaroslav? Towards the mountains? It didn't matter. Any second now they'd be caught.

An axe whizzed past Imogen's shoulder, slicing into a nearby tree. *That was supposed to hit me*, she thought, as a second axe cartwheeled by.

She was focusing so hard on running, she hardly noticed the velecours galloping alongside.

Glancing back, she saw Samo. He was getting closer, dodging around wayward branches, hurdling over logs. His gaze was locked on her.

But taking her eyes off the ground was a mistake. Imogen tripped over a rock and fell, sprawling across the forest floor.

'Got you,' Samo growled and his shadow fell upon her. Imogen was face down, exhausted. She couldn't run any more.

'Step away,' said a voice that wasn't her mother's.

Imogen rolled on to her back.

The voice was familiar. She'd heard it before, although she wasn't sure where.

She didn't dare turn to look at the speaker. Above, the trees flailed their branches, as if they too wanted the Yezdetz to leave.

Samo peered up at the owner of the voice. 'Who are you?' he asked.

In one hand, he was holding a dagger. In the other hand, he held something with wings.

Oh, bum-snot, thought Imogen. *He's got the moth.*

'I said, step away,' said the speaker once more.

Samo retreated, face twitching with annoyance. The other Yezdetz had caught up too and they emerged from the trees, gripping axes and swords and knives.

Imogen tried to shuffle away on her bottom. Her pursuers weren't looking at her. They were looking at the person behind her – the one who'd told them to back off.

'This is nothing to do with you,' snarled Samo. 'These are my prisoners.'

Imogen couldn't take the suspense any longer. She turned and looked up. There were Mum and Marie. There were Frieda and Fred. And there, above them all, balanced on the branch of a sturdy oak, was a shape that Imogen knew well.

The figure in the tree held a bow and arrow: string taut,

arrow point out. Imogen recognised the archer's dark eyes, green clothes and hair tied in two knots.

It was Lofkinye.

CHAPTER 43

'You've got no right to hunt in these woods,' said Lofkinye.

Confusion crossed Samo's pale face. 'We're not hunting.'

'They're our prisoners!' cried Anneshka, who had caught up with the Yezdetz.

'Looks like hunting to me,' said Lofkinye. She only had to release her fingers and the arrow would fire at Samo's chest. 'I'll give you five seconds to run.'

'You won't get away with this,' barked Anneshka. 'We'll return and—'

'Four seconds,' cut in Lofkinye.

But Samo's eyes were fixed on Imogen. He held the moth key above her. 'Drop something?' he murmured.

'Excuse me,' called Mum. 'Can I have that?'

'Three seconds!' shouted Lofkinye.

Samo turned to leave. He smirked at Mum over his shoulder. 'Without me,' he muttered, 'you're trapped.'

'One second till I shoot!' warned Lofkinye. Her bow string was pulled very tight.

And, with the mechanical moth clasped in his fingers, Samo slunk off between the trees. Anneshka went with him, flouncing and scowling and kicking up fallen leaves. The remaining Yezdetz followed.

Imogen lay still while their footsteps faded. Fred and Frieda rummaged through the undergrowth and when Imogen was sure that their pursuers had gone, she clambered to her feet.

She almost felt embarrassed for Lofkinye to have seen her so vulnerable. Something within her always wanted to impress her friend.

Mum looked up at Lofkinye, who had lowered herself to sit on the branch. Her feet dangled above their heads.

'Thank you for sending them away,' said Mum. 'It was – *you were* – great!'

Lofkinye shrugged her shoulders. 'That's all right,' she said. She was eyeing the sisters, a grin spreading over her face. 'I wasn't expecting to see *you* in these woods.'

'Lofkinye, you saved us!' cried Marie.

Mum looked from Marie to their rescuer. 'Do you . . . know each other?'

Lofkinye slipped from the tree, landing like a cat on the ground. 'It's a long story,' she said as she straightened. 'You must be their mother?'

Mum smiled, but Marie suddenly looked worried. 'How will we get home without the moth?' she asked.

'I'm not sure, darling,' Mum said gently. 'But we've got enough problems to solve. That one will have to wait.'

Imogen was too excited to form proper sentences. All her words came gushing out: 'Anneshka broke into our world and Miro was king and he fought the krootymoosh and then Mark went funny and—'

Lofkinye laughed. 'It sounds like we have a lot to catch up on. Would you like to come up?'

'Yes, please!' squeaked Marie, still bouncing.

'Up?' Mum looked a little shellshocked.

'To my tree house.' Lofkinye grinned and Imogen felt proud to call this woman her friend. She was so brave and clever and kind. Lofkinye would know what to do about Anneshka. Lofkinye would know how to fix Mark.

'A tree house?' cried Mum. 'Thank you, thank you, that would be . . . thank you!'

Now Imogen laughed too. In her rush to escape from Anneshka, she'd almost forgotten. Not only was this Mum's first time meeting Lofkinye – it was her first time being *in this world*.

And, although Imogen carried the weight of Mark's illness and the fear of Anneshka, she couldn't help it. Her whole being filled with joy.

The sudden arrival of three strangers did not go unnoticed in the Kolsaney Forests. As Imogen, Marie and Mum followed Lofkinye, they were watched by the trees.

The forest shifted behind the children as they made their way through it. Some of the trees were heavy with berries, red as Christmas baubles. They lowered these gleaming ornaments, hiding the children from view.

When the Yezdetz returned to that part of the forest, searching for Imogen and Marie, the trees scattered leaves over the children's footsteps. So, no matter how hard the Yezdetz tried, they always lost the trail.

'Anneshka will be furious if we don't find them,' muttered Ulf, one of the red-trousered men.

By nightfall, the trees were victorious. The Yezdetz had walked many miles, only to find that they were back in the same place they'd started.

Anger radiated off Samo like a poisonous gas. He knew he'd been tricked, and the trees could taste his fury.

Samo took hold of a young horse chestnut, growing close to its mother tree. And, without saying a word, he tore the sapling from the earth.

CHAPTER 44

Lofkinye's tree house was spread over four different trees, with the biggest trunk growing through the middle. The floor was supported on broad branches. More branches held up the roof.

Imogen stepped inside and allowed herself to relax . . . just a little. They seemed to have escaped from the Yezdetz. They seemed to be in a safe place. And, even better, they were in a world where a cure for Mark might exist.

The tree house had changed since Imogen's last visit. Repairs had been made to the stairs. The house smelled of tree resin. Fresh sap oozed from the walls.

Everything seemed a little brighter, a little richer.

Imogen should have been used to this feeling – after all, it was the third time she'd done it. But travelling between worlds made something stir in her stomach: a nameless excitement that was not quite attached to any one thing, but to everything all at once.

Marie and Mum came up next and Mum's face was a picture. Her eyes flicked from the dried herbs in the kitchen,

to the bowls of gleaming berries by the sink.

'It's – it's – it's . . .' Mum was grasping for the right words and Imogen couldn't read her expression. But after a few seconds of staring, Mum's face cracked into a smile. Imogen couldn't help reflecting the grin. 'It's lovely,' Mum managed at last.

'Thank you,' said Lofkinye, entering the house. She took off her long green jacket and hung it, along with her bow and quiver, on a branch by the front door. 'Things have been good in the forests since the mountain got back its heart.'

'Lofkinye,' whispered Marie. 'What if the people who were chasing us come back? What if they attack your tree house?'

'I am fairly sure we lost them,' said Lofkinye. 'They must not be familiar with these woods.'

Imogen glanced out of the closest window, peering down at the forest floor. She couldn't see any sign of Anneshka or Samo or any of the Yezdetz . . .

She lifted her gaze to the tree canopy. It was impossible to see Yaroslav. But in a gap between flaming leaves, a blue mountain peeped through.

'And what about Yaroslav?' asked Imogen. 'Are things going well there too? How is Miro?'

Lofkinye gave her a sharp look. 'You don't know? He's been missing for months.'

Imogen's joy faded fast. 'What?'

'He hasn't been seen since the duel with the krootymoosh.'

Imogen could only shake her head. How could that be?

She thought that Miro had been spotted, travelling downriver with Konya and Kazimira on an enormous leaf. It had never crossed her mind that he'd still be out there . . .

'Miro's adviser isn't happy,' continued Lofkinye. 'If Miro doesn't come back soon, they'll have to find a new king . . . and a new king might want a new adviser.'

Imogen remembered Miro's adviser. He wore colourful clothing and a big stretchy grin, like he'd eaten something disgusting and was trying to smile his way through it. 'Do you mean Patoleezal?' she asked.

'Yes!' said Lofkinye. 'That's his name.'

'But what's happened to Miro?' asked Marie.

Lofkinye looked concerned. 'There are plenty of rumours, but nobody knows the truth . . . I hope the little prince is all right.'

There was a ruckus outside the tree house; the desperate flapping of wings. Through a window, Imogen saw Frieda's face. She had her head angled sideways so one eye could see in. Fred was behind her. They were perched on the balcony, asking to be let in.

Lofkinye rushed out and clapped her hands. 'Hoosh, off you go!'

Fred and Frieda stared at her. They were far too tame to be scared off.

'Lofkinye, they're our friends!' cried Marie.

Lofkinye poked her head back inside. 'They're what?'

'Their names are Fred and Frieda.'

'But velecours are supposed to be wild!'

Mum started laughing – so much she could hardly breathe. 'They sleep in the bath,' she gasped.

Lofkinye stepped back inside the tree house. Then she bolted the door. 'I see,' she said, and she watched the giant birds through the window. 'Well, Fred and Frieda, *as you call them*, will have to wait outside.'

CHAPTER 45

Lofkinye, Imogen, Marie and Mum talked for many hours. And while they talked, they ate forest berries, with bread and bowls of meaty stew.

Lofkinye told them about her new position as a forest elder. It was a mark of the highest respect to be a lesni elder at such a young age.

She also spoke of the adventures she'd shared with Imogen and Marie, of their journey to meet the king of the skret. Mum heard this story with amazement, and more than a little concern. She kept thanking Lofkinye for keeping the girls safe, as if she was stuck on repeat.

As the four of them talked, eyes appeared in the trees that held up Lofkinye's home. The eyes were of varying sizes with slit pupils and bark lids.

'Oh, there's an eyeball,' said Mum. Her voice sounded high and strained, as if remarking on an unexpectedly large pet dog.

Lofkinye glanced up at a branch, which acted as a beam in the roof. Eyes were popping open at one end of the wood, small as grapes and clustering close. 'It's just the forest witch,' said Lofkinye. 'She'll have a good look and then leave.'

Imogen and the forest witch were not on good terms. The witch had attacked Zuby, Imogen's friend. She had to fight the urge to jab her finger in the nearest eyeball.

Finally, the girls and Mum got down to the serious business of discussing why they were here. 'We are sort of looking for something,' said Imogen.

'And sort of running away,' said Marie.

Together, they told Lofkinye the full story – about Anneshka turning up and making threats, about Mark becoming ill and their quest to find a cure.

Lofkinye looked puzzled when they mentioned the yedleek.

'So, *you've* never heard of these monsters?' asked Mum.

Imogen's heart sank. Lofkinye was so wise . . . surely, she knew everything?

'It's not a beast we have in the forests. You could ask in Yaroslav? Perhaps someone there will be able to help.'

'Thank you,' said Mum. 'That's what we'll do. I was hoping to find a local doctor.' She glanced out of a window, where the light was beginning to fade. 'Lofkinye,' Mum continued. 'Is there any chance we could stay until morning?'

'Those who helped return the heart of the mountain are always welcome in my home.' Lofkinye gave Imogen and Marie a significant look.

After the stew and berries, they settled by the tree house's stove. Lofkinye lit the fire and the girls sat close. Imogen enjoyed being cocooned and warm, surrounded by people she loved.

Mum and Lofkinye took the comfy chairs. Outside, the darkness pressed in. Imogen hoped that Fred and Frieda were okay on the balcony. They'd gone very quiet, which probably meant they were asleep.

'Do you think there's time for a story?' asked Marie in her most angelic voice.

Mum started to shake her head, but Lofkinye replied, 'Oh yes.'

Imogen wriggled with excitement and Marie shuffled close.

'This story was not passed down through generations,' said Lofkinye. 'It wasn't handed from adult to child – but rather it was passed sideways. It is a tale carried by merchants and drifters and pilgrims. Stories travel further than people . . . Don't you forget that.'

Mum settled back into her chair. She wanted to send them to bed early, Imogen could tell, but she would not interrupt Lofkinye's tale.

'Many thousands of years ago,' said Lofkinye, 'in a land faraway, there was a king called Radko. He was a terrible man, whose only love was for battle. No matter how much land and power he had, he always wanted more.

'Radko built a great empire, roaming from realm to realm, conquering every place that he found, slaughtering those who dared to resist. His reputation was so fearsome that most people fled when his army approached.'

An eyeball appeared in the trunk behind the stove. It had a mournful expression, like the eye of a huge hunting dog. Imogen wondered if it had come for the story.

'At one point, it seemed like Radko ruled the whole world,' said Lofkinye. 'But there was one kingdom he hadn't yet captured. Nedobyt, a city in the Nameless Mountains. By all accounts, it's a fine-looking place.

'Radko wanted that kingdom so badly. He wanted the houses, built into cliffs. He wanted the enchanted springs. He wanted to master its snĕehoolarks, who live high on the snowy peaks.'

Lofkinye shifted in her fireside chair and the stove-light danced on her tawny-brown face.

'But, unlike the other lands that Radko had marched upon, the people of Nedobyt didn't flee. The mountains protect their city. They are enormous, much bigger than the mountains around here, and impassable apart from a chasm. It is the only way in.'

The little stove clinked and ticked as its metal expanded with heat. The droopy eyeball in the tree trunk blinked. Imogen and Marie waited for Lofkinye to go on.

'Radko stood at the end of the ravine, dressed in his finest armour, backed by his much-feared army. "I am Radko the Conqueror," he roared, his voice carrying down the ravine. "I've conquered the lands to the north and the west. Now, I will conquer you."

'But Radko had underestimated Nedobyt. Many of his

soldiers perished in the ravine. Some say the cliffs fell on his warriors. Others say the people of Nedobyt summoned the devil himself. I've even heard rumours that it was the slipskins who swooped in and saved the day.'

'What are slipskins?' whispered Marie.

'You haven't heard of the slipskins? Oh, you're missing out on a treat.' Lofkinye's smile glinted in the firelight. 'The slipskins were grand magicians. They had mastered the power, sought by many, of turning into animals.'

'Wow,' breathed Marie.

Imogen thought of all the things she'd turn into if she had such powers – a snĕehoolark or a velecour or perhaps a really fast horse.

'Once, there were many slipskins,' said Lofkinye, 'and Nedobyt was the centre of their art. But in recent years I've heard less of them. Perhaps they were always a myth . . .

'Let us return to Radko. This is his story, after all. Radko was so used to winning that he didn't know when to stop. He thought that if he sacrificed enough soldiers, eventually, they'd break through.

'A steady stream of warriors marched into the ravine. They died in their hundreds, then their thousands. But still, Radko didn't cease. "More, send more of them," he commanded.'

Imogen thought of Anneshka. She didn't care about other people either – even those who were supposed to be on her side.

'Radko sent every last soldier down the chasm. He

destroyed his own army, and, so the story goes, he was suddenly overwhelmed with regret. Seeing the bodies piled up, he realised what he had done.'

Lofkinye raised a sceptical eyebrow. 'I'd say it was more likely that he finally realised he'd lost . . . Legend has it that after the battle, Radko wandered into the Marshes of Mokzhadee. His world-spanning empire fell apart. And Radko was never seen again.'

Imogen and Marie were silent. Mum had fallen asleep. And, all around them, the tree house creaked.

'It is a very old story,' said Lofkinye. 'But the truth still stands. No matter how mighty a person becomes, they are never too mighty to fall.'

CHAPTER 46

A knock on the front door startled Mum, who had slept through the end of Lofkinye's tale. 'What is it?' she gasped, suddenly awake and afraid.

Lofkinye picked up a small knife and stalked towards her front door.

Imogen and Marie moved closer to their mother.

Please don't let it be the Yezdetz, thought Imogen. *Please don't let them find us!*

Lofkinye pressed her ear to the wood, and Marie, Mum and Imogen watched. Imogen could hear the velecours on the balcony and the wind swishing through the trees.

'Child of the forests,' said a voice from outside. 'May I come in?'

Imogen's blood ran cold.

That was not the Yezdetz.

It was not a friend either.

Lofkinye unbolted and opened the door. 'Ochi?' she gasped. 'Is that you?' She opened the door wider and a cloaked figure hobbled through.

The witch's skin was as white and crinkly as old tissues. Under one arm, she carried a chicken.

Ochi took Lofkinye's arm and shuffled towards the stove. Mum offered the witch her chair and she accepted, knees creaking as she sat.

'What happened?' asked Lofkinye. 'I've never seen you so – so—'

'Old?' The witch rested her head against the back of the seat, as if she was too exhausted to go on. 'I'll take a cup of that nice berry tea, if there's any left.'

Imogen watched from a little distance, as Mum, Marie and Lofkinye fussed over the witch. She couldn't help feeling that Ochi was putting on a show. The witch may look weak and frail, but she was the same woman underneath. Being old does not make you good.

Lofkinye handed her guest a steaming cup. 'What's going on?' she asked. 'Why do you appear like this?'

Ochi sipped the tea. 'Anneshka Mazanar,' she said.

Mum reached for Marie.

The eyeball in the trunk behind the stove swivelled and stared at Imogen. 'Ah, there you are,' said Ochi, who was now eyeing her too. 'I thought you couldn't have gone far.'

'Why are you here?' said Imogen flatly.

'Imogen!' exclaimed Mum.

'It's all right,' said Ochi. 'The child and I know each other . . . don't we, Imogen?'

The witch set the chicken on her lap and drank deeply

from her cup. Finally, when the chicken was settled, Ochi told her tale.

'Anneshka came to my cottage,' said the witch. 'I thought she was after my help: a new prophecy or a potion . . . but she smashed almost half of my pots, setting all those souls free!'

Mum, Marie and Lofkinye looked confused. Imogen was confused too. She knew that the witch sold prophecies . . . She didn't know what payment she took.

Ochi caught sight of their faces. 'Oh, the souls are given freely, taken only when a customer dies.'

Imogen didn't think taking other people's souls was okay, no matter how nicely you asked. Surely, if souls existed, they ought to be allowed to do what they liked, not be imprisoned in pots.

'Each soul I collect extends my life,' continued Ochi. 'But the spell has been damaged beyond repair. I can no longer shed my old body.' She gestured at her own shrivelled limbs. 'Not even when I leave my house. Had any more souls been released I would have – I might have – died!'

Lofkinye was very still, watching the old lady talk.

Mum stood with one hand over her heart.

Marie held Mum's other hand tight.

'So, you see,' said Ochi. 'Anneshka is no ally of mine.'

'But you gave her the prophecy!' cried Imogen, unable to contain her rage. 'You started this whole thing! Why couldn't you have told Anneshka she was destined to be something peaceful, like a sheep farmer or – or an optician?'

Lofkinye snorted. 'The child has a point.'

The witch only smiled, displaying toothless gums. 'I am merely a messenger. A humble servant of fate.'

Imogen couldn't help herself. 'You didn't do anything to save Marie from Anneshka! You tried to kill Zuby in the circle of trees! You only care about your stupid pots and your trees and your – your – your chicken!'

Imogen stood, panting, surprised by the heat of her own rage.

The droopy eyeball in the trunk blinked.

'I want revenge,' Ochi whispered. 'Revenge for the souls Anneshka released.'

'Some would say you should seek it yourself,' replied Lofkinye. She seemed to be coming round to Imogen's way of thinking.

'Alas,' rasped the witch. 'I would gladly, but, as you can see, I am too old.'

'Look, Mrs Ochi,' said Mum. 'I'm very sorry to hear what happened to your pots, but my partner is in hospital and my children have been through enough. If you're looking for assistance, I'm afraid you'll have to find someone else.'

Ochi looked up at Mum, craning her turtle-like neck. 'Your youngest child was in Anneshka's prophecy. Their fates were bound and I do not think it is over . . . not yet.'

'I don't want to help Anneshka!' cried Marie.

'It's okay, darling,' soothed Mum.

'Maybe I should put this another way,' said Ochi. Her

voice hardened, as if she'd decided to drop the sweet-old-lady act. 'Anneshka won't stop hunting you, or your children, until she has got what she wants. And she will never have that. It will never be enough. If you wish to live out your lives in peace, you must stop her. *Kill* Anneshka.'

Mum glanced nervously at the old woman. 'I'm not sure we want anyone dead.'

Imogen wished that Lofkinye would throw Ochi out of the tree house – via the rope ladder or by some rougher means.

'In truth, I have not come to make demands,' said Ochi, her voice softening again. 'The stars have already set your course, and you cannot change it. I come to offer assistance. From now on, any enemy of Anneshka Mazanar is a true friend of mine.'

Imogen narrowed her eyes. She did not trust the witch one bit.

'I have already helped to shield you from the Yezdetz. I asked the trees to hide this part of the woods. Anneshka and her soldiers won't find you, so long as you're in this house.' Ochi's gaze flicked between Imogen and Marie. 'And I hear you seek a cure for your father?'

Imogen froze.

'Mark?' cried Marie. 'Do you know what's making him sick?'

'It is not an illness,' said Ochi. 'I'm afraid it's more complex than that. He is carrying yedleek eggs.'

Imogen felt as if the floor to the tree house had just

given way and she was falling – falling to the forest floor below.

'He's what?' Mum's tone was cold.

'It happens very rarely,' said Ochi, 'once in a millennium. The yedleek decide not to eat a victim, but to use them as a vessel instead. They plant their eggs in the human's gut and there they stay for months. It is a slow process, and very little studied, but eventually the victim will fall into a sleep-like state.'

Imogen sank on to a footstool. Her legs suddenly felt very tired. She thought of Mark, lying in his hospital bed, connected to all those machines.

'When the eggs hatch,' said Ochi, 'it is not a pleasant sight. The young yedleek eat their victim. Then they move underground . . . ready to begin a new hive.'

Mum looked at the old lady as if she was out of her mind. 'You think Mark has parasites?'

Ochi nodded, stroking the chicken on her lap. 'I believe there is a cure, a way of flushing the eggs out, without damaging the human carrier. But the answer is not in my books. If the remedy is recorded anywhere, it would be in the Great Library of Nedobyt.'

'The Great Library?' Mum repeated. She seemed to be in shock. 'But I need to speak to a doctor.'

'Pah! A physician?' The old woman waved her hand. 'Those meddlers won't be any help. You need to go to Nedobyt – to the largest book collection in the world.'

Imogen glanced at Lofkinye, wondering if she'd heard of this place.

'Ochi makes a good point,' said Lofkinye. 'That library is the home of many answers. If the knowledge you seek is anywhere, it will be in the Great Library.'

'Where is Nedobyt?' Marie whispered.

'A very long way from here,' said Lofkinye. 'Beyond the mountains, beyond the Lowlands, beyond Mokzhadee. It's the city from the story, only accessible by a narrow ravine.'

'We can't go there!' cried Mum.

'I will help you from my cottage,' said Ochi.

Imogen scowled at the old woman. 'Fat lot of good that will do.'

'You would be surprised how much I can do from my house.' Ochi waggled a bony finger. 'You see, I have the trees . . .'

'Do you make the trees walk?' asked Marie.

Ochi laughed, a wheezing chuckle, as if there was a hole in her throat. 'Goodness, child. Is that what happens in your world? No, that is not what I meant. The trees here are connected, deep in the soil, by their roots and the fungus between. It is an underground network, through which information is passed. How else do you think I keep an eye on things?'

Imogen looked at the eyeballs in the branch above the witch's head.

'Trees can be very helpful,' continued Ochi. 'And, if you're going to cross the Marshes of Mokzhadee, enter Nedobyt Library and find a cure before your father is eaten by yedleek, you're going to need all the help you can get.'

'Aren't those marshes dangerous?' said Lofkinye.

The witch nodded. 'Mokzhadee dissolves everything – soil, rocks, memories. Stay on the marshes long enough and they'll dissolve you . . . No, no. You have to go the long way round.'

'But we don't have time!' cried Imogen. Mum's words echoed in her head. *The doctors say Mark's deteriorating quickly. He can't go on like this . . .*

'Better hurry then,' said the forest witch. She got up from her seat and tucked the chicken in the crook of her arm. Then she reached for the front door. 'When you need me, look to the trees.'

CHAPTER 47

That night Imogen had a dream. While she was tucked up in a tree house, deep in the Kolsaney Forests, her mind transported her to a hospital room.

There was a bed and medical equipment. There was a person lying in the bed.

As Imogen got closer, she saw it was Mark. And there was a yedleek hand reaching from his chest.

Mark was struggling against the monster, but the clay fingers clawed at his flesh.

Imogen tried to move, tried to help him, but the hospital machinery pinned her to the spot. Wires wrapped round her ankles, tubes held her in place.

The yedleek's head arose next. Its eyes were white with fire. Its mouth was a terrible pit.

Imogen didn't know what to do. She reached for the button that said 'press for assistance' but the hospital equipment still had her in its grip.

Up came the yedleek's stony shoulders, up came its arms and legs. The more of the yedleek that emerged, the less of

Mark there seemed to be left.

Finally, the rock monster stood over him. Mark had gone very still. His limbs flopped off the sides of the mattress, his body seemed empty and flat . . . as if the monster had been wearing him, as if Mark was an old coat.

Then slowly, ever so slowly, the yedleek turned Imogen's way. Her ears were filled with a hot roaring. Her nose burned with the stench of smoke.

Fire shot from the top of the yedleek.

And Imogen screamed and screamed.

She woke up tangled in the covers. Marie was standing over her bed. 'Imogen,' she said. 'Are you all right?'

Imogen struggled free from the sheets.

'You were making all kinds of weird sounds.'

'Sorry. I – I was dreaming.'

'It's okay. I have nightmares too.'

Imogen looked around the room. It was wooden, with patchwork blankets and a thick rug on the floor. A branch wove in and out of the ceiling. She was in Lofkinye's tree house. She was safe.

And there was still time to save Mark from the yedleek. Still time to find the library and discover the cure. Although they had to be quick.

'Shall we go and sit with the velecours?' Marie suggested. 'Until Mum and Lofkinye wake up?'

The sisters crept through the tree house, out on to the balcony. Fred and Frieda greeted them with excited noises and much flapping of wings. Imogen was glad to see them too.

The girls sat for a while, watching the velecours preen. They seemed to be happy and Imogen wondered if they knew this was their real home.

Once, she had thought of the forests as a forbidding place. Now, as she stood on Lofkinye's balcony, she felt grateful for the protection of the trees.

'How are we going to get to Nedobyt Library?' asked Marie. 'Even if we do learn about a cure, then we have to actually find it, and get it back to our world.'

Imogen peered at the autumn leaves, as they stained the morning light. 'Ponies?' she suggested.

'Do you think that will be fast enough?' said Marie.

Imogen had no idea. And despite her tranquil surroundings, the image from her dream still lingered: a yedleek breaking out of Mark's chest.

It wasn't just Mark they had to worry about. Surely, if the eggs really hatched, if they started a new colony, eventually they'd need more humans to eat . . .

'If only we had a car,' said Marie. 'Or a super-charged horse.'

Imogen smiled. 'If only we were slipskins. Then we could turn ourselves into something that runs fast – like a lion or a cheetah.'

'If only you could fly,' said a voice from behind. It was Lofkinye, standing at the front door. She was wearing a simple green nightdress and a waistcoat of many different furs.

'Fly?' said Imogen, wondering if this was a joke.

But Lofkinye didn't laugh. 'I was thinking about it,' she continued. 'Perhaps you could fly your velecours to Nedobyt.'

Imogen looked at Fred and Frieda. The birds were squabbling over a piece of fruit.

'It's not something I'd usually approve of,' said Lofkinye, 'but these velecours are different. They are tame. With some reins and saddles, you should be able to steer them.'

Imogen's heart lifted at the thought. She had flown on a velecour before, and it was scary, but it had also been fun.

'It would be the fastest and safest route to Nedobyt. You could fly right over the marsh, without having to touch down. No need to take the Long Road.'

Mum's face appeared at the nearest window. 'What's all this?' she asked.

Imogen, Marie and Mum had to wait a little while for the velecours to grow and for their flying to improve. They spent hours getting the birds used to carrying riders, building up the strength of their wings.

Imogen said they couldn't wait much longer – Mark didn't have any time. But Lofkinye was insistent that, even allowing for some velecour training, this was the swiftest way.

And Lofkinye was an excellent teacher. She understood

animals well, as all good hunters do. She had old horse saddles and reins adapted to fit Fred and Frieda.

Together, they helped the birds get used to their new kit. They picked it up surprisingly quickly. After all, Imogen had already been training them in the bathroom to do circus tricks. Compared to that, learning to turn left or right with reins was easy.

'I've never seen velecours like it,' said Lofkinye, after a long day. 'What did you do?'

'Fed them slugs,' said Imogen.

Lofkinye shook her head in disbelief. 'They probably think you're their parents.'

'Maybe we are,' said Marie, with a self-important wriggle.

Mum took some convincing that flying on velecours was a good idea. Lofkinye added a few safety features to the saddles, like straps that attached to the riders' waists, so if they fell, they would dangle beneath the birds, rather than plummet straight to their deaths.

'I'm not sure about this,' Mum said. 'Those birds are wild animals.'

Lofkinye looked at Mum long and hard before replying: 'Children are wild creatures too.'

She lent them some clothes for the journey – things she'd borrowed from her cousins and friends. There were rabbit-skin boots with fur on the inside, coats oiled for protection from the rain.

They stuffed small packs with food for the journey:

berries and salted meat, twice-baked biscuits and honeycomb chunks.

'How will I ever repay you?' gasped Mum, when everything was bundled up.

Lofkinye grinned. 'Survive.'

The day before they planned to leave, Imogen felt her nerves stir. She was a little afraid of flying such a long distance. She hoped that Fred and Frieda would be up to it. She hoped that they'd make it in good time.

And, although she tried not to think of it, she couldn't forget the nightmare about Mark and the yedleek. It was there, waiting in quiet moments – the image of what would happen if they failed.

CHAPTER 48

Miro had been wandering the Marshes of Mokzhadee for a very long time. He no longer remembered where he was going. He no longer remembered who he was.

One day, he found a thing in the water that he hadn't come across before. He waded around it several times before he could identify it. 'It's a tree,' said Miro, stepping back.

'No,' said the girl. 'Tree's a drink.'

'That's tea,' said Miro, although he wasn't sure.

'TREEEEEEEEE STUUUUMP,' said Panovník, the bog troll, reaching out to touch the knobbly wood.

And the troll was right, because the tree had been cut way above Miro's head. It must have been very old. Miro guessed that it would take fifty people, all holding hands, to encircle it.

The trunk was covered in moss, lichen and mushrooms. They grew, as vibrant as coral, all over the bark. Miro studied it up close, running his fingers over some soft fleecy stuff, inspecting tiny orange fungus cups. There was even some lichen, that looked like a beard, hanging down from the top.

When Miro's skin made contact with the wood, he felt something very strange. A slow sort of drumming that seemed to come from within the dead tree.

Someone had carved steps into the edge of the stump and Miro started to climb. Behind him, the bog troll growled.

'What's wrong?' asked Miro, glancing over his shoulder.

Today, the troll was about the same height as him, with hairy violets sprouting from its head and water cascading down its back. 'NOOOOOOOOT FOOR YOUUUU-UUUUUU,' it groaned.

'I just want a look,' said Miro, and he kept climbing, gripping with dirty fingers and bare toes.

Although it was only a stump, the dead tree was the tallest thing on the marshes. There must have been a good view from the top.

The girl followed Miro, crying, 'I want to count the tree rings!' The giant cat came too, scrabbling up the steps. Only the bog troll stayed in the water.

At the top, Miro could see for hundreds of miles. The whole world was spread before him – a sea of reeds and rushes, islets and glimmering pools.

The girl crouched to count the tree rings. The cat sniffed a yellow mushroom.

'COOOMME DOOOOOOOWWWN,' moaned the bog troll. Its neck had lengthened, so it could peek over the top of the stump.

'One minute,' said Miro. 'I want to see the view.'

But it was not really the view that held his attention. The heartwood, the very centre of the stump, stuck out higher than the rest. It had been carved into a smooth, curving chair.

Miro stepped closer to the seat.

Mushrooms had grown at the top and beetles were nestled in the cracks. Their wings were iridescent so, from a distance, it looked like the armrests were studded with jewels.

'What is *that*?' whispered Miro.

'NOOT FOOR YOUUUUUUUU,' repeated the troll and it extended its arms so it could haul itself on to the enormous stump.

Something flickered inside Miro . . .

He remembered a room with paint flaking off the walls and pillars shaped like river sprites. King Ctibor was at the far end, slumped on a throne.

'You look nothing like your father,' snarled Ctibor. 'Who are you? Who are you *really*?'

The memory burned bright as marsh gas and Miro staggered backwards, scorched by what he'd seen. But he was transfixed by the chair cut from heartwood.

A second memory washed over him . . .

He saw a room full of mirrors. There had been a throne in there too. Miro had sat on it and people had called him 'King'. He hadn't felt like a king. He hadn't felt like himself.

The memory drained away and Miro sank to his knees. After all these months of forgetting, this was very hard . . .

The bog troll stood before him, growing taller and more terrible by the second.

'One hundred and eighty,' cried the girl, who was still counting rings in the wood.

Miro ignored them both because here came a third memory, rushing at him like a wave. He braced himself for impact—

There were two thrones. Miro remembered. Flags hung from the ceiling and tapestries lined the walls. This was Castle Yaroslav and the people on the thrones were his parents.

His mother . . .

His father . . .

The bog troll roared and the marshes vibrated. Miro and the girl both covered their ears. A flock of wading birds took to the sky.

Then the troll stomped its feet on the tree stump and the whole thing quaked, knocking the children sideways. Miro rolled to the edge, while the girl tumbled overboard. The giant cat dug her claws into the wood.

Miro looked up and the troll was enormous. 'WHHHHAAAAAAAAAAT ARRREEEEE YOUUUUU DOOOINNNNNGGG?' it roared.

Miro wished he had an answer. He wanted to see that memory again. He scrunched his eyes shut and – *there* – he could see his parents. He remembered; their faces were clear. His mother had brown eyes and she wore her hair plaited. Her ears poked out, just like his did. Her face was gentle and round. His father had much sharper features. He might've looked harsh, even scary, if it wasn't for his smile. Miro knew his father's smile was like his own.

'Miro,' called his memory mother. 'My little Miro, come here.'

And this vision unlocked a floodgate.

Miro couldn't stop remembering . . . There was his father, reading him a bedtime story, there was his mother playing chess. Now Miro could remember the feel of her hands, her finger tracing a line down his forehead, between his eyes, to the tip of his nose. He could remember the words that she sang: *My little Miro, fly swift as a falcon* . . .

The memories kept coming, like a river bursting its banks. They flooded every inch of Miro and he remembered, he remembered . . . The cool drinks his father brought him when he had a fever. The special tea he made when he had a cold. Sadness rose in Miro. 'They're gone,' he choked, eyes still shut. 'They're dead – my parents . . .'

At the same time, he was filled with a truth, a certainty he hadn't felt for years. His parents had loved him. And, even though they were gone, their love was not.

Miro could feel it now, bringing him back to himself.

'I'm not supposed to be on these marshes,' he cried. His lower lip began to shake. How could he have forgotten?

Miro opened his eyes.

The heartwood chair was before him and he felt sure now – this wasn't any old seat. This was *a throne*.

The bog troll lumbered across the tree stump. It had made

itself too tall, and its limbs bent at awkward angles as it threw itself on to the throne.

And, finally, Miro understood.

This was the high seat of Mokzhadee and the troll was the warden of these lands. 'NOOOT FOOR YOUUUUUUU,' Panovník rumbled, reclining in its mushroom-framed throne.

Miro nodded. He had no interest in being king – of this place or any other.

He got to his feet and turned in a circle, scanning the horizon and, in one direction, he noticed an uneven spine. 'The Nameless Mountains,' he whispered, feeling their tug at his heart.

'I am not here for your throne,' Miro said to the bog troll. 'I – I remember now. I've been wasting time, but I'm trying to get to those mountains. I want to meet my mother's mothers. I want to see her childhood home.'

The girl, who had mounted a nearby islet, let out an angry shriek. 'I was counting the tree rings, and that monster ruined it! Now I'll have to start again!'

'TWEEEEEEELLVE THOUUUUUSAAAANDDDD YEAAAARSSS,' said the troll king. 'THHHAAAAT'SSSS THE AAAGGEE OF THIS TREEEEEEEEEEE.'

Miro slid down the edge of the stump, landing in the water with a splash. 'We haven't got time to count tree rings,' he said. 'We've got a long march ahead.'

Konya, the giant cat, leaped to Miro's side. The girl, whose real name was Kazimira, gave the bog troll one final scowl, before trudging after Miro, over grassy knolls and between patches of reeds, towards the distant mountains.

Miro turned, just once, as he walked away from the throne. Panovník was still sitting on it. The troll didn't seem like it meant to follow. Miro gave it a low sweeping bow. The troll king didn't say anything, but it nodded farewell.

CHAPTER 49

Dawn broke over the Kolsaney Forests. In a clearing, deep in the woods, two velecours and four humans stood close.

Fred and Frieda were fitted with ornate saddles, reins and bridles. Imogen, Marie and Mum were dressed in borrowed clothing – tunics, long coats and fur boots. They carried small packs for the journey.

The fourth human was Lofkinye. 'All right,' she said. 'Let's get you up.'

Imogen found mounting Frieda a lot easier than mounting a wild velecour. Lofkinye was holding the reins and the velecour had been through this in training.

After Imogen had clambered into position, Frieda twisted her long neck and blinked at her rider, as if to say: *What took you so long?*

Then Imogen leaned down to help Marie, feeling slightly unnerved by Frieda's watchful eye. 'We're doing our best,' she muttered.

Mum stood close, with her hands out to catch the girls

should either of them slip.

Mum won't be able to do that when we're flying, thought Imogen. And the thought made her stomach squirm.

There was a lot of bum shuffling, but, eventually, Marie was seated in front of Imogen, her legs tucked behind Frieda's wings.

Lofkinye tied the safety rope round Imogen's waist, then she did the same with Marie.

'Can we tie the birds together?' asked Mum. 'So they don't get lost?'

'It's better to trust them,' said Lofkinye. 'The more things we tie around them, the more difficult it is for them to move.'

'But if we get separated over the marshes . . .'

. . . *we're done for*, thought Imogen, and her limbs turned to jelly.

'You have to let them fly,' said Lofkinye, and Imogen wasn't sure now if she was talking about children or birds.

Perhaps Mum was right; this was too dangerous. The velecours were too young. With a rush of anxiety, Imogen wished she was standing with both feet on the ground.

But Lofkinye gave Mum her most level gaze. 'These are the tamest velecours I've ever met. They won't let you down, trust me. This is the best way to Nedobyt.'

Mum seemed to swallow with great effort. 'Okay,' she said.

Lofkinye kept hold of the reins as Mum climbed up on Fred. He was flightier than his sister, and he shifted on his feet.

When Imogen, Marie and Mum were all perched on the velecours, Lofkinye handed them the reins.

'May the stars watch over your journey,' she said. Imogen held Frieda's reins on either side of Marie, wrapping the leather twice round her wrists.

She was sweating in her layers. They were too warm for the autumn forest. It didn't help that she was buzzing with nerves.

'To Nedobyt!' cried Lofkinye.

'To save Mark!' added Marie.

Lofkinye ran at Frieda, squawking and whooshing her arms. Frieda started jogging across the clearing and Imogen almost fell backwards, before remembering to grip on with her thighs.

The girls lurched across the open ground. 'Hold on to the saddle,' cried Imogen, as Frieda picked up speed.

The velecour extended her wings and beat them – slowly at first, as if testing them out – then faster, faster, each wingbeat catching more air.

Imogen felt the briefest sensation of weightlessness, before they were back on the earth. *Crunch, crunch, crunch* went Frieda's feet on dry leaves.

They were near the edge of the clearing and the closest tree had an eye. The eye seemed to get wider as the velecour approached, and the trunk leaned away from the charging bird. They were on course for a collision.

Frieda flapped harder. The tree shut its eye and Imogen forgot to breathe.

'Come on, Frieda,' cried Marie. 'You can do it!'

And Frieda could.

They took off just before the first line of trees. There were branches – branches – leaves – branches. Imogen was struck on all sides before they burst through the canopy, in an eruption of foliage.

'Wahoooo!' cried Marie and she raised both hands as if she was on a fairground ride.

Imogen's stomach seemed to have been left on the ground. It didn't matter that she'd flown on a velecour before, or that Frieda was a bird she knew well. She was totally terrified.

Fred burst through the canopy behind them, with Mum still perched on his back and leaves exploding around her like orange confetti. Mum was lying over the saddle, hugging Fred's neck with her arms.

She straightened when they were clear of the trees, and looked about for the girls. 'Imogen, Marie,' she called. 'Are you all right?'

'We're fine,' replied Marie and she gave Mum a wave, as Frieda carried them up.

Imogen only managed a nod.

The wind whistled in her ears. The sky was vast and pastel-coloured, flushed with the first dawn light.

Down in the clearing, Lofkinye looked small; a lone figure standing on an unwooded island among an ocean of trees.

CHAPTER 50

Anneshka was in her old bedroom in Yaroslav, at the top of her parents' house. It was not a place she enjoyed being. She did not like her parents very much.

'England is not the greatest kingdom,' said Anneshka, staring out of the window at the rows of tiled roofs. 'All of this nonsense about Stonehenge and technology . . . It was a foolish mistake.'

Her mother stood stiff at the end of the bed. She did not offer any words of comfort – did not say that Anneshka had done well. The clock of stars lay on a pillow.

'Perhaps Ochi was right,' muttered Anneshka. 'Perhaps I should accept my place in Vodnislav, as the princess of that miserable land.' Just saying those words out loud made her feel small and sad.

Anneshka's mother spoke at last. 'When you were born, the stars said you were destined for greatness.'

'I know,' snapped Anneshka. 'Don't you think that I've tried? It's not my fault the Yezdetz lost the girl in the forest.'

'Greatness – *true greatness* – does not come easily,' said her mother.

Anneshka felt a rush of fury. Perhaps she should have Samo kill her mother. He was waiting at the front of the house . . .

Her thoughts were interrupted by a chiming, like the striking of a miniature bell. Anneshka turned to look at the clock.

The jewelled stars moved in circles, the painted moon inched into view, and the hatch at the top of the clock opened. Anneshka jumped on to the bed, keen to get a closer look.

A wooden bird flew out of the hatch, wings hinging up and down. It was painted in gaudy colours. And there were two children sitting on its back.

They looked a lot like Marie and her sister.

Anneshka wanted to snatch the little figures and stamp on them until they were splinters. She resisted the urge. Instead, she watched with her mother, as the bird turned in a circle and flew back into the clock.

'Another useless sign,' said Anneshka. 'The stars are not on my side.'

But Anneshka's mother shuffled towards the window. What was the old dragon doing now?

'There,' she said, pointing.

'What?'

'Fate,' her mother replied.

Anneshka stood up and joined her mother at the window. Flying above the forests, hardly visible in the dawn light, was the outline of two velecours. They seemed to be travelling away from Yaroslav, towards the mountain pass. It was hard to tell, but it looked like there was something on their backs.

Anneshka's breath caught in her throat. 'The children. Do you think . . .? Is it them?'

Anneshka's mother took her by the shoulders and gave her a little shake. 'The stars said you were destined for greatness,' she hissed. 'All you have to do, is *trust* them. Stop trying to work things out. Let the clock show you the way.'

Anneshka took a shuddering breath.

Perhaps her mother was right . . .

Perhaps it could be that simple . . .

She must go after Marie. Even if it was not what the child intended, she would lead Anneshka to greatness. That was what the clock of stars said.

Anneshka threw her bedroom window open and leaned out, looking down the sloping tiled roof. Samo was standing on the cobbles below.

'Samo,' called Anneshka. 'We're going beyond the mountains. Ready your people! I want to leave with every soldier you have.'

CHAPTER 51

Frieda flew in large circles, carrying Imogen and Marie ever higher like a backwards helter-skelter. Fred and Mum followed, just a few loops behind.

Frieda called to her brother and Fred replied. More squawks joined them, rising from the Kolsaney Forests. It was a raucous, riotous chorus – hundreds of giant birds shrieking *hello*.

The valley spread out beneath Imogen. Yaroslav gleamed in the early morning light. Flame-coloured forests lined the foothills. And *there* were the Twin Brothers: the huge mountains that stood on either side of the pass. That was the way they must go.

Imogen tugged gently on Frieda's reins. To her relief, Frieda responded, angling her wings towards the pass. Mum must have done the same thing because Fred pulled up alongside them.

'You know,' said Mum, shouting to be heard. 'If you forget about the speed and the height and the fact that you two aren't old enough to ride an electric scooter, let alone a wild animal, it's actually quite . . . exhilarating!'

Imogen laughed. She knew exactly what Mum meant. Once she got used to the wind in her ears and the emptiness beneath her feet, her fear was replaced by fierce joy. She was *flying*! And she was moving in the right direction – towards Nedobyt, towards finding a cure for Mark.

They soared between the Twin Brothers, where the snow lay thick on the ground. A dark shape was visible against the white below them. It moved on all fours with great lumbering strides, but it seemed to pause and look up when the velecours passed overhead.

'A bear!' cried Marie. And Imogen couldn't help wondering if it was a bear that she'd met before.

Soon, they were flying above the Lowlands; a patchwork of meadows and streams. The velecours swooped lower and Imogen could make out more detail. She could see hay stacked up in fields, a water-wheel turning in the river, and a cluster of houses nearby.

'Isn't that Perla's village?' asked Marie.

Imogen's heart leaped at the thought, but only fisherfolk seemed to be about and their attention was directed downwards – at the river and their circular boats – not up at the giant birds.

Imogen's stomach did a flip as the velecours swooped lower still. 'Helllllloooo!' she cried, unable to help herself.

A group of fisherfolk glanced up, tilting their oilskin hats. At first, they just stared, open-mouthed. Then one of the women started waving and Imogen and Marie waved back. 'Hello, hello!' they called.

It was much faster travelling by velecour than by pony or on foot. By mid-morning, the Lowlands were changing. The river that Imogen had been following widened and the edges became indistinct.

It looked like they were flying over a flood plain, where water mixed freely with land. *These must be the marshes that Ochi warned us about*, thought Imogen. Fred and Frieda lifted higher, perhaps sensing the power of the place and not wishing to be drawn too close.

It was a nowhere-land. Imogen could see that. There were no buildings, no farms, no people, and very few trees. Everything about the marshes was abstract – smudges of brown and bristling reeds, great washes of blue with intricate veins and flecks of lurid green.

And yet, the higher they soared, the more magnificent Mokzhadee seemed. Hundreds of streams fed the edges, like capillaries in a living being. Parts of the landscape looked marbled, swirling with different tones. Other parts were speckled with islands, creating a mottled effect.

Imogen peered over Marie's shoulder, past Frieda's bobbing head, and there, on the horizon, were mountains – hundreds of them. Even from this far away, it was clear that they dwarfed the mountains around Yaroslav. The Twin Brothers were hillocks compared to those peaks.

'The Nameless Mountains,' whispered Imogen. She steered Frieda towards the hazy alps and wondered what Mum was making of all this. It must be a surprise, having spent many months thinking this world didn't exist, to see it unfold like a map.

And despite the bad things that had brought them here – Anneshka and the Yezdetz, Mark and the yedleek – Imogen hoped that her mum was impressed.

For hours, they flew across the marshes. They flew until Imogen's face was numb from the wind. She was glad of her many layers, of her squirrel-fur mittens and rabbit-skin boots. They flew until her fingers were clenched into fists from gripping the velecour's reins. In front of her, Marie shivered in her borrowed coat.

'Almost there,' Imogen called to her sister, who nodded stiffly in reply. *After all*, thought Imogen, *how big can marshes be?*

But Imogen hadn't reckoned with the Marshes of Mokzhadee. The wetland stretched on and on. Ochi had warned them not to land here. She said the marshes made people forget. So, despite her weariness, Imogen encouraged Frieda to keep going.

Mum and Fred flew above them, with Fred's feet tucked close to his belly. Mum's boots dangled on either side of the velecour's glossy chest.

Below, there were small flecks that looked like cattle, moving across the great wash. Imogen guessed they were buvol, wild cows that she'd heard about.

Separate from the herd of cattle, Imogen spotted four dots. Two looked like they could be human. *That's strange*, she mused. *I thought there were no people on the marshes . . .*

One of the dots was much bigger than the others. Squinting, Imogen thought she could make out the shape of an ogre – or some kind of swampy troll.

But a flock of wading birds chose that moment to take off. Thousands of wings flickered beneath the velecours, blocking Imogen's view of the marsh. She tried to steer Frieda around the waders, keen to get a better glimpse of the troll – or whatever it was – but she only succeeded in getting stuck in the middle of the flock.

All around, she could hear the soft clapping of thousands of wings. They were small birds with long beaks, and they didn't even turn their heads to look at the velecour that had appeared in their midst. They simply manoeuvred sideways to make room for Frieda's great wings, as if they were all connected, as if they knew exactly where each other was.

It was strangely calming, this acceptance into such a vast flock. Imogen and Marie took in the spectacle in silence.

When the wading birds flew down, heading back to their marshland home, the four dots were no longer visible.

Oh well, thought Imogen. *I'm sure it was no one I know.*

CHAPTER 52

The sun was low in the sky when the velecours neared the Nameless Mountains, and Imogen was frozen solid. Even in her warm clothes, she shivered. Marie was shivering too.

Beyond the first row of mountains was another, and another beyond that. So it went on for as far as Imogen could see.

She wondered how deep into the mountains they'd have to travel before they reached the city of Nedobyt. She hoped they'd arrive in time for supper. Her stomach was grumbling.

'We need to go higher to clear those peaks,' called Mum, pulling Fred up alongside his sister. 'I'll go first. Follow me.'

Fred and Mum flew higher, and it looked like very hard work. Imogen wondered if the velecours were tired. This was, by far, the furthest they'd ever gone.

Frieda and the girls followed. As they rose, the wind picked up, running its cold fingers through Imogen's hair, tugging at her long coat. She narrowed her eyes to protective slits.

'Are you okay?' she called to Marie.

'Tired,' Marie shouted back.

When they neared the first row of mountains, the wind came in a sudden blast. It caught Frieda off guard and the velecour wobbled. Imogen and Marie screamed, but Frieda managed to steady herself with a few frantic flaps.

If they didn't pull up quickly, they'd collide with the nearest slope. Imogen encouraged Frieda to fly higher, but with each metre they climbed, the wind seemed to strengthen, coming in uneven gusts.

Imogen didn't understand. When she looked at the sky from the ground, it always seemed so calm. Now she was up here, higher than she'd ever been, and there was a violent movement of air. It buffeted the velecours and snatched the breath from Imogen's lips.

Frieda fought to stay airborne and Imogen's heart seemed to rise to her throat. The rope Lofkinye had tied round the girls' middles wouldn't save them if Frieda was knocked from the sky.

'Imogeeeen,' cried Marie. 'What's going on?'

Ahead, Fred was also struggling. He flapped wildly, not nimble enough to respond to the constantly shifting winds. Mum clung to his back, glancing over her shoulder to look at the girls.

The first row of mountains sailed towards them like granite tanker ships. And that was when Imogen realised – much like a boat cutting waves through an ocean, the mountains were stirring up the wind. The sudden appearance of rock must have created some kind of *turbulence*. That was what they called it on planes.

'We can't fly through this,' Imogen shouted to her mother. 'We have to land!'

But the wind tore at her words.

Even worse, Marie's hair came loose from its ties, and started batting Imogen in the face.

Another gust caught Frieda, and the bird jerked sideways. Marie grabbed the front of the saddle. Imogen grabbed Marie.

And then the velecour fell.

'Muuuuuuuuuuuum!' shrieked Marie.

Both girls were screaming,

screaming and spinning,

in a vortex of feathers and wings.

Imogen's arms were wrapped round her sister,

legs squeezing the velecour tight.

Frieda squawked and flapped.

Hair lashed Imogen's face,

and the ground . . .

the ground rushed up.

Imogen was still screaming when Frieda extended her wings. The girls were thrown forwards, but the saddle stopped them from falling off.

Imogen did not dare unclench her limbs.

They were much lower now, beneath the mountains' brows. And Imogen did not try to resist as Frieda sailed to the ground.

Chapter 53

Frieda landed at the foot of the Nameless Mountains. Fred touched down nearby. It wasn't the most elegant landing, and Mum leaped from her saddle, running towards the girls. 'Are you injured?' she called.

Imogen and Marie slid off Frieda. 'We're fine,' gasped Imogen. 'We're – we're fine.'

Mum threw her arms around them. 'Thank God,' she cried.

For a moment, they all simply held each other, too wind-blasted to speak.

'Frieda,' said Marie. 'Is she going to be okay?'

The giant bird was panting, tongue lolling out of her beak. Imogen and Marie examined her wings. There were no obvious injuries – although there were some gaps where there used to be feathers. 'Poor Frieda,' cooed Marie.

Fred plodded to his sister, clucking. Frieda clucked back. They seemed to be checking each other over, and Imogen felt bad that they had pushed the birds. 'It was too much for them,' she said. 'Too much flying, too much wind.'

'They've done well to get us this far,' said Mum. 'But you're right . . . We'll have to walk to Nedobyt.' She glanced at their surroundings and Imogen did the same.

They were standing on a patch of grassland. The area was open to the elements, with a few thorny shrubs and bent trees.

To their right were the marshes, a vast expanse of blue and green. Birds with long legs waded in the shallows, disappearing into forests of reeds. Imogen was a little afraid of the wetlands now she'd heard how dangerous they could be.

To their left were the mountains. They were a bit scary too. They were so massive, their peaks seemed to touch the sky. Against this great bulk of rock and ice, Imogen felt minnow-small.

The first row of mountains rose sharply, creating something like a cliff. A narrow chasm cut through the rock. *The entrance to Nedobyt*, thought Imogen. And she remembered the soldiers from the story, who had died when they entered the ravine. She hoped that whatever had killed them was no longer here . . .

'What are we going to do?' asked Marie, twisting the sleeve of her coat. The sun was setting over the marshes, turning the sky neon pink.

'We don't have a lot of choice,' said Mum. 'It's getting too late to wander about. We'd better find somewhere to sleep.'

'Out here?' peeped Marie. 'In the dark?'

'It's okay,' said Mum, trying to be cheery. 'It'll be just like a camping trip.'

Yes, thought Imogen. *It's just like when we go camping, except we've got no tent or sleeping bags and we're in a totally different world with bears and wolves and who knows what else.*

They walked a little closer to the mountains, away from the sprawling marsh where great swarms of flies were emerging. The insects were gathering in such numbers, they changed the quality of the light. The sun's last rays seemed to waver between millions of midge wings.

Luckily, the insects didn't show any sign of wanting to leave the bog. They stuck close to the marsh's boundaries, a good distance from Mum and the girls.

Mum stopped beneath a lonely tree, with leaves of burnished gold. 'This is as good a spot as any,' she said, as if she was choosing a place to sit on the beach.

Dropping her load at the base of the tree, she started setting up camp. Imogen and Marie shed their packs too. Lofkinye had given them food, blankets and water in tightly sealed skins.

Mum spread out a blanket and the three of them sat on it. Fred and Frieda stayed close, searching for grubs in the grass.

Mum passed around twice-baked biscuits and honey. The girls ate greedily, with Mum punctuating the silence every so often to say things like, 'Well, isn't this an adventure?'

Her words were probably meant to be reassuring, and at home they might have been. But, beneath the blank stare of the marshes and the gathering gloom of the night, they fell a little flat.

Strange noises were rising from the wetlands – honks, peeps, mewls and a hiss. Imogen thought she heard wings beating against water, the sound of furry bodies moving between dry reeds.

'I wonder what's out there,' she whispered.

'I don't,' said Marie.

At least they were on the right side of the marshes, with hundreds of miles between them and the Yezdetz.

'Hey, Marie,' said Imogen. 'I'd like to see Anneshka try to follow us here.'

And tomorrow we will reach the Great Library, thought Imogen. *Tomorrow we will discover Mark's cure.* She held on to that thought.

After they'd finished eating, they wrapped themselves in blankets and huddled very close, tree branches stretching overhead.

Imogen was just slipping into unconsciousness, when she felt something move against her leg. Mum must have felt something similar. 'Oh,' she cried. 'What is that?'

It was hard to see properly in the darkness, but the tree seemed to be lifting its roots. Imogen could see their outlines, snaking between the grass.

Imogen's first instinct was to get to her feet – to run as far as she could. The last time she'd seen tree roots moving, they'd been used as a weapon of attack.

But, this time, the tree didn't seem aggressive. It moved

slowly and with great care. Imogen could hear creaking and ripping as the rootlets broke free from the earth.

Mum and the girls sat motionless with tree roots snaking all around. The roots kept rising and joining, winding and wrapping, until they'd formed a wonky circle, with the humans at the centre of the nest.

'Do you think it's Ochi?' Marie whispered.

'I – I have no idea,' said Mum.

A small eyeball opened in the root beside her, no bigger than a one-penny coin. The forest witch was watching . . . and, this time, Imogen felt glad.

They settled down to sleep once more, with the velecours clucking nearby. And so it was, that Imogen, Marie and Mum spent the night cradled in a rowan tree's arms.

CHAPTER 54

The next day, they woke early. Mum passed around breakfast – a parcel of fruit that looked like blackberries, although they were as large as plums.

Once the berries had been devoured, and the girls' fingers were stained crimson with juice, they reattached their blankets to their packs and said goodbye to the little tree.

Fred and Frieda had been foraging at the edge of the marsh. When they saw that their humans were leaving, they swallowed whatever was in their beaks and tottered after them.

The mountains were just as impressive at dawn as they had been the night before. Their tops were lost in the clouds, their great immensity only separated by the ravine.

Imogen, Marie and Mum paused at the entrance to the chasm. There was a chill draught that seemed to come from within, as if the mountains were breathing. It ruffled Imogen's hair and tugged at her clothes.

'This must be where Radko the Conqueror stood,' said Marie in her smallest voice. 'What do you think killed his soldiers?'

'Oh, it's just a story, darling,' said Mum.

It's never just a story, thought Imogen. But there was no other way to enter Nedobyt.

She hitched her pack higher up her shoulders and stepped into the chasm. Cool air swirled around her. Rock pressed in from either side.

Imogen was a speck of dust on the breath of the mountains, a seed, a grain of sand.

And yet, she would not just roll over and do as the stars wished.

The stars have already set your course, said a memory of Ochi. *And you cannot change it.*

'We will see about that,' muttered Imogen. She remembered what Mark had told her, about how scientists adjusted their ideas with new evidence.

Perhaps, thought Imogen, *even the stars change their minds . . .*

And so, Imogen, Marie and Mum began the walk through the mountain ravine, with the velecours toddling behind. Imogen found herself moving swiftly. Fear was chasing behind her. Hope was leading her on.

In some places, the ravine was wide – wide enough to fit a bus. In one spot, it became so narrow that a boulder had fallen and got stuck, suspended above their heads.

'Let me go first,' said Mum, overtaking Imogen. 'I'm sure it's fine . . . but just in case.'

Marie started humming, as she did when she was nervous. Imogen joined in.

'I thought you found humming annoying?' said Mum. Marie looked surprised too. She and Imogen used to have arguments about this.

'I've changed my mind,' said Imogen, and she went back to humming.

'I know this sounds silly,' said Mum, as the ravine twisted to the left, 'but now that we're here, I almost don't believe in our world.'

Imogen knew what Mum meant. Against the solidness of the mountains and the black rock of the ravine, their little house and Grandma's bungalow felt like a distant dream.

Imogen's thoughts turned to Mark. She hoped that he was still safe in hospital. She hoped that they weren't too late.

She remembered a spring night, when she and Mark had driven to the Haberdash Gardens. No one else wanted to wake before dawn to see the meteor shower. It was just the two of them.

They'd sat at the edge of Mum's tent, shivering and squinting at the sky. Mark had seemed a bit quiet. At the time, Imogen hadn't known why – hadn't known about the yedleek.

'Meteors are tiny,' Imogen had said, hoping to stun Mark out of his trance. 'They're dust-sized particles that catch fire. Did you know that?'

Mark nodded.

A light had sailed across the sky, drawing a white line in the darkness. It was followed by another, with a longer tail. A third light zipped overhead. Blink and you'd miss it.

Meteors.

Imogen had jumped out of the tent. 'I saw it!' she'd cried. 'I saw a meteor shower!' She felt such elation, such a lifting of spirits – as if it was *her* who had shot across the sky. She turned to Mark, who was still sitting. 'Did you see it?'

'I saw it,' he had replied. Although he was looking at her – not the stars. 'How can something so small shine so brightly?' And, at last, he was smiling.

Imogen tucked the memory away and kept walking through the ravine. She hoped that she would have the chance to go meteor-spotting with her stepdad again.

CHAPTER 55

The ravine twisted and widened. Up ahead, there was a figure on a ledge. She wore golden armour and a helmet shaped like a bird of prey. In one hand she held a bow and there were arrows at her back.

'Stop, girls!' cried Mum, and she took a few steps in reverse.

But the archer did not attack. In fact, she waved her hand, signalling that they should pass.

Imogen, Marie, Mum and the velecours kept walking. 'We must be getting close to the city,' Mum whispered. 'Stay close.'

There were more archers up ahead, perched high on rocky shelves. They wore helmets shaped like birds, with metal wings swept back above their ears.

None of the gold-clad archers paid much attention to the new arrivals. When they did glance down, they simply gestured for the travellers to go on.

Imogen's pace quickened. Approaching Nedobyt meant one thing – the famous library and, hopefully, a cure for Mark.

As the ravine widened even further, she got her first glimpse of the city. It was set in a valley between mighty mountains, a narrow space among all that stone.

The buildings looked more grown than built. They clung to the mountainsides, in rising layers that reminded Imogen of mushrooms on a tree.

'Wow,' said Marie. 'Is this Nedobyt?'

The girls were half running, eager to arrive. 'Don't get too far ahead,' Mum was calling, but neither girl slowed.

They passed the last group of archers and entered the valley. Now they were a bit closer, Imogen could make out the buildings' foundations, anchored deep in the rocks.

She gulped and wiggled her toes, fighting the dizziness that came from looking that high.

Steps were cut into the cliffs between the buildings, creating vertical paths. Some of the paths were so lofty, there were birds flying underneath. This was not a city built for those with a fear of heights.

Mum had caught up with the girls now. 'If I was a betting woman,' she murmured, 'I'd say this is the greatest kingdom.'

Imogen was inclined to agree. It was more striking than Yaroslav, with its buildings perched like nests – even more breath-taking than Valkahá.

At the base of the valley was a park, or perhaps it was some kind of common. Here, trees and flowers grew in great numbers, protected from the harshest mountain winds.

Children played and adults talked among the parkland.

Imogen watched them, curious. Short capes seemed to be in fashion, with narrow trousers and tall lace-up boots.

There were lots of different people, all sharing smiles and greetings. It reminded Imogen of her own world, although it was more magnificent.

Some of the locals had pale skin, like Imogen and Marie. Other people were Black. Many had golden complexions and dark hair, much like Miro did.

Miro . . .

Imogen couldn't help wondering where her friend was.

But Marie and Mum had already started walking through the park, and Imogen trotted to catch up.

Fred and Frieda clucked and darted off between the trees. 'Frieda!' cried Marie, 'Fred, come back!'

'Leave them,' said Mum. 'They'll be okay. I doubt you can take giant birds into the library . . . and this is probably an excellent place to find slugs. We'll catch up with them later.'

As Imogen watched the young birds trot deeper into the park, she noticed two glass-topped buildings on the far side. She could just about make out glittering domes. Could one of those be the library?

Around the edge of the park was a wrought-iron fence, punctuated by gates. The gates were marked with street names; such as 'Glassblowers Avenue' or 'Snow Bunting Lane'. Behind these elaborate entrances, paths wound up the rock face.

I suppose it's good to know where you're going, thought Imogen, *before you start climbing*.

She paced along the edge of the park, reading the names over the gates. Buildings sprouted from the mountains above her. The steep stone steps were the only way to reach them – unless you were a bird or a mountain goat.

'Breathless Boulevard' said one of the gates. Imogen didn't fancy going up that. Another was called 'Musicians' Way'.

'How will we find the library?' asked Marie.

'We might need to ask someone,' said Mum.

There were plenty of people around, but they all seemed very busy. They were stringing up lanterns and setting tables between the trees in the park. It looked like they were preparing for a big outdoor feast.

Imogen walked a little further, following the fence. And, as if by magic, the words above the next gate read: 'The Great Library of Nedobyt'.

'Mum, I've found it!' cried Imogen.

The wrought iron was bent into curly letters. The gate was the grandest one yet, with archers standing on either side. Like the guards in the ravine, they wore light armour and helmets shaped like birds.

The path to the library wound up behind them, with dense trees on either side. It climbed abruptly, before disappearing behind a wooded slope.

Mum walked towards the gate, but the archers blocked her way. 'Oh,' said Mum. 'Can't we go there? We need to borrow a book.'

The archers didn't look at her as they replied. 'The library is out of bounds.'

'I thought libraries are supposed to be for everyone,' said Marie.

Now the archer turned his gaze her way. 'The people have no need of books.'

'Says who?' asked Mum, getting flustered.

'Mage Bohoosh,' the archer replied.

'Mage what?'

'He's the one who makes the rules, madam. He might not be Nedobyt's finest leader, but he does his best.'

'Too much knowledge is dangerous,' said the other archer, metal beak glinting above his eyes. 'It's for your own good, madam. Why don't you go and prepare for the festival?'

'If we don't find the book that we need,' said Marie, 'my stepdad might die! Please, won't you let us in?'

But Imogen could see that the archers were decided. There was no point in arguing.

Mum and the girls retreated. They crouched beside the fence, just out of the guards' line of sight. 'How are we going to get past them?' muttered Imogen.

'We can't, Imogen,' said Mum. 'Didn't you hear?'

Three eyes appeared above Mum's head. They were lodged in the trunk of a pale tree that stood on their side of the fence.

'Ochi,' whispered Marie.

CHAPTER 56

'Look, Mum,' said Imogen. 'Behind you.'

Mum turned and three more eyes opened, stacked up the centre of the trunk. 'If that's Ochi, spying on us, she can blooming well go away.'

The eyes all rolled skywards, in a synchronised movement. Imogen followed, looking up, but she saw nothing other than narrow branches, threaded with yellow leaves. A cluster of trees grew near her, and more – a whole woodland – stood on the other side of the fence.

'Ochi is trying to tell us something,' said Imogen. 'But I don't understand what.'

'Oh!' squeaked Marie, and Imogen turned to see her sister dangling in the air.

For a horrible moment, Imogen thought Ochi had betrayed them, but the trees weren't hurting Marie. Their branches were clasped round her ankles and they seemed to be lifting her up.

Mum seized Marie's hands and pulled downwards.

'No, Mum,' said Imogen. 'Don't. I think they're trying to help.'

It took a lot of branches to hold Marie, for these trees had narrow limbs. They looked like silver birches, with white trunks that turned red at their twig tips.

Together, the trees passed Marie over the fence, and higher, until she was in the canopy. Imogen could just about see her between the jigsaw of leaves.

The archers patrolled the library gate. They were far enough away not to notice the strange goings-on in the trees.

The people in the park also seemed oblivious; too busy to see a girl cresting the woods. But a toddler raised his finger in Marie's direction. 'Papa!' he cried.

'Shush,' said the child's father. 'Papa's got his hands full.' The man was halfway up a ladder, tying lanterns to a park tree, and he did not turn.

Roots pushed up under Imogen's feet and she lost her balance. She was caught by a low-hanging branch. Several more trees reached for her and Imogen rose over the pointy-tipped fence, clearing it by a few inches.

'Ouch!' said Mum, as the same thing happened to her.

It wasn't very comfortable, being passed from tree to tree. Their branches were hard and knobbly and they didn't seem to think twice about leaving Imogen swinging at a difficult angle, pack hanging off her back.

Imogen was lifted past more bark-rimmed eyes. The canopy parted, letting her through, until she was face down in the treetops, staring at the ground.

She turned herself over, so she could see up. A mountain gazed at her and there was a waterfall, running down its slope.

Mum emerged between Marie and Imogen, feet breaking the canopy first. When her face surfaced, she looked very nervous.

The trees continued passing them, closer to the archers and the library gate. Imogen caught glimpses of the guards between twigs and foliage.

It was difficult knowing how to arrange your body while all this was going on. You had to be relaxed so the trees could handle you. But you couldn't go completely floppy, or you'd slip between branches to the ground.

One tree even tried to carry Imogen by her hair, before she tugged it free.

'What's that?' cried one of the archers. He stepped away from the gate, peering into the trees.

He was right beneath Imogen. One noise and he was sure to look up.

The birches stopped moving. Imogen didn't dare breathe.

The archer turned and called back to his companions. 'There's no one here. Must be the squirrels.'

The trees started moving again slowly, very slowly. Imogen, Marie and Mum travelled up, along the edge of the path.

There was a branch digging into Imogen's shoulder, and another one jabbing the back of her thigh.

Finally, they turned the corner, and were out of sight of

the guards. The trees passed their human packages downwards, setting them on the stone path.

Imogen was placed on her side. Marie was almost planted on her head. Mum struggled with the branches until they agreed to set her down feet first.

'Thank you,' Marie whispered to the trees. The birches straightened, waving their leaves.

Imogen got to her feet and dusted down her long coat. The path ahead was very steep, with moss braided over the steps; a sure sign that it hadn't been used – at least for a little while.

'Well,' whispered Mum, straightening her pack. 'I suppose we had better climb that.'

I don't like the look of it, thought Imogen. *But if this is the path we must take to save Mark, then I will certainly try.*

CHAPTER 57

The steps sliced up the side of the mountain. The higher they climbed, the shorter the birch trees became until, at last, they were no taller than Imogen.

Mum led the way, stopping regularly to check that the girls were okay and so they could all catch their breath.

Imogen faced the path when they did this, pretending to inspect the tiny plants that grew in the cracks between steps. The truth was, looking the other way made her feel funny. She glimpsed it once – the cut-away drop of the mountain, the reddish cluster of trees already

so

far

down.

It made Imogen dizzy, as if she was back on a velecour, flying high. Except *now* there was no comforting body beneath her, no broad wings to catch the air – just her own wobbly legs and the near-vertical steps.

Her mouth went dry at the thought.

'There's no rush,' called Mum. 'Just take one step at a

time, girls.'

Imogen wiped the sweat from her face and continued to climb.

The steps narrowed and turned a corner, disappearing behind rocks, and here, tucked out of sight, was a patch of flat ground – a green ledge on the side of the mountain.

Imogen, Marie and Mum staggered on to it, too puffed out to speak. When Imogen's breathing steadied, she looked at her surroundings more closely. The ledge was large, about the size of Grandma's bungalow, and it felt secret; hidden from view.

There was a pool in one corner, with moss-fringed edges. On the other side of the ledge was a building. Imogen hadn't noticed it at first because it was a similar colour to the rock and, like the other structures in Nedobyt, it clung to the mountainside.

The entrance was small, but the rest of the building towered upwards and fanned out like a mushroom with many different caps. There were lamps on either side of the doorway, shaped like big droopy flowers.

This must be the library. We've made it! thought Imogen, with a surge of relief.

Imogen turned to ask Mum if they could go in, and saw she was stooping by the pool, splashing water on her face.

'Ah, that feels good,' Mum muttered. Then she cupped her hands and drank. 'I'm so thirsty,' she said. 'Water never tasted this sweet.'

Imogen was thirsty too so she knelt at her mum's side and

peered into the pool. The water was clear and shy fish glinted, hiding behind watercress.

Mimicking her mum, Imogen cupped her hands in the liquid. It slopped and sparkled in her palms. Imogen lifted it to her lips, but Mum did something that made her pause. Mum sat back on her haunches and used her foot – yes, *her foot* – to scratch her ear.

Imogen did a double take. 'Mum?'

'What, darling?'

Marie giggled. 'That looked weird.'

But things were about to get a lot weirder.

Mum wrinkled her nose, as if she had an itch and a very long hair sprouted out of her cheek. No, not a hair . . . a whisker. Imogen parted her hands and the water leaked out between her fingers. 'Mum!' she cried, alarmed.

More whiskers sprouted from Mum's face. They must have been itchy because Mum tried to scratch them – but again, she scratched with her toes.

Marie ran to Imogen's side. She wasn't giggling any more. Mum's face was warping and changing, as if something moved under her skin. 'What's happening?' squealed Marie.

Mum looked panicked too. She held up her hands and fur peeked out from her sleeves. It was spreading quickly – thick tufts of honey-coloured fuzz. Then her nails pinged off, and in their place grew claws.

'Mum!' yelped Marie.

Mum moved away from the pool, scrabbling on all fours

in a movement that could only be described as a hop. Imogen raised a hand to her mouth, biting her fist to stifle a scream, because, as Mum moved, she kept changing.

Fur spread up her neck and her front teeth grew too long for her mouth. Then, with a whistling shriek – not unlike a steam train – Mum's arms shot up her sleeves, her head whooshed down her collar and her feet vanished from her boots.

'Muuuum!' wailed Marie.

But there was no reply.

For Mum had disappeared.

CHAPTER 58

All that was left of Mum was a pile of crumpled clothing. Imogen stared at the heap, unable to process what she'd just seen.

There was a lump . . . a strange bulge under the fabric. Imogen started rummaging through, tearing Mum's clothes when she had to, tossing the empty boots aside.

The lump wriggled and thrashed, until all the clothes had been removed except for Mum's shirt. Imogen lifted the collar and peeped nervously inside.

Staring back at her from under the linen was a creature that looked a lot like a rabbit, except it had black-tipped ears and a golden-brown coat. It was much bigger than a normal rabbit too, with long and springy back legs. It was, Imogen realised, some kind of hare.

'Imogen, you don't think . . .' whispered Marie.

'Oh no,' said Imogen. 'Oh no, no, no!'

But no matter how many times she said it, the real answer was *oh yes*.

'Mum?' asked Marie, helping the hare out of Mum's shirt.

The hare twitched her nose.

'This cannot be happening,' exclaimed Imogen. 'I need Mum – *human* Mum!'

The hare hopped towards the pool and peered in. She must have caught sight of her own reflection because she sprang back and bolted to the other side of the ledge. But she didn't stop there; she ran back again, circling the girls like a furry rocket.

Imogen couldn't turn fast enough to keep up. The hare – also known as 'Mum' – hurtled round the ledge, ears pinned back, legs propelling her on. She was clearly in a state of high panic.

'Stop it, Mum!' cried Imogen. 'Please stop!'

It took the hare several minutes to slow to a gambolling trot. Finally, she bounded in a circle, like a dog chasing her tail. And she did have one – a tail, that is.

Marie got on to all fours, right in front of the hare, and gently lifted one of the creature's long ears. 'Mum?' Marie called into the ear. 'Are you okay?'

The hare scrabbled away, covering her ears with her front paws. She gave Marie a look that reminded Imogen of the face Mum pulled when they'd done something wrong.

'I think those big ears are sensitive,' said Imogen. 'We shouldn't shout into them.' She took a few deep breaths and closed her eyes, trying to fight the rising panic.

'Is our mum a slipskin?' whispered Marie.

It took Imogen a moment to remember what a slipskin

was. *Legendary magicians, shape-shifters.* 'No, I don't think so,' she said. 'Mum's not magic . . . she's . . . Mum.'

'It was the water,' said Marie. 'Maybe if she has some more, she'll turn back.' Marie dipped her hands into the pool, offering the hare a drink. The little animal lapped it up and the sisters waited.

But nothing happened.

'What if she never changes?' gasped Marie. 'We're orphans!'

Imogen tutted. 'Don't say that.'

The golden hare seemed to be listening, ears cocked in their direction.

'Mum's not dead,' Imogen continued, 'she's just . . . different. We'll find a way to fix her.'

Just like we'll find a way to fix Mark, she thought. She didn't want to start listing their problems out loud. It only made her feel worse. But she couldn't help thinking of the people who might help them and how far away they were: Grandma, Mrs Haberdash, Lofkinye, Miro . . . None of them were in this kingdom; some of them weren't even in this world!

But there was one person who hadn't given up.

Mum-the-hare hopped towards the library, tail flashing white with each stride. The lamps on either side of the doors glowed.

The hare paused at the entrance and glanced back at the sisters, just as Mum had done when they were climbing up. *Just take one step at a time, girls . . .*

Imogen locked eyes with her sister. 'I suppose, since we're here . . .'

'We might as well stick to the plan!' finished Marie.

'We're coming, Mum,' called Imogen and she pulled the heavy doors open. She could have sworn the hare nodded, before bounding into the library.

CHAPTER 59

Imogen and Marie followed their mum through the double doors, into a wood-panelled room. There was no furniture, other than a desk, and there were more flower lamps, hanging from the walls.

Their leaves and petals were made from glass, and little beads dangled down. Something burned at the centre of the flowers and the room was pink in their glow.

The desk looked a bit like the one in Imogen's local library. It was stacked with books and empty tea cups. There was a chair too, but no one was sitting on it.

Instead, there was a note, written in a scrawl that leaned so far to the right, the words seemed to race off the page. Imogen read it aloud:

> Short-staffed, doing my best.
> Many books in need of my help.
>
> If you really must talk to a
> librarian, simply follow the . . .

'Follow the what?' asked Marie.

'I don't know,' said Imogen. The final words seemed to butt up against the edge of the paper, as if the author had run out of space.

She glanced down at the place where the note had been, and saw that a piece of string was looped round the desk leg. Mum sniffed the string, then prodded it with her paw.

Imogen knelt and picked it up. 'It feels like garden twine,' she said. She looked at where it led . . .

The string trailed along the floor and disappeared down a dark passage. Imogen sighed. 'Nothing is ever easy, is it?' she muttered. The books and, presumably, the librarian, must be through there.

Imogen, Marie and Mum followed the string down the corridor, and it led them to a tall, thin room. Every wall was lined with bookshelves, which curved to fit the bowed shape of the walls. There was no natural light – no windows or skylights – just hundreds of soft-burning lamps.

The room smelled of paper and parchment, of leather bindings and wood. The books here looked old, and there were ladders attached to the shelves, so people could reach the ones near the top.

Imogen and Marie stood, staring, on the cusp of the room. 'Wow,' whispered Marie. 'It does look like a library . . . But how will we find the right book?'

'Librarian,' replied Imogen and she followed the string,

which trailed across the floorboards, looping around bookshelves and sometimes through them, tying itself in knots, before disappearing through a door on the far side of the chamber.

The girls and the hare followed the string up some stairs and into another room. This one was also full of books, although it was slightly more chaotic – with stacks of them on the floor.

The sections here had labels. Imogen read a few as she passed: *The Study of Stones & Strata*, *Epic Poems & Ancient Tales*. Still there was no sign of the librarian.

On they went, following the thread.

Mum stayed close, hopping over fallen manuscripts and sniffing dusty shelves. *At least she's calmer now*, thought Imogen.

The string grew thicker, and, by the time they left the fourth room, it was more like a rope than a thread.

Eventually, they reached a room where there seemed to have been an avalanche of books. Imogen paused at the door. Mrs Nelson, her local librarian, would have been raging if she'd seen books being treated like this. They were splayed out, spines broken, pages crumpled and bent.

The book mountain was so enormous, it filled the room from wall to wall, almost touching the high ceiling. Into this pile went the rope, disappearing between books.

Imogen and Marie started climbing. Mum hopped behind them, ears pricked.

The rope re-emerged near the ceiling. It was hooked over

the chandelier, which was made from dozens of mini glass flowers. Then it ran down the other side of the book mountain and out through the open door.

This side of the book stack was too steep – there was no use in trying to climb down. So Imogen and Marie slid down on their bottoms, creating a landslide of books. They whooped as they skidded towards the exit, chased by tumbling hardbacks and a cloud of dust.

Together, they whizzed through the door.

Mum surfed on a large book behind them. Her ears flapped and her eyes bulged.

'That was amazing!' cried Marie, dusting off her trousers.

Mum looked a little less sure.

They followed the rope deeper into the library, past a room where books were kept in cabinets. Each cabinet had a label: *Forgotten Peoples*, *Prayer Books*, *Maps*.

The rope was thigh-thick now, and it seemed to be made of matted wool.

'This is the strangest library I've ever been to,' said Imogen, keeping her voice low in case the librarian was close.

And it was a good thing she did because the next room they entered had a bookcase in the centre – a very tall one. The rope was coiled around the bottom, like a snake, before rising up one side, right to the top, where, much to Imogen's surprise, she saw a pair of dangling feet. There was someone sitting on top of the bookcase.

CHAPTER 60

'Hello?' called Imogen, to the person on the bookcase. The feet parted and a face appeared between them, peering down at the girls. It was an old man and, from the looks of things, he wasn't happy. 'Argh!' he cried. 'What do you want?'

He was sitting on the top shelf, with very bad posture.

'We'd like to borrow . . . a book,' said Marie.

The man started climbing down the bookcase and Imogen was stunned to see that the thing they'd been following was attached to his face. It was not a string or a rope – but a very long beard.

When the man reached the floor, he unfurled his body. He wore a deep blue robe and a pointy blue hat. He looked more like a magician than a librarian.

Imogen wondered if they'd got the wrong person. 'Are you in charge of the books?' she asked.

'I am Grand Librarian Otakar,' he answered, tossing his beard over one shoulder and sticking out his sunken chest. 'I'm also Librarian-in-Waiting, Deputy Book Handler,

maintenance, the cleaner and a great many other things . . . And you must be *cust-o-mers*.' He seemed to struggle with the last word.

'Yes,' said Imogen. 'Have you got anything about yedleek?'

Grand Librarian Otakar rolled his eyes to the left, as if he was flicking through an invisible catalogue. 'Creatures of the deep with humanoid bodies and flaming heads, move swiftly through stone, slowly through air, height: eight feet, if you don't count the flames, genus *Rockus*, species *ignis*.'

He paused and blinked, as if he'd been somewhere else. 'I'm sorry, what was the question?'

'A book,' said Imogen, less certainly. 'Do you have one about yedleek?'

'Oh yes,' said Otakar. 'I've got a whole section.'

'Great,' said Imogen, brightening. 'Where is it?'

'I don't have time to show you,' cried Otakar, and he gestured at the books on the floor. 'There's only me and there's so much to do. This library won't take care of itself.'

'But . . . we don't know how to find it.'

The librarian's pink-rimmed eyes slid from Imogen to Marie to their mother, who was still a hare.

'Well, I don't know why you're telling me. That's way outside my remit. I'm employed to look after the books and to serve the library's members.' His eyes swivelled back to Imogen. 'You don't look much like a book.'

'We could be members?' said Marie, hopeful.

'No,' snapped Otakar. 'There's only one. And that's Mage Bohoosh.'

Imogen thought of the rooms they'd passed through. There must have been thousands of books, perhaps millions. All of that was for one person? 'That's so greedy,' said Imogen, before she could stop herself.

'I'm sure Mage Bohoosh wouldn't mind us borrowing one book,' said Marie, trying a softer way in. 'We'd look after it very well.'

The librarian straightened his hat, which was, Imogen noticed, tied with string under his chin. 'Impossible,' he said. 'It's against regulations. Besides, there's no time. I have important work to do, sorting manuscripts.'

Marie looked at him sideways. 'What if we helped you? We're pretty good with books, actually. We're kind of . . . librarians-in-training.'

Imogen gave a tiny head shake. What was Marie talking about? They weren't anything close to librarians and they didn't have time to sort books.

'Interesting,' mused the old man.

'But since there's two of us,' continued Marie, pulling her most angelic face, 'I think we should be allowed to borrow *two* books. One about yedleek and one about how to turn animals into people.'

Mum scratched her chin with her hind paw.

'That book . . . Why do you want that book?' The librarian

glanced about, as if expecting someone else to walk in. 'It's not supposed to be read.'

'You said it yourself,' said Marie. 'You can't do all this by yourself. Please, let us help.'

Imogen could almost see a wonky halo, hovering above Marie's head.

'Well,' said the old man, 'I *would* be grateful for an extra pair of hands . . . And it's not often that my path crosses that of other librarians.'

He circled the bookcase several times, unwinding his coiled-up beard. Then he marched out of the room, gesturing for the girls to follow.

'What are you doing?' Imogen whispered to her sister.

'It's a trick that I learned from Anneshka,' said Marie. 'Find out what people want, then make them think that you have it.'

Imogen couldn't decide if she was annoyed or impressed. 'But we're not librarians,' she whispered. 'And we don't have time for this. We've got to get back to Mark before the yedleek hatch and eat him!'

'No point rushing home without the cure,' hissed Marie, and Imogen knew she was right. They didn't have any choice. She just hoped they were able to find it before it was too late . . .

And so the sisters followed Grand Librarian Otakar, back the way they had come, taking care not to step on his beard. The glass lamps glowed all about them. The floorboards creaked underfoot, and Mum-the-hare stayed close.

The old man led the girls to the room that contained the mountain of books. He rolled up his baggy sleeves and waved at the enormous pile. 'This is the room that needs sorting,' he said. 'Alphabetical, by author's surname.'

'But—' Imogen wanted to protest. She couldn't – they couldn't – it was too much!

The book mountain loomed before them, and Imogen's heart sank. This was *way* worse than the chores Imogen did for Mum, way worse than washing up.

And, surely, by the time they'd finished, it would be too late to save Mark. Imogen's nightmare about the yedleek hauling itself out of Mark's chest was still very fresh in her mind . . .

Marie swallowed and lifted her eyes, right to the top of the pile. 'All of it?' she squeaked.

'It shouldn't be a problem for two librarians,' said Otakar, and his expression wasn't unkind. 'A fair price for the loan of two books.'

CHAPTER 61

Imogen and Marie tackled the book mountain the only way that they could – one book at a time. They made piles for each letter of the alphabet, and sorted the books into the relevant stack.

The librarian brought them food, sharing his rations. The food got lifted to the library in a basket that was connected to the city by a rope.

'Don't you ever leave?' asked Imogen, noting the man's spindly legs and pinkish-grey skin. He'd been out of the sunlight for too long. He looked like an uncooked prawn.

'Of course not!' cried the librarian. 'I'm totally committed to this job.' He passed around crispy fried meatballs, soft bread and tangy white cheese that he said was made from the milk of mountain goats. There was even a jar of sweet pickle.

The people who filled the basket thought the librarian was alone so, although the food was nice, it wasn't enough. Yet it took away the worst of the girls' hunger and gave them enough energy to keep sorting books. When she was peckish, Mum hopped out to the ledge and nibbled grass.

Without any windows in the library, it was hard to tell when it was night. But, once a day, Otakar led the girls to the Reading Nook – a little alcove with comfy armchairs. This space was separated from the rest of the library by a heavy curtain. And here, the girls and the hare slept.

On the first day, Marie hummed as they worked, and Imogen joined in. Mum helped by nudging the books with her front paws and nose.

They talked about Mark and the things they did with him. 'I like it when we watch films on the sofa,' said Marie. 'At the end, sometimes, I pretend to be asleep and Mark carries me all the way upstairs.'

'I *knew* you were faking it!' cried Imogen. She picked up another dusty book. 'I like it when he makes campfires, and when he drives us in his silly squished car – even when he goes really slowly . . . It's funny how things that used to be annoying seem sort of nice when you know they won't happen again.'

'Imogen, don't say that,' Marie whispered.

'Sorry,' said Imogen. 'You're right. I'm sure we'll be back with Mark in no time.' But there was a hollow pit in her stomach that said otherwise.

On the second day, Marie hummed a bit less. The girls' eyes were tired from the dim light, their backs were sore from picking up books, and their bellies grumbled for more food.

'How long do we have before the yedleek hatch?' asked Marie.

Imogen didn't know. She'd lost track of time since their hospital visit . . . She just hoped they had enough left.

Mum hopped in a circle, which meant *Hurry up!*

On the third day, they worked in silence. Imogen was so sick of sorting books that she wanted to pack it all in – to run back down the side of the mountain, find the velecours and fly home.

'Who cares if the books are in alphabetical order,' she cried, tossing the one she'd been holding across the room. 'It's not like anyone's ever going to read them! It's just that crusty old librarian and Mage Bohoosh – whoever he is!'

But then Imogen thought of Mark, lying in hospital. There was no one in their world who could save him . . .

And they needed to work out a way to help Mum. She couldn't stay as a hare forever. So Imogen kept sorting books.

'Very good,' said Otakar, that evening. 'Your librarian skills are clearly well honed.'

'Please can we see the book about yedleek?' asked Marie. 'We won't take it until we've finished, we just want to have a look.'

The librarian blinked with his mole-rat eyes. 'I know that the work isn't easy. But I'm afraid I can't help you, not yet – not until the whole pile has been sorted. Being a librarian is not for the faint-hearted, you know.'

CHAPTER 62

While Imogen and Marie waded through books in the library, Miro had crossed the Marshes of Mokzhadee, with memories of his mother leading him on.

He had walked to the foot of the Nameless Mountains, ignoring the hollow pain in his tummy and the thirst that made his lips crack.

The mountains towered above him. Their hulking shoulders were cloaked in white, glinting against the pale sky. Miro felt a strange tug at his heart. He didn't know why – the mountains were just rock and ice. How could something so without meaning make him feel so much?

Miro led Kazimira and Konya through the narrow ravine. His memories of his mother were so clear now, she seemed to be standing at his back, whispering words of encouragement. He could almost feel her breath on his cheek.

Keep going, little Miro. Nedobyt is a safe place. You will be welcomed there . . .

He wondered when he'd get to meet his grandmas – the queens who ruled Nedobyt. Perhaps he'd meet his mother's brother and some of her cousins? The thought of meeting even one relative made Miro walk faster.

He noticed archers at either side of the ravine. They were the first humans, other than Kazimira, that Miro had seen for months and, spotting them perched up there, on impossibly small bits of rock, Miro couldn't help wondering if they were less human – and more mountain goats.

The ravine came to an abrupt end and Miro stepped into a valley. Before him was a city and, just like Yaroslav, it was surrounded by peaks. But that is where the similarities ended. This valley was narrow and the city seemed to have fallen between the cracks, as if it had been dropped down the side of a mountain and no one had been able to pull it back out.

Most of the buildings sprouted from the rock face. Their walls were painted and smooth. At the bottom of the valley, on the small slice of flat land, were many trees and flowers. It looked like a large common, and there were children playing at the closest edge.

Miro took it all in with a dazed acceptance. 'Nedobyt,' he whispered. 'My mother's home . . .'

'Is this it?' asked Kazimira, but her face gave her away. Her eyes shone with wonder as they flicked from the cliffside buildings to the glistening snow-capped peaks and the silver waterfalls that threaded dark rock.

'I'll go and ask for directions,' said Miro and he started walking towards the children. Konya loped at his side.

'I'll stay here and rest,' called Kazimira, sitting down at the end of the ravine.

The children were dressed up as animals; one wore a wolf mask, another had antlers, the smallest wore a fake beaver tail. They paused as Miro and Konya approached. Miro thought they looked afraid, and he realised that he must look very odd. His clothes were rags, dyed green by the marshes. Konya's fur was matted and wild. There was even a bit of woolgrass in her tail.

Miro wished the children knew that his mother was from here, and that he wasn't as strange as he seemed, but he was bone-weary so he focused on the essentials. 'Which way to the Royal Palace?' he asked.

The boy in the wolf's mask didn't seem to have heard. 'What are you supposed to be?' he asked.

'Be?' Miro didn't understand.

'You're dressed up for the festival, like us.'

'Oh . . .' Miro looked down at his filthy bare feet. Then he looked at the children again. Beside the wolf-boy stood a blonde girl, with antlers attached to her headband. Miro guessed she was pretending to be a deer.

The third child was much younger – a boy in a furry brown suit, with a beaver tail trailing on the ground. His black hair was curly and cropped.

All three were waiting for an answer.

'Erm . . . I'm dressed as a bog troll,' said Miro, hoping it would be enough to stop the children asking any further questions. He didn't have the energy for the truth. He just needed to get to the palace.

'A bog troll?' cried the deer-girl. Her eyes bulged with barely suppressed laughter. The boys started laughing too and the tips of Miro's ears felt hot.

Konya tilted her big whiskered head, trying to work out what all the fuss was about.

'Right,' muttered Miro. He started walking away.

'It's over there,' said the wolf-boy, between bursts of laughter, and he pointed across the common, towards a cluster of glass domes shaped like teardrops.

Miro started walking, ears still burning. This isn't how he imagined his arrival in Nedobyt would be . . .

Kazimira trotted to catch up with him, sticking out her tongue as she passed the other children. 'When Daddy arrives, I'll have them executed,' she said.

Miro gave a little smile. In some ways, Kazimira reminded him of his younger self. 'I don't think that'll be necessary,' he muttered. 'Thank you anyway.'

But the local children weren't done yet. They bounded after Miro, Konya and the princess. 'You can't go into the Royal Palace,' said the smallest boy. 'The gardens around it are enchanted. Mage Bohoosh put a spell on the place.'

Miro kept walking, shaking his head. He'd come too far to be put off by tricks.

'It wasn't Mage Bohoosh,' said the deer-girl. 'He's not a good enough magician for that.'

'My mam says he did it,' said the small boy. 'He did it to keep people out of the palace. She says it helps him stay in power.'

Miro stopped walking. Weren't his grandmothers in charge? He was so tired that his thoughts were blurry, as if seen through very thick glass.

Grandmother Olga and Granny Nela . . . Surely, they couldn't be . . . dead?

'You'll get turned into a flower,' said the deer-girl, standing in Miro's way. 'Only members of the royal family – and their servants – can enter the enchanted gardens.'

'It happened to my uncle,' said the boy in the wolf mask. 'He got caught by the spell. Now he's a pink orchid. My aunt is still furious.'

'It happens to all intruders,' said the deer-girl in a matter-of-fact voice.

But I'm not an intruder, thought Miro. He didn't have the energy to say it out loud. He wished the children would move out of his way and let him get to the palace.

'Well, that's fine,' said Kazimira and she crossed her grubby arms. 'Because this boy *is* a member of the royal family. His mother was Sofia Sokol. Now, all of you, step aside!'

Konya let out a low hiss.

The children in fancy dress fell quiet and Miro fidgeted.

'Are you really a prince?' asked the small boy.

'No,' said the deer-girl. 'Clearly not.'

Miro felt a wave of anger – *how dare they question my*

lineage? – followed by an even bigger wave of shame – *of course they don't believe me, why would they? I don't know anything about this place.*

But his mother's ghost called him on.

He could almost see her, walking through the common, glancing back to see if he was coming. Miro pushed his hair from his eyes, darted around the deer-girl, and followed.

'Hey, everyone!' cried the boy in the wolf mask, raising his voice to a shout. 'The bog boy's going into the Royal Palace! Come see him get turned into a flower!'

CHAPTER 63

By the time Miro, Kazimira and Konya reached Nedobyt Royal Palace, they were being followed by a small crowd. There were children, shouting words of encouragement. There were adults, pretending that they had come to supervise the youngsters.

Miro's mind was bursting with memories. Some were his own, of being sung to by his mother, of being held, wrapped in her arms.

Some were the things she'd said about her own childhood. Grandmother Olga and Granny Nela were famous walkers. When they had a tough decision to make, they would go hiking in the mountains, disappearing for days.

When the queens returned, they'd always have a new way of solving the problem that no one had suggested yet.

Miro was the grandchild of mountain women. These were his mountains too.

How could he have forgotten?

It was as if all the things other people had said, about *who he was* and *what he'd become*, had pushed his mother's stories from his head.

People had said that Miro couldn't be king, that he was too much like his uncle.

Others had said that it would be better if both his parents were from Yaroslav. They wanted him to have light eyes and fair skin.

Patoleezal had said that he must be the king, that he couldn't choose his destiny.

They were wrong. *All of them.*

And now Miro's mother's stories were coming back to him, like presents she'd wrapped and put away, waiting for the moment that he was ready to receive them.

'I remember,' he whispered.

He was standing at the entrance to the Royal Palace Garden. Within it was the palace itself. It was made entirely from stone, apart from the crystal-domed roof.

Miro had never seen a building like it. It was beautiful. He couldn't be sure from this distance, but it looked like the domes were constructed from thousands of diamond-shaped panes.

Behind the palace was another, similar, building – although it wasn't quite so grand.

A stone slab marked the threshold to the garden.

'Nobody sets foot in there and lives,' said the girl with deer antlers on her head.

The garden was full of mountain orchids. And they were

in bloom, despite it being the wrong time of year. Miro had the feeling they were *always* in bloom. 'Are all those flowers . . . people?' he asked.

'Uh-huh,' said the small boy with the beaver tail, appearing at Miro's side. 'I've never seen it happen before though. This will be my first time.' Miro wished he didn't sound quite so excited.

A path led through the flowers, to the Royal Palace entrance. Both the garden and the building inside it were quiet . . . as if waiting to see what Miro would do.

'Are you sure you want to do this?' said the wolf-boy. He lifted his whiskered mask and Miro saw his face. It was rounder than Miro's, but his complexion was similar. Miro paused. It was the first time he'd been in a place where many of the people looked like him.

'There will be no going back once you step into the garden,' the boy continued. 'I wouldn't risk it, if I was you . . .'

And, suddenly, Miro felt so full of fear that he almost turned and ran.

'Don't do it,' cried a voice from the crowd.

'Get on with it,' shouted someone else.

People say all sorts of things, said the voice of his mother. *Let them. They cannot change you.*

Miro turned to Kazimira. Her face was very pale. 'I want to go home to my daddy,' she said. 'I want – I want—'

'I know,' Miro sighed.

'But what if you get turned into an orchid?' said Kazimira. She almost sounded concerned.

'I'll be all right,' Miro whispered, so only Kazimira could hear. 'This is my mother's homeland, remember.'

It isn't your *home though, is it?* said a little voice in his head.

Miro stared at his feet, toenails hardly visible beneath layers of grime. The truth was, he didn't know. His surname was Krishnov, inherited from his father . . . and he'd never even visited Nedobyt.

That meant he was more Krishnov than Sokol . . . didn't it? You can't be two things at once.

But Miro's famous grandmothers might be inside that palace, with its ornate stone entrance and glittering roof. He wanted so desperately to meet them.

Miro lifted one leg. His heel hovered, a few inches above the garden path. His heart was beating so loud, he was sure that other people must be able to hear it.

He lowered his foot.

Nothing happened.

He moved his other foot to join it.

Still, nothing changed.

Konya nudged Miro with her velvety nose and he took another step into the garden, fear knotting tight in his chest. 'He's doing it!' cried a voice from the crowd. 'Bog boy's breaking into the palace!'

Miro glanced at his hands, checking that they hadn't turned into leaves. *There* were his fingers, as normal. *There* were his arms and his legs.

He let out a high-pitched giggle – more out of relief than anything else.

And then he started to walk, arms spread wide as if on a tightrope. The knot in his chest was loosening and the crowd was chanting, 'Bog boy, bog boy!'

Either side of him, orchids bobbed their heads, filling the air with their delicate scent.

His mother's ghost drifted ahead. *Keep going, little Miro. You're doing so well.*

A pair of mice scampered across the path and Miro almost tripped, trying not to squash them. His body wasn't working as it used to. He was so tired. He'd been in the marshes for too long.

But it was all right. He was almost there . . .

There were no soldiers guarding the Royal Palace, none of the gold-clad archers that had watched from the sides of the ravine.

The entrance loomed above Miro, with curving patterns cut into the stone. He reached for the knocker and, before he could touch it, the doors creaked apart.

There was an audible intake of breath from the crowd. 'He's a real Sokol,' shrieked one voice.

There were no servants beyond the doors, no sign of anyone who might have let Miro in.

He hesitated, heart hammering.

'What are you waiting for?' shouted Kazimira, from the far side of the enchanted garden. 'I want food and a hot drink. Go and speak to your family!'

Konya stood at the princess's side, watching Miro with her penetrating eyes.

'I am a true Sokol,' said Miro. And with that he stepped between the doors, into his grandmothers' home.

CHAPTER 64

Inside the palace, it was bright. The ceiling was a dome, sparkling with thousands of glass panes, and it seemed to not only let the light in, but to *magnify* it.

The entrance hall was empty; a circular space surrounded by arches.

'Hello?' Miro called, his voice echoing.

'And who do we have here?' asked a deep voice.

Miro felt as if the speaker stood right behind him, whispering into his ear. But when he turned, there was no one there.

'I – I'm Miroslav,' he replied. 'Sofia Sokol's son.'

The doors creaked shut behind him and Miro stood in the hall alone. He turned, wondering where the speaker might be.

'Ahhhh,' said the voice, and this time it came from the left.

Miro had a feeling that the invisible man was circling him, taking him in from all angles. He wished that he wasn't wearing rags. He wished that he'd taken some time to wash in a stream, to scrub the slug-mint from his face. He was sure that all of his shortcomings were more visible in the magnified light.

'I have crossed the Marshes of Mokzhadee,' said Miro. 'I have duelled the krootymoosh. And now I have come to see my grandmothers. Will you tell them I am here?'

'You are very welcome.' The voice drew further away. 'Very welcome indeed . . . My name is Grand Mage Bohoosh. Please, follow me.'

A man stepped out from under one of the archways. He was dressed head-to-toe in grey, with a cloak slung over one shoulder, as if he'd been caught in a gale. It was hard to see his face properly in the blinding light.

'This way,' said Bohoosh, walking under the arch.

Miro paused. There was a ringing in his ears that was probably the result of being very hungry. Food had been hard to find since he'd left the marshes.

He followed the man into a large room that also had a domed roof. It was some kind of orangery or sunroom. There were trees with citrus fruits and plants with fat, waxy leaves.

From the looks of things, there had been a celebration the night before. Wine glasses were strewn on every surface, along with half-eaten tartlets and big stuffed dates. Miro had to stop himself from taking one. He hadn't had food like *that* in a long time.

'Please, sit down,' said the man. He helped Miro to a chair, but he moved it in too quickly, so it struck the back of Miro's knees. He half fell on to the seat.

The mage sat opposite and gestured at the rubbish. 'Apologies for the mess, Miroslav. There was a bit of a get-together last night. The servants really ought to have tidied it up.' His eyes darted over Miro. 'So . . . you're Princess Sofia's son?'

Miro's heart boinged in his chest. Hearing his mother's name in another person's mouth made her feel more present – more alive.

'Y-yes,' he whispered, mouth dry.

Bohoosh was grey all over – grey tunic, grey hair and pale greyish skin. The only exceptions were his dark bushy eyebrows and the middle of his cheeks, which shone pink.

He looked shabby considering he was a Grand Mage . . . although, Miro had to admit, he had never met a magician before.

Bohoosh's appearance was more that of an uncle who always meant very well, but who drank too much at parties and made embarrassing speeches before midnight.

Miro could well believe that whatever powers Bohoosh held, they were not very impressive ones.

The mage noticed Miro staring, and gave him a jolly smile. 'As the Grand Mage of Nedobyt, I commend you on being the first human to cross the marshes. What a clever chap you must be. All of Nedobyt rejoices in your arrival and extends various hospitalities. And you're just in time for the festival. My powers – indeed, the whole Royal Palace – is at your service.'

'Where are my grandmothers?' asked Miro.

The mage's smile froze. 'You haven't heard? Your grandmothers are missing. Haven't been seen these last three years . . .'

'What?' Miro's stomach plummeted.

'Yes, I'm afraid it is true.' Bohoosh pulled a serious face, but there was still a cheery gleam in his eyes.

'What about my mother's brother? And her cousins? Hana and Durko?'

'All gone,' said the mage.

'Gone where?' cried Miro. He could feel all the hope that had sustained him on the marshes draining away.

I'm still alone, he thought. Even after reaching his mother's homeland, even after getting into the palace . . . He wished Konya was with him. He even wished for Kazimira.

'If I knew that, I would have sought them,' said Bohoosh. 'But I'm afraid the Sokol Dynasty is over. The queens have disappeared . . . You are the last of the line.' He lowered his voice to a whisper, and something like triumph flashed in his eyes. 'And, let's face it, you didn't even grow up here.'

Miro felt dizzy. 'I think – I think I need to lie down.'

Bohoosh clicked his fingers and two servants, dressed in muted colours, rushed to Miro's side. They supported him under his elbows and steered him out of the room.

CHAPTER 65

The next morning, Miro was woken by a shaft of light on his face. It was the sun, shining through the glass roof. Miro was wrapped in a quilt, lying on a mattress so soft, it felt as if it had half-swallowed him.

He shielded his eyes and squinted at the domed ceiling. The sky was ice blue and he could see a white mountain peak. Then Miro remembered.

He remembered his trudge across the marshes, the throne made from heartwood, the violet spiders, the bog troll who'd helped him survive.

He remembered Princess Kazimira eating suckers like they were going out of fashion, and Konya pouncing on fish.

He remembered their arrival in Nedobyt, the smell of wild orchids, Mage Bohoosh's voice and, with a slicing sensation, he remembered that his family were gone.

He was the last Krishnov.

The last Sokol.

The last everything.

Miro gasped. It was too painful. He couldn't keep going, couldn't pick himself up yet again.

And here came the final memory. Miro remembered being washed by servants, then being carried and laid on this bed. He had cried himself to sleep, thinking of the grandmothers that he would never meet – of the love that he'd never feel.

The sun shone stronger, coming in through the ceiling and Miro closed his eyes. 'Mother, I need you,' he croaked, leaning into the ray. The sun was warm, like a hand reaching down, cupping the side of his face. And Miro couldn't help feeling that his mother was with him.

A knock startled him out of his trance. 'Your Highness?' said a voice, from outside the bedroom. 'It's Lída, the palace steward. May I come in?'

Miro cleared his throat. 'Yes.'

The door opened and a woman entered the bedroom. She was wearing the grey-green of the palace servants, but there was extra lace on her collar and sleeves, suggesting that she was important. And she was. Miro knew all about stewards. They were a king or queen's representative – the person who made sure things got done.

He wondered if Lída had worked for his grandmothers, before she served Mage Bohoosh.

'Did you sleep well, Your Highness?' asked Lída.

Miro nodded. 'My friends,' he said, thinking of Kazimira and Konya. 'Did they – are they here?'

'The young princess and her sněehoolark are in the Guest Palace.'

'I expect Kazimira will want to return to King Ctibor,' said Miro, and that slicing pain was still there.

There was a time, not so long ago, when Miro had hoped that Ctibor might think of *him* as a son. But Ctibor did not care for anyone outside his family . . . and Miro could no longer forget.

'We will organise a carriage to take the princess to her father,' said Lída. 'This time, she should take the Long Road.'

Miro's throat tightened at the thought of Kazimira leaving.

The sun was fully up now and its rays poured in through the dome. They illuminated every inch of the bed, every floating speck of dust.

'Mage Bohoosh says you can stay in the palace,' said Lída. She started rearranging some ornaments on a side table, turning so Miro couldn't see her face.

'It's the festival this evening,' she continued. 'Should be quite a sight. Everyone dresses as animals, in honour of the slipskins. Of course, there haven't been any slipskins for years now, but the festival is still popular. You know what people are like . . .'

Apparently satisfied with the layout of the ornaments, she turned to face Miro again. 'I'll organise your costume, Miroslav. Perhaps a little lion or a wolf.'

Miro shook his head. 'I don't want a costume.'

'What about a rider?' said Lída. 'Shall we send a message to your home? Mage Bohoosh thinks it would be wise, and I must say I agree.'

'Home.' The word escaped Miro's lips without him thinking.

'Yes, your home in Yaroslav,' said Lída, as if she was speaking to a much younger child. 'Your Chief Adviser has been searching for you.'

Miro thought of Patoleezal, his elastic smile stretching tight enough to snap. Patoleezal only wanted Miro back for one reason – so that he could continue to rule through him.

'Mage Bohoosh suggests you leave after the festival. I'll tell him it's all been agreed. We can organise supplies and horses, and an armed escort, of course.'

Miro looked straight at the woman now, his attention focused on her words. He had been a puppet for long enough to know when decisions were being made on his behalf.

'Oh, and I must ask,' continued Steward Lída, 'because the servants are curious. Did you really spend all those months on the marshes? How did you survive on that wasteland?'

The sun was still shining through the ceiling and its light was being split by the glass, creating a rainbow on Miro's bed. He moved his hand so the colours shone on his skin.

'It's not a wasteland,' said Miro.

'What?' said Lída.

The rainbow extended across Miro's face. 'The marshes. They're not a waste. Not a wasteland.'

Lída was standing with her back pressed against the wall, as if afraid of the light.

'I will stay for the festival,' said Miro. 'I'm tired . . . But, after that, I'm going to search for my grandmothers. And if that means staying in Nedobyt, so be it.'

Lída's face twitched. 'Your Highness? But your grandmothers . . . they are gone.'

'People don't just *disappear*,' said Miro. 'You can tell Mage Bohoosh that.'

CHAPTER 66

It must have been the morning, because Imogen and Marie were still asleep. They were tangled together in the Reading Nook, in Nedobyt Library.

The armchairs had been pushed to meet; curtain drawn.

Mum lay behind Marie, nose by her neck, as if they were hugging. In reality, Mum was too small to give anyone a hug, on account of her being a hare.

Imogen was woken by men's voices, and, at first, she thought the librarian was speaking to himself. It wouldn't be the first time . . .

But one of the voices was definitely a stranger's – and they didn't seem to realise that there were people on the other side of the curtain.

'I don't know where he came from, he just turned up,' said the stranger. 'Claims that he crossed the marshes, although we both know that's impossible.'

'Hmmm,' said the voice of the librarian. 'Mokzhadee, the vast unknowable marshes, cannot be built upon or farmed. The wetland is excellent habitat for—'

'Forgive me,' said the stranger. 'I do hate to interrupt, but I've heard enough about swamps.'

'Oh, but it's not a swamp,' said Otakar. 'Swamps are defined by their forests and the marshes have very few trees.'

He sounded like he was reading the information, but Imogen guessed he was not. Grand Librarian Otakar knew a great many things.

'You are a first-rate book-keeper,' said the stranger. 'The city is very grateful for all that you do. You really are a pillar of Nedobyt . . . a rock.' The speaker seemed a little distracted. 'Marvellous job. All this parchment and ink and, erm . . . Thing is, old chap, I'm in a bit of a tight spot. I'm here because I need a book.'

Imogen pushed the blanket off her body, making sure not to disturb Mum and Marie. Then she eased her legs sideways until her toes touched the floor.

'Of course,' mumbled Otakar. 'I live to serve. Are you after a book for the boy? What is the child's name, may I ask?'

'Miroslav Krishnov,' muttered the stranger. 'And no, no, the book's not for him.'

Imogen almost jumped with surprise. *Miro?* He was here – in the city? Now she was listening intently, not wanting to miss a word.

'He claims he's the son of Sofia Sokol,' said the stranger. 'You know, the princess who married abroad. Yaroslav . . . was that where she went? God only knows why she did it, although

I hear their sausages and dumplings are good. Anyway . . . I digress. Whatever this boy is, he can't stay.'

There was a silence and Imogen tried not to breathe. She didn't know why, but she didn't want this man to know she was listening. She prayed he wouldn't look behind the curtain.

'But the boy has every right to be here,' said Grand Librarian Otakar. 'And he could be just what Nedobyt needs. Why, when Princess Sofia was a child—'

'Balderdash!' shouted the stranger, all his charming bluster gone. 'I am Grand Mage Bohoosh! I can do anything that I want! Do not lecture me, you puffed-up popinjay!'

Imogen lowered her body to the floor. She had to get a look at this man. She crawled to the curtain that hid the Reading Nook from view, and lifted the hem.

'And if Miroslav won't leave of his own free will,' continued the mage, 'I have other ways of making him disappear.'

Pressing her face to the floorboards, Imogen peeped under the curtain. The stranger was dressed in grey, and was a deeply average-looking man. He had unbrushed grey hair and dark eyebrows, a long face and a smug little mouth.

He looked very little like a magician . . . Is that what a mage was supposed to be?

Indeed, out of the two men, it was the librarian who looked more like a conjurer – with his billowing robes and pointy hat.

Otakar was turning in circles so his long beard got tied

up in knots. 'But how will you make him disappear?' asked the librarian.

'Never you mind,' said Bohoosh. 'Everyone will be merry at the festival . . . far too merry to worry about a foreign-born princeling.' He looked at Otakar as if he had only just realised that he'd been speaking out loud. 'I shouldn't be telling you this, old fellow –' and he glanced about at the book-filled room – 'but who are you going to tell?'

Otakar looked horrified. He kept scrunching his eyes in long blinks, as if he was trying to shut the mage out.

Bohoosh clapped him hard on the back. 'Don't go all funny on me, Otakar. It's just politics . . . Nothing for you to get flustered about. Stick to the books, that's my advice.'

Imogen couldn't believe her ears. Mage Bohoosh stepped closer to the curtain and Imogen saw that his slippers had long curly tips, like the shoes of a jester.

You can learn a lot about a person from their shoes, said Grandma's voice in Imogen's head.

'Anyway, I'm here to collect the book about slipskins,' announced Bohoosh. 'It needs destroying, and urgently.'

'Destroying?' whispered Otakar. 'But it's the only one of its kind. I thought you wanted it protecting.'

Imogen agreed with the librarian. Destroying books was bad. But Otakar did have quite a few of them, and he was speaking as if Mage Bohoosh had asked him to kill his first-born child.

'There's no choice,' snapped Bohoosh, and his curly shoes

paced closer. 'That book contains information that is . . . best known by me. It would be dangerous in other people's hands.'

The librarian hesitated for a long time. 'I'm afraid it's missing,' he said at last.

'What?' cried Mage Bohoosh. 'How can it be missing? No one but me has access to this place.'

'Oh, it's here,' said Otakar. 'I put it somewhere safe – so safe that I can't remember where . . .'

'Find the slipskin book,' shouted Bohoosh. 'Find it or I'll have this whole building burned down. If that's the only way to make sure the book is destroyed, so be it.'

Imogen couldn't see Otakar's face, but he had gone very quiet and still. 'Yes, Grand Mage Bohoosh,' he muttered. 'Of course, Grand Mage Bohoosh.'

And, with that, the mage and his curly-tipped shoes turned and walked out of the room.

CHAPTER 67

When the footsteps had faded, Imogen pulled back the curtain. The librarian was standing in the middle of the room and, for a minute, he was so still, she was worried that something had happened to him.

But he snapped back to life when he saw her. 'You shouldn't have heard that,' he gasped.

'Mage Bohoosh is going to do something to Miro, isn't he?' cried Imogen.

The librarian looked confused.

'Miroslav Krishnov,' said Imogen, impatient.

'Oh, yes – maybe – I don't know,' said Otakar. 'He *has* done unsavoury things in the past, but he's normally too busy partying to achieve anything much . . . He's certainly going to burn down my library if I don't find that slipskin book. I can't believe I've lost track of it. There's just too much work to be done! Too many books!'

His face was lined with worry. He started rummaging through the book mountain, checking each cover before setting it aside.

Imogen woke Marie and her hare-mum, and told them what she'd just overheard. 'Miro's in Nedobyt?' cried Marie, eyes lighting up. 'Can we go and see him?'

'I think we might have to,' said Imogen. 'We have to warn him about Mage Bohoosh before the festival. Otakar, when does the festival begin?'

'Tonight,' said the librarian.

'Bum-snot!' cried Imogen. 'We have to go now!'

'But what about the books?' said Marie. 'The one for Mum and for Mark?'

Both sisters turned to the librarian, who was searching through the pile of hardbacks in an ever more frantic fashion.

'Grand Librarian Otakar,' called Marie. 'Please, can we have our books?'

The librarian paused and looked at the girls, as if he'd forgotten they were there. 'No, of course not!' he snapped. 'The book Mage Bohoosh wants destroying is the same one you've asked for. It explains the rules of slipskin magic. You can't *both* have it at once.'

'That's not fair!' cried Imogen. 'We asked for it first!' She couldn't stand to think of her mum being stuck as an animal – especially after all the book sorting they'd done.

'Slipskin magic?' Marie frowned. 'But our mum isn't a slipskin. She just drank the wrong water.'

Otakar glanced at the golden hare. 'Being a slipskin isn't something you're born with. It's something that is learned, that is lived. All those who drink from the magic spring change species. You need the correct spell to turn back. And the correct spell is in the missing book.'

Mum ran towards the librarian and rose on to her back legs, pawing at the bottom of his robe. She was clearly asking for his help. But Otakar shook his head. 'Honestly, I don't know where that book is! And, even if I did, I have to sacrifice it to save the others.'

'Once you know the right spell, are you a slipskin?' asked Marie. 'Could I be a slipskin too?'

Imogen didn't know why Marie was still asking questions. None of this mattered right now. Time was running out to save Mark from the yedleek – and to alert Miro too.

The librarian sniffed. 'There is far more to it than that. These days, those who call themselves "slipskins" are nothing more than cheap performers. A true slipskin can not only change species, they can choose which animal they become. What's more, they can change back at will . . . No. There has not been a true slipskin in Nedobyt for years.'

Imogen considered attacking Otakar. Between her and Marie, they might be able to hold him down. They could refuse to release him until he gave them the books.

But then they'd be little better than Mage Bohoosh . . .

Otakar was still talking, with a faraway expression on his face. 'Young mages used to study every letter of that book. Sadly, it is an ancient art, and today the youth of Nedobyt show little interest. They do not train as slipskins. They hardly read any more. Such a rich heritage is wasted upon them.'

Imogen's anger bubbled up. 'That's not true,' she cried. 'If the book and the magic water are both here, and no one's allowed up the path, people don't have any choice. It's no wonder the slipskins died out.'

The librarian stroked his long beard. 'Hmm,' he murmured. 'It is an interesting point . . . Still, keeping people out of my library does keep the lovely books safe.'

'Does it?' asked Imogen, stepping closer. 'Mage Bohoosh said he'd burn the whole lot. And no one out there is going to stop him because – why would they? – they can't even borrow books!'

'Please, Otakar, won't you help us?' pressed Marie.

The librarian hugged his beard to his chest and rocked from side to side. 'You haven't finished sorting this room . . .'

'But we can't stay any longer,' cried Imogen. 'We have to go and warn Miro. And if we don't have the book about slipskins, our mother will always be a hare! And if we don't have the book about yedleek, our stepdad is going to die! Why should people care about books if you won't let them be read – if you won't allow the knowledge inside to save us?'

The librarian gulped. He looked guilty; his mouth shaped like a little 'o'. 'Have I made a terrible mistake,' he whispered, 'allowing Bohoosh to seal the library off?'

Imogen, Marie and the hare exchanged glances. The answer seemed obvious enough.

'Perhaps libraries are a bit like slipskin magic,' said Marie, in her gentlest voice. 'They exist when they're shared with lots of people . . . they die out if they're hidden away.'

The librarian's face crumpled. 'W-where did you read that?'

Marie pressed her lips together. 'Please can we borrow the books?'

Otakar closed his eyes for a moment, taking a tremulous breath. 'I suppose you *are* librarians in training . . .' He hurried towards the door, beard swooshing on the floorboards. 'One moment,' he called as he left the room.

When Otakar returned, he was gripping a thick book, bound in dark leather. He held it up so Imogen and Marie could read the cover in the light from the glass lamps:

ON YEDLEEK

'Take it,' said Otakar. 'Take it! Everything you said is true . . . Books are for reading, for doing good. I think that perhaps, like my manuscripts, I have been alone for too long.'

Imogen clasped her fingers round the cover, knowing that this was a shared prize. It had taken her and Marie's combined efforts to talk Otakar round. She held the book lower, so Mum could see it too.

'You must go and tip off your friend,' said the librarian. 'I will search for the slipskin book and bring it to you. On that you have my word.'

Imogen nodded solemnly. 'Thank you, Grand Librarian

Otakar.' He was taking a very big risk. When Mage Bohoosh didn't get the book he'd demanded, this whole library might be destroyed.

Otakar seemed to be thinking the same thing. 'If Miroslav Krishnov is who he says he is, we won't have to put up with Mage Bohoosh for much longer.'

'What do you mean?' asked Marie.

'The boy has a claim to the throne,' said Otakar. 'That's why Bohoosh wants him gone. For years folk have been saying there's no one better – they say Bohoosh is all that we've got.' Otakar shook his head, making his beard sway from side to side.

'We allowed him to sit in the Royal Palace, drinking wine and entertaining his friends, getting rich at the expense of the people.' Otakar was getting quite worked up now and colour flushed his pale prawny skin.

'As with the library, Bohoosh doesn't let people enter the palace – has anyone who tries turned into a flower. He's got no right to do that! Just like he has no right to terrorise these books.' The librarian blinked at the sisters. 'You *must* protect Miroslav.'

Marie ran at Otakar and gave him a hug. The old man froze, as if ice had been poured on his head. But, after a moment, he softened.

'Erm, yes,' he said as he patted Marie's hair. 'Now, I shall continue my hunt. You had better run. Whatever Bohoosh is planning for Miroslav, it sounds like it's happening soon.'

CHAPTER 68

Anneshka Mazanar was riding on the Long Road, flanked by a mighty army. Ahead of her stood the Nameless Mountains. To her left were the cursed marshes, with their endless water and weeds.

The Long Road was a narrow trade route that skirted the wetland. It was not designed for such a military force, so Anneshka's soldiers had to march in a line, snaking over a distance of several miles.

At the head of the army were the Yezdetz. Samo had sent word to his homeland, in the north, summoning the rest of his kin and the great war elk that they rode into battle.

Anneshka was not keen on the elk. They were always snorting and their poo stank to the stars. Still, it was worth it to have the Yezdetz beside her, dressed in their armour and furs. Many of them carried spears and longswords. Others, like Gunilla, favoured axes and shields.

Behind these warriors came a legion of red-jacketed soldiers. Most of them were on horseback; others marched on foot. They had been given to Anneshka by Patoleezal.

The Chief Adviser was a slippery man, who Anneshka did not trust, but he seemed keen to be her ally – and she would take what fighters she could get.

Patoleezal was probably nervous about his position, what with Miroslav being gone. In return for the loan of his soldiers, Anneshka had promised Patoleezal a key role in her new empire. Naturally, she'd also be Queen of Yaroslav – a small addition to her territories.

At the back of the line came the soldiers of Vodnislav, given by King Ctibor to Anneshka's cause. The old fool still believed she was his daughter. And, while he continued his search for Kazimira, he'd let Anneshka take every fighter he had.

Among Ctibor's soldiers were both humans and skret, clinking in their chainmail. Ctibor had also given Anneshka battering rams and catapults, which had to be pulled by thirty horses each.

But the most powerful machine of all was strapped to Anneshka's saddle: the clock of stars, wrapped in its velvet bag. It was the clock that had shown Anneshka what to do.

First, it had shown her Marie, riding on a velecour, and Anneshka had followed the child beyond the mountains. She would follow the child to the ends of the earth, if it meant she'd fulfil her destiny.

Samo had interrogated the Lowland fisherfolk, and they had told him that two giant birds had been seen flying towards the Marshes of Mokzhadee. So Anneshka's army had marched south.

Then the clock had shown Anneshka a mountain falcon, the symbol of Nedobyt.

Ha! thought Anneshka. *The child has gone to the Nameless Mountains. Does she imagine she'll be safe there? If so, she underestimates me.*

Nedobyt was famous for its library, for its beauty and its magic. Could it be the greatest kingdom? Or would Marie lead Anneshka somewhere greater still?

She meant to take the city either way. It would be a fine capital for her empire.

'Your Majesty,' said one of the Yezdetz, interrupting her thoughts. It was a scout who'd been riding ahead. His war elk was panting from the gallop.

Anneshka eyed the beast's massive antlers and wrinkled her nose at its big foaming mouth. It really was hideous.

'We are making good time,' the scout continued. 'If we march through the night, we'll reach the ravine before daybreak. It would give us an element of surprise.'

Anneshka nodded. 'Then that is exactly what we'll do.'

CHAPTER 69

M iro had no idea that a great army was marching towards Nedobyt. Nor did he know that Imogen and Marie were so close and searching for him.

It was late afternoon, just a few hours before the festival, and Mage Bohoosh had invited Miro to have tea in the Guest Palace.

These lodgings were built in the same style as the Royal Palace, with stone walls and domed glass roofs, but they were outside the enchanted gardens, so Konya and Kazimira could attend.

Miro arrived early, and found Kazimira putting the final touches on her outfit. She had been washed and no longer looked like an angry swamp fairy. In fact, she looked like her old self. Well, almost . . .

The princess had requested a sněehoolark costume for the festival and a maid was busy painting whiskers on her face. Her hair had been combed and wrapped around wires so it held the shape of two pointy ears.

'How do I look?' she asked, when Miro walked in.

'Erm . . . like a giant cat?' he said, hoping this was the right answer. He had to admit, she looked good. It made him slightly regret his refusal to wear a costume himself.

But Miro didn't want to do anything that Steward Lída or Mage Bohoosh suggested. He'd had enough of being controlled and, for a few days at least, Miro was determined to be himself . . . whatever that meant.

Kazimira beamed. 'That's what I am!' She gave a sickly sweet miaow.

Konya, the *real* sněehoolark, was sitting by the fireplace.

Kazimira dismissed the maid. She seemed to have no problem slipping between the role of sněehoolark and princess.

'I heard about your family,' said Kazimira. 'Why didn't anyone tell you that your grandmothers were missing? All that walking across the marshes . . . and they're not even here.'

'I don't know,' said Miro. 'I invited them to my coronation, but they never replied, and I thought perhaps they didn't want to see me . . . Maybe they never received my message.'

Kazimira pushed her lips into a thoughtful pout. 'I'm missing,' she said. 'Daddy doesn't know where I am. But I bet he hasn't given up – just like he never gave up on Pavla. When he receives my letter, he'll send fifty soldiers to collect me. That's what families do . . . So you can't give up on your grandmothers. You have to find out where they've gone.'

Miro stared at the cat-girl. He thought it was the wisest

thing she'd ever said. 'Thanks, Kazimira,' he mumbled. 'I'm going to look for my family. That's my plan, I just—'

He was interrupted by a terrible scream. It had come from the princess herself.

'What?' asked Miro, suddenly on high alert.

The cat-girl raised a trembling finger and pointed to a corner of the room. 'A rat!' she cried.

Miro turned and saw a tiny mouse cleaning its whiskers. Kazimira hopped on to her bed. 'There's a rat in my room!'

The mouse froze, aware that it had been spotted.

'That's not a rat,' said Miro. 'It's a mouse. I'll – I'll call back the maid.'

But there was no need because the difference between a snĕehoolark and a princess in a costume was about to become very clear. Konya sprang into action.

The mouse shot across the floor like a wind-up toy, and Konya skidded after it.

'RAAAAAAAAAT!' shrieked Kazimira, jumping on the bed. 'HELP! THERE'S A RAAAAT!'

Miro didn't know what to do. He was a little afraid of mice himself.

The mouse zigzagged and jumped to avoid the snĕehoolark's paws, before disappearing into a hole at the base of the wall.

Konya, for all her usual grace, did not see the wall coming. She crashed into it, nose first, so that her back legs seemed to scrunch into her front.

A maid burst in, brandishing a broom. 'Where is it?' she cried.

'It was a mouse,' said Miro, pointing at the tiny hole and the accordioned cat.

The maid let out a huff. 'That's it. I'm setting a trap.' She tucked a stray hair behind her ear. 'Oh, and I was coming to tell you – Mage Bohoosh will see you now. He's in the Reception Room.'

CHAPTER 70

M age Bohoosh was sitting in the largest room of the Guest Palace. Pink cheeks glowing, grey hair ruffled, as if he'd got dressed in a storm.

A table was laid with a glass tea-set and delicate wafer biscuits. Miro eyed the teapot. It was made from special glass that didn't crack with hot water and he could see the tea sloshing inside. Tiny purple flowers floated in the water, turning it indigo.

Miro also spied a plate of syrup-dipped figs, a speciality of Nedobyt and a favourite of his mother's. From the looks of things, Bohoosh had already eaten most of them.

'Ah, Miroslav, Kazimira, greetings!' cried the mage.

There was a disarming chaos about the man that made him hard to dislike. But Miro was not entirely convinced. There was something about the mage that didn't feel genuine . . .

Bohoosh was looking at Miro. 'I hear that you plan to stay?'

'Yes, my relatives may still be alive,' replied Miro. 'I'm going to do everything I can to find them.'

'That's the spirit,' said the mage, although his eyes twinkled a bit less. 'There's nothing a positive attitude can't achieve . . . except perhaps bringing back the dead.'

'I'm staying with him,' said Kazimira, twirling her fake sněehoolark tail.

'Really?' gasped Miro, staring at the princess. This was news to him.

'Got to help you find your grand-mummies,' she said. 'Isn't that obvious?'

Miro's heart swelled, just a little. He turned back to Mage Bohoosh. 'Thank you for your hospitality,' he said. 'We really are very grateful.'

'Not at all,' said Bohoosh. 'In fact, I've got you a gift.' He gestured to a pile of feathers that were draped over a chair.

Miro realised it was a costume, and felt a hot curl of annoyance. He'd already told Lída that he didn't want to dress up.

'I believe it used to be your mother's,' said the mage.

The annoyance fizzled out. 'My mother's?'

The mage rolled back his sleeves and held up the feathered thing. The garment appeared to be a cape, lined with silk.

Dappled grey feathers hung from the sleeves so that when the wearer stood with their arms extended, it would look like they had wings.

'Apparently, when your mother was a girl, she loved mountain falcons. And now you can have her costume,' said Bohoosh, still clutching it, 'so long as you promise to return

328

to the palace for the tasting of the waters this evening. It's a very important part of the festival. The waters are drawn from all the springs around Nedobyt and I would hate for you to miss out.'

Miro had no interest in mineral water, and he already felt that Bohoosh and Lída were bossing him about . . . but he *really* wanted to touch his mother's cape. 'Yes, Mage Bohoosh,' he said. 'We'll make sure we're back in time.'

The mage handed the costume to Miro, letting go a little too soon, so the cape fell and Miro had to pick it up off the floor. He slipped it over his shoulders. Its warmth reminded him of his mother's embrace.

'And don't you look charming?' said Bohoosh to Kazimira.

'I'm a sněehoolark, miaow,' she replied in a simpering voice.

'Where were my grandmothers last seen?' asked Miro.

The mage rolled his eyes to the domed roof, as if thinking very hard . . . or perhaps trying to remember what he had for breakfast.

'Heading deeper into the mountains,' said the mage, eventually. 'Yes, that's it. I'm quite sure. They were last seen heading into the mountains. I do wish I could help, old chap.'

'They were going walking?' said Miro.

'I suppose so,' mumbled Bohoosh. 'The old dears were obsessed – used to hike out before dawn. Strange habit when you think of it. Reminds me of something I once read by a poet . . . something about rambling and jeopardy. No doubt your grandmothers got lost and took a fatal fall.'

Miro's blood froze at the thought.

But if his grandmothers knew the mountains so well, it seemed unlikely . . . didn't it?

Kazimira started on the wafer biscuits. Bohoosh finished the figs.

Miro watched the Grand Mage chewing. He'd stopped assuming that adults had his best interests at heart . . . especially adults that were sitting pretty in his grandmothers' home. But he needed to keep the mage onside – needed more time to work out what was going on.

'Now, children,' said Bohoosh, changing tone. 'I bet you'd like to see some magic!'

'Yes!' cried Kazimira. She clapped her hands.

Bohoosh began chanting a spell. He wriggled his fingers at the glass teapot and it lifted an inch from the tray. 'Hah!' cried Bohoosh. 'You see! There's still life in this old mage yet!'

He kept chanting and the teapot rose higher. Mage Bohoosh wafted it closer to a cup. But the pot wobbled and sloshed tea across the table. 'Oh, bother,' he muttered. 'I've been practising that.'

'It's all right,' said Miro. 'I don't mind pouring the tea.'

'Ah, you are a kind boy . . . No wonder Patoleezal is so keen to see you returned.'

'I'm not going back there,' Miro repeated.

Mage Bohoosh sipped his drink with narrowed eyes.

CHAPTER 71

The marsh-gas lanterns of Nedobyt were lit, illuminating the sides of the mountains. They were placed at the doors of glassblowers' workshops, nine hundred feet above the valley floor. They were clustered around ancient springs. There were even glass lanterns on the zigzag steps that cut down the vertical slopes.

Dancers, acrobats and musicians filled the common. A band of men were dressed as firebirds, spinning and breathing flames.

Tables had been set out between the trees, decked with tablecloths and autumn leaves, ready for the feast that came at midnight.

People gathered, wearing their animal costumes – snails and snakes and buvol. There was even a man in a purple tunic with extra limbs sewn to his sides, pretending to be a marsh spider.

The humans weren't the only ones gathering. Small birds came to roost in the trees, chattering in the blue dusk. Moths blurred between branches. And beyond that were the first early stars.

Skret joined the human celebrations, having travelled down from their caves. The skret were mountain creatures, smaller than adult humans, with very sharp teeth and cup-sized eyes.

Many of them were dressed up as people. Their bald heads were covered by hats. Yet there was no disguising their long claws, which glinted beneath trouser legs and sleeves. They might have looked funny to you or me, but the joke was definitely on the humans.

And, through this flamboyant crowd, two children dashed. 'Your Highness, come back,' called Steward Lída, but her voice was already lost in the throng.

Miro was giddy with excitement. He had decided to put his problems aside for one night and enjoy the festival. He was wearing his mother's cape, extending his arms like wings as he ran.

It was as if a spell had been cast across the city. A spell that allowed you to forget – forget about your worries – forget who you were supposed to be.

Miro would go back to Bohoosh and Lída. He would taste the waters, as they wished. But first he wanted to see the festival, like his mother used to do when she was young.

He dodged between an old man who was dressed as a turtle and a woman dressed as a bear.

Kazimira ran beside him, giggling. Konya galloped behind, dodging between festivalgoers and pale trees. 'I am a sněehoolark,' cried Kazimira, 'hear me ROOOAAR!'

She sounded so unlike a sněehoolark, that Miro started to laugh. Then the laugh became uncontrollable and he had to stop running to catch his breath.

Kazimira paused by his side. 'What's so funny?' she demanded.

But she didn't wait for an answer. She had spotted a man dressed as a toadstool. He wore white stockings and an enormous red hat, and he was handing out mushroom-shaped lollies.

'I want sweets!' shouted the princess, and she dragged Miro towards the man.

Miro was sure that they'd have to pay and neither of them had any money, but the mushroom man handed them a glossy lolly each.

'Daddy would never let me do this,' said Kazimira, licking the sticky sweet. She almost looked cute in her sněehoolark costume. 'He'd never let me be with all these strangers. He says that's how little princesses get kidnapped.'

Miro nodded. He thought he understood. He'd been kept indoors for a long time too – kept separate from the people he was supposed to rule.

Kazimira licked her lolly and smiled. 'Perhaps Daddy isn't right about *everything*.'

Miro, Konya and the princess wandered through the festival, observing the celebrations and joining in where they could. They marvelled at a troupe of jugglers. Konya's tail flicked from side to side as she watched the flying batons.

Then the children helped themselves to a plate of sweet fried balls. Miro didn't know what the treats were, but they were delicious. They were crunchy on the outside, soft and mushy within.

'There you are,' said a voice from behind. Miro turned to see Steward Lída. She was wearing a fluffy white dress and black stockings. On her head was a fleecy bonnet. She was dressed as a sheep.

'It is time to taste the waters with Mage Bohoosh. He's in the Guest Palace, waiting for you.'

Miro and Kazimira both groaned.

On the other side of the park, two different children had arrived. They didn't have any costumes. And a golden hare stood at their feet.

On their backs they carried a pack each, with provisions attached – water skins, extra clothes and blankets. They also carried a book.

Otakar had wrapped the yedleek book in fabric, and Imogen had tied it to her pack. They hadn't had a chance to read it yet; they were in too much of a rush.

'How are we going to find Miro?' asked Marie, eyes scanning the crowd. 'There are so many people, and they're all in fancy dress!'

The festivalgoers didn't expect there to be a hare in the park and several almost stepped on Mum, so Marie picked Mum up and tucked her into her hood.

'I don't know,' said Imogen. 'But we'd better start searching right away.'

At a little distance, Imogen spotted a pair of enormous birds. Fred and Frieda were tottering through the crowd, sniffing people's costumes and pecking the grass.

A woman with a food stall tossed two pastries towards the velecours. Fred and Frieda gobbled up the offerings. They, at least, seemed to be okay.

'Come on,' said Imogen to her sister. 'We have to warn Miro that something's going on, before Mage Bohoosh makes him disappear.'

CHAPTER 72

Mage Bohoosh was waiting for Miro in the Guest Palace. He was sitting between two large tropical plants, looking more alert than usual. He wasn't dressed up as anything. He wore his normal grey clothes. On the table at his side were three crystal glasses, filled with water.

Lída ushered Miro and Kazimira forwards. Konya followed at her own pace. No one dared to usher a sněehoolark.

It was warm in the Reception Room and Miro slipped off his falcon cape. Kazimira was still dressed as a sněehoolark, fake tail dragging behind.

'Ahh,' said Bohoosh, 'so good to see you!' He opened his hands in a welcoming gesture and his sleeve caught one of the glasses. The glass wobbled, but Lída managed to catch it.

'I want to go out and play,' complained Kazimira.

'Afterwards, my dear,' said Bohoosh. 'You must try the waters. It's tradition.'

Through the domed ceiling, Miro could see marsh lights, hundreds of them twinkling down the sides of the mountains. He wanted to rejoin the festival too, but he thought playing along with Mage Bohoosh might be the fastest way to get there.

Steward Lída handed the first glass to Miro. The water was salty, not very nice, but he didn't want to offend anyone so he swallowed.

'Well done,' said Bohoosh, raising his bushy eyebrows. 'A true Sokol always takes the waters.'

Miro handed the glass to Kazimira so she could do the same. 'What is it?' she asked.

'Special water,' said Lída and she gave the princess an encouraging smile. 'From one of the sacred mountain springs.'

Kazimira took a big gulp. 'Tastes like trout,' she announced.

Let's get this over with, thought Miro. He could hear the festival music, even through the thick palace walls, and it reminded him of what he was missing.

As he reached for the second glass, Bohoosh leaned forwards, eyes glinting. Miro drank and, this time, it was disgusting. The water tasted like old eggs. Miro's eyes watered, but he made himself swallow. He couldn't make himself say it was nice.

'Very good for the digestion,' said Lída.

Miro handed the glass to Kazimira. He thought the princess wouldn't want it, but she drank long and deep.

'Try the third drink,' said Bohoosh. 'You'll like this one.'

Miro sniffed the water and it had no scent. He sipped and found it was sweet. His stomach grumbled as the water went down. *Right, that's done*, he thought and he handed the glass to Kazimira.

The princess drank most of it and held out the last drops for Konya.

'Oh,' quavered Lída, 'I'm not sure that's a good idea.'

'Kitty's thirsty,' said Kazimira.

Konya sniffed at the glass. Then her pink tongue lapped up the last of the liquid.

'Good kitty,' said Kazimira, beaming.

Beneath her fleecy bonnet, Lída's face was stern. Kazimira sniggered and Miro laughed too. It was funny seeing Lída's face turn red – especially when she was dressed as a sheep.

But neither child laughed at what happened next.

The gurgling in Miro's stomach was getting stronger and, for a split second, he thought he'd be sick. *Uh-oh.* 'Can we go now?' he asked, a little weakly.

'It's working,' whispered Mage Bohoosh. 'Just like it worked for the others.' Both adults backed away and Miro didn't understand . . .

Then he felt a terrible prickling, spreading up his back. It was as if someone was driving pins into his skin. And still the water gurgled in his belly.

'I'm bubbling!' cried Kazimira, looking down at her stomach. 'What's going on?'

Something had been wrong with that third glass of water . . .

Konya was affected by it too. She backed away until her

tail hit the wall. Still trying to retreat, she reared on to her hind legs, front paws boxing an invisible enemy.

Miro managed to look back at the Grand Mage and Steward Lída. They were sheltering behind potted plants, as if they expected the children to explode.

'Bohoosh has betrayed us,' Miro said, his words slurring. The prickling sensation spread down his arms and up the back of his neck. 'They've poisoned us! We're dying!'

CHAPTER 73

But Miro didn't die. He stumbled, catching the edge of the table for support. All three glasses fell off and smashed. 'Konya,' he gasped.

The giant cat's body was stretching and shrinking as if she was made out of dumpling dough. In places, her fur was falling out.

'Kitty!' cried Kazimira, but she didn't look so good herself. Her eyes were big – far too big – and they were moving apart, migrating across her face. Her whole body was warping and a green rash spread up her neck. Shrieking, the princess clutched her throat.

Miro couldn't watch any longer. His own pain was too intense. It felt like his body was a sack of leeches. Yet, beneath the agony, Miro knew that the squirming things were not leeches. They were his muscles – extending and shifting, searching for a new place to attach. His ligaments and bones were rearranging themselves. And still, his skin prickled.

Miro started screaming now too. Because *there*, bristling

beneath his shirt, were feathers – hundreds of them, packed tight under linen.

Miro wanted to flee, but with a final excruciating twist, his body collapsed in on itself. His head shot down through his collar. His hands shot up his sleeves.

What was happening?

For a moment, Miro lay still, panting. Then he tried to stand and found that he couldn't. His limbs were bound tight by his shirt. It was like being inside a straitjacket.

He was trapped in his own clothing, with his face pressed against a seam.

The pain had ceased. His bones had stopped shifting. His skin no longer stung.

But he couldn't stay stuck like this, so he clawed – really clawed – and the fabric ripped apart. With a final scramble, he burst free and skidded across the flagstone floor.

Miro should have been embarrassed, lying there without any clothes, but his mind had stopped caring about such things.

He didn't move. Right in front of his eyes was a frog. It was standing on a pile of scrunched-up clothes and it looked furious. It was bright green and about the same size as a gherkin, with the same bobbly skin.

And Miro was struck by unlooked-for knowledge. This was Kazimira. She'd turned into a frog.

So the water wasn't poisonous . . .

Yet it wasn't normal spring water either.

At least Konya will still be herself, thought Miro. *Snĕehoolarks are already animals; you can't turn them into animals again.*

But in the corner, where Miro had last seen the giant cat, there was a naked woman. She was standing still, with her eyes flicking right and left.

'Look at the snĕehoolark,' groaned Bohoosh. 'What are we going to do with it?'

The woman's long hair covered her body, but it was clear that her limbs were tensed. She looked as if she was preparing to pounce. *Konya!* Miro cried in his head.

If the water had turned Kazimira into a frog and Konya into a human . . . what had Miro become? He looked at his feet and saw why it had been so easy to shred his shirt.

Instead of feet, he had talons.

Miro screamed and it came out as a screech.

Steward Lída was shouting, 'GET THEM OUT GET THEM OUT GET THEM OUT!'

Miro's thoughts flew faster than comets. Some of the thoughts were his own – *This can't be happening; I can't be a bird!*

Some of his thoughts seemed to belong to someone else – *Swoop, fly, get out, get free.*

When he tried to run, his legs didn't move. Instead, his arms, which were actually wings, extended above his head. His wingtips almost met in the middle and, with one powerful downward thrust, Miro's claws left the floor.

It was that easy. His body knew what to do.

With another thrust, Miro flew round the room, narrowly missing the potted plants.

Inside him, the bird voice was taking over. *Swoop, fly, get out, get free.*

Miro was no longer thinking about the festival. He wasn't thinking about his grandmothers either. All he knew was he couldn't stay here. He couldn't be boxed in this room.

He beat his wings, gathering as much power as he could. *Swoop, fly, get out, get free.* With one final stroke, he smashed upwards, through the centre of the domed roof.

Glass shattered and Miro blasted out of the Guest Palace.

Swoop, fly, get out, get free.

Bohoosh yelled from below, but Miro did not care. He could smell the night, feel the wind. He was a creature of air and light.

Swoop, fly, get out, get free.

No walls could contain him, no glass keep him in. He was a sharp-eyed nomad, a weapon with wings. He was nobody's prey. Miro soared over the palace and the lantern-lit common.

The mountains rose steep on either side.

Swoop, fly, get out, get free.

He was Miro and he was a Krishnov. He was an Sokol too. But most of all, yes, above all else, he was a mountain falcon.

CHAPTER 74

Miro flew between the mountains. He screeched and it echoed off rock. He beat his wings and soared higher. The moon rose to meet him, unfurling a carpet of light. Miro followed it away from Nedobyt.

This was it. This was freedom. This is what he'd been born to do.

His sight was better than it used to be. He could see very faraway things as if they'd been outlined with a sharp pencil. He saw a distant peak with a slanting top. It was Mount Kerrub, home of the skret.

He saw a vole darting between moon shadows. The falcon voice said, *hunt, catch, kill.* Miro's talons twitched in response.

No, said his old voice. *Fly on.*

He followed the steady rise of a mountain, where the wind teased the snow into glittering dunes, until the land dropped beneath him, giving way to a sheer cliff.

But Miro was not afraid. Quite the opposite.

He decided to fly higher.

His wings propelled him like a swimmer, with his shoulders

doing most of the work. He built up a rhythm, rising through the cold air, until, at the last moment, he pulled his wings close and flipped his belly so it faced the stars – before spinning round again.

He twirled for the joy of it. Because he could. He could go any way that he wished. Not only left or right, but up or down. He could pirouette, he could hover, he could dive.

The falcon voice in his head was growing louder. *Soar, fly, hunt, kill.*

But there was another voice, a quieter one, at risk of dying out. *I am here for a reason . . .*

Miro flew on.

The air above the mountains was dancing, and Miro's wings had to constantly adjust so he could ride the choppy waves. He didn't have to think about it. His body was built for gales.

Perhaps he would stay as a falcon forever, flying on the back of the wind, giving names to the mountains as he passed them, forgetting the names of his family and friends.

A group of dots climbed a white slope. With his falcon eyes, Miro could see they were sněehoolarks. One of them put back her head and yowled.

It reminded Miro of Konya . . .

Konya, who was no longer a giant cat.

It reminded him of Kazimira, who was no longer a little girl.

It reminded Miro of the moment when they had all transformed. Bohoosh had been saying something to Lída: *It's working, just like it worked for the others . . .*

And the thought struck Miro so suddenly that it almost made him drop from the sky. What 'others' had Bohoosh been talking about?

The air around Miro sparkled with flecks of ice and he knew that the thought was worth chasing.

Mage Bohoosh and Steward Lída have done this before.

What if Miro's family were not missing or dead – but trapped in animal form?

Miro didn't know how much time it would take for him to forget about his human self, to become stuck as a falcon with no hope of turning back, but he suspected he didn't have long. Perhaps it was already happening. Perhaps he was already too late!

Soar, fly, hunt, kill, wind under wings, eyes to the ground, seek scurrying, seek shadows, seek movement on snow.

He'd never find his family like this. He had to – he had to –

Soar, fly, hunt, kill . . .

CHAPTER 75

Imogen and Marie searched for Miro in every corner of the park. The night-time festival was in full swing, with music and feasting between the trees. The girls hunted behind stalls and under tables. They peered between dancers who spun in their butterfly cloaks.

But it was no use. Even if Miro was at the festival, they probably wouldn't recognise him. Not if he was wearing a costume, not if his face was masked.

'Maybe we're too late,' said Marie. 'Maybe Bohoosh made Miro disappear.' Mum-the-hare was still snug in Marie's hood, peeping over her shoulder.

'Miaow,' said a human voice.

Imogen almost jumped out of her skin. The sound had come from a low bush. She crouched down and peered into it.

There was a woman hiding among the leaves. From the looks of things, the woman was naked. Although most of her body was covered by her ankle-length hair.

Was this part of the festival? Taking your clothes off and hiding in shrubs?

'Miaow-roslav,' said the woman. She looked shocked by the sound of her own voice.

'A-are you okay?' Marie asked, squatting at Imogen's side. 'Have you seen our friend, Miro, somewhere?'

The woman raised her amber eyes to the sky.

She doesn't understand what we're saying, thought Imogen. But something was very familiar about the woman's face. She had strong features and intense eyes.

The woman held one hand close to her chest. She opened her fingers, revealing a very small, very green and very poisonous-looking frog.

Imogen didn't know what to say. This was all pretty strange.

'It's miiiaaaoow, miaow, me,' said the woman, as if she was struggling to find the right words. 'Miaow – it's miaow – it's Konya!'

Imogen almost rocked backwards with surprise.

'Konya?' cried Marie.

'Konya,' said the woman, more confident this time.

'B-but, what happened to you?' gasped Imogen.

The woman scrunched up her face. 'Magic water,' she growled.

Imogen couldn't take all this in. Had Konya been changed like their mother? Did she drink from the pool by the library too?

Marie worked it out a bit quicker. 'Mage Bohoosh did this, didn't he?'

Konya glanced at the people in costumes as they walked past her hiding place. 'Ran . . . we ran from him.'

So *this* is what Bohoosh had been planning.

Konya held the frog out towards the girls. Mum clambered on to Marie's shoulder. She had one ear up and one ear flopped down. It was an investigative pose.

'Purr-incess,' said Konya.

The frog opened its mouth and out came a squeak.

Imogen stared. 'What? You don't mean . . . *That's* Princess Kazimira?'

Konya was smiling and Imogen could see that her incisors, while human, were very sharp.

Kazimira squeaked again. *Peep-peep, peep-peep, peeeep!* It was pathetic really. A minuscule sound.

Imogen remembered how Kazimira had behaved when she was human, and she couldn't help feeling that she liked the princess better as a frog.

'What about Miro?' asked Marie. 'Where is he?'

Konya looked up once more. 'Too late,' she whispered. 'He is gone.'

Imogen hung her head. They should have left the library sooner. They should have been faster warning their friend . . . After everything he'd done for them.

Konya looked sad too. She shivered beneath the bush.

'You must be cold without your fur,' said Marie.

'Miaow,' Konya replied.

'Wait,' cried Imogen. 'I've got an idea!' She removed her

351

pack and rummaged about until she found Mum's old clothes – the ones she'd been wearing before she turned into a hare. 'Here. You can wear these.'

The girls waited in silence as Konya got dressed, shielding her as best as they could. The trousers were a little bit short, but the rest of Mum's clothes fitted well.

'What did Miro turn into?' asked Imogen.

'Bird,' Konya replied. 'Flew out through the Guest Palace roof.' She seemed to be finding her voice and she told the girls what had happened.

'We'll never find Miro in that shape,' said Marie, eyes scanning the starlit sky. 'He could be miles away. He could be anywhere.'

CHAPTER 76

Miro wasn't sure what made him go back. It was difficult, turning his rudder-like tail, tilting his wind-sharpened wings, forcing his falcon-self to do as his boy-self willed.

And yet – and yet – Miro's beak cut an arc through the air, until he faced the way he had come. He couldn't keep flying forever. He had to return to Nedobyt.

I travelled across the marshes for a reason. I chose to walk a path that no others have walked.

I did not choose the sinking bogs. I did not choose the hunger or the fear.

And yet, I chose to go on. I survived clouds of midges, lived off suckers and befriended a troll.

'But you are the king of the mountains,' howled the wind – or, at least, Miro thought that it did.

No, I am not, called his inner voice. He was not king of anything, nor did he wish to be. He did not have to prove things to others.

Falcon eyes scanning the horizon, Miro searched for

Nedobyt. The mountains were a toothy crust of ice and black rock. The stars jittered on the edge of their seats.

Miro wanted to be part of this world. He wanted to be *in* it. Not on top.

He thought of his experience from the marshes – how he'd been connected to the reeds and the woolgrass, to the wading birds, to the water and the fish.

He wasn't alone. He never would be.

He flew faster, wings slicing through the night.

Below, he could see light radiating from a crack between the mountains. It was an unnatural, human-made light . . . The lanterns of the festival.

And Miro was filled with indescribable joy. He had felt it on the marshes and he felt it again – the sheer ecstasy of having a small place in something so big and so wondrous as the world.

He hovered above Nedobyt, and, even though the city was a mile below, he could see every person as if they were across the street. His vision was sharpened to pinpoints.

I came here for a reason, said Miro's inner voice. He was no longer sure if it was Miro the boy or the falcon. *I came to find my family*.

And with that, he started to dive.

Miro plummeted towards Nedobyt, towards the birch trees and revellers and the glowing palaces. The lantern-lit mountains on either side of the city seemed dangerously close, but Miro did not pull back.

The earth rose to meet him, the sky tore apart. Miro's

wings were folded close to his body. He was an air cleaver, a star splitter.

And, despite the efforts of the wind, which pulled at his feathers, despite his own fear and doubts, Miro clung on to one thought as he dropped.

Not alone.

A funny feeling bubbled in his belly.

He thought of how the marshes had sustained him. How there'd seemed fewer dividers between water and land, between fur and moss and skin.

A muscle in Miro's shoulder twitched, and he knew he had to get to the ground. His body was a few heartbeats away from rearranging itself.

There are so many connections between us, said Miro's inner voice.

That did it. A clump of his feathers fell out, shedding easily in the wind.

All the times that Miro had been set apart from other people – been told he was superior, or that he wasn't enough – it was nonsense. He could see that now.

The dividers between things were, at best, flexible; at worst they were an illusion made by people with something to gain. People like Bohoosh and Patoleezal, like his uncle and King Ctibor.

Miro flew like a meteor, feathers trailing in his wake. He could feel his bones and muscles releasing, reaching and binding anew.

He didn't want to crash into the palaces. He searched, desperate, for a safe place to land. The birch trees were whizzing closer and Miro wanted to scream with the pain, but he couldn't; he was still mostly falcon.

There are so many connections . . .

He fought to keep hold of that image – of the marshes, of the mingling of life.

Meanwhile, Miro's dive was becoming a crash landing. He turned into the descent, hoping his tail would stabilise him, trying to extend his wings.

But there was more finger than feather, more arm than wing. *Uh-oh*, he was changing too fast.

Stars smudged.

Branches reached.

Human faces looked up,

small but getting bigger,

pointing and fleeing,

as a falcon-rocket hurtled their way.

Miro was on the edge of consciousness. The pain of the transformation made lights explode behind his eyes – *ping, ping* – off they went.

He was soluble,

he was fluid,

he was falling.

Branches buffeted his shoulders – sides – feet.

Miro landed on the earth with a thump that knocked the air from his lungs. He was still shifting, part-boy, part-feathered-thing. Blinking, he found that his vision was blurry – no, not blurry, just human.

Miro gasped and his chest heaved. Crawling, his knees scuffed grass. He was stiff and battered, as if he'd fallen from the stars.

There were people standing nearby. 'It's a child,' said one of them.

'It was a bird a second ago!'

Miro looked down and saw hands, human hands. His feathers had burst from him and were scattered on the ground. And his skin – his real skin – had returned.

'It's a slipskin!' cried another voice.

Miro had landed at the edge of the common, near the palaces. His transformation was complete . . . and it had been witnessed by half of the city. Even better, he wasn't wearing any clothes.

How humiliating, thought the boy part of his brain.

Who cares, thought the falcon. *Soar, fly, hunt, kill –*

Miro looked up at the curious faces. They were all dressed as animals, wearing feathers and fur, but it was clear that they were human underneath. Costumes. It was still the festival.

'Has anyone got a spare cloak?' asked Miro. 'There's someone that I need to find.'

CHAPTER 77

I mogen saw a star fall from the sky – no, not a star, a large bird – no, not a bird, but a child in bird's clothing who was shedding his feathers as he fell.

People were screaming in that corner of the park and running, to avoid being crushed. Musicians stopped playing their instruments. Many faces turned up.

The falling child twisted and turned in mid-air, arms flailing as if trying to flap wings. It was hard to see by the light of the lanterns, but Imogen caught sight of his face and her insides seemed to go liquid. 'Is that Miro?' she gasped.

'It is!' cried Marie, who was at Imogen's side.

'He's going to die!' Konya yelled.

But the falling boy was slowed by tree branches and Imogen prayed it was enough. She started running towards him as he hit the ground.

Marie and Mum-the-hare ran too. Konya-the-woman followed, carrying Kazimira-the-frog in one hand.

Mum was the fastest, springing out of Marie's hood. She

nipped between people's ankles like an Olympic skier whizzing between flags.

A crowd had formed around the spot where Miro had landed and Imogen had some difficulty squeezing through. She ducked between the furry chests and feathered elbows.

'Excuse me – can I just – can I . . .' She squidged her way past a woman dressed as an elephant, batting her fabric trunk aside.

And there was Miro. He was panting, on all fours. Someone had thrown a cloak on his back. Mum-the-hare was circling him, not quite sure what to make of it all.

'Miro!' cried Imogen. 'Are you okay?' She scrambled to his side. People were keeping their distance, as if they thought he might be dangerous.

Miro didn't reply and Imogen was afraid that he was seriously hurt. Perhaps he'd broken some bones. He crouched under the cloak, breathing hard.

Miro turned his face slowly. 'Imogen?'

It *was* Miro, that much was clear. But he looked different – thinner and older – more like Miro's older brother than the boy that Imogen knew.

'W-w-what are you doing here?' he mumbled. 'Didn't you – I thought you'd gone home?'

'Miro!' squeaked Marie as she burst out of the crowd. 'We went home and then we had to come back.'

A smile snuck across Miro's face. He looked weary and

there were scratches on his cheeks, probably from the trees that had broken his fall. 'I don't understand,' he said. 'But I'm glad. I'm glad to see you.'

You might not say that if you knew why we were here, Imogen thought.

'We're happy to see you too,' said Marie.

'We heard about the duel with Surovetz,' added Imogen. 'It sounds like you were very brave. And you helped distract the krootymoosh – it gave us time to get out of the mines. We didn't even get the chance to say thank you!'

Imogen half expected Miro to puff himself up and say, *Yes, I was rather brave.* But Miro looked at her with a faraway expression, as if he hadn't even heard what she said.

'The duel?' he whispered. 'That was a long time ago.'

Imogen wondered what he meant. It had been about half a year. It wasn't *that* long . . . not really. She hadn't even started Year Eight.

Miro wrapped his cloak tighter round his shoulders before getting to his feet. He groaned as his back straightened and, when he was upright, he wobbled. The girls grabbed his arms to steady him.

'Thanks,' said Miro, 'I just need a moment.'

'He's a slipskin!' cried one of the onlookers.

Miro's eyes flicked in their direction, but he didn't respond.

'Were you . . . a bird?' asked Imogen.

Miro looked at her with his far-apart eyes. 'A mountain falcon, since you ask.'

360

'Wow,' said Marie. 'How did you change? You don't even have the slipskin book!'

Miro shivered in the cloak. 'I don't know. It all happened so quickly . . .'

The golden hare was hopping near the children, scrabbling at Miro's feet. Marie picked her up under her front paws, so her long back legs dangled down. 'This is our mum,' said Marie. 'She's pleased to meet you.'

The hare stared at Miro with her protruding eyes. Then she scrabbled in Marie's grip until one paw was extended towards the boy.

Miro took the paw and kissed it. Imogen suppressed a laugh. She was pretty sure Mum had intended for Miro to shake her paw, but there you go. Things were different in this world.

'It's an honour to meet you,' said Miro. He glanced at Imogen and Marie. 'You didn't tell me your mother was a hare?'

'She isn't normally,' said Imogen.

'Did she get tricked by Mage Bohoosh too?'

'No,' muttered Imogen. 'Although he is the reason we're here. He said he was planning to make you disappear. We came to warn you, but it looks like we were too late . . . Bohoosh must have thought you'd be stuck as a bird.'

Konya-the-woman stepped forwards. 'Miaow-roslav,' she said. 'It is I.'

Miro blanched. 'Konya? How did you escape Bohoosh?'

Konya gave a luxurious shrug. 'I ran. Brought this little purr-incess with me.' She held out a long-nailed hand, with the toxic green frog in the centre.

Kazimira croaked and, for a moment, Imogen was afraid that Konya would eat the frog. But Konya pushed her hair back, allowing Kazimira to hop on to her shoulder. 'Good froggy,' purred Konya.

'Bohoosh is going to pay for this,' spat Miro.

He started limping towards a glass-topped building that bordered this corner of the park. The crowd parted to let him through.

'I must speak with Mage Bohoosh, in the Guest Palace,' Miro called over his shoulder. 'I think he's turned people into animals before. I think that's what he did to my family.'

CHAPTER 78

M iro strode towards the Guest Palace, with Imogen and Marie in tow. Mum bounded beside them. Konya brought up the rear, with Kazimira-the-frog balanced on her shoulder.

Imogen thought they'd be told to wait outside, but the guards clearly recognised Miro. 'They're with me,' he said and the guards stood aside.

The ragtag band of children and animals set off down an arched corridor. At the end of the passage, Miro opened the door into a circular room. It reminded Imogen of a massive conservatory: warm and full of thick-leaved plants.

There seemed to be a party going on. The guests were dressed as animals, just like the festivalgoers outside. But they'd taken off most of their costumes – uncomfortable clawed feet and itchy furred cloaks. They were almost human once more.

Only one person wore no fancy dress. Imogen recognised his long curly shoes. It was the man who'd come to the library – Mage Bohoosh.

He lounged on a bench, at the centre of the room, with a great many pillows about him. People were crowded close, passing cheese and pouring wine.

'And I said,' cried Bohoosh, 'it looks like a llama to me!' Everyone around him laughed.

'Bohoosh,' shouted Miro and the room fell quiet.

The Grand Mage lifted his head. His mouth opened . . . and closed.

Someone slurped wine in the silence that followed. Then a woman, dressed as a sheep, broke the hush. 'Miroslav!' she cried. 'You're . . . *you*!'

Miro advanced on the mage. 'What have you done to my family?' he demanded.

Bohoosh shrank into the bench, as if hoping the cushions would consume him. 'I am but a servant of the crown.'

The woman in sheep's clothing pointed at Mum. 'No hares are allowed in the palace!'

But Miro would not be put off. 'You turned my grandmothers into animals, didn't you?'

'What piffle,' said Bohoosh. 'What absolute tosh! You know I'm not much of a mage.'

'Lies,' snarled Miro. 'You're a good mage when it suits you.'

Konya-the-woman paced behind Miro. If she'd still got a tail, it would have been flicking.

Marie scooped up Mum and held her out with both hands. 'This is our mother,' she said to Mage Bohoosh. 'Do you know the spell to make her human again?'

'Those things carry disease,' cried a partygoer with a mouth full of Stilton.

'And this froggy,' said Konya, pointing at the green creature that clung to her neck. 'Turn her back into a princess.'

'Can you do it?' said Imogen, eyes fixed on Bohoosh.

'Of course not!' he snapped. 'I'm no slipskin. I am just a humble mage, doing my best to keep this kingdom running. Isn't that right, Steward Lída?'

The sheep-woman gave a prim nod.

Imogen scowled at them both. She knew that wasn't true. Bohoosh had turned Miro into a falcon. He wanted the slipskin book destroyed. There was nothing humble about him.

Marie placed her mother on the ground and the hare scratched her ear with her back paw.

'It's Miroslav you should be asking,' said Bohoosh. 'How he transformed into a boy is beyond me.' Then he gestured at Konya. 'Besides, I don't see any problem. Your sněehoolark is less dangerous like that.'

Konya lunged at the mage.

Bohoosh scrambled to his feet, keeping the bench between him and the furious woman.

'Dangerous?' screamed Konya. 'I'll show him dangerous. I'll claw him to death! I'll eat his face!'

Imogen rushed to pick up Kazimira, who had fallen from Konya's neck. There were a lot of big feet on that floor. And if there's one thing worse than being a frog, it's being a flat frog.

'I'll make him into pâté!' shouted Konya. 'Come on, old man, don't you want to play?' It took several people to restrain her.

'Once an animal, always an animal,' said Lída.

'Always an animal?' said Miro. 'Is that what you hoped would happen to me – that I'd be trapped as a falcon, unable to turn back?'

Mage Bohoosh took a big glug of wine, not even bothering to respond.

'Fetch the guards,' cried Lída. 'Miroslav and his friends are no longer welcome. It's time for you children to leave.'

CHAPTER 79

B ut any attempt to call the guards was drowned out by a loud trumpeting. It seemed to be coming from the corridor leading to the big plant-filled room.

The partygoers were ruffled, not sure if they should be afraid. Bohoosh stayed behind his bench.

Imogen placed Kazimira on her shoulder. Mum stayed close to Marie. Whatever was coming, it was making a lot of noise.

Finally, the door flung open and a skret stood on the other side. The fanfare blasted behind him, and it was all that Imogen could hear. The sound seemed to reverberate about the room, circling round and round. Mum clamped her paws over her ears.

The skret was dressed in human clothing. The ends of his shoes had been sawn off to make way for his claws. A feathered cap was set on his bald head.

He was, Imogen realised, in fancy dress as a human. And, as the skret stepped into the lamplight, Imogen felt a surge of recognition.

She recognised the skret's yellow eyes.

She recognised the way that he stood.

Above all, she recognised his teeth.

Unlike the other skret, who had small triangular gnashers, this one had long bottom teeth that stuck out from his mouth like tusks.

'Zuby?' asked Imogen. But the trumpeting was too loud.

More skret entered the room. They were also wearing human costumes and blowing into shiny brass instruments, like trumpets with extra pipes. They kept making their bright brash sound, until Zuby raised his hand.

'I present, the Královna's Chief Moth Keeper,' called one of the musicians, gesturing at Zuby. Imogen had met the Král of Klenot Mountain. He was the king of that place. She guessed that Královna was something similar; perhaps a queen of the local skret.

Imogen still remembered Zuby's parting words from the last time they'd met. *I have a little quest of my own . . .* Was this the quest he'd been planning? Joining the skret of the Nameless Mountains?

If so, it must have gone well for him to be in charge of the moths. Imogen knew it was an important job – one of the most trusted positions among skret.

Zuby bowed to Mage Bohoosh. 'My Lord,' he said in his crackle-hiss voice. 'I come bearing ill news.'

Bohoosh did not bow back. 'Ill news? I'm not sure I want to receive it.' The partygoers murmured their agreement.

Imogen and Marie, Miro and Konya, all stood very still.

'I received a moth a few hours ago,' said Zuby. 'It had travelled a very long way, carrying an important message for the Královna of the Nameless Mountains.'

There was stirring among the partygoers. Bohoosh looked nervous too.

'The moth was sent by the Maudree Král, who rules a realm near Yaroslav. He wanted to warn the Královna of a great danger heading her way.'

'What danger?' cried Lída, removing her sheepy bonnet.

'A great swarm of humans is marching towards us – a terrible army.'

Bohoosh's wine-stained lips quivered. 'Who are they?' he asked. 'What do they want?'

'I sent moths to investigate,' said Zuby. 'They say the army is on the Long Road, and they're carrying mixed banners . . . but the ones out in front show a green crown.'

Imogen had seen that mark before. 'Anneshka!' she cried. 'That's her logo!'

Now Zuby looked her way. His round eyes seemed to grow even rounder. They flicked between Imogen, Miro and Marie. 'Little humans?' he gasped. 'You are here?'

'Why would anyone march on Nedobyt?' cried one of the party guests. 'We are not at war!'

Zuby shrugged his shoulders. 'Do humans ever need a reason to attack?'

Imogen glanced at her sister, who had gone very pale.

Surely, thought Imogen, *Anneshka hadn't come all this way – hundreds of miles, assembling an army – just to find Marie?*

'We estimate that there are ten thousand soldiers,' said Zuby. 'At this rate, they'll reach the ravine before dawn.'

'That is not good,' whispered Konya.

'We are doomed,' cried Mage Bohoosh. 'We'll never stand against such numbers. There are too many, too many by far!'

Imogen felt fear stir in her stomach, like a small animal waking up. She'd never seen an army, never been in a battle, and she didn't want to do either.

'The Královna has left the festival,' said Zuby. 'She's retreating to her mountain-top cave. But she asked me to share this message, and to make a suggestion to *you*, Grand Mage. Now might be a good time to close the ravine.'

A deathly hush fell on the room.

'Yes,' cried Imogen, breaking the silence, 'that's a good idea! Is that how Nedobyt defeated Radko the Conqueror? Did they shut the ravine?'

Bohoosh gave a smile that wasn't a smile, but more of a grimace. 'Miroslav's grandmothers were the last ones who knew how to do it. When they vanished, the secret vanished too. I tried to get them to tell me before they . . . disappeared. But they were stubborn old biddies. Never knew what was best.'

There was a long guilty pause, where all eyes seemed to be fixed on the mage. And then, as if speaking to himself, he muttered, 'The party is over, Bohoosh.'

CHAPTER 80

The Grand Mage shook his head. 'It is lost,' he whispered. 'Nedobyt is lost.' He removed a glass bottle from his robe and held it to the light.

'Bohoosh,' said Miro. There was a warning in his voice. 'What did you do to my grandmothers?'

The partygoers observed the mage and the boy. Some of them looked excited, as if watching a gossipy TV show. Others looked terrified. A few filled their pockets with great handfuls of cheese and started to edge out of the room.

Zuby and the skret musicians looked confused. This clearly wasn't the response they'd expected.

'Ladies and gentlemen,' said Bohoosh, lifting the glass bottle to his lips. 'I have very much enjoyed the festivities . . . the company, the wine and the cheese. But now I am afraid I must be leaving.' He drank the bottle in one swig. 'For – as I'm sure you have already realised – you are all going to die.'

And, with that, Bohoosh started to change. The party guests fled the room, screaming. Many of the skret left too.

Imogen wondered if they should do the same. Mum-the-hare certainly seemed to think so. She was nipping at Imogen's and Marie's ankles, trying to herd them out of the door.

But Miro leaped at Bohoosh, shouting, 'Tell me what you did to my family!' Imogen couldn't leave him like this. She rushed to Miro's side, with Marie and Konya hot on her heels. Together, they tried to restrain the mage.

It was no good. Bohoosh was thrashing and bucking, his body expanding under Imogen's grip. Dark fur sprouted from his neck. His curly shoes tore open as his feet morphed into hooves.

'What did you do to my family?' cried Miro.

Bohoosh answered in a deep bellow that made the glass ceiling vibrate. It wasn't a reply, so much as a moo. Imogen and the others backed off. There was no point trying to restrain *that*.

For Bohoosh had changed into some kind of bull.

Seeing this, the remaining skret musicians took the opportunity to leave. Only Zuby remained, staring in horror at what the Grand Mage had become.

Bohoosh lowered his head and charged across the room, through the arched entrance and down the stone corridor. Judging by the distant screams, Bohoosh kept on charging – out of the palace and across the festival-filled park.

'Mage Bohoosh!' cried a voice. 'Don't leave me!' Imogen turned to see Konya twisting Lída's arms behind her back.

The woman was wriggling as Konya held her pinned to the floor. 'Let me go, you filthy beast!'

Miro crouched next to her. 'Come on now, Lída,' he said. 'I've had enough of these lies. Won't you tell me what happened to my grandmothers?'

'Mice,' screamed Steward Lída. 'They're MICE!'

CHAPTER 81

M iro led his friends through the Guest Palace. Imogen kept asking where they were going, but Miro only walked faster.

He led them across a cold courtyard, where the stars blinked overhead. He led them down stone steps and through big lamp-lit rooms.

Imogen, Marie, Mum and Konya trotted after him, with Imogen still carrying Kazimira-the-frog.

She tried not to think of Zuby's message – of Anneshka's soldiers coming with the morning light. But every time she looked up through one of the glass domes, the sky looked a little less black.

Where was Zuby anyway? Had he stayed behind? Imogen glanced over her shoulder . . .

There was so much going on, so many questions and dangers, it was impossible to keep track of it all: mice and bulls and mountain falcons, Anneshka's approaching army, Mark's approaching end.

Finally, Miro led them into a room with a big bed and

swirly furniture. 'This is where Kazimira has been sleeping,' he said.

The frog leaped from Imogen's shoulder on to the enormous bed. Mum-the-hare hopped up beside her. Konya kept watch by the door.

Imogen and Marie both shed their packs, glad to be free of them.

Meanwhile, Miro turned the room upside down. He opened a chest and pulled out quilted blankets. He rifled through drawers of clothes – dresses with frills and ribbons went flying.

Imogen and Marie exchanged glances. What was going on with their friend? Hadn't he understood Zuby's message? There was an army marching their way!

Finally, Miro wriggled under the bed until only his feet stuck out. 'Ah-ha!' he cried.

'What is it?' asked Imogen, crouching nearby.

Miro wormed out from under the bed and in his hand was a cage, no bigger than a jewellery box. There was a stump of hard cheese at one end and a metal contraption at the other.

'Mouse trap,' said Miro, placing the cage on the floor. 'The maid said she was going to set one in here.' And, sure enough, there were two mice in the cage. It wasn't the kind of trap that killed things and the mice seemed to be unharmed.

'Oh look, they're cute ones,' said Marie, squatting next to Miro. Imogen was inclined to agree. The mice were brown, with soft white bellies and eyes that gleamed like plastic beads.

Konya walked over – a little too fast.

'No,' shouted Miro and he shielded the mice with his arms. 'They're not for eating. Stay back.'

Konya went very still, eyes locked on the cage. 'I was only going to nibble their tails.'

'Maybe you should wait outside,' said Miro.

'I'll stay,' said Konya. 'You might need my purr-tection.' She slunk back to the door.

'Miro,' said Imogen, trying to go carefully. 'I know that woman said your grandmas are mice, but what makes you think they are *these* mice?'

It was a sensible question, she thought. In a building as big and old (and full of cheese) as this palace, there must be hundreds of rodents.

'They came to see me and Kazimira,' said Miro. 'As if they had something to say . . .'

He waited until Konya was settled, before holding the trap level with his face. 'Hello,' he whispered. 'Are you my grandmothers? Was Sofia Sokol your child?'

One of the mice crept forwards. It had a pink nose and one cloudy eye. With its front paws wrapped around the bars of the cage, it looked at Miro and – there was no mistaking it – the mouse gave a nod.

Imogen's jaw dropped.

'Did you see that?' cried Marie.

Miro started gasping as if he'd been kicked in the stomach. His eyes widened and his face went very pale. 'Miro?' asked Marie. He put down the cage and scrabbled across the floor.

'I thought – they didn't – love me,' wheezed Miro. 'I thought—'

Imogen watched with horror. What was happening to her friend?

'It's the worry creatures,' whispered Marie.

Imogen stared. Miro had worry creatures too? She could hardly believe it . . . Was this how it looked when they attacked?

She pushed the questions aside. Her friend needed help.

Imogen shuffled towards him. 'Miro,' she said. 'Try to breathe in through your nose.' She placed a hand on his back, tentative at first, and then firmer, so he knew she was there.

Miro sucked in the air. 'That's it,' said Imogen. 'And now breathe out through your mouth.' Miro did as she said. 'Slowly,' said Imogen, 'do it slowly.'

The mice squeaked, while Imogen rubbed Miro's back. Eventually, the colour returned to his face and his breathing grew calmer again. 'Well done,' said Imogen. 'You did really well.'

Miro crawled towards the mouse trap, arms still trembling. He picked it up once more, so the mice were level with his eyes. 'Olga . . .' he whispered. 'Granny Nela?'

The mice squeaked their replies. 'I thought – when you didn't reply to my letters – I thought I'd done something wrong,' said Miro. 'I thought you'd forgotten about me.' Tears rolled down his face, big blubby tears that fell each time he blinked.

The mice's squeaking became insistent. *It's not true, it's not true!* their cries seemed to say.

'They haven't forgotten about you,' said Marie.

Imogen chewed the inside of her cheek. Miro deserved a nice family. He deserved it more than anyone she knew. She just hoped they'd be able to turn the mice back into people.

'Can you change them, Miro?' asked Marie. 'Like how you changed yourself?'

'I don't think so,' he replied. 'I hardly know what happened. One minute I was flying . . . the next, I just fell.'

'It looked amazing,' said Marie, with genuine feeling.

Imogen nodded her agreement.

Miro turned his attention back to the caged mice. 'Bohoosh did this to you, didn't he?' he muttered, and he pulled at the little trap door until it wrenched free. 'He turned you into mice so he could have fun and throw parties in the palace.'

The mice scampered out of their prison and up Miro's arm, still squeaking. They ran around his neck. 'That tickles!' cried Miro, but he stayed very still. It would be too easy to squash the little creatures.

'There's a spell to turn people back into humans,' said Marie, glancing anxiously at Mum. 'It's in a book. The librarian is searching for it . . . Bohoosh wanted it destroyed.'

'And now we know why,' added Imogen. 'He didn't want

379

you or your grandmas to be changed back and stop him from being in charge.'

Miro held out his arm so the mice could run down it. 'What librarian?' he asked. 'What book?'

'The book about slipskin magic,' said Marie. 'The spell we need is inside . . . But we don't know how long it'll take Otakar to find it.'

There was a knock on the bedchamber door. 'Who is it?' called Imogen.

Konya let out a hiss.

The door eased open and Zuby stuck his head through the gap. He surveyed the scene – the frog and the hare on the bed, the children kneeling with two mice, the rather fierce-looking woman who guarded the door.

'Is there space in here for one more?' asked the skret.

CHAPTER 82

There was much talking between Zuby and the children. They had a lot to catch up on and, as they talked, their stories overlapped.

'And then Mark got taken to hospital.'

'And the island turned out to be a troll!'

'And the Královna needed a moth keeper, so she asked me if I'd like to stay.'

After several minutes of excited interruptions, they all started to calm down. When Imogen heard how Miro had survived on the marshes, she was very impressed.

Zuby told the children about his 'quest'. He'd taken the Long Road to Nedobyt, before heading to Mount Kerrub, home of the local skret. Imogen was glad Zuby was happy.

Then she and Marie explained what had happened to Mark – how the yedleek were getting ready to hatch – how they'd kill Mark when they did.

Miro's face dropped when he heard this. 'But . . . I like Mark,' he whispered.

The girls told their friends about Anneshka appearing in their world and making threats.

'She thinks you will lead her to greatness?' asked Zuby, scratching his bald head.

'Even if I did know which kingdom was the greatest, I'd never tell *her*,' said Marie.

'Perhaps you don't have to,' said Zuby. 'Perhaps that's why she's followed you. After all, you have led her to Nedobyt. It doesn't get much greater than this.'

Imogen's stomach twisted at the thought. Could Nedobyt really be the greatest kingdom? Had Marie accidentally completed the prophecy?

'We don't always know that it's happening,' said Zuby, 'when we're fulfilling our fate.'

'No,' cried Marie, voice wobbling. 'No, that can't be right!'

Imogen wanted to say, *Of course not, Zuby is talking rubbish.* But the more she thought about it, the more she was afraid he was correct. 'Nedobyt does seem to have a lot of magic,' she said, not daring to look Marie in the eye.

'The mountains are spectacular,' said Zuby.

'And the snĕehoolarks,' added Konya.

Miro glowed. 'My mother was from Nedobyt.'

'No, no, no!' cried Marie, face flushing. 'I should never have come here!'

'It's not your fault,' said Zuby, as he laid a palm on Marie's back. 'The stars, they shape our fates. We can only consider the options we have left. That's what matters, little human.'

Kazimira and Mum were still sitting on the bed, heads flicking left and right. They might not be able to speak, but they were certainly listening.

'We need to make a plan,' said Miro, pacing. 'Anneshka will be here soon. My grandmas know how to protect Nedobyt and I'm sure they would tell us, if they weren't mice. Do you think we should help this librarian search for the slipskin book?'

'I don't know,' said Imogen. She felt a little overwhelmed by the scale and number of problems. She glanced up at the glass ceiling. It was still dark outside, but there was a blueness creeping in at the edges.

'You should retreat,' rasped Zuby. 'Go deeper into the mountains, to the skret caves in Mount Kerrub.'

'And surrender Nedobyt to Anneshka?' said Miro.

'I don't see what choice you have.'

'No,' cried Konya, from her post by the door. 'We must assemble our own soldiers. We must fight!'

While the debate continued, Marie untied the yedleek book from Imogen's pack. She sat on the end of the bed and opened the first page on her lap.

'Speak to the Královna,' said Zuby. 'I'm sure she'd let you shelter in her caves. She is a good and just ruler. You only have to ask.'

'I'm not in charge of this city,' said Miro. 'I wasn't even born here!'

The mice squeaked as if to disagree. And, all the while, the sky was lightening.

'Hey,' said Marie. 'I think I've found the cure for Mark.'

Everyone looked her way – three humans, one skret, two mice, a golden hare and a small green frog.

Imogen rushed to Marie's side. 'Show me.'

Marie pointed to a word on the page. 'What is lichen?' she asked.

Imogen remembered a terrible joke that Mark had told long ago. 'I'm liking the lichen,' he'd said, touching some grey-green strands that were growing on a tree. 'Lichen the lichen . . . get it?'

Imogen had not laughed, so Mark had switched into serious mode. He'd explained that lichen was part plant, part mushroom – two things living as one.

'Some lichen can survive in space,' Mark had said. 'Not bad for a small stringy thing.'

Ever since, when Imogen had seen lichen, she'd thought about it floating through the cosmos, on its way to visit the stars.

'That is lichen,' said Imogen, pointing to an illustration in the book. The drawing showed a yellow blob with wiggly edges, shaped a bit like a shell. The title said: *Maiden's Kiss Lichen.*

The only thing to wake a sleeping prince, thought Imogen.

She and Miro crowded round, and Marie read the words out loud: 'To flush out the eggs of a yedleek, apothecaries must make an infusion of water and Maiden's Kiss lichen. The victim must drink this concoction.'

Imogen looked up from the book, heart thudding. 'Lichen,' she whispered. 'That's the cure?'

'Maiden's Kiss is very rare,' said Marie, continuing to read. 'It can only be found in the clear air near a Sertze Bahnoh, growing in the warmth of the stone.'

'What is a Sertze Bahnoh?' said Miro.

A smile flitted over Zuby's face. 'The one I've heard of is the world's largest sertze.' The skret put one hand to his chest, as if he was about to sing a national anthem. But, much to Imogen's relief, the skret did not break into song. 'I have never had the honour of seeing it,' said Zuby. 'It's a very powerful stone.'

'Zuby, where is it?' cried Marie.

'Why, it's on the marshes,' he replied. 'Don't you humans know anything?'

CHAPTER 83

That same night, on the other side of the mountain ravine, Anneshka and her army set up camp. It was a short march from here to Nedobyt, and they needed to rest before the fighting began.

Kegs of beer had been opened. Cauldrons had been hoisted above fires and broth had been consumed.

The soldiers were superstitious so they camped as far from the marsh as they could, wedged between its boundary and the base of the mountains. They said the bog swallowed all who set foot on it – said it was guarded by a man-eating troll.

Some of the warriors were already sleeping in their low-lying tents. Others stayed up, talking, drinking and playing dice. They preferred not to sleep this close to Mokzhadee. Who knew what might wander out . . .

The army chiefs slept in pavilions, with Anneshka's in the middle. Hers was the most luxurious shelter, with furs carpeting the floor. She even had a feather-stuffed bed.

Anneshka peered out at the camp and the marshes. *When I am queen of these parts, I'll have the swamp drained*, she thought. *It's such a disgusting place.*

Then she kicked off her silk slippers and climbed into bed. It was very late, almost morning, and she wanted to get a few hours of sleep. The clock of stars lay next to her pillow.

Anneshka allowed her mind to wander to Nedobyt; the mountain city rich in magic.

If that *really was* the greatest kingdom, if Anneshka had successfully tracked Marie, then her prophecy was almost complete. After everything she'd been through . . . she had finally found her place.

Just as Anneshka was dozing off, the clock began to chime. She rolled over so she could see it, and the little hatch sprang open.

'What more could you have to say?' asked Anneshka. But she watched as a wooden man wheeled out. He looked ordinary enough – a long face, messy hair, curly shoes.

Yet, when the figure bent over, horns hinged from his neck. By the time the man had finished rearranging himself, he looked a lot like a bull.

The mini bull dipped its head and charged, clattering back into the clock.

Anneshka wriggled deeper under her covers, wondering what it might mean. Was it a promise of victory? A show of her army's strength?

She would work it out in the morning. For now, she needed to rest.

And so Anneshka drifted to sleep, dreaming of a great horned bull.

CHAPTER 84

'There's a giant sertze out on the marshes?' cried Miro. The sun had risen now. Its light poured in through the ceiling, filling every inch of the Guest Palace chamber.

'Of course,' said Zuby. 'How else do you think the marshes are so full of life? The Sertze Bahnoh beats for the marshfish and the waders, for the otters and the midges and the bats, for the woolgrass and the hairy violets, for the great intermingling of life.'

The skret was stood like a preacher, clawed hands up by his head. He talked with such passion that Imogen wished she could see the sertze for herself. She pictured it full of starlight, like a miniature sun, feeding energy to the wetland.

'If I was a rare kind of lichen,' rasped Zuby, 'I'd grow near that sertze too.'

'But I spent months out there,' cried Miro. 'And I never saw a magic stone.'

'No,' said Zuby, 'you wouldn't have done. The heart of the

marshes is submerged. Legend has it that it's buried beneath an ancient stump . . . although that seems unlikely. There are hardly any trees out there.'

'Excuse me?' said Miro. He stood up very quickly, as if someone had yanked him to his feet.

'It's buried beneath an old tree stump,' said Zuby.

'But I've been there!' Miro exclaimed.

And there was that tilting feeling – something Imogen had experienced before – the feeling of things sliding together, of events clicking into place . . . As if the sisters and Miro had been meant to meet, as if they were all parts of the same instrument.

'That's amazing!' piped Marie, almost dropping the book in her excitement. 'Just tell us the way to the tree stump, and we'll go and get the Maiden's Kiss!'

Miro hesitated. 'Erm . . . There aren't many landmarks on the marshes . . . it all sort of merges into one.'

There was a knock on the door and a servant stepped inside. 'Your Highness,' he said, with a bow. 'A letter arrived at the Royal Palace. It was brought by a soldier on an elk. And the archers say an army has been spotted, camped on the other side of the ravine.'

Imogen's whole body felt cold – despite the fact that it was warm in the palace, despite the fact she was surrounded by friends.

'I wanted to tell Mage Bohoosh,' said the servant, 'but I can't find him anywhere . . . Here is the letter. It's addressed to you.'

'Thank you,' said Miro.

The wax seal on the letter was stamped with a crown. Miro broke it and unfurled the parchment. Imogen shuffled closer, keen to read for herself.

Dear Miroslav,

Fancy meeting you here. For all of these months, I had thought you were dead.

Now I hear that you've taken charge of Nedobyt. It seems that no matter how far I travel, no matter how many masks I tear off, the face underneath is always yours.

Prince of Yaroslav – boy king – champion . . . What is it now . . . bog boy?

I am sure you know why I write. I am here with my army at the mouth of the ravine. Your city is but a catapult's throw away.

Hand over Nedobyt, give me the throne. It will be the crown jewel of my empire. And so long as you surrender, nobody needs to die.

Oh, and I want Marie too.

Should you fail to comply with either request, my soldiers will kill every man, woman and child. There will be no survivors in Nedobyt. Of that, you can be sure.

I will wait until noon for your reply.

Anneshka Mazanar
Supreme Queen of Yaroslav,
Heir to the Lowland Throne,
Conqueror of Nedobyt

'Queen of Yaroslav?' gasped Imogen.

But that wasn't Miro's first concern. 'Who told Anneshka I'm in charge?' he cried. 'I never agreed to rule Nedobyt . . . Why can't she go somewhere else and leave me alone for once?'

'I know the feeling,' whispered Marie, pressing her lips together. 'Anneshka must think Nedobyt is the greatest kingdom . . . I'm so sorry, Miro. I think Zuby is right. Anneshka has followed me here.'

Imogen flopped down on the bed, next to the hare and frog. *I have no idea what to do,* she thought. *I'm totally out of my depth.*

Kazimira-the-frog was sleeping, making squeaky snores. Mum snuggled against Imogen's side.

'I've got to hand myself over, haven't I?' said Marie. 'I can't let everyone die, or become slaves to Anneshka.'

'No!' cried Imogen, still lying on the bed. 'Marie, you can't!'

'It's me who should be handing myself over,' muttered Miro.

'But just think what Anneshka would do if she ruled Nedobyt,' said Marie. 'If she got hold of that magic pool, she'd turn everyone she didn't like into slugs. Then she'd have even more power!'

Despite the bright morning sunlight, Imogen's eyes felt

heavy. She'd been awake all night and wanted nothing more than to sleep – to wake up and discover that this whole thing had been a horrible nightmare.

'Don't despair,' croaked Zuby. 'Anneshka still wants Marie.'

'Zuby, that's a bad thing,' said Miro.

'You could turn it to your advantage,' said the skret.

Imogen sat up. 'How?'

'Why don't we send you somewhere else?' said Zuby, tapping at the side of his nose. 'Somewhere you've got to go . . .'

All three children were staring at him as if he'd spoken in another tongue.

'Oooh,' said Konya, stepping away from the door. 'That's good – that's very good! The skret is suggesting you take the bad woman to the marshland!'

Imogen's brain was so tired, it took some time for the idea to sink in. Lure Anneshka away from Nedobyt . . . But would she fall for it? Didn't she already have what she wanted? Nedobyt was as good as hers.

Ochi's words drifted through Imogen's head . . . *Anneshka won't stop hunting you until she has got what she wants. And she will never have that. It will never be enough.*

'You want me to be bait?' Marie whispered.

Mum made a grunting sound and lashed out with her back legs. It didn't take magical powers to understand what that meant. She did not like this plan.

'I could go with you to fetch the lichen for Mark,' said

Zuby. 'Didn't the book say it grows near the Sertze Bahnoh? Well, I could help you find it. We skret are more sensitive than you humans. I should be able to feel when we're close.'

'That's very kind, Zuby, but—'

'It would be a diversion,' cut in Miro. 'You'd distract Anneshka, while I worked out how to close the ravine.'

Imogen looked at her friend. He did have a point . . . 'It's a good plan,' she said, ignoring her hare-mother's protests. 'But how will we get past the army?'

Marie started tying her hair into a bun. She looked a little less nervous – a little more ready for action. 'I've got an idea,' she said.

CHAPTER 85

I mogen, Marie and Zuby stood at the mouth of the ravine, at the edge of the enemy's camp. A clump of blackthorn and squat trees shielded them from view.

They were joined by Fred and Frieda, who were doing their best to appear small – legs folded beneath them, bodies huddled to the ground. The velecours looked plumper and glossier than ever. They must have eaten well in the park.

And slotted into Marie's hood was a golden hare. The hare's nose stuck over the top of the fabric; her black-tipped ears pointed up.

Imogen peeped between the branches of a tree. 'What do you see?' whispered Marie.

'I don't know, it's difficult—' The tree parted its boughs. 'Thank you,' muttered Imogen. She was surprised that Ochi had kept her word. The trees were still being helpful.

Between twigs and thorns, Imogen saw Anneshka's army. Flags shimmered in the morning light. There were rough tents on the outskirts, more luxurious-looking pavilions further in.

They were crammed on the narrow stretch of land between marsh and mountains.

'There are soldiers,' whispered Imogen. 'Lots of them . . .'

An eye appeared in the trunk next to Imogen's head. Ochi was watching too.

Small fires were dotted across the site; lines of smoke connecting earth and sky. About thirty paces from Imogen's hiding place, a group huddled round one such fire, talking and heating pots over the flames.

Most of the fighters were human, but Imogen could see a few skret in chainmail. King Ctibor must have lent them to his 'daughter's' cause. Imogen saw soldiers from Yaroslav too; their red jackets stood out. There were many other uniforms she didn't recognise.

'They've got horses,' she said, 'and . . . something else.' She didn't know the names of the tall deer with antlers and shaggy coats. Anneshka must have amassed her army from far and wide.

Imogen pulled back from the trees. 'I think we'd better go,' she said.

Marie nodded, biting her lip. 'How will we know if Anneshka is following?'

'We won't,' said Imogen. 'She doesn't have any velecours so she'll be much slower. We'll just have to make sure she sees you and hope she takes the bait . . . rather than attacking Nedobyt.'

Imogen and Marie climbed on to Frieda, with Marie in front and Mum-the-hare still secured in her hood.

Zuby climbed on to Fred and the velecour twisted his neck. 'Hello there,' croaked Zuby.

Fred stared. He wasn't used to such a well-clawed passenger.

'Doesn't feel natural,' muttered Zuby. 'Skret should have both feet on stone.' Fred beat his wings and lifted his chest, and Zuby almost slid off. 'Argh!' he exclaimed. 'This is worse than a horse!'

Imogen grabbed Frieda's reins and the velecour swerved out of hiding. Stalking towards them was a small band of soldiers. They must have heard the girls talking. Their hands were on the hilts of their swords.

Uh-oh, thought Imogen. *Now we're in trouble.*

Frieda ran as velecours do – fast, and in an unexpected direction. She bolted towards the soldiers and both girls screamed. The soldiers screamed too, scattering as the giant bird hurtled their way.

Frieda's feet pounded on the ground. Mum's ears flapped as Frieda ran, batting Imogen in the face.

'Come on, Frieda,' called Marie, as the velecour spread her wings.

Once again, Imogen could feel the bird's powerful muscles straining.

Frieda took off before the first cluster of tents.

Imogen ignored the flip in her belly, wrapping the reins round her wrists. To her left, she could see Fred and Zuby, also flying. Below, was the tightly packed camp.

They flew over a fire and smoke blew in Imogen's face.

She shut her eyes, and when she opened them, every soldier seemed to be looking up.

'It's two girls and a skret,' a voice shouted.

'She's the one Anneshka wants!'

Yes, that's it, thought Imogen. *Go and tell your mistress . . .*

Below, more soldiers scrabbled out of their tents. Some drew swords, others reached for bows.

'Faster, Frieda!' urged Marie.

If they got shot, there would be no saving Mark – no saving themselves – and Imogen couldn't bear to think of the velecours being injured.

An arrow whistled past Frieda's wingtip, singing as it curved overhead, before diving down on the other side of the bird. Frieda squawked and beat her wings harder.

Now they were flying over the marshes, low and with great speed. Imogen glanced back and saw the full size of the encampment. There were thousands of tents and makeshift shelters, catapults, cooking stations and carriages. It was more like a town than a temporary base.

Arrows hissed through the air behind the sisters, but they were out of range. The missiles fell into the wetland below.

'We did it!' cried Marie, punching the air.

Imogen set her face to the wind and encouraged the velecour on.

CHAPTER 86

'Any sign of her?' asked Marie, who couldn't see back past Imogen.

Imogen glanced over her shoulder. No one was visible on the marshes. That wasn't a surprise. It would take Anneshka several minutes to assemble a guard or ready her horse or whatever it was that she did. And, even then, she'd be much slower on horseback than they were in the air.

'Anneshka is coming,' muttered Imogen. 'I'm sure of it. But we'll be off the marshes before she gets close.'

Mum-the-hare placed her front paws on Marie's shoulders and sniffed the air, whiskers twitching.

'Zuby, can you feel the sertze?' called Marie.

Perched on Fred, the skret's cloak flapped from his neck. His head was hunched into his shoulders. His eyes bulged even more than they normally did. 'Yes,' he replied. 'It is faint though. We have some distance to go.'

'That's okay,' said Imogen. 'You take the lead.' And she steered Frieda aside so Fred could go first.

Imogen had to work hard to keep Frieda low. The velecour

wanted to soar with the clouds, where her broad wings were at their most effective.

But Zuby needed to be able to feel the Sertze Bahnoh and Imogen wanted to see the marsh. She hoped the tree stump was as big as Miro had described. He did occasionally exaggerate.

'You're doing well, Frieda,' said Marie, giving the velecour a pat.

After they had been flying for a while, Imogen noticed that Marie had gone quiet and she was resting against Imogen's chest. Leaning forwards a little, she saw that her sister was asleep.

Imogen decided not to wake her. With her arms around her, she would stop Marie slipping off. And having been up all night, it was a good idea to take a nap.

Mum-the-hare was safely nestled in Marie's hood, her eyes slowly closing, long ears pressed flat against her back.

The warmth of the velecour, and the steady wingbeats, was incredibly soothing. Imogen had to work hard not to fall asleep herself.

She hadn't stayed up this long since a sleepover at her friend's house. And, even then, they had drifted off before the dawn.

Imogen bit her lip to keep herself conscious, and peered at the marshes below.

As before, she saw hundreds of grassy knolls poking above the surface. She also saw huge spiderwebs cloaking the reeds.

'The sertze is getting stronger,' said Zuby. 'I suspect we are close.'

Imogen couldn't help thinking of Mark . . . wondering if they were too late. The nightmare about the yedleek hadn't left her imagination. But neither had the memories of Mark making campfires, of Mark and Mum holding hands, of Mark waking Imogen early so they could go and watch meteors.

Imogen *had* to find the Maiden's Kiss lichen. She *had* to find the tree stump.

Zuby steered Fred lower and veered to the left.

Marie stirred as Frieda also flew down. 'Where are we?' she mumbled.

'The heartbeat, I can feel it!' called Zuby.

'Over there,' cried Imogen, pointing to a dark ring in the marsh. If she hadn't known better, she would have said it was a hole.

She encouraged Frieda to descend further and the velecour dipped her wings, landing on a tuft of earth. Imogen and Marie scrambled off the bird. Mum sprang out of Marie's hood.

And there was the ancient tree stump. It was taller and wider than a house. Steps had been carved into the edge and, on top, there was some kind of seat.

The stump's bark was covered in crusts of lichen, sprouting mushrooms and velvet moss. Finding the right lichen would take some time.

Zuby splashed closer to the tree stump and crouched in the water at its base. Then, he stuck his head under, bottom up.

'What's he doing?' asked Marie.

The skret surfaced, gasping. 'The Sertze Bahnoh! It's under the stump!'

Imogen waded to Zuby's side, water rushing into her boots. She put her palms on the tree stump. And *there*, beneath the shivering breeze and the shake-shake of the tall grasses, beneath the warbling birds, she could feel a steady beat.

It was as if the stump had a pulse, but Imogen knew that wasn't quite right. The rhythm came from the Sertze Bahnoh, the heart of Mokzhadee.

'The tree must have grown on top of the sertze,' said Zuby. He patted the trunk. 'Perhaps that's why this stump survives. Either way, the sertze keeps this land so healthy, so –' he breathed in through his nose – 'full of life. Can you smell it?'

Imogen took a tentative sniff. She could smell rotting things and bird poo. 'Kind of,' she said, wondering if that was what Zuby meant.

Her eyes wandered back to the horizon. She couldn't help checking for Anneshka. And, this time, she saw something – a dark dot. It was hard to tell if it was coming closer.

It can't be Anneshka, thought Imogen. *Not yet* . . .

Mum-the-hare had climbed the steps and was standing on top of the stump. She rose on to her back legs, like a meerkat. 'What is it, Mum?' asked Marie.

The hare twitched her whiskers before letting out a high-pitched whistle.

Imogen had never heard Mum make that sound, but she knew it was a warning – the kind of noise one hare makes to another when a hawk is approaching their nest.

'Shall we find that lichen?' said Imogen, fear tightening her throat.

'Quite right,' said Zuby, 'quite right.' But he didn't move to help. He just stood, marvelling at the tree stump and the stone buried beneath.

The sisters shuffled around the stump, moving in opposite directions, and Imogen thought back to the yedleek book. The illustration had shown a yolk-yellow lichen, thick, with wavy edges. That was what she needed to spot.

Imogen's eyes scanned the bark. In some places, it was slimy. In others, it was cracked like scales. Most of it was hidden by things growing.

The lichen was so colourful; acid orange and mint green. The mushrooms were unusual too. Some were candyfloss pink and frilly, with white gills underneath. Many of them grew in layers, and Imogen thought they looked like a mini version of Nedobyt, clinging to the stump.

But there was no sign of the Maiden's Kiss – the lichen that would save Mark.

Imogen squinted at the horizon and the dark blob was bigger. She gulped.

Better keep looking . . .

She checked the bark above her head and the bits by her knees, seeking glimpses of yellow. She lifted floppy mushrooms to see if the lichen was underneath. She was so focused on her search, that she almost bumped into her sister.

'Oh!' cried Imogen. They had come full circle.

'It's not here,' said Marie. 'What if the book got it wrong?'

Imogen didn't reply. She could hear an unsettling sound . . . a soft roar like a distant waterfall. She looked down and realised that her knees were no longer submerged. The marsh water was ebbing, as if drawn by a tide.

And it wasn't just the water. The little islands were shuffling too, being dragged towards the oncoming shape.

'I-Imogen.' Marie quailed. 'What is that?'

'I think we're about to meet Miro's bog troll,' said Imogen, 'unless we find the lichen fast.'

CHAPTER 87

M iro was alone in the bedchamber. Well, almost alone. Two mice stood on a table by the bed. A frog rested on a plump cushion. A fierce, long-haired woman stood watch by the door.

'All right,' sighed Miro. 'What do I do now?'

There were only two hours until noon, when Anneshka had threatened to invade. That was assuming she didn't follow the girls across the marshes.

There will be no survivors . . . Anneshka's letter had promised. Miro shivered at the thought. He couldn't let it come to that.

There was a tentative knock on the door and he turned. 'Hello?' he called.

Konya held the door open and a palace servant stepped through. 'Your Highness,' said the woman, bowing. 'You have a visitor. We tried telling him that you weren't available but he wouldn't go. He started making a scene . . . I think he was reciting from a book.'

'Erm, all right,' said Miro. 'Let him in.'

There was a jostling on the other side of the door and an

old man entered the room. He was dressed in baggy robes and had a cone-shaped hat tied to his head, with moons and stars sewn on. His beard almost reached his ankles and he'd tucked it into his belt.

'King Miroslav,' said the old man. 'I am glad to see you're still with us. I have brought the book for your friends.'

Miro was so surprised by the man's appearance that, at first, he didn't understand.

'The book?'

'*The book*,' the man whispered. 'I am Grand Librarian Otakar . . . You might have heard of me?'

'Oh,' said Miro. 'Thank you. You've come just in time. Is it the book about changing mice into people?'

'That, and a great many other things.' Otakar removed a book from the folds of his robe. 'It was requested by Imogen and Marie. I had hoped to find them here.' His eyes flicked around the room.

'I'm afraid they had to go out,' said Miro, 'but if you leave the book with me, I'll make sure they get it.'

'Excellent.' Otakar held the book out and Miro took it with both hands. The writing on the cover was large and flowing, as if the letters had been spun from silk.

SLIPPING YOUR SKIN
A Practical Guide

'I had to turn the library upside down to find it,' said Otakar. 'It will take months to put everything back. And I cut my beard. Couldn't get myself out of the building with my hair tied up in the shelves.'

'Thank you, Grand Librarian,' said Miro, who was keen to start reading straight away. 'Your help is greatly appreciated.'

'I am so delighted to meet you,' said Otakar. 'Are you to be our next king?'

The question caught Miro off guard. 'Err, no, I am not here to rule.'

The librarian looked disappointed. 'I was hoping that, with your permission, I might reopen the library.'

'I am sure that you can,' said Miro, not really understanding what Otakar meant. Why had the library been closed? 'I don't mean to be rude, Grand Librarian, but there's an army at the entrance to Nedobyt and I need to focus on that.'

Otakar nodded vigorously. Yet he still didn't take the hint.

'Oi, Mr Librarian,' said Konya. 'He's asking you to leave.'

'Ah!' cried Otakar. 'Of course, I shall be off! It has been an honour to meet you, King Miroslav.' And with that, he shuffled out of the room.

Miro was left with the uncomfortable feeling that people had already formed expectations – things that they wanted from him. He had hoped to shed such pressures when he left Yaroslav, but they seemed to have followed him.

Miro glanced at the mice. There was no time for thinking

about these things . . . He had to turn his grandmothers back into people. He sat on the edge of the mattress and opened the slipskin book.

CHAPTER 88

The first thing Miro noticed, was the book had no paragraphs. It was page after page of handwritten text, as if the author had gushed out everything without even pausing to draw breath.

If you wish to control which creature you turn into, you must learn its ways; study its most intricate habits, fear its very worst fears.

The second thing Miro noticed, was the book had no chapters. It would be impossible to skip to the most relevant bit.

What was worse, there didn't seem to be any logic to the way it was structured. Notes on animal behaviour were mixed with recipes and remedies.

One should avoid eating thistles when one is a goat. They won't digest nearly so easily as you imagine.

The information on turning animals into people could be anywhere . . . Miro would have to read the whole thing. And he'd never been a very fast reader.

With less than two hours until noon, he took a deep breath and began.

Several times, he considered giving up. But then he caught sight of the mice, watching him from the table. Their shiny black eyes were so full of hope . . . Miro couldn't let them down. He couldn't let his friends down either, or the people of Nedobyt. He must find a way to close the ravine, and for that, he needed his grandmothers to be humans again.

Miro rubbed his tired eyes and stared at the page.

Avoiding predators . . .
Making a peregrine nest . . .
Where blue bears go to hibernate . . .

None of that was right.

Kazimira kept hopping on to the page. 'No, Kazimira,' grumbled Miro and he lifted up the frog. 'I can't read when you're sitting on the book.'

'Miaow-roslav,' said Konya, rolling her shoulders and licking her lips. 'I am hungry. I'm going to hunt.'

'You could ask for some food from the kitchens,' called Miro, but Konya had already left the room.

Miro went back to his reading and the next title made him stop in his tracks:

*A Spell to Help the Uninitiated
Return to Their Original Shape*

There it was. The secret he'd been searching for, wedged between advice on hibernation and regurgitation. Miro bent closer to the page and read the words out loud:

*'Slipskins and catkins and flotsam and jetsam
Flowers and algae and spiders and mud
You are a part of the marshes
Return to your truest shape.'*

Miro glanced at the mice. They were standing close to the front of the table, paws wrapped over the edge. His grandmothers were listening.

Kazimira was listening too. She blinked one eye after the other, directing her froggy stare Miro's way. He pressed his finger to the page and read on:

*'Glaciers and rivers and melt-water minerals
Ravens and rowans and rocks and blue ice
You are a part of the mountains
Return to your truest shape.'*

As Miro read, he was reminded of what he'd felt on the marshes – of the great dissolving of things. In Mokzhadee, he'd felt *held* by the landscape, part of a great swampy soup.

Miro had remembered that feeling when he'd been a falcon, just before he'd started to change.

Was that why he'd been able to turn back into a human, when most other people got stuck? Had his time in Mokzhadee changed him forever?

One mouse closed its eyes. At first, Miro thought it was going to sleep, but it didn't curl up. It was thinking. The other mouse did the same.

Perhaps he'd read the spell wrong. Miro lifted the book, about to read it again.

Then he heard a scuffle.

He glanced at his grandmothers and his heart seemed to flutter up his throat, like a wild bird trying to break free.

It was working.

CHAPTER 89

O ne of the mice was as big as a cat. The other was stretching out like a ferret. Miro bounced off the bed, caught in a flurry of excitement.

'Don't stop thinking about connections!' he cried, afraid that his grandmothers might get stuck.

The extended mice loped on to the bed – for the table was already too small for their rapidly inflating bodies. Their fur was moulting away, their tails and whiskers shrinking.

Thinking they might want some privacy, Miro lifted the bedcover and the mice scurried underneath. He tried to stand patiently as the veiled shapes wriggled and grew.

He felt like his insides were wriggling with them. It was working. It was *really* working!

'Argh,' cried one of the things under the cover. It was a very human-like sound.

'Grandmother?' breathed Miro.

The edge of the cover lifted and a head poked out. It had grey hair and wrinkle-hemmed eyes. It was, without any doubt, a human. 'Would you be so kind as to fetch me a robe?' said the head.

Miro almost jumped out of his skin. He didn't know why he was surprised. This was exactly what he'd been trying to achieve.

'Y-yes, Grandmother. Of course, Grandmother.' He searched the chest of drawers and found a couple of linen sheets. Grabbing them, he lifted the edge of the cover and pushed the sheets underneath.

After some squirming, and a shout of 'Oi, that's my head!', two old ladies emerged. Even wrapped in bedsheets, there was something about them that commanded respect.

One woman was tall with a proud chin and a golden complexion, much like Miro's. The other was shorter and rounder and looked rather frail. She had a haze of white hair, deep brown skin and soft umber eyes.

Miro wanted to look at their faces forever – to commit every detail to memory. He wanted to tell them how he'd travelled through the Lowlands and across the Marshes of Mokzhadee, how he'd always wanted to visit them, how, when he was small, he used to sing a special song each time their letters arrived.

But the only thing that came out of his mouth was, 'Grandmother Olga, Granny Nela! It's me!'

'Miroslav!' laughed the tall woman, Granny Nela. 'Come here.' She hugged his face into her bony shoulder and Miro breathed her in. She smelled faintly of biscuits and lavender – not like a mouse at all.

'How you have *grown*,' she muttered and she held him at arm's length. 'Why, you're all legs and angles, just like your mother was at your age.'

The shorter woman, Grandmother Olga, barged between them. 'My turn,' she said and she gave Miro a surprisingly firm hug. She smelled . . . familiar . . .

For a flickering moment, Miro was caught in a memory. He was back in Castle Yaroslav, in his mother's dressing room. 'It's white pine and juniper,' his mother had said, holding out a bottle for Miro to sniff. 'True mountain scents. I have it transported all the way from Nedobyt.'

That was what Grandmother Olga smelled like. Miro wondered how she'd got hold of the perfume when she was shaped like a mouse.

'There's no need for introductions,' said Olga to Miro. 'We know who you are. We have always known . . . Come now, there is much to discuss.'

'Tush, Olga!' cried Nela. 'Can't you let the child rest? He's been up all night!'

'Absolutely not,' said Olga. 'The enemy is at our gates.'

'We don't have gates.'

'Exactly,' said Olga, with a sniff. 'There is no time to lose.'

Miro watched his grandmothers with an anxious smile. They had an easy way with each other, as people do when they've been married a long time.

Yet Miro hardly knew these women. He only remembered meeting them once, before his parents had died. Now that meeting felt like a dream. Apart from their letters and his mother's tales, these women were strangers to him.

'You have done very well,' said Nela. Her eyes were fixed on Miro. 'Thank you for helping us change back. We couldn't have done it without you.'

Miro wanted, more than anything, to impress his grandmothers so he did what Patoleezal had taught him. He swept one hand forwards and bowed. 'It is an honour to have been able to assist you,' he said.

'Good gracious, child, what are you doing?' snapped Olga.

Miro craned his neck, back still bent. 'I'm . . . bowing?'

'Enough of that,' said Olga. 'We have to stop this army – and quickly.'

Miro straightened, embarrassed. 'It was a very nice bow, Miro,' said Nela. She spoke as if she was reassuring a toddler and that made Miro feel even more foolish.

'There is very little time,' announced Olga. 'We must close the ravine.' She raised her eyebrows at Miro. 'And when I say *we*, I mean *you*.' Despite her apparent fragility, it was clear that Olga was the grandmother in charge.

Miro gulped. After all the excitement of the festival, the shock of being turned into a bird, the struggle to turn himself back, the joy of seeing Imogen and Marie, and the argument with Bohoosh . . . Miro was very tired.

'Me?' he asked, trying to calm his nerves. 'But I don't know how.'

'It's easy,' said Olga and, as she pulled him close, Miro noticed that one of her eyes was cloudy. He had to bend so she could whisper in his ear: 'You must wake up the mountains, Miroslav.'

CHAPTER 90

'*That* is a bog troll?' said Zuby, squinting across the marsh. His eyes were excellent in darkness, but not so good in the light.

'I think so,' said Imogen. The dark blob was definitely moving closer, and she could see that it was growing in size.

The earth pulled from under her heels, like sand being dragged between waves.

Fred and Frieda squawked, clearly spooked by the thing that was coming their way.

'Little humans, I think we should go!' cried Zuby. He grabbed the velecours by their reins.

'We can't leave without Mark's cure!' said Marie.

'You mean you haven't found it?' croaked Zuby. 'What have you been doing?'

Imogen felt a flash of rage. That was a bit rich from a skret who'd been standing with his head underwater.

The islets were wobbling now – not with the beat of the sertze, but with the bog troll's strides.

Miro said we shouldn't get on the wrong side of Panovník,

thought Imogen, remembering her friend's story about the marsh. Judging by the speed at which the troll was approaching, they already had.

'We haven't checked the top of the tree stump,' said Marie, and she ran up the steps. Imogen scrabbled after her. Mum-the-hare was already up there, looking for the Maiden's Kiss.

The throne was as bizarre as Miro's description. It rose from the middle of the stump, like the mast of a wrecked ship, standing proud of the waves.

Desperate, the sisters searched for the yellow lichen, tearing off bits of moss in their haste.

The rushing noise grew louder, and now Imogen could see what it was. Gallons of water were being sucked from the reedbeds, into the charging troll. It was like a waterfall – only this one was flowing backwards. Mud and grass moved with it, providing the materials Panovník needed to swell.

A great many animals were disturbed by the upsurge. A huge flock of wading birds burst from the reeds. There were more of them than Imogen had imagined. They filled the sky with their wings.

When the curtain of birds parted, Imogen thought she could see fish, flipping out of the water. There was even a mist around the troll's running legs – a gathering of midges, startled out of their daytime slumber by the shaking of their beds.

The marshes were frothing with life, and most of it seemed to be in a rush to get out of the bog troll's way.

'Imogen, I think I've found it,' yelled Marie. She pointed to a golden piece of lichen that grew on the back of the throne. Its edges were wiggly, as the illustration had shown.

Imogen couldn't believe it – couldn't believe that this fleshy thing, that was no larger than her palm and no thicker than her ear – *this* had the power to destroy yedleek?

It looked so unremarkable, so easily missed.

'It's just like the picture in the book,' said Marie. She had to shout to be heard above the rumble of rising water and Imogen knew Panovník was close.

Marie wriggled her fingers under the lichen, working to remove it. 'Put it here,' cried Imogen, opening a purse at her belt. Marie pushed the lichen in.

'The velecours!' cried Zuby, and Imogen turned just in time to see Fred and Frieda fleeing. Zuby was dragging behind them, reins wrapped round his wrists.

'No!' screamed Marie. 'Frieda, come back!'

The birds took off with Zuby dangling.

Imogen watched them leave, feeling more than a little bit sick. The sisters and the hare were stranded.

Then a damp-algae stink filled Imogen's nostrils. The roar of water filled her ears, and a shadow fell across the tree stump.

Imogen didn't dare look.

But she had to.

She turned slowly; her body reluctant to obey.

And there was Panovník.

The bog troll towered above the dead tree, head blocking the sun.

Marie screamed with terror. Mum sprinted around the girls, as if she could form a protective circle, if only she ran fast enough.

But there was no sheltering from this monster.

'NOOOOOT FOOOOOR YOOOOOOOUUUU,' boomed the troll in a voice deep and terrible.

Its face was made from leaves and reeds. Streams ran from its eyeholes and toadspawn hung from its nose. Imogen could feel the spray from its waterlogged body. She could see the marsh life up close. Lizards and insects, small fish and birds – they were scrabbling out of Panovník's legs.

'W-w-we're not here for your throne,' cried Marie, but the troll didn't seem to hear. She was like a mouse squeaking at its feet.

Imogen took Marie's hand and the girls backed away, until their heels found the edge of the stump.

'USSSUUURRRRRPEERRRRS WIIILL DIEEEEE-EEEEEEE.' The troll raised a bone-crushing fist.

Imogen's heart pattered. This was it. The end.

She squeezed Marie's hand a little tighter.

Mum let out a whistling shriek.

'Don't you dare kill my prophecy,' screamed a voice.

Imogen's world seemed to slow.

She knew that voice. It had followed her across worlds, through her waking hours and her worst dreams. And now it had followed them over the marshes.

Anneshka Mazanar.

CHAPTER 91

Miro pulled back from his grandmother. 'Wake up the mountains? W-what? How?'

'Climb the three peaks that flank the ravine,' said Olga, as if this was the simplest thing in the world. 'And knock on each of their tops. I would do it myself – indeed, I was once quite the mountain woman – but, alas, those days are behind me.'

'You want me to . . . knock on the mountains?'

'Quite right,' said Olga. 'None of this namby-pamby tapping. A nice firm whack.' She smacked the end of the bed.

Miro didn't want to be rude, but he had hoped his grandmothers would know how to close some secret, hidden gates. Knocking on the top of a mountain sounded about as useful as asking for help from a frog.

. . . Frog?

Miro had almost forgotten about Kazimira. She was still sitting on her pillow, was still an amphibian.

Croak, she said, looking downcast. Although, perhaps that was how frogs always looked.

Why didn't Kazimira change back with the spell? wondered Miro.

Olga and Nela were waiting for Miro's response. 'Three mountains,' repeated Olga. 'Do you think you can manage that?'

'I'll try,' said Miro. 'But what will it do?'

His grandmothers exchanged knowing glances. Before either of them could answer, the bedroom door opened and Konya's head poked through the gap. Her eyes flicked around the chamber, finally settling on Nela and Olga. 'Are you the mice?' she asked.

'They are the queens of this kingdom,' said Miro, wishing Konya would show some respect.

The woman who used to be a snĕehoolark slunk into the room. There was a slightly scared-looking cook behind her, carrying a platter of raw fish.

'I went to the kitchens,' said Konya. 'As you suggested, Miaow-roslav.' She popped a chunk of fish in her mouth. 'Mmmm, delicious . . . By the way, the humans are panicking. News of the army has spread.'

'How do you know?' asked Miro.

'They were talking in the kitchens,' Konya replied.

Everyone turned to the cook. He gulped, still balancing the fish platter. 'It's just that without Mage Bohoosh, there's no one in charge. How are we going to defend ourselves? Who will close the ravine?'

'No one in charge?' said Nela.

The cook's eyes darted to the old ladies, wrapped in linen bedsheets. His eyes were so wide that they almost popped out of his head. 'Your Majesties!' he gasped. 'Y-y-you're back!'

'Everyone must leave the city,' said Nela. 'Seek refuge with the skret. The Královna's caves are deep in the mountains . . . We'll see to this army. Won't we, dear?'

Olga nodded and smiled, looking much calmer than Miro felt.

'Please will you tell the guards for us?' asked Nela. 'Make sure the message gets spread?'

The cook nodded and started backing away. Konya took the platter from him as he left the room.

'I heard another rumour,' said Konya, face-planting the pile of fish. She chewed for a long while before going on. 'Anneshka's army is purr-paring to march. It is almost noon . . . we might not have enough time to get everyone out of Nedobyt.'

But if Anneshka's soldiers arrived before people had escaped, there'd be a bloodbath. The thought made Miro's palms feel all sweaty. 'It didn't work then?' he asked. 'Imogen and Marie's plan . . . it failed?'

'No one seems to have seen Anneshka,' said Konya. She stretched her neck, luxuriating in the movement. 'But the army still rallies. The scouts say the chief is a bearded man. He me-miaow-must be her second-in-command.'

Miro reached for his rings, before remembering they'd

been lost on the marshes. Instead, he twisted his fingers. This was bad news. Very bad news indeed.

Miro had hoped that if the girls distracted Anneshka, she'd make her army stay put – at least for a little while. He hadn't counted on her having a deputy.

But his grandmothers did not seem to be ruffled. 'Konya, you are clearly a good friend to Miroslav,' said Olga. 'For that, we are already in your debt. Good friends are difficult to find.'

Konya continued to stretch, reaching with her arms and arching her back, but she did not contradict the queen.

'We have no right to ask anything of you,' continued Olga. 'But I ask a favour because I must.'

Miro couldn't help wondering at the tone of reverence with which Olga spoke. Especially since when Olga was a mouse and Konya had been a giant cat, Konya had tried to eat her.

'Would you speak with your kin?' the old lady asked.

Konya stopped stretching and focused her attention on the women. 'My kin?'

'The wild snĕehoolarks, who roam the Nameless Mountains.' Olga held Konya's gaze. 'We used to be on good terms with the giant cats. Some of our people left offerings . . . and we all share the same land. Would the wild snĕehoolarks come to our aid?'

Konya's eyes darted to Miro. 'I am supposed to stay with him.'

It was true. Perla had asked Konya to protect Miro, and

Konya had done just that. She had caught fish and shared her heat on the marshes. She had stayed with him through midge-blizzards and sinking bogs. *She is*, thought Miro, *an excellent friend . . . if a little intimidating.*

'Many will be at risk if that army reaches Nedobyt,' said Olga. 'Including Miroslav. Including other children. And, if this Anneshka becomes Queen of Nedobyt, she might not be the type of neighbour the sněehoolarks are used to. She may allow the hunting of your kin.'

It was a good point. Miro hadn't thought about what Anneshka would do to animals in the places she conquered. Anneshka could be very cruel . . . and why should that end with people?

He glanced at Kazimira-the-frog. She was still watching, still taking it all in.

Konya stood erect now, eyes unblinking and wide. 'I will do it,' she said. 'I will speak with the wild sněehoolarks.'

'Thank you,' said Olga, and then she did the most extraordinary thing. The great Queen of Nedobyt bowed. Nela did the same.

Even more extraordinary, Konya bowed back. It was a small movement, a graceful dip, but still . . .

Miro had never seen the sněehoolark bowing – not in human or giant cat shape.

Oh, said a small voice in his head. *Is this what it means to rule?*

CHAPTER 92

Q ueen Olga straightened, gripping the closest bedpost for support. Then she turned to face Miro. 'Will you help your friend resume her normal shape?'

Miro felt more exhausted than ever. What he wouldn't give to close his eyes. But the thought of Anneshka's army storming into Nedobyt and slaughtering people was more than enough to clear his drowsiness.

'There's a spell,' he said to Konya, picking up the slipskin book. 'I'll read it to you now . . . *Slipskins and catkins and flotsam and jetsam, flowers and algae and spiders and mud . . .*'

The change happened faster for Konya. She closed her eyes, focusing her attention inwards, or perhaps reaching out to the world. Fur started growing on her forehead, spreading down her nose and across her cheeks. Her ears migrated upwards. Her teeth sharpened into fangs.

A few seconds later, Konya was yowling and shredding her clothes. Instead of a woman, there was a sněehoolark – amber-eyed, thick-furred, with extravagant whiskers. Her ears were tufted. Her tail was fiercely striped.

'Konya!' cried Miro, 'You're back!'

The snĕehoolark bounded towards him and Miro felt a wobble of fear. She was a *very* big cat. But she only nuzzled his stomach and Miro returned the embrace.

Konya had always been Konya, even when she was a woman. She had always been ferocious and loyal. But, somehow, she was *even more* Konya in this body. Her shape finally suited her soul.

Miro glanced at Kazimira. If only the same could be said for the princess . . . She was very much still a frog and Miro didn't understand why.

'Please, take our message to the wild snĕehoolarks,' said Olga to the giant cat. 'Whatever their decision, we are very grateful for your help.'

And, with that, Konya sprang out of the room.

Now Olga directed her attention at Miro. 'Miroslav, you had better go too.'

Miro wished, with every fibre of his body, that he could take a nap. His brain felt scrambled. His eyelids seemed to lift tiny weights.

Nela shook her grey head. 'It's too late, Olga. Didn't you hear what Konya said? The army is preparing to march – perhaps they've already set off. You're asking the impossible of the boy. He'll never climb three mountains before the soldiers arrive.'

'We'll send more people,' cried Olga. 'They can do one mountain each.'

'Olga,' said Nela. 'Even the fastest couldn't climb a mountain that quickly, not even if they ran all the way.'

Olga scowled and sat on the edge of the bed. Miro's chest hurt to look at her. She appeared even smaller and frailer sitting down.

Above, the sun poured its gold through the glass.

Miro rubbed his tired eyes. He had survived his trek across the marshes. Of that he was very glad. He'd finally found his family. For that he was grateful too.

He wasn't about to give it all up because of Anneshka Mazanar . . .

'What if I didn't run,' said Miro.

Both women looked his way.

'What if, instead, I flew?'

CHAPTER 93

By the time that Miro and his grandmothers walked through the common, the festival atmosphere had vanished. Instead, there was an air of suppressed panic.

Long gone were the jugglers and dancers. Instead, folk dragged hand-drawn carts, piled high with their belongings and those people who were unable to walk.

There were no more cheerful costumes. Most were dressed for the road, wrapped in shawls and wearing mittens. Some had young children strapped to their backs.

A few were carrying weapons. Perhaps they intended to stay and fight.

'It's a hard trek to the skret caves,' muttered Nela and, for the first time, she looked afraid. 'Especially with little ones. I do hope they make it in time.'

'Shouldn't you be going with them?' whispered Miro. He didn't want his grandmothers to get hurt.

'No, Miroslav,' said Nela. 'We are Nedobyt's queens.'

Miro couldn't help thinking of the other rulers he'd known. His uncle, King Ctibor, the five queens . . .. He didn't think

431

they'd have taken the same approach. They always put themselves first.

Miro and his grandmothers kept going, making their way through the valley. On either side, cliffs towered above them, with buildings clinging to the rock.

All the marsh-gas lanterns had been extinguished and thousands of people were visible as dots, inching down the near-vertical paths in the sharp midday light. Most were moving towards the common and the trail that led deeper into the mountains.

Eventually, Miro and his grandmothers stood at the city-side entrance to the ravine. The spot was guarded by several gold-clad archers, who all saluted their queens.

'I'll tell you one thing,' said Nela. 'It's colder when you're not covered in fur.'

'It's the tail I miss the most,' replied Olga. 'Really helped with my balance. Much better than a walking stick.'

Miro didn't know how they could keep chatting as if a vast army wasn't marching towards them, as if they weren't on the cusp of an unwinnable war, as if they weren't all about to be butchered.

Beneath his grandmothers' talk, Miro could feel a faint drumming; a tremble rising up through the soles of his boots. It was, Miro realised, the marching of many thousands of feet.

His stomach seemed to desert him.

Anneshka's army was on the move.

'Although I can't say I miss being that small,' said Nela.

'Remember when I got stuck in a chamber pot? Thought I'd had it. Thought I'd drown in—'

Is this what happens when you become an adult? wondered Miro. *Do you stop being afraid?*

Grandma Olga seemed to read his mind. 'There's no point getting flustered, Miroslav,' she murmured, so the archers wouldn't hear. 'Panic is contagious. Remember that.'

Miro nodded, but his eyes were on the ravine. Its sides clinked with pebbles; tiny rocks that had been dislodged by the vibrating earth.

Nela held out a glass bottle she'd taken from Bohoosh's chamber in the Royal Palace. 'Fly swift,' she said, pressing the bottle into Miro's hand.

'I – I will do my very best,' he said in a hoarse voice. 'I want to make you proud.'

Nela stooped so her face was level with Miro's. She was much taller than her wife. 'We're already proud of you, Miroslav. We were proud from the moment you were born.'

Miro felt as though his grandmother had lifted him – as though he was floating an inch above the ground. *From the very first moment he was born?*

Olga looked pensive. Then she shrugged, adding, 'Even though you were a screamer for the first year of your life. Now, bottoms up, Miroslav.'

Miro drank the sweet water. He felt it whoosh down his throat, gurgling as it entered his stomach. He hiccupped and burped and was about to apologise, when his body started to shift.

It happened faster this time, as if the magic knew its way round. Negative thoughts swirled in Miro's head. *What if I turn into an earthworm? What if I turn into a snail?*

Miro batted the thoughts away and Granny Nela started to sing. 'My little Miro, fly swift as a falcon.' That was his mother's lullaby!

Hundreds of feathers stiffened beneath Miro's skin, pressing up ready to sprout.

'You make the world come alive . . . You give the wind form, give it feathers and wings. You give the stars their bright eyes.'

Miro's spine shuttered like a telescope, folding in on itself. His legs shrank. His bones hollowed out. It hurt – really hurt – and Miro tried to control it.

Bad thoughts came with the pain. *What if I can't wake the mountains? What if I'm not fast enough? Anneshka's army will storm Nedobyt . . .*

But Granny Nela's voice cut through. 'My little Miro, fly swift as a falcon, and know that you are adored. You are the valleys and you are the summits. You've made a nest in my heart.'

The lullaby reminded Miro of his mother and he tried to focus on that – tried to conjure her face. He imagined her shining with a soft golden radiance. The bad thoughts seemed to bounce off her, seemed to melt in the brilliance of her light.

Granny Nela was still singing, but Miro couldn't make out the words. His whole body was contorting and, try as he might, he was not in control.

My little Miro . . .

His clothes pushed against his face and Miro scrabbled with his feet. As he burst free from his tunic, he could feel the strength in his shoulders, could sense the violence of his claws.

Finally, his transformation was complete. 'I am a falcon,' he cried and it came out as a screech.

Nela was beaming. Olga dabbed her eyes.

Miro lifted his wings and all it took was one thrust. His feathers caught the air.

'Fly swift,' called Nela.

And with his claws tucked against his belly, Miro rose.

When he glanced down, he could have sworn that there were three figures – three women watching him soar. One was Grandmother Olga, the second was Granny Nela, the third . . .

Her face was so familiar and yet . . .

Miro blinked several times, his mind struggling to trust his eyes. But falcon eyes do not lie. The third woman was made out of starlight.

CHAPTER 94

Miro flew up the first mountain. It was sheltered from the worst of the wind and easy enough to ascend.

Staying close to the slope, his eyes needled the rocks and vegetation that soon turned to snow and ice. He couldn't help keeping a lookout for small creatures. His boy-self might be exhausted, but his falcon-self wanted to *soar, fly, hunt, kill* . . .

Miro landed on the peak, talons out. Glancing across the mountain's shoulder, he caught his first sight of the enemy – a dark mass at the other end of the ravine. His falcon eyes could make out the details, even though the army was at least one mile down.

Foot soldiers were the first to funnel into the chasm. Behind them came mounted soldiers, on horses and antlered elk. There were riders with crossbows. There were standard-bearers too, carrying Anneshka's crown flags.

It reminded Miro of the toys in his tower; the ones he'd had in Castle Yaroslav. Back then, he'd owned many stone warriors, each no bigger than his thumb. He'd enjoyed lining them up in his chamber, getting them to stand in just the right way.

But these soldiers were no playthings. They carried real weapons, real orders to kill.

Oh, Stars, thought Miro. *I hope this works.*

Shouts from the army chief echoed up the ravine. At the centre of this great throng were catapults and battering rams. Anneshka would not need such weapons to bring Nedobyt to its knees. The foot soldiers alone could do that . . .

No. Miro would not let it happen. He scrabbled at the ice with his claws. When he found bare rock, he hammered on it with his beak.

Wake, mountain, wake, we have need of you.

Then Miro launched back into the air, gliding towards the second peak. It was connected to the first by a narrow ridge. His tail twitched, stabilising him over the slipstreams.

Once again, he scrabbled at the ice until his claws found rock. Then he pecked at it several times and stamped with his talons, just in case.

He didn't know what would happen when he'd completed this ritual – or, indeed, if it would really work – but he would sooner fall from the sky than fail because he hadn't done *exactly* as his grandmothers had told him.

Below, the army poured into the ravine: an unfaltering, unstoppable force. At the other end of the chasm was Nedobyt, its elegant buildings splaying out from the valley's every crease; its glass-topped palaces gleaming like crystal-winged beetles.

Even from here, Miro could see townsfolk funnelling out of the city, up the steep mountain path. Nothing seemed to be standing between them and the approaching soldiers. Although Miro knew the archers would do their best.

Rising, Miro soared across the ravine. The army cut a grey river beneath him, helmets shining.

He hoped his grandmothers had returned to the Royal Palace. He hoped that Imogen and Marie were safe. He thought, once again, of his mother.

As he approached the third pinnacle, it took some skill not to be thrown off course. This mountain was by far the highest and the air around it seethed.

Ice crystals swirled in the wind and Miro was caught in a shimmering cloud. When it cleared, he swooped down, perching on the mountain's tip. Here he dug, wings folded, shoulders hunched, until he found rock. *Thud, thud, thud.* He stomped with his foot.

Miro was about to tap with his beak, when the ground beneath him trembled. Snow skittered down the sides of the mountain.

Surely, that couldn't have been caused by the soldiers . . .

Miro flapped his wings and managed to stabilise himself. *It's an earthquake*, he thought, and for a moment, he was afraid.

But then a thought flew into his mind. *Wake up the mountains* . . . Was this what his grandmothers had meant?

The snow beneath him was shivering and shifting, falling

away in great chunks. Miro couldn't balance any longer. He lifted into the sky.

Looking down, he saw a huge ice-misted eyeball, embedded in rock.

He screeched and flew higher. There was a second eye beside it. And the thing he'd been sitting on wasn't a peak. It was a nose – a great stone snout, with nostrils as big as caverns.

From a bird's-eye view things were clearer, although it would be invisible to the soldiers below. Miro wasn't looking at a dead lump of rock. He was looking at the face of a living creature. And it was looking at him.

The guardian of Nedobyt was awake.

CHAPTER 95

The face in the mountain blinked, and the icicles that fringed each eyelid clinked.

Miro flapped his wings on instinct, rising higher. This creature, whatever it was, was enormous. It seemed to be buried in the mountain and it was trying to escape.

The mountain shuddered, filling the sky with its groans. Deep ice cracked, stone ground on stone, and immense frosted shoulders emerged.

No . . . Miro realised. *The giant isn't buried in the mountain. It* is *the mountain.*

He screeched with fear and in celebration. The two peaks on the other side of the ravine were also rumbling. Trees and bushes came loose, sliding down their slopes.

The mountains were coming to life.

One landslide fell into the ravine, crushing a group of soldiers. The wind was loud and Miro couldn't hear their screams. He was screaming too – in a way that only mountain falcons could – a high-pitched, ear-shredding shriek.

The three giants yawned and stretched, shaking off their

snowy veils. Icicles splintered from their spines. Rubble tumbled down their legs. They hadn't been woken for thousands of years, not since Miro's ancestors had knocked on their peaks, seeking protection from Radko the Conqueror.

Yet, for mountain giants, a millennium is but a short nap.

Their kind had been born from volcanoes, had risen from liquid rock. Their quartz bones were crystallised magma. Their faces were glacier-carved.

Miro watched as the tallest giant straightened. She was heavy-browed with piercing white eyes. Her lower limbs were clothed in moss and lichen. Her arms were thick with ice.

At her full height, the tip of her head brushed the clouds. And, always, ribbons of snow swirled, wreathing her body in glittering mist.

She was terrifying . . . the biggest thing that Miro had ever seen.

She was also beautiful.

The giants turned to each other, nodding their silent greetings. When they were done, the tallest rolled her ice-eyes towards Miro.

Miro hung in the air. He was caught in the grip of the ages, and it was all he could do to hover, returning the giant's cold stare. Shaped as a mountain falcon, he was unable to speak, unable to request her help.

But the giantess didn't need such trifling things as words and questions. She was a force of nature. And she knew why she was awake.

The mountain giants roared and everything trembled. Every rock and tree, every snowflake and upland stream. Even the stars, sleeping in their daytime beds, were stirred by the call.

Miro tried not to think of the connections – tried not to think of how united the world was by that juddering, earth-shaking sound. This was *not* a good time to start changing into a boy.

As the roar faded, rippling out across the chains of mountains, across the city and the marsh, many of the soldiers turned and fled. The horses and elk panicked too. They stampeded back the way they had come, throwing off their riders.

But some of the soldiers ran towards Nedobyt. Others were already there, bearing down on the townsfolk as they tried to escape. The archers, though greatly outnumbered, were doing all they could to defend their people.

In the ravine, crossbows were fired at the giantesses. Battering rams thumped their stone feet. The mountain giants responded by stamping, triggering rockfalls, and crushing any warriors who refused to flee.

Miro had to look away. He didn't want the soldiers to die, but this was no longer in his hands, and he could not make them retreat.

His mind returned to his grandmothers and the people of Nedobyt. Had he saved them? Was he too late? Miro angled his body towards the city and, once again, he started to dive.

CHAPTER 96

Anneshka Mazanar was sitting on a big colourful bird. Imogen couldn't believe what she was seeing. How had that woman got her hands on a velecour – and a tame one too?

'The child is mine,' she snarled.

Mum lunged with her front paws, challenging Anneshka to a fight.

'No, Mum,' hissed Imogen and she scooped up the hare with both hands.

The bog troll lowered its fist. It seemed confused by this new arrival. 'WHHAAAAAAAATT ARRRRREEEEE YOUUUUUUUUUUUUU?'

Anneshka's gown was encrusted with metal sequins – or was it a kind of armour? On her head was a jewel-studded crown.

'I am your queen,' she announced and she slid from the velecour, landing with a splash. 'Ruler of everything between earth and sky, of every city and mountain, every village and marsh.'

As she waded towards the tree stump, her velecour started to change. Its beak shrank into its head, its wings withered into arms. A few seconds later, Bohoosh stood naked and shivering.

So . . . the mage had joined forces with Anneshka. And, from the looks of things, he was a competent slipskin. That must be why he'd wanted the book destroyed – to keep all the magic to himself.

The bog troll put back its head and roared, 'MMYYYYYYYYY MAAAAARRRRRSSSSSHHHHH.'

Anneshka threw a small bottle to Bohoosh. 'Kill the monster,' she commanded. 'I will take care of the child.'

Bohoosh swigged, and once again, he began to transform.

Imogen and Marie didn't stay to watch. They dashed across the tree stump, taking shelter in the only place they could: behind the heartwood throne.

Anneshka stalked up the steps. Her gown was magnificent, even drenched in marsh water. The metal sequins clinked as she moved. 'Hello, Marie,' she purred. 'Did you think you could escape?'

Marie was breathing quickly with her eyes scrunched tight, as if she could shut out Anneshka.

Imogen scanned the sky, searching for Frieda and Fred, but the velecours were gone. Her hands still gripped on to Mum.

Anneshka approached the centre of the stump. 'Or perhaps you thought I'd wander the marshes? Outstay my welcome and lose my mind?'

Imogen glanced at the edge of the tree. Could they jump off it?

Mum started thrashing about.

'I haven't come to hurt you,' said Anneshka, drawing a dagger from her belt. 'I only want the greatest kingdom. It's Nedobyt, is it not? Tell me the answer to the riddle . . . I want the truth this time.'

Anneshka will never have what she wants. Imogen remembered Ochi's words. *It will never be enough . . . If you wish to live out your lives in peace, you must stop her.*

Behind Anneshka, Mage Bohoosh had finished his transformation. He was a bull again, with horns wider than his body. His shoulders looked very strong.

The bog troll shifted its great bulk to face Bohoosh. The bull stamped his front hoof and charged.

At the same time, Anneshka lunged round the throne. The girls ran in the other direction, sprinting for the steps. But Imogen's foot slid on something slippery and, as she tried to steady herself, Mum broke free from her arms.

The golden hare galloped towards Anneshka. Rearing on to her hind legs, she boxed the woman's shins, sending sequins flying.

'What have we here?' laughed Anneshka. She leaned down and seized Mum by the ears.

'No!' gasped Imogen.

'Mum,' whispered Marie.

'Tell me which kingdom is the greatest,' cried Anneshka.

She gave Mum a shake. 'Tell me, or I'll skin your bunny.'

Imogen's world narrowed. There was no bog troll, no buvol, no marsh. There was only her mother. And that knife in Anneshka's right hand.

She wouldn't, thought Imogen. *She can't!*

Imogen took a few steps across the tree stump. Anneshka pressed the blade to the hare's throat. 'Don't you move any closer.'

Imogen froze, heart pounding. Mum's back paws scrabbled and kicked. Somewhere – it felt like it was very far away – the bog troll clashed with the bull.

'Marie,' sang Anneshka. 'I'm waiting . . .'

Marie's head was lowered in defeat. Only her lips moved, as if she was muttering a spell.

'Say something,' begged Imogen.

But her sister seemed to be somewhere else.

Imogen wondered if she was reliving the moment when Anneshka had killed the old queen. Marie had seen it all, had heard the queen's last words, and now she was about to witness the same thing happening to their mother.

Marie lifted her gaze. 'It's this one,' she said.

Anneshka wrinkled her nose.

'This kingdom is the greatest,' Marie repeated.

Imogen felt very sick. There was no way Anneshka would fall for that.

'This place is a wilderness,' snapped Anneshka. 'Do you take me for a fool?'

'There's a sertze,' said Marie. 'A big one, beneath the throne.'

Anneshka's eyes flicked towards the heartwood seat in the middle of the stump. It was resplendent with beetle wings and fungus. 'Throne?'

Marie raised her voice to be heard. 'This is the throne of Mokzhadee. The one who sits on it commands the Sertze Bahnoh and all of its power.'

No, thought Imogen, recalling Miro's story. *Those who sit on it get killed by the troll.*

Ah . . .

Was that Marie's plan?

Imogen only had a fraction of a second to marvel at her sister's cleverness. For the troll had heard Marie's words too. Panovník started lumbering towards the tree stump.

'All of its power?' said Anneshka, a smile quirking her lips.

'NOOOOOOOOOOOOOO,' bellowed the bog troll.

Imogen wanted to jump off the stump, to get out of the troll's path. But Anneshka still had hold of her mother. Anneshka raised one defiant eyebrow, took a few steps – and then sat.

CHAPTER 97

Beneath the sounds of the howling wind, the trampling mountains and the breaking of stone, Miro could hear people screaming.

The sound tore at his chest as, in falcon form, he hurtled towards the valley.

The archers of Nedobyt had climbed down from their cliffs and formed a line, near the ravine entrance. In one synchronised movement, they pulled back their bow strings and rained arrows on the attackers.

Miro had to swerve to avoid getting caught in their fire.

At the heart of the common, a row of cavalry and elk-riders were charging at unarmed townsfolk. A man with a sharp beard led the assault, sitting on the most enormous war elk. And Miro knew that *this* was the army's chief.

Among the townsfolk were Miro's grandmothers. They were shouting at the warriors, trying to make them stop. But the riders paid no attention. They cut people down as they ran.

Fly swift, fly swift . . .

Miro flew faster as swords collided with flesh. His grandmothers were backing away, clutching each other's hands. The army chief galloped towards the queens and Miro pulled in his wings.

Air splitting,

talons reaching,

fly swift, fly swift.

The chief raised his sword above Olga's head.

Miro's beak was an arrow,

and, as the sword fell,

Miro attacked,

claws ripping the rider's face.

The army chief fell from his saddle and the elk swerved. The man was a lump on the ground. Miro crash-landed beside him and this time it hurt. Pain shot up one of his wings.

The man grabbed his sword and got to his feet. He was breathing heavily and blood poured from the cuts that Miro had made.

'I am Samo Boyovník,' said the warrior, directing his fierce gaze at Miro. 'Know me and die.'

Miro tried to lift his wings and found that he couldn't. His left wing was bent at a sickening angle. It dragged on the ground as he tried to flee.

Miro needed to change back into a human. He reached into his memory, into the marshes, tried to remember what it was like to connect . . .

But he was too tired, in too much pain, and Samo was almost upon him.

'Miroslav,' cried Granny Nela, and Miro reached for her with his unbroken wing. He couldn't fly. Could hardly walk.

Again, Samo raised his sword. Blood was glooping from the cuts on his pale face. His eyes were wide and he roared as he swung back the blade.

Then Samo was hit by a wild thing. A tornado with claws and teeth. People nearby were shrieking and Miro wasn't sure if it was the townsfolk or the soldiers.

Samo fell and Miro realised that the thing fighting him was a snĕehoolark. Not just any snĕehoolark – it was Konya!

Miro twisted his neck and saw that there were more giant cats entering the valley. They threw themselves at the soldiers, snarling. Some of them were even bigger than Konya, with scars on their faces and bristling fur. Miro almost fainted with relief.

The wild snĕehoolarks had come.

The sight of the giant cats was enough to make some of the cavalry and elk-riders retreat. But many stayed to fight. A tall woman was battling with an axe in each hand. The cats circled her. The woman screamed a war cry and attacked.

Miro's grandmothers were shouting at the townsfolk, telling them to run. Some of them did just that. Others joined the fight, arming themselves with things they'd packed for their journey – walking canes and blunt kitchen knives.

There was much yelling and yowling and blood. Miro

screeched as a sword plunged into a sněehoolark. Another cat seized the aggressor by the neck, shaking him until he went still.

Among the chaos, Miro thought he saw a man armoured in books. They were strapped all over his body, covers flapping as he swung his sword.

The man turned and Miro realised it was Otakar, the Grand Librarian. In one hand, he held a blade. In the other, he grasped a hardback, which he was using to knock people out.

Fingers grasped Miro and he was about to defend himself, when a familiar voice said, 'It's only me, Miroslav.'

Granny Nela! She lifted him up.

The sněehoolarks were furious fighters. But even they couldn't all escape death. There were three giant cat bodies on the ground, alongside the bodies of soldiers and the citizens of Nedobyt.

Miro wanted to make it stop.

Behind the warring people and sněehoolarks were the mountain giants. They were closing the ravine with their colossal bodies, forcing hundreds of soldiers to flee.

Then Miro caught sight of Samo, crouched low and brandishing his sword. He was circling Konya. She was circling him back. Samo's movements were liquid, each footstep part of a dance.

Miro flapped in Granny Nela's hands, but it was no use. His wing was injured and he was too exhausted to escape from her grip. *Konya*, he screamed in his head.

Samo lunged at the sněehoolark, narrowly missing her chest. Miro's heart was fluttering fast.

But the sněehoolark showed no fear. She lashed out, tail swishing. The next time Samo attacked, he caught her hind leg and Konya yowled.

Konya – no!

Miro scrabbled to be free, but it was no use. The pain in his wing was too much. A group of riderless horses galloped in front of him, blocking his view, and Granny Nela backed away.

CHAPTER 98

Imogen and Marie crouched low on the tree stump, trying to shield their heads. Anneshka was sitting on the heartwood throne and the bog troll was coming to get her.

Panovník's footsteps rattled through Imogen; its bellow filled her brain and there was only one thought that cut through. *Has Anneshka let go of my mum?*

Imogen scrunched her body, bracing for the troll's impact . . .

But it didn't come.

Panovník fell, as if its hamstrings had been cut. 'Look!' cried Imogen, nudging Marie.

The bog troll folded into the marshes, clumps of mud sliding from its back. 'MYYYYYYYYY THHRRRRROO-OOOOONE,' it howled.

'It's working!' shrieked Anneshka. 'I can feel the sertze's power! This is my destiny!' She still held Mum and the knife.

'Uh-oh,' whispered Imogen. She knew something bad had just happened. She knew that this was bigger than her or Marie.

But the same thought kept on repeating: *How can I make Anneshka let go of Mum?*

The hare thrashed, trying to break free.

'I will bend the world to my will,' bellowed Anneshka, and she spoke with many voices; a multiplying of her power.

From within the tree stump came a sludgy-green light. It lit up the jewelled beetles in the throne's armrests. It illuminated the mushrooms that framed the seat. It gushed from cracks in the wood.

And Imogen realised – although she didn't fully understand – that something was happening with the Sertze Bahnoh, the stone buried deep in the stump. Sitting on the throne had triggered it.

Imogen tried to run at Anneshka and found that she couldn't. It was as if the air around the throne had gone thick. But Imogen *had* to save her mother. It couldn't end like this.

So she tried the only thing she hadn't tried yet. She threw herself on to her knees and pressed her hands against the stump.

'Ochi,' she screamed, 'I know you can hear me. You promised to help! Help us now!'

'There is only one ruler of Mokzhadeeeeee,' roared Anneshka. And now she was filled with light too. Her whole face glowed algae green.

The troll dragged itself up the steps. Most of its body had

fallen into the marsh. It was smaller, much smaller, and it moved as if crawling through sand, while reaching towards its throne.

Anneshka held Mum up with one hand. In her other, the knife glinted. Mum struggled and squealed. 'And now,' roared Anneshka, 'you will see what happens to those who stand against me.'

'No!' screamed Marie.

But over the cry of her sister, over the churning of the marsh, Imogen heard a cackle. It echoed across the pale sky. At first, she thought the laugh came from Anneshka. Then an eye opened in the wood by her hand.

'Ochi?' Imogen whispered.

The eye winked.

More eyeballs appeared on the tree stump. There were hundreds, in all shapes and sizes. They popped open, swivelling in their sockets. They clustered around the green shining throne.

Anneshka screamed and jumped to her feet. She started stamping on the eyeballs, golden hare flailing in her grip.

A root rose from the marshes, and Imogen grabbed her sister. They held each other tight.

'W-w-what's happening?' shouted Marie.

Imogen wasn't sure.

Did that root belong to the stump? Was the 'dead' tree still connected to Ochi's underground web?

The root snaked across the tree stump and seized Anneshka

by the throat. She hacked at it with her dagger, but the roots were very old and thick.

'Release the hare,' shouted Imogen.

Anneshka's hand unclenched and Mum scrabbled free. Marie scooped her up.

'Drop the dagger,' commanded Imogen, and Anneshka did that too.

She let out a gargle of defiance, half-choked by the root round her neck. More roots wrapped about her legs and her body, dragging her backwards, forcing her to sit.

'It's okay, Ochi,' shouted Imogen. 'You can stop now.'

But the laughter still resounded across the sky. And the stump's roots did not retreat. As Anneshka was held on the heartwood throne, she was filled again with green light.

The bog troll lay still, not far from the seat. It was now the shape and size of a man – albeit a man dressed in weeds. Stems and leaves twitched off his body. A grass snake squirmed free from his back.

There seemed to be some kind of exchange occurring; a switch between Anneshka and the troll. Anneshka was trying to stop it, was scrabbling to get off the throne, but the roots bound her fast.

'No,' she shrieked. 'Noooo! MARIE, HELP MEEEEEE!'

Marie looked horror-struck, but there was nothing she could do to save her old enemy.

Weeds and mud crept towards Anneshka. They plastered her arms – shoulders – neck – burying the human, hiding the flesh.

Imogen felt a twinge of pity when she saw the fear in Anneshka's eyes. 'What's happening to her?' whimpered Marie.

White flowers sprouted from Anneshka's head. They grew in a circle, meeting at the front like a crown.

'MYYYYYY MAAAAARRSSSSHHH,' growled Anneshka.

The light of the Sertze Bahnoh faded. It was over. It had made its new queen. The roots binding her relaxed, before slithering back into the water, tucking themselves out of sight.

Finally, Anneshka stood. The only parts of her that weren't coated in marsh-stuff were her bright violet eyes.

She lurched across the tree stump.

Imogen and Marie shrank as she passed, keeping Mum tucked between them.

But Anneshka didn't notice the sisters. It was as though she'd been put into a trance. She clambered down the steps with stiff mud-caked limbs and, without so much as a backwards glance, she started to walk away.

A shellfish wriggled out of the marshes, scaled Anneshka's leg and latched on to her shoulder.

Grassy knolls shifted . . .

Birds sang from the reeds . . .

And the wetland saluted its queen.

'All hail, Anneshka Mazanar,' whispered Imogen. 'Ruler of Mokzhadee.'

CHAPTER 99

'Is Anneshka a bog troll?' asked Marie.

Anneshka was small now, a distant figure heading towards the horizon. Soon, she would be indistinguishable from the enormity of the marsh.

'I suppose . . .' There was a wobble in Imogen's throat, a ringing in her ears.

After all of the noise and the fighting, all of the shouting and fear, the marshes were so very peaceful. As if nothing had happened.

One clue that this was not true was Bohoosh, who was still shaped like a bull. He was slumped, motionless in the marsh. He must have been killed by the troll.

Imogen tried to adjust her position so she blocked the sight from Marie. The last thing her sister needed was to see a dead body.

But as reality dawned on her, she realised she didn't feel so brilliant herself. She had to fight hard to steady her breathing. There was no reason to panic, not now Anneshka was gone.

They had the Maiden's Kiss lichen. That was a good thing. Marie and Mum were safe. That was good too. But they were stuck on the Marshes of Mokzhadee, with no quick route off. That was bad – very bad.

The hare nestled against Imogen and she ran her fingers through the animal's fur. How she longed for it to be *her* hair that was being smoothed, how she longed to hear her mother's voice.

Human Mum could always find some words of comfort . . .

Marie wrapped her arms around Imogen, and it helped. For a moment, they stayed entwined.

Then shocked tears started running down Imogen's face. Marie was crying too.

'I really thought she'd kill Mum,' sobbed Marie. 'I thought it'd be like in Valkahá when Anneshka and Surovetz cut the queen's throat. Bad things just keep happening . . . I can see it in my head, Imogen. The old queen keeps on dying. It's echoing on and on.'

'It's okay,' whispered Imogen. 'It's not – it's not happening now. Mum's safe. Anneshka has gone and you – you were amazing! How did you get the idea to say all that stuff about the sertze?'

Marie pulled back. Her eyes were pink-rimmed, but her mouth showed the very start of a smile. 'It was my destiny,' she said. 'I didn't have any choice . . . I had to lead Anneshka to the greatest kingdom.'

Imogen gazed at the surrounding marshland. This place

did have the most powerful sertze – it *was* rich in life. But a nation of wading birds and marshfish was certainly not what Anneshka had in mind.

'I used Anneshka's trick,' said Marie, and her smile spread to her eyes. 'I told you about it before . . . remember? Find out what people want. Make them think you have it.'

The golden hare lifted her ears. Even though Mum could no longer speak human, she seemed to be listening.

'I knew that Anneshka wanted more power,' Marie continued, 'and I knew the troll protected the throne. I thought that, perhaps, they would fight for it. I didn't know Anneshka would—' Marie glanced at the horizon, lower lip trembling. 'I feel a bit sorry for her . . . Is that weird?'

Imogen shook her head. She had no idea what 'weird' meant any more.

Marie sniffed and wiped her nose. 'But if Anneshka's a bog troll,' she said, 'then what exactly is that?' She pointed at a man who was sprawled on his back, on the other side of the tree stump.

Imogen got a start when she saw him. She'd forgotten about Panovník.

The girls crawled closer, with Mum hopping at their heels.

So, this was the core of a bog troll? When you shed all the things that built up over time, when you stripped off the mud and the reeds . . . this was what you had left?

A soft creature – furless – without shell or claws.

It was a human. He was white-skinned and narrow-faced,

with a line between his eyebrows. His dark hair was streaked with grey.

Marie gave him a prod. 'Excuse me?'

The man's eyes snapped open.

Both sisters screamed and Mum leaped into the air.

'I remember,' he rasped through cracked lips.

Imogen leaned in. 'Remember what?' The man did not smell good, but she wanted to hear and his voice was very quiet.

'For so long, I'd forgotten . . .'

Mum and Marie leaned in too.

'I am not Panovník the bog troll. I am Radko the Conqueror . . . I remember . . .'

Imogen met Marie's gaze. Radko was the man from the story; the ancient king whose empire had spanned half the world. He'd sent all his soldiers to their deaths. Then, when his army was destroyed, he had fled.

Everyone thought he had perished . . .

That's what the old story said.

Imogen looked back at the man. He must have been kept alive by the marshes and the Sertze Bahnoh, preserved and trapped as a troll, until he lost all memory of being human.

She was staring at a face that was thousands of years old. Yet he didn't look much older than Mark.

Mark . . . was he still alive? Preserved by the hospital machines?

Radko drew a rattling breath. 'I came here after a battle . . .

I wandered and got lost . . . I saw the throne on the tree stump.'

Imogen could guess what happened next. 'You sat on it, didn't you?' she said.

'Let it be known,' breathed Radko. His voice was barely a whisper – a breeze running through hollow reeds. 'You cannot conquer the marshes . . . cannot own these lands . . . for this place is living. This place owns you.'

Mum lifted a paw to his cheek and the man seemed to look beyond the clouds.

With a slow release of breath, Radko the Conqueror was free.

CHAPTER 100

With a final burst of strength that he didn't know he possessed, Miro broke free from his grandmother's grip.

'Miroslav!' cried Granny Nela. 'No! It isn't safe!'

But Miro-the-falcon scrambled across the grass, towards Konya.

The last of the riderless horses stampeded across the battlefield and Miro saw he was too late. The fight between Samo and Konya was over.

Samo lay on his back, bloodied . . . and dead.

Konya stood over him, panting.

Miro screeched and Konya turned her head towards him. Her eyes were lit by a savage energy and, for a moment, Miro was afraid.

Konya?

The snĕehoolark blinked and the bloodlust cleared from her eyes. She limped towards Miro and licked his feathered face.

Miro was almost knocked backwards by the force of

her greeting but he was glad – so glad – that she was alive.

When Konya was done licking, Miro noticed a glint of silver in the grass. It lay next to Samo's body, as if it had tumbled out of his pocket.

Miro shuffled closer, injured wing stinging, and Konya followed too.

Together, they peered down at the silver thing. It was a crumpled lump of metal on a very fine chain. Samo must have fallen on it.

It looked a little like a crushed insect. One of its antennae had snapped off and its wings were bent at awkward angles.

But it wasn't a living creature . . . Only an ornament.

Granny Nela and Grandmother Olga approached their grandson. 'The worst is over,' Olga said. Miro looked around and saw she was right.

The vast majority of the townsfolk had escaped from the soldiers. The sněehoolarks had seen to that. And, while many of the giant cats were injured, very few were dead. The remaining sněehoolarks were resting and licking their wounds.

Grand Librarian Otakar was with them. He was injured, although he seemed to be in good spirits.

Further away were the gold-clad archers. They had removed their helmets, but they were still on watch, guarding the enemy soldiers who'd been wise enough to surrender.

Yet too many had died for Miro to feel relieved. He wished

he had been able to stop the army sooner. He hung his head, overwhelmed.

'We must arrange funerals for these people,' said Grandmother Olga. 'And the snĕehoolarks too. Nedobyt has suffered a great loss.'

Granny Nela scooped up Miro, being careful not to touch his damaged wing. 'If you hadn't woken the mountains, we would all be dead,' she whispered. 'Don't you forget it, Miroslav.'

'It's true,' said Grandmother Olga. 'You did well. Very well indeed.'

Miro lifted his head. If he had been human, he would have said something – or perhaps, returned the embrace.

Beside the ravine, the mountain giants were going back to their original positions. They folded their immense limbs beneath their bodies, gathering trees round their feet. For a long time, Miro, his grandmothers, and the people of Nedobyt stood and watched.

When the last giant had made herself comfortable, she let out a long breath that came out as a breeze. Songbirds settled on her slopes and waterfalls tumbled down her back. With all of the wild snĕehoolarks and the folk of Nedobyt gazing on, the mountain giants returned to their sleep.

CHAPTER 101

Two girls roamed the marshes. They jumped between grassy mounds. They'd left behind a dead warlord, a dead mage and a throne.

The tallest girl had short hair and smudges of freckles that ran across her pale cheeks like warpaint. Tied to her belt was a purse with a very rare lichen inside. Her name was Imogen.

The smallest girl had pinkish skin and wild red hair. Sometimes she hummed as she wandered. Sometimes she was quiet. Her name was Marie.

A hare hopped beside the sisters. It had golden fur, a white belly and black-tipped ears.

On the first day of walking, the girls fixed their eyes on the mountains. Imogen knew that if they kept going in that direction, eventually they'd reach the edge of the marsh.

They drank bog water when they were thirsty. They had no means of catching the fish.

At night, when the midges came swarming, the girls crawled under spiderwebs. A boy had once told them that the webs offered protection, although Imogen wasn't sure who the boy had been.

On the second day of walking, Imogen grew very hungry. She'd give anything for a bar of chocolate. She'd even eat a pack of nuts. But there was neither option on the marshes.

Instead, she picked a flower and stuffed it into her mouth. It tasted funny so she spat it back out. If only she could eat grass, like the hare did.

After three days, both girls were weak. 'Perhaps we should have stayed at the tree stump,' said Marie.

'No good now,' muttered Imogen, surveying her surroundings. There were little islands in every direction and she couldn't see beyond them. Hunger was turning her vision soft.

'Where are we walking to anyway?' asked Marie.

Imogen's mind showed her the inside of a hospital. There was a man lying on a bed. He had tubes going into his body, and there were bleepy machines and flashing lights. The man was very sick . . . but Imogen couldn't remember what was wrong. All she knew was she had to reach him.

'I think we're going to hospital,' she murmured, crawling up the side of an islet. She planned to lie there, just for a moment, just while she gathered her strength.

Marie came and lay next to her. The golden hare too. It clambered on to Imogen's chest, sharing its soft furry heat. Imogen could hear Marie breathe in and out, in and out . . .

'We have to remember,' Marie whispered.

'Remember what?'

'Who we are.'

Imogen looked up at the wispy cloud sky. 'How are we supposed to do that?'

'Tell each other stories,' said Marie. 'Shall we try?' She didn't wait for an answer. 'Do you remember when Mum used to read to us? We'd climb into her bed and listen until we were sleepy.'

Imogen thought she could remember being inside a burrow. There had been fairy lights and stacks of books. And, nestled between the sisters, there'd been a huge talking hare.

'Now it's your turn,' said Marie.

Imogen sucked in her cheeks. There was a gnawing pain in her belly. She'd never been this hungry. Not even when she forgot her lunchbox. Not even when she was poorly and kept being sick – ah, yes, there was a memory.

'Once I had a virus and Mum came to collect me from school,' said Imogen. 'She made me something special to eat . . . I think it was chicken soup. Mum was a really good cook.'

'She was,' Marie agreed. 'What happened to her?'

The golden hare lifted her head.

'I think she's probably at work,' said Imogen. 'Don't worry, she'll be home this evening . . . I'm in charge until then.'

Imogen smiled because thinking of Mum made her happy. Exhausted, she closed her eyes. The sun wasn't strong, but it did give some heat. And then, with a smile still lingering, Imogen fell asleep.

CHAPTER 102

Miro flew over the marshes on the back of a tame velecour. He scanned the grassy islands. *There* was a forest of woolgrass. *There* was a herd of buvol.

But there was no sign of Marie or Imogen.

Soon after the battle, Zuby had returned to Nedobyt. He'd been dragged there by Fred and Frieda. The poor skret had been in quite a state. He'd explained what had happened on the marshes. He didn't know the girls' fate.

Miro had wanted to go straight off to find them, but his grandmothers said it wasn't allowed. They forced him to have some food and water, to get a few hours of sleep, and to have his injured arm bandaged before he was permitted to leave.

Then Miro took off, riding Frieda, with Fred tethered at his side.

In some ways, the search would have been easier as a falcon – his eyes were much sharper in that form. But falcons cannot fly with one wing bandaged, nor ride velecours.

Every evening, Miro returned to Nedobyt, exhausted in body and in mind. He didn't dare spend a night on the marshes, in case he forgot why he was there.

Every morning, he set off before dawn.

On the third day of searching, when the sun hung low, Miro saw a flock of wading birds. They took off from the reedbeds with a flicker of white feathers.

Something must have disturbed them, thought Miro, and he steered the velecours closer.

When the wading birds cleared, he saw two figures on an islet, shouting and waving their arms.

'Hello! We're down here!' shouted Imogen.

Marie was beside her, jumping on the spot. The golden hare was thumping her back legs – her contribution to making some noise.

Miro's heart lifted at the sight of them. Still holding the reins, he waved back.

The velecours splashed on to the marshes and Imogen saw a boy dismount. In one hand he clutched the birds' leashes. The other arm was in some kind of sling.

He had far-apart eyes, dark olive skin and a mop of curly brown hair. Imogen liked his face the instant she saw it. She hoped that, one day, they could be friends.

But the boy already seemed to know who they were. 'Imogen, Marie, I found you!' he cried. He waded towards them, and the velecours toddled in his wake.

Imogen didn't know what was happening – not really – not any more – but she had the distinct feeling that they were being rescued and she was very, very glad.

CHAPTER 103

Imogen woke up. The sky was bright above her and, for a moment, she thought she was outside. Her limbs felt very stiff, as if she'd walked a very long way.

Where was she? How long had she been asleep?

She rubbed her eyes and looked again. There was glass between her and the clouds. And she was lying on a big comfy bed.

Memories came rolling towards her with an unstoppable force.

Days spent walking on the marshes . . .

Anneshka turning into a troll . . .

Hunting for Maiden's Kiss, the only known cure for Mark . . .

Imogen reached for the purse. That was where she'd put the lichen. But the purse and belt were no longer at her waist. 'The lichen!' she gasped, sitting upright.

'It's okay, Imogen, I've got it,' said a voice.

It belonged to a woman. She was sitting on a chair and she looked like she'd been reading, but she'd glanced up when Imogen spoke.

Imogen recognised the woman. She knew her hair and her eyes and her mouth. But her brain couldn't fit it together, couldn't summon the name.

It was only when the woman scratched her ear, in the way that a rabbit might do, that it all clicked into place. 'Mum?'

Mum stood up, not bothering to stop her book from falling off her lap.

They ran to each other. 'Mum, you're *you!*'

Mum smoothed Imogen's hair and planted kisses on her head. 'Your friend Miro read out the spell,' she whispered.

'Where are we?' said Marie's voice, and Imogen turned to see her sister, propped up in the bed. Marie's hair stuck out at funny angles, as if she'd been electrocuted. But, other than that, she looked okay.

When Marie saw Mum, she hopped out of bed. There was much hugging and squeezing and laughter.

'Where's Miro?' asked Imogen.

'He's been very busy,' said Mum. 'He turned himself into a falcon and managed to close the ravine, saving the people of Nedobyt. Then he changed into a boy again, without even needing a spell.'

Miro is a real slipskin, thought Imogen. She would never have guessed that the young prince she'd first met in Yaroslav, who lived all alone in his tower and who didn't know how to make friends, would turn out to be a magician.

There was a tray at the girls' bedside, with stuffed dates

and hot tea. Mum took the crystal teapot and poured the girls a drink each. 'Here,' she said. 'You must be starving.'

Neither sister needed telling twice. They ate dates stuffed with nuts and honey, dates stuffed with herby soft cheese, and they slurped the warm tea, not stopping until everything had gone.

'I'd better let the others know you're awake,' said Mum, and she popped out through the chamber door.

Imogen took in her surroundings – properly this time. Above her was a domed glass ceiling. There were glass lamps around the room, balanced on elegant furniture. They must be inside one of the palaces.

'How is Konya?' asked Marie, when Mum returned. 'Did Miro fix her too?'

'Yes, she's a sněehoolark . . . She's quite intimidating like that.'

'She was quite intimidating as a woman,' said Imogen. 'What about Kazimira?'

Mum's smile faded. 'I'm afraid the spell didn't work for her.'

They were quiet for a while, all sitting on the edge of the bed. Imogen wondered what was wrong with the princess. She couldn't imagine that King Ctibor would be happy to have his daughter returned as a frog.

'What was it like being a hare?' asked Marie.

Mum scrunched her forehead. 'I feel much more like myself as a human,' she said. 'There were moments, when I was a hare – it was like I had another self – and that self was taking over. The only thing that stopped me from letting it happen was seeing you two girls. I knew I had to stay with you and do what I could to keep you safe.'

'And how do you feel now?' asked Imogen.

'I feel like my old self,' said Mum. 'That is, I feel human again. I'm not sure, if I'm entirely honest, that I'll ever be quite the same. Some experiences . . . they change you.'

Imogen felt a bit sad, hearing that.

Mum must have noticed the shift in her expression. 'Not necessarily in a bad way,' Mum added. 'These events make us who we are. Just as I'm sure all your adventures have shaped and reshaped you.'

Marie folded her legs beneath her, so she was scrunched up small on the bed. 'What if we don't like how we've changed?' she whispered. 'What if we want to change back?'

At first, Imogen didn't understand her sister. Then she remembered what she'd said on the marsh:

I can see it in my head, Imogen . . . The old queen keeps on dying. It's echoing on and on.

Mum looked at Marie – really looked. 'You have been through a lot, my darling. But no feeling lasts forever . . . I promise that. What is it you're worried about?'

'The old Queen of Valkahá,' said Marie, voice cracking. 'I keep seeing her . . . keep seeing her die. And I didn't stop Anneshka from doing it. I just stood there . . .'

Mum hesitated, mouth forming silent words. Finally, she

seemed to settle on one. 'Marie,' she said. 'It wasn't your fault. Sometimes bad things *just happen*, and they're nothing to do with you. You can't . . . you can't always stop them. In fact, it's often dangerous to try.'

Marie stared at the bed. 'But I want to stop thinking about it.'

'Talking it through might help,' Mum suggested. 'You can always chat to me, you know . . . and perhaps, if you'd like, we could talk to a therapist?'

Marie gave the world's smallest nod.

Talking to Mum seems a lot easier, thought Imogen, *now that she listens and believes what we say.*

Their conversation was interrupted by a loud squawk. And who should come running into the chamber but Frieda and Fred.

The velecours launched themselves at the bed. They were far too big for it, almost fully grown, but Mum did not try to stop them.

Frieda rubbed her long neck against Imogen. Fred settled down between the girls, squawking to himself.

'Hello?' said a voice at the door. Imogen looked up to see Miro, his hair so long it almost hid his eyes.

'Miro!' cried Marie. The sisters sprang off the bed and ran to greet their friend.

CHAPTER 104

A sense of joy settled on Nedobyt, warm and bright as the sun. From archers and monks to musicians and glaziers, everyone was happy to be alive.

Anneshka had underestimated the Nameless Mountains and the magic of Nedobyt. She had also underestimated the desire of its people to be free.

And now everyone knew the truth about Bohoosh, the city would not be the same. He'd exiled or killed the other slipskins, and hidden the tools for new ones to train.

He'd kept the Royal Palace from its citizens too. It was Bohoosh who'd enchanted the garden.

After he died, the orchids disappeared. In their place stood hundreds of people – folk who'd dared to seek answers from the mage. Now, they poured out of the garden, stretching their renewed arms and legs.

Some of the people of Nedobyt wondered how Bohoosh had fooled them for so long. Had he cast a spell on the whole valley? Queen Olga and Queen Nela did not think so . . .

Bohoosh had spent so long partying and showing how

useless he could be that many people had believed him to be harmless. *Oh, he can't be plotting anything terrible*, they thought, *he can't even brush his own hair.*

But there was nothing harmless about him.

Miro thought of how Bohoosh had pretended that his magic was too weak to pour tea. And all that time he'd been keeping hundreds of people trapped as mountain flowers.

Miro remembered how the mage had said that he was 'no slipskin'. Meanwhile, he'd been hoarding the magic for himself. His lack of competence had been a distraction.

'There is nothing more dangerous,' said Granny Nela, 'than a ridiculous ruler.'

That evening, there was a celebration in Nedobyt. It was held in the library. It was not only a celebration of the kingdom's victory, but of the library's grand opening.

Otakar welcomed people into the building, dressed in his fanciest robes. The books had not yet been sorted, but that was all right. The library doors were left open, the marsh-gas lamps turned up full.

Everyone was allowed to explore the cabinets, taking out and flicking through books.

'Does touching the parchment damage it?' asked a visitor.

'Oh, never mind that,' said Otakar. 'Would you like to borrow a book?'

It wasn't long before someone started playing music on an old guitar with many strings. Some of the people began dancing. Others pressed against the edge of the room, backs against bookcases, laughing and passing round drinks.

Miro helped himself to nibbles, occasionally giving a treat to the frog who was perched on his shoulder. His grandmothers were busy speaking with people, answering their many questions.

Zuby was also at the party, and he joined in with the dance. A cloud of moths twirled above him, following their keeper round the room.

Even the insects are celebrating, thought Miro as he nibbled a goat's cheese tartlet.

'Excuse me,' said a voice from nearby. 'But are you Miroslav Sokol?'

Miro glanced down to see a small boy. 'Erm, yes. Yes, I am.'

The boy sucked on his lower lip, apparently fighting to get his question out. 'Is it true that you are a slipskin? Can I be a slipskin too?'

Miro recalled the feel of the wind beneath his feathers, the hollow lightness of his bones . . .

'Of course,' he said to the younger child. 'I will show you how.'

CHAPTER 105

Imogen, Marie and their mother stood at the library entrance. They were already in their travelling clothes: fleece-lined tunics and wool trousers, warm hats and furry boots.

Fred and Frieda were waiting in the park, hundreds of metres below. They were saddled and ready to carry the girls and their mother home.

'I'm afraid we can't stay long,' said Mum. 'It's time to say your goodbyes.'

Although it made her sad, Imogen understood. They had to get back to Mark. Every moment they lingered could mean they arrived too late.

Since her time on the marsh, her memories of Mark seemed more vivid. It made her even more anxious to get back – to give him the cure that they'd found.

Imogen stepped into the library, with Mum and Marie at her heels. Together, they followed the sound of music through the dusty rooms.

There were people talking and studying books. One little

girl carried a stack of hardbacks that was almost as tall as herself.

As the party noises grew louder, Imogen heard a rhythmic stomping and scuffing of feet. Dancing. There was dancing in the library!

When she entered the biggest room, she saw a mass of people, skipping and swinging round. The marsh-gas lamps burned bright as fallen stars, illuminating the dancers' faces and the rows of books that lined the walls.

Queen Olga and Queen Nela were at the far end of the room, surrounded by a crowd. The old ladies' dresses were beautiful, tied at the waists with gold bands. 'I'll go and thank Miro's grandmas,' said Mum, hurrying to join the queue.

Marie dashed off to find Zuby, who was in the centre of the dance. The moths fluttering above his head made the skret easy to locate, even among all the bodies.

At first, Imogen didn't spot Miro, tucked in the corner as he was. He wasn't alone – quite the opposite. A group of children had gathered round.

Imogen made her way over. 'Hello,' she said, feeling shy, although she wasn't sure why.

Miro grinned. 'Ah, Imogen! I was wondering when you would arrive.' He turned to the little gathering. 'I'm sorry, I have to talk with my friend.'

There were groans and sighs from the other children, but, with a little encouragement, they dispersed.

'Is Kazimira staying with you?' asked Imogen, noticing the frog on Miro's shoulder.

'Peep, peep!' said the amphibian.

'Not for long,' Miro replied. 'We received word from King Ctibor. He's coming to pick her up . . . I didn't mention that she's a frog in my letter. I couldn't find the right words.'

Imogen didn't think Ctibor would take the news well. 'Why didn't the spell work for Kazimira?' she asked. 'It worked for Konya and Mum . . .'

'I'm not entirely sure,' said Miro. 'But I've been reading the slipskin book and I do have a theory.'

He took Kazimira off his shoulder and held her at arm's length, so she wouldn't hear what he was about to say. Then he whispered into Imogen's ear: 'To change back, you have to sense the connections between you and the rest of the world. The spell helps people do this. But not Kazimira, it seems. I don't think she's ready . . . not yet.'

Imogen lowered her voice too. 'She still thinks she's above everyone else?'

Miro shrugged. 'It's just a theory.'

'Peeeeep!' said the frog.

'Poor Kazimira,' whispered Imogen. 'Hopefully, she'll understand soon.'

The dancing in the library was growing wilder, with more people joining in. Otakar was skipping down the middle, swinging his beard above his head.

'Do you think *you'll* stay in Nedobyt?' asked Imogen.

Miro nodded and his curly hair bounced. 'It feels good to be here. Next, I want to find my uncle and my mother's cousins. Bohoosh turned them into animals too.'

'Are you sure you won't miss Yaroslav?'

'No . . . I am not sure.' Miro glanced at his grandmothers, who were talking to Imogen's mum. 'But Nedobyt feels like my home.'

A plate of syrup-dipped figs was being passed round the room. Imogen and Miro both took one. The fig burst with sweetness in Imogen's mouth.

'I'm happy that you're happy,' she said, words thick with sugar. 'Will you help your grandmothers rule?'

Miro licked his fingers before replying. 'No. I'm renouncing my royal titles . . . I wish to train as a slipskin mage.'

Imogen was surprised to hear that. She'd never really imagined that Miro would become anything other than a king. If she was totally honest, when they'd first met, she didn't think he'd be a very good one. But Miro had changed a lot since then.

'I'm sure your parents would be proud, Miro.'

He gave her a secret smile.

'What about you?' he asked. 'Can't you stay a little longer? At least until the party's over?'

Imogen wished that the answer was 'yes'. She would love to spend more time with her friend. But she couldn't forget about her stepdad.

'We can't,' she said. 'Mark needs us. We have to get the

lichen to him.' Just saying the words out loud made her want to begin the journey right away.

Miro looked a little disappointed, but he took the news well enough. 'You two always appear just when I need you,' he said. 'And then you're gone again.'

'Perhaps we're lucky charms,' joked Imogen.

Miro met her gaze. 'No. It's more than that . . . You're my best friends.'

Imogen shifted, awkward. She didn't like it when things went serious. 'You're my best friend too,' she mumbled.

'Little humans,' called Zuby, careering towards them. 'I have something for you.' Marie was with him; her face bright red and beaming. She must have been dancing as well.

The skret hurried away from the cluster of people, followed by a blizzard of moths. Imogen, Marie and Miro trailed after him, into a quieter room.

When they were all standing together, Zuby turned his orb-shaped eyes on the sisters. 'I hear that you plan to return home this evening, back through the door in the tree. Well, I've been talking to someone and, it seems, they are willing to help.'

Down from the whirl of insects flew a silver-grey moth. It wavered about Zuby's bald head, before landing on his outstretched hand.

'The shadow moth!' cried Marie.

Imogen couldn't believe it. With all that had been going on, she hadn't thought about how they'd find the door in the tree – how they'd make it open without the mechanical moth.

She was *very* glad to see her old friend, the Mezi Můra. 'Thank you, Zuby!' she cried. 'Thank you, shadow moth!'

Zuby held the insect a little higher. 'Fly with courage and speed and the will of the stars. May you show them a way to a kingdom that's theirs.'

The moth opened and closed its wings to show it was thinking. Its antennae were shaped like feathers, and it had a soft velvety body.

'Girls?' came Mum's voice from the doorway. 'Girls, it's time to go.'

CHAPTER 106

Imogen and Marie flew over the marshes, sitting on Frieda's back. The velecour's wings beat steadily, soaring on currents of air.

Imogen turned to see Mum and Fred flying beside them, silhouetted against the full moon. The stars twinkled all around, keeping them company.

The shadow moth fluttered ahead of the velecours, leading the way to the door in the tree. Its darting flight might have looked haphazard, but it knew where it must go.

As they travelled away from the Nameless Mountains, Imogen thought of her best friend. For a reason that she couldn't quite name, she felt sure he'd be okay.

'Look at the marshes,' called Mum.

Imogen and Marie both peered down. The moon and the stars were reflected in the water, creating a doubling of light. Most of the animals were quiet now. The breeze blew waves through the reeds so the marsh seemed to whisper and sigh.

It was beautiful. *Truly beautiful.*

Yet Imogen was glad they were travelling at altitude.

Even from this height, she could see that the midges were about.

To the west, the Long Road was visible, stretching out like a long brown snake. On it, Imogen spotted a familiar shape. She couldn't resist. She steered Frieda closer.

'It's Konya!' cried Marie, pointing. 'Hey, Konya! We're up here!'

The snĕehoolark stopped running and looked up. Then she threw back her head and yowled. It was an eerie sound – somewhere between a howl and a miaow.

Imogen and Marie howled back, their cries echoing across the night.

'Good luck, Konya!' called Marie, and Frieda swooped higher, leaving the snĕehoolark behind.

'She must be on her way to see Perla,' said Imogen, 'back to the Lowlands again.'

By the time they sailed over that kingdom, Imogen was cold and tired. The shadow moth must have been tired too, but it didn't hesitate. It led them above meandering rivers, sloping hills and quiet villages.

Imogen was relieved when she saw the outline of the Twin Brothers, black against the deep blue of the sky. She knew that once they passed that way, the end of their journey was close.

The moth and the velecours soared between the mountains, and Yaroslav came into view. The city seemed to be sleeping, with very few lights visible.

Imogen's pulse quickened at the sight of it. She'd had many adventures in Yaroslav, and part of her would always want to be there, always want to return.

Around the city, were the Kolsaney Forests. Most of the leaves seemed to have fallen, which made Imogen wonder how long they'd been away.

The moth dropped down through the treetops.

Frieda and Fred swooped after it, extending their broad feathered wings. The last autumn leaves tumbled as the giant birds passed through the canopy, landing on the forest floor.

Imogen and Marie slipped from the saddle. It felt strange, planting both feet on the ground. Imogen was so used to bobbing with the velecour's wingbeats, the earth seemed to float beneath her still.

She leaned against Frieda for a moment, steadying herself.

And *there* was the door in the tree. It was hard to make out in the moonlight, but Imogen recognised its shape – a shadow against the dark of the tree. Leaf litter had gathered at the threshold. The keyhole shone with light.

The moth zigzagged towards it.

'Thank you, shadow moth,' whispered Imogen. She knew the tree would have remained hidden if it wasn't for the insect's help.

Mum was busy removing the velecours' harnesses and saddles. 'What are we going to do with Fred and Frieda?' asked Imogen. 'They're too big to fit through the door.'

The velecours answered her question by walking away. They

clucked to each other, as if they were happy to be back, as if they recognised the forests as their home.

'Well, goodbye to you too,' called Mum.

Imogen squinted, and there, in the distance, she saw more velecours moving between the trees. Fred and Frieda padded towards them.

'Frieda! Fred!' cried Marie and she took a few steps after them.

'No,' said Mum. 'Let them go. That is their family.'

Imogen knew Mum was right, but still, as she watched the birds fade into the forests, she felt a little tug on her heart. 'Goodbye, Fred. Goodbye, Frieda,' she whispered.

She turned her attention to the door in the tree. The moth was resting on the door's smooth wood. After a moment, it crawled towards the glowing keyhole.

'It must be day on the other side,' said Imogen.

The moth moved its antennae in circles, and it seemed to mean *follow me*. Then it folded its wings across its body, and wriggled through the little opening.

The door in the tree clicked open.

Mum did one final check of the purse at her belt, making sure the lichen was still safe inside. And, with that, Imogen, Marie and their mother stepped through the door between worlds.

CHAPTER 107

In Mum's bedroom, the fairy lights were on, casting their pinkish glow. There were extra pillows by the headboard and books were stacked up at the side of the bed.

Imogen and Marie were nestled under the duvet, surrounded by Marie's colouring pencils. She was busy drawing in her sketchpad, with the tip of her tongue peeping out between her lips.

'Time for a story,' Mum muttered as she searched through her piles of books. 'Which one shall we pick?'

'Something with lots of adventure,' said Imogen.

'Where the baddies get what they deserve!' cried Marie.

Grandma was perched on the end of the bed, with Mog curled up on her lap. Normally, Mog wasn't allowed on the bed. But this was a special treat.

'I want a story with blood and guts,' said Grandma. 'Why don't I tell the one about the time their great-grandad got his arm stuck in an industrial rolling machine?'

Mum gave Grandma a significant look. 'No, we're not doing that.'

'All right, suit yourself,' huffed Grandma.

While Mum was selecting a story, Marie worked on her sketch. She was drawing Anneshka on the heartwood throne, colouring her in so she glowed green.

Imogen peeked at the image, admiring the careful shading. 'Do you think we'll have any more adventures?' she said. 'Do you think . . . is this the end?'

'I'm not sure I want any more adventures where Mark almost dies,' whispered Marie.

'No,' said Imogen, 'I mean the fun bits – where we sleep in a tree house and fly on giant birds and have a friend who's a magician.'

Marie stopped scribbling and met Imogen's eyes. 'Oh, I hope so,' she said.

'I'll let you in on a secret,' hissed Grandma, who must have been listening in. 'You can have adventures in this world. Not the same as the ones that you've had . . . but adventures nonetheless. There is danger and excitement in everyday life. There are monsters and heroes too.'

Imogen cocked her head. She wasn't sure what Grandma was getting at.

'Do you mean on TV?' asked Marie, reaching for a different shade of green.

'Ah, never mind,' sighed Grandma. 'Life is wasted on the young.'

Mum clambered into bed empty-handed. She seemed to have given up on choosing a book. The girls scooted up to make space.

'Once upon a time,' said their mother. 'In a land very far away, there were two young sisters. They didn't have any superpowers. They weren't princesses or magicians. But they were very good at working together. Together, they could achieve anything.'

Imogen wriggled deeper under the duvet, letting the softness envelop her.

'They lived on the edge of an enormous marsh, where a great many things grew. There was magic in those marshes. There was—'

The bedroom door eased open and Mark poked his head through the gap. 'Sorry to interrupt,' he said. 'Is there room in here for one more?' He was carrying a tray with mugs of hot chocolate.

'There's always room for the man with the drinks,' said Grandma.

Imogen, Marie and Mum shuffled up. Mark put the tray on the bedside table. Then he squished in next to them, passing round the mugs.

Mark was wearing the jumper that Imogen liked, the one that smelled of coffee and wool. It no longer carried the scent of yedleek. Neither did Mark himself.

The Maiden's Kiss lichen had worked its magic and, after doing more tests, the doctors were totally baffled. They didn't understand how it had happened, but they said Mark was cured.

Imogen watched Mark drink. A dot of whipped cream

was stuck to his nose. *It's good to have him with us*, she thought. *Good to have Grandma and Mog.*

Imogen didn't want it to just be her, Mum and Marie – not today, not any more. Having everyone squidged into one bed felt right. It felt like home.

'I've not missed the story, have I?' asked Mark.

'No,' said Imogen and she wrapped her fingers round her hot chocolate. 'It's just getting started.'

EPILOGUE

The clock of stars stopped ticking. All pacts had been honoured. All prophecies fulfilled.

The timepiece lay on the cusp of the marshes. It had remained here since Anneshka's army retreated, and, in the chaos that followed their defeat, the clock had been knocked to the ground.

After a few days, it had started raining and the Marshes of Mokzhadee swelled.

Water swallowed the lowest-lying islands. Pools swamped the nearby earth . . . And things that had been on dry land were no longer out of reach.

Abandoned army tents and cooking utensils, discarded chicken bones and knives – it all got lifted by the water, all got swept into the marsh.

The clock of stars was no exception. Slowly, ever so slowly, the water carried it into the reeds.

Even here, at the edge of the wetland, the power of the Sertze Bahnoh could be felt; the measured *thump-thump* of its heartbeat, the relentless thrusting of life.

495

Many months later, the clock was tucked at the foot of some woolgrass. It was spring, and everything was growing, trying to take up more room.

One of the wading birds found the timepiece and decided it was a good place to make a nest. Insects crawled across star-jewels. A mouse chewed at the little hatch.

And so it was that the clock of stars fell asleep – far away from its maker, far from the witch who had claimed it as her own – taking with it all of its secrets of deep time and futures untold.

Thank you to . . .

Joe, who has kept me watered, fed and cheered throughout the writing of this book – and who I first told, ten years ago, 'I think I might like to write stories again.' I couldn't have written them without you.

My parents, my sisters, my great-aunt and my friends. Thank you for the pep talks, the PR and all your support.

Lucy Rogers for coaxing this book out of me. You've made it so much better. And you've made it happen faster than I feared was possible.

Nick Lake and Claire Wilson, for everything you've done over the past four years. It might sound melodramatic, but it's true so I'm writing it down – you have changed my life.

Chris Riddell for all the beautiful, terrifying and funny illustrations.

Aisha Bushby, for your insightful feedback. Thank you also to Lela Burbridge, for reading and critiquing in record time. Many thanks to Helen and Becky for the conversations about children and PTSD.

The Conservative leadership of the United Kingdom, who have provided plenty of villain-spiration.

I'd like to thank the whole team at HarperCollins, including Julia Bruce, Leena Lane, Jane Hammett, Tina Mories, Alex Cowan, Sarah Lough, Sandy Officer, Jasmeet Fyfe, Aisling Beddy, Elorine Grant, Hannah Marshall and Matt Kelly. Especial thanks go to Laure Gysemans, who has dealt with more emails about italics than anyone should ever have to. Thank you also to Safae El-Ouahabi.

And finally, thank you to my readers. Hearing from you and meeting you has been the highlight of my year.